A former history lecturer, Edward Marston was born and brought up in South Wales and educated at Oxford University. Since 1966 he has worked as a full-time writer, and has written over forty original plays for radio, television and theatre, as well as children's books, literary criticism and novels. He was recently shortlisted for the prestigious Edgar Award for Best Mystery Novel and is the author of eleven hugely popular Domesday mysteries, also published by Headline.

Also by Edward Marston

The Restoration mysteries

The King's Evil

The Domesday mysteries

The Amorous Nightingale

Edward Marston

HEADLINE

First published in hardback in 2000
by HEADLINE BOOK PUBLISHING

First published in paperback in 2001
by HEADLINE BOOK PUBLISHING

10 9 8 7 6 5 4 3 2

ISBN 0 7472 6256 X

Typeset by Letterpart Ltd
Reigate, Surrey

Printed and bound in Great Britain by
Clays Ltd, St Ives plc.

HEADLINE BOOK PUBLISHING
A division of Hodder Headline
338 Euston Road
London NW1 3BH

www.headline.co.uk
www.hodderheadline.com

To my own amorous nightingale

Moll Davis performed the song (My Lodging is on the Cold Ground) so charmingly that, not long after, it raised her from a bed on the Cold Ground, to a Bed Royal.

John Downes, *Roscius Anglicanus*

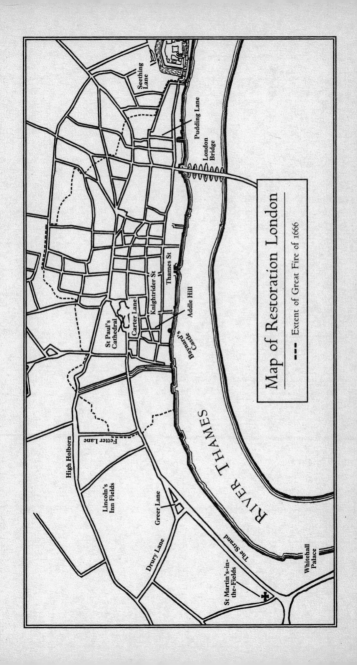

Chapter One

Christopher Redmayne found conversations with his elder brother rather trying at the best of times. When there was a mirror at hand, it was well nigh impossible to have a meaningful exchange with Henry for he was continually preening himself, adjusting his wig, fidgeting with his attire, experimenting with a series of facial expressions and generally ignoring the person or persons unfortunate enough to be in his presence at such a moment of total self-absorption. Though he found such behaviour extremely irritating, Christopher schooled himself to be patient.

'What manner of man is this Mr Hartwell?' he asked.

'Jasper?' said Henry dismissively. 'He's an arrant fool.'

'I thought that he was a friend of yours.'

'A mere acquaintance. I'd never list Jasper Hartwell among my intimates. It would damage my reputation.' He tried the wig at a slightly different angle and raised an inquisitive eyebrow. 'How does this look?'

'Fine,' said Christopher wearily. 'It looks fine.'

'Does it make me handsome and faintly satanic?'

'You look like Henry Redmayne and he is both of those things with many other distinctive traits besides. Could we put your appearance to one side for a moment and discuss this Mr Hartwell?'

'But appearance is everything, my dear brother.'

'I would dispute that.'

'Well, do not do so in front of Jasper,' warned his brother, striking a peevish note. 'In fact, I would advise you to dispute nothing in the presence of your potential client. Agree with everything he says, however vapid or inane. Jasper is all outward show. If you think that your dear brother leans a little towards vanity – a crime I readily confess – wait until

1

you meet Jasper Hartwell. He puts me in the shade. Jasper makes Narcissus seem like a martyr to modesty.'

'What of his inner nature?'

'He doesn't have one.'

'He must, Henry.'

'Why?'

'Every man has a true centre to his being.'

'Jasper is the exception to the rule.'

Henry Redmayne decided that his waistcoat was not being displayed to the best advantage and fiddled with his coat for several minutes. Christopher suppressed a sigh and waited. They were in the hall of Henry's house in Bedford Street, preparing to leave for a visit to the theatre, a pleasurable occasion which also had a commercial purpose, since Christopher was to be introduced to someone who might well be interested in employing him as the architect to design his new London abode. The fact that he had to rely on his brother for the introduction brought a number of anxieties in its wake. When Henry turned his attention back to his wig, Christopher tried to probe for more detail.

'I hope that Mr Hartwell proves a more reliable client,' he said.

'Reliable?' echoed the other.

'Profoundly grateful as I am for your help, I have to admit that your introductions have not always borne fruit.'

'What do you mean?' returned Henry, rounding on him. 'Did I not secure a valuable commission for you from Sir Ambrose Northcott?'

'You did, indeed.'

'Was it not the start of your career as an aspiring architect?'

'Undoubtedly.'

'And were not your services generously rewarded?'

'They were, Henry. The fee was paid in full. Unfortunately, the house was never built so that all of my work went to waste.'

'Don't blame me, Christopher. How was I to know that Sir Ambrose would be unguarded enough to let himself be murdered? It was an unforeseen hazard. The point is that, out of the kindness of my filial heart, I presented you with a golden opportunity.' He gave a loud sniff. 'A modicum of thanks is in order, I fancy.'

'I have already said how deeply grateful I am, Henry. Grateful for the introductions to Sir Ambrose Northcott and, more recently, to that other friend, acquaintance, crony, drinking companion, associate, call him what you will, Lord Staines.'

'Fulke is part of my inner circle.'

'So I assumed.'

'A man on whom I pattern myself.'

'I deduced that from his air of dissipation.'

Henry stiffened. 'Fulke Rowett, tenth Baron Staines, is a splendid fellow in every particular. Had circumstances been more propitious, he could have looked to be the next warden of the Cinque Ports. You can surely not complain about Lord Staines. You designed a beautiful house for him and it stands to this day as a worthy example of your talent.'

'The house was built,' agreed Christopher, 'but the architect's fee was never paid. Nor was that of the builder.'

'A temporary problem in raising finance,' said Henry airily. 'I'm sure that Fulke will soon rectify this situation.'

'Not while he is still on his Irish estates. For that is where he fled when we tried to seek payment. And we were two among many, Henry. The queue of his creditors would stretch from here to Land's End. Lord Staines may be a splendid fellow but he is also impulsive, extravagant, irresponsible and up to his neck in debt.'

'Even the best horse stumbles at times.'

'This one fell at the first jump.'

'What are you saying?' demanded Henry, putting his hands on his hips as he went on the attack. 'Are you telling me that your brother should not put himself out to advance your interests, to honour the promise I gave to Father to lend all the help I could in your search for gainful and satisfying employment?'

3

'No, Henry,' said Christopher with an appeasing smile, 'that is not my meaning at all. I simply wish to remind you that my experience has hitherto been somewhat chequered. My first client was killed and my second took to his heels when the question of payment was raised. All I am seeking to do is to establish that Mr Hartwell is more dependable.'

'Have no worries on that score.'

'How can I be sure?'

'Jasper has no intention of being murdered, nor does he have any Irish estates which can act as a refuge from his creditors. Arrant fool he may be, but he is as rich as Croesus and more likely to pay you twice the fee you ask out of sheer benevolence. Does that answer your question?'

'Not entirely.'

'How do you like my new coat?' said Henry, courting the mirror once more. 'Does it not lend a certain dignity?'

'Dignity *and* elegance.'

'Truly, my tailor has ennobled me.'

'You could pass for an earl, if not a duke.'

'Dignity, elegance, nobility. The quintessence of Henry Redmayne.'

'Coming back to Mr Hartwell . . .'

'Now, which hat shall I wear? The choice is crucial.'

'What is your own position with regard to him?'

'Jasper? We exchange polite nods of greeting. Nothing more.'

'I was talking about your pecuniary relationship,' said Christopher, trying to catch his attention. 'If so be it, this afternoon's meeting does produce a commission for me, you are rightly entitled to a fee for effecting the introduction. I would prefer that you agreed the amount with me beforehand rather than with Mr Hartwell.'

Henry was shocked. 'What I do, I do out of brotherly love.'

'I'm delighted to hear it.'

'I seek nothing in terms of monetary recompense.'

'That is very altruistic of you, Henry,' said the other politely, 'but I am bound to recall the way that you brokered the deal with Sir Ambrose Northcott. Brotherly love was ever your cry on that occasion, too, but it did not stop you from arranging to have a percentage of my fee paid surreptitiously to you.'

'Sir Ambrose thrust the money upon me. What could I do?'

'Be more honest with your brother.'

'I was, I am and evermore will be.'

'So no understanding has been reached with Mr Hartwell?'

'None, Christopher. I give you my word.'

'Then I will hold you to it.'

'That will not be necessary.' He scrutinised his appearance in the mirror. 'Have you ever seen a finer sight? I do believe that I will outshine the King himself this afternoon. Henry Redmayne – Baron Cynosure.'

Christopher let him twist and turn in admiration for a couple of minutes before speaking. He loved his elder brother. With all his faults and foibles, Henry Redmayne was an endearing man in many ways. Both of them were tall, slim and handsome but the resemblance ended there. While Christopher's face shone with health, Henry's pale and ravished countenance betokened a life of studied degeneracy. The former's luxuriant dark brown curling locks had a reddish hue, whereas the latter's rapidly thinning hair obliged him to seek the cover of an expensive periwig. The earnest manner of the younger brother was in complete contrast to the easy cynicism of his sibling. One was dedicated to his work as an architect, the other to a life of idle pleasure. They inhabited quite separate worlds.

Christopher knew the futility of even attempting to reform his brother. He had grown so accustomed to Henry's sybaritic existence that he hardly recognised it as a vice any more. Someone else in the family, however, was less tolerant of Henry's shortcomings.

'I had a letter from Father this morning,' said Christopher.

'Why does the old gentleman always write to you, not to me?'

'Because I always have the grace to reply.'

'So do I,' retorted Henry petulantly, 'when his missives are civil. But that is all too rare, I fear. If only Father could forget – albeit briefly – that he is Dean of Gloucester. He will insist on treating a letter as a pulpit from which he can denounce me for my sins.'

'Then do not give him cause for that denunciation.'

'Would you have me betray my instincts?'

'I would have you exercise a little discretion,' advised Christopher. 'Father wrote to tell me that he intends to visit London shortly and means to call on both of us. Especially on you.'

'Why me?' gasped Henry, flying into a mild panic. 'Are there not sinners enough in the county of Gloucester to keep him busy? The last thing I need is a prying parent, watching over my shoulder, calling me to account. I'll not be *judged*, Christopher!' he declared, waving an arm. 'Keep the old gentleman away from me. Tell him that I have temporarily quit the city. Tell him that I am performing military service abroad on behalf of my country. Tell him that I am on a pilgrimage to Jerusalem. Tell him anything you choose, but save me from his damnable sermons!'

'Father has a right to call on you.'

'What about *my* rights?' wailed the other. 'And my freedom?'

'It is the use to which you put that freedom which is bringing Father to London. I say no more,' added Christopher. 'I simply wished to give you fair warning.'

Henry shivered involuntarily. 'Of impending catastrophe,' he moaned. 'They say that disasters come in threes. First we had the Great Plague. Then the Great Fire. Now we have the Great Visitation from the Dean of Gloucester, descending out of heaven in a blaze of righteous indignation like an avenging thunderbolt.'

'You can hardly compare Father's visit with the plague and the fire. They were disasters that affected the whole city. The only person likely to suffer this time is you, Henry.'

'I am already sweating as if I have the plague and

smouldering as if I am trapped in the fire. Let us away, Christopher,' he ordered, pulling open the door of a closet to extract a broad-brimmed hat whose crown was bedecked with plumes. 'Father coming to London? How can I enjoy myself when I have this dire threat hanging over me? It has made every part about me quiver with apprehension.'

He confronted the mirror for the last time in order to place the hat at the correct angle. Standing at his elbow, Christopher checked his own appearance. He was smart, well groomed and dressed in the latest fashion but his attire had nothing of the vivid colour and ostentation of Henry's. The latter favoured a vermilion coat, whose large cuffs were adorned with an intricate pattern, over a waistcoat of red and gold silk. The breeches were dark blue above a pair of mauve stockings. Even the butterfly bows on his shoes were a minor work of art. Christopher estimated that his brother had lavished more on his apparel for an afternoon at the theatre than the young architect spent in six months.

Henry grimaced and stroked his wispy moustache.

'I suppose that I will pass muster,' he said dully.

'A moment ago, you were boasting that you would out-dazzle the King himself in your fine array.'

'That was before I heard the tidings about Father.'

'Are they so unsettling?' said Christopher.

'Terrifying!' He swung on his heel and headed for the door. 'Still, there's no help for it. Come, brother. This afternoon's business may at least give me a chance to impress Father.' Sailing through the front door, he gave a curt nod to the servant who held it open for them. 'I'll secure that commission for you and Christopher Redmayne can continue his valuable work of helping to rebuild this ruined city.'

'Nothing would please me more, Henry.'

'Sing my praises to Father.'

Christopher grinned. 'Like a heavenly choir.'

He fell in beside his brother as they strolled towards Drury Lane, the one marching purposefully with a confident stride while the other strutted importantly and assumed an expression of total disdain.

'We should have taken a carriage,' decided Henry.

'For so short a journey? A needless indulgence.'

'Indulgence is a mark of good character.'

'And bad housekeeping,' argued Christopher. 'Why spend money on the unnecessary when it might be saved for the truly essential?'

'Cutting a dash *is* truly essential.'

'We must agree to differ on that, Henry. As on so many other things.' A thought struck him. 'By the way, you have not told me the name of the play we are about to see.'

'It is irrelevant.'

'Does it have no title?'

'Who cares?'

'I do,' said Christopher seriously.

'Forget the play,' decreed Henry with a lordly gesture of his hand. 'Remember that you are not going to the theatre to watch a troupe of mangy actors, practising their craft. You are there to ensnare Jasper Hartwell in order to part the fool from as much of his undeserved wealth as you can. As for me,' he said, revelling in the attention he was getting from passersby, 'I never visit a theatre for the purpose of seeing. I am there simply to *be seen*.'

The two brothers moved on, linked by ties of blood but separated by almost everything else, walking side by side towards a critical meeting with a potential client, mixing hope with enjoyment, ambition with display, sensitivity with arrogance, serenely unaware of the perils that lay in wait for them at The Theatre Royal.

Chapter Two

Jonathan Bale looked up at the house and emitted a reverential sigh.

'There it is,' he said, pointing a finger. 'Study it well, boys.'

'Why?' asked Oliver.

'Because this is where he once lived. Over twenty years ago, the Lord Protector, as he became, moved from Long Acre to Drury Lane and made his home right here. He sent for his family to join him from Ely. Think on that, Oliver,' he said, with a hand on his son's shoulder. 'The man whose name you bear graced this house with his presence.'

'Was he a good man, Father?'

'A great one.'

'Then why didn't he become King?'

'He did. In all but name.'

'But we have a real King now.'

Jonathan pursed his lips and nodded sadly.

'What about me, Father?' piped up Richard Bale, the younger of the two brothers. 'You told me that I was named after a Cromwell.'

'You were,' explained his father. 'You were so christened because the Lord Protector's son was called Richard. When his father died, he inherited his title and his power.'

'Was he as great a man as his father?' wondered Richard.

'Alas, no.'

'Nobody was as great as Oliver Cromwell,' boasted the older boy. 'That's why I carry his name. I mean to be great myself.'

'You already are,' teased Richard. 'A great fool.'

Oliver bridled. 'Who are you calling a fool?'

'Nobody,' said Jonathan firmly, quelling the argument before it could even begin. 'Now, look at the house and remember the man who once owned it. We must keep his memory bright in our hearts. England owes so much to him. He is sorely missed.'

'What about his son, Richard?' said his namesake.

'Well, yes . . .' Jonathan tried to keep disappointment out of his voice. 'Richard Cromwell is missed, too, but in a different way. His achievements fell short of his father's. That was only to be expected.'

'Where is he now, Father?'

'Somewhere in France.'

'Why?'

'Richard Cromwell is in exile.'

'What does that mean?'

'He is not allowed to live in this country.'

'But you said that he was Lord Protector.'

'For a time.'

'What happened?'

Jonathan shrugged. 'That's a long story,' he said softly. 'When you are old enough to understand it, I'll tell it to you.'

'*I* understand it,' asserted Oliver, inflating his little chest. 'It's quite simple. Oliver Cromwell was famous, which is why I was christened after him. His son was hopeless so Richard was the right name for you.'

'That's not true!' protested his brother.

'It certainly isn't,' confirmed Jonathan.

'They called him Tumbledown Dick,' said Oliver, grinning wickedly at his sibling. 'That's how useless he was. Just like you, Richard. You're Tumbledown Dick Bale!'

'No!' wailed Richard.

'That's enough!' said Jonathan sternly. 'There'll be no mockery of the Cromwell family. Both of you should be justly proud of the names you bear.' He shook Oliver hard. 'Don't ever let me hear you making fun of your brother again. You'll answer to me, if you do.'

The boy nodded penitently. 'Yes, Father.'

'There is no shame in being called after Richard Cromwell.'

'Why didn't he become King?' asked the younger boy.

Jonathan let the question hang in the air. Directing the

gaze of both sons to the house once more, he reflected on the changes that had occurred during their short lifetimes. Oliver was almost ten now, born and baptised when the Lord Protector was still alive. Richard was three years younger, named after a man whose own rule was brief, inglorious and mired in controversy. Both sons had grown up under a restored monarch, Charles II, a King who showed all the arrogance of the Stuart dynasty and who, in Jonathan's opinion, had devalued the whole concept of royalty by his scandalous behaviour. A devout Puritan like Jonathan Bale was bound to wonder if the plague, decimating the population of London, and the subsequent fire, destroying most of the buildings within the city walls, had been visited on the capital by a God who was appalled at the corruption and depravity that were the distinctive hallmarks of the Restoration.

The three of them were returning home after a long walk. Now in his late thirties, Jonathan was a big, solid man with a prominent nose acting as a focal point in a large face. The two warts on his cheek and the livid scar across his forehead gave him a slightly sinister appearance, but his children loved him devotedly and thought their father the most handsome of men. Long years as a shipwright had developed his muscles and broadened his back, visible assets in his role as a parish constable. Only the bold or the very foolish made the mistake of taking on Jonathan Bale in any form of combat.

He loomed over the two boys like a galleon between two rowing boats. Proud of his sons, he was keen to acquaint them with the history of their city and the significance of their names. The fashionable house outside which the trio were standing was at the Holborn end of Drury Lane, a respectable, residential neighbourhood with an abundance of flowers and trees to please the eye and to reinforce the sense of leisured wealth. The area presented a sharp contrast to their own ward of Baynard's Castle. Untouched by the Great Fire of the previous year, Drury Lane and its environs were highly popular with the rich and the powerful. Addle Hill, on the other hand, where Jonathan and Sarah Bale and their sons lived, comprised more modest dwellings. It had been largely gutted by fire and Jonathan had had to rebuild his home before they could move back into it.

'Let us go,' he said quietly. 'We have seen enough.'

'Who owns the house now, Father?' said Oliver.

'Nobody of importance.'

The boys fell in beside him as he strode off down Drury Lane, unable to match his long stride and all but scurrying to keep pace with him. They had reached the long bend in the thoroughfare when the sound of an approaching carriage made them turn. It came rumbling at speed from the direction of Holborn, the rasping sound of its huge wheels augmented by the urgent clatter of the horses' hooves. The coachman did not spare them a glance but one of the occupants leaned forward with interest. As the vehicle went past, the smiling face of a young woman appeared at the window and a delicate hand waved in greeting. Jonathan lifted a rough palm in response.

'Who was that?' asked Richard, hugely impressed that his father should know anyone who travelled in such style. 'The lady waved to you.'

'It was Mary Hibbert,' said Jonathan.

'She was very pretty.'

'Yes. Mary takes after her mother.'

'Is she a friend of yours?'

'I know the Hibbert family well. They used to live not far from us in Carter Lane. Good, kind, decent, God-fearing people.' A distant regret intruded. 'Mary was a dutiful daughter at first. But times have changed.'

'What do you mean, Father?' said Oliver.

Jonathan shook his head dismissively. The coach had now slowed to pick its way through the crowd that was converging on Bridges Street. Recognising one of the occupants of the vehicle, several people cheered or gesticulated excitedly. A few young men ran alongside the coach to peer in. Richard surveyed the scene with increased awe.

'Is Mary Hibbert famous?' he asked.

'No,' replied his father.

12

'Then why is everyone waving to her?'
'I suspect that there is another lady in the coach.'
'Who?'
'Nobody you need concern yourself with, Richard.'
'Is the other lady famous?' said Oliver.
'That is not the word that I would use.'
'Who is she, Father?'
'Tell us,' said Richard. 'Who is the famous lady?'
'And where are all those people going?'

Jonathan raised a disapproving eyebrow before shepherding his sons down a sidestreet in order to avoid the gathering crowd.

'To the theatre,' he said.

Christopher Redmayne caught only the merest glimpse of her as she alighted from the coach and made her way through a circle of admirers. When she and her companion entered the building by means of a rear door, there was a collective sigh of disappointment, immediately replaced by an anticipatory glee as those same gentlemen realised that they would soon view her again upon the stage. There was an involuntary surge towards the front entrance of the theatre. Christopher and his brother waited while it spent its force.

Henry watched the stampede with wry amusement.

'Did any woman ever lead so many men by their pizzles?' he observed. 'Truly, their brains are in their breeches when she is near.'

'Who is the lady?' asked Christopher.

'Who else but the toast of London? The uncrowned queen of the stage. A veritable angel in human guise. She is the prettiest piece of flesh in Christendom and I speak as a connoisseur of such creatures. I'll hold you six to four that she could tempt a saint, let alone a Pope or an Archbishop. Yes,' Henry added with a wild laugh, 'she might even make our dear father abandon his piety and dance naked around the cloisters of Gloucester Cathedral with a rose between his teeth.'

'Does this paragon have a name?'

'Several. Most call her the royal nightingale.'

'Nightingale?'

'Wait until you hear her sing.'

'Can she act as well?'

'Sublimely. Upon any man with red blood in his veins.'

'And her real name?'

'Harriet Gow. She is the sole reason for this mêlée, this undignified scramble you see before us. Whenever the adorable Harriet Gow appears in a play, the gallants of the town positively fight to get into the theatre.'

Christopher smiled. 'I'm surprised that you don't join in the brawl, Henry. It is unlike you to forego the opportunity of feasting your eyes on a young lady of such fabled beauty.'

'What?' said Henry, recoiling slightly. 'Run with the herd and get my new coat creased? Never! Besides, I have standards. Henry Redmayne never chases any woman. I make them come crawling to me.' He tossed his head and set his wig trembling in the sunshine. 'As for the delectable Harriet, gorgeous as she may be, I would never waste my shot on a target that is already beyond my reach.'

'Beyond your reach?'

'Did you not catch her nickname?'

'The nightingale.'

'The *royal* nightingale.'

'Ah!' said Christopher, understanding him. 'The King himself has also succumbed to her charms. That explains your unaccustomed restraint. Miss Gow is spoken for.'

'Doubly so. For she is Mrs Harriet Gow.'

'Married, then?'

'Yes, Christopher. I would need to be a congenital idiot to compete with a King *and* a husband.'

'You have done so in the past.'

'An aberration,' said Henry, anxious to consign the unpleasant reminder to oblivion. 'How was I to know that that particular lady was already warming two beds? Forget the wretch. She deserves no rightful place among my *amours*.'

'If you say so, Henry.'

'I do say so. With vehemence.' He spotted a familiar figure and softened his tone at once. 'Here comes the very person we seek. Jasper Hartwell, as large as life and twice as odious. Smile and fawn upon him, Christopher. His pockets are as deep as his ignorance.' Henry beamed and fell on the newcomer. 'Jasper, my dear fellow!' he said, grasping him by the arm. 'How nice to see you again. Allow me to present my brother, the brilliant architect, Christopher Redmayne.'

'Oh,' returned the other, displaying a row of uneven teeth. 'Is this the young genius of whom you spoke so fondly, Henry?' He squinted at Christopher. 'Pleased to make your acquaintance, Mr Redmayne.'

'Your servant, Mr Hartwell,' replied Christopher politely.

'Well, now, isn't this a happy coincidence?'

'Chance meetings are always the most productive,' said Henry easily. 'But why have we come to watch a play when a far more dramatic sight confronts us? You look quite superb, Jasper. A sartorial sensation. Elegance Incarnate. Is he not, Christopher?'

'Indeed,' said his brother.

'Have you ever seen a coat better cut? Scrutinise him well, brother. Admire the sheer artistry. Jasper Hartwell wears nothing but the best and that means keeping a score of Parisian tailors at his command. The periwig is a triumph – Chedreux at his finest.'

Henry continued to pour out the flattery in large doses and Jasper Hartwell lapped it up greedily. Christopher smiled obediently when he really wanted to laugh with derision. Jasper Hartwell's apparel was, to his eye, frankly ludicrous. The man himself was short, plump and ill-favoured, features that were exposed rather than offset by his attire. He wore a scarlet coat that was slightly waisted with a short flared skirt, made of a garish purple material, falling just below his hips. The coat was collarless and fastened from neck to hem by gold buttons, as were the back slit and the low horizontal pockets. Close-fitting to the elbow, the sleeves had deep turned-back cuffs fastened and decorated with a plethora of buttons.

Around the neck was a linen cravat with a lace border. Across the body was a wide baldrick, supporting the sword, while the waist was entwined in a silk sash, fringed at both ends. Instead of giving him the military appearance at which he aimed, the outfit emphasised his complete unsuitability for any physical activity. The square-toed shoes were objects of scorn in themselves, fastened over the long tongues with straps, large square buckles and limp ribbon loops with an orange hue. It was as if the tailors of Paris had conspired to wreak their revenge on the perceived lack of taste of the English.

If his clothing invited ridicule, Jasper Hartwell's wig provoked open-mouthed wonder. It was enormous. Made of ginger hair, it rose up in a series of massive curls until it added almost a foot to his height. The wig fell down on to both shoulders, ending in two long corkscrew locks that could be tied at the back. Perched on top of this hirsute mountain was a large, low-crowned hat, festooned with coloured feather plumes. Out of it all, gleaming with pleasure, loomed the podgy face of Jasper Hartwell, powdered to an almost deathly whiteness and looking less like the visage of a human being than that of an amiable pig thrust headlong through a ginger bush.

Christopher's hopes were dashed. Expecting to court a potential employer, he was instead meeting a man of such overweening vanity that he made Henry Redmayne seem self-effacing. If the commission were forthcoming, what sort of house would Jasper Hartwell instruct his architect to build? In all probability, it would be an expression of the owner himself, gaudy, fatuous, over-elaborate and inimical to every precept of style and symmetry. Christopher was crestfallen. It would violate his principles to design such a house for such a client.

Yet in one sentence, his prospects were suddenly resurrected. Leaning forward until his hat wobbled precariously atop its eminence, Hartwell gave him a confiding smile and a first whiff of his bad breath.

'Henry has shown me your drawings, Mr Redmayne,' he

said with a note of respect, 'and I declare, I think them the best I ever beheld.'

Christopher was dumbfounded. His brother winked at him.

'First, however,' added Hartwell, 'let us see the play.'

'And then?' pressed Henry. 'We will come to composition?'

'Of course.'

It was over as simply as that.

Formerly a riding school, The Theatre Royal occupied a site in Bridges Street off Drury Lane. The conversion of the old building was a signal success, the only complaint being that the corridors to the pit and the boxes were too narrow. None of the patrons criticised the interior. It was circular in shape, the walls lined with boxes that were divided from each other to ensure privacy and equipped with rows of seats. As befitted a theatre that was known as The King's House, the prime position was taken by the royal box, overlooking the stage from the ideal angle and offering greater luxury to those who reclined there. The pit, the large central space on the ground floor, was the domain of those unable to afford a box or too late to find one still available.

It was Christopher Redmayne's first visit to the theatre and its architecture intrigued him. Nobody would ever have guessed that horses were once schooled around its circumference. Jasper Hartwell led the way to a box where he was welcomed loudly by half-a-dozen cronies at various stages of drunkenness. Henry knew them all but Christopher hardly caught their names above the hubbub. Sitting between his brother and his client, he let his gaze rove around the interior.

'The builders have done a fine job,' he remarked.

'At a cost,' noted Henry.

'Oh?'

'I had it from Tom Killigrew himself. The projected cost was fifteen hundred pounds but it had risen to almost two and a half thousand by the time the renovations were complete. Tom was most unhappy about that. He keeps a tight hand on his purse.'

17

'The money was well spent,' said Christopher, looking upward. 'I do like that glazed cupola. It lends distinction and adds light.'

Henry grimaced. 'It also lets in the rain. Be grateful that we came on a fine day. A *very* fine day, Christopher. Our fish is landed before we even set sail. We can feed off Jasper Hartwell until we burst.'

'*We*, Henry? I thought that I was to be his architect.'

'Yes, yes, but you must allow me some reflected glory.'

'Feeding suggests more than glory.'

'Stop haggling over a damnable verb!'

Henry accepted the glass of wine that was handed to him and joined in the badinage with the others. When some new guests came lurching into the box to take up their seats, the level of jollity reached a new pitch of intensity. Jasper Hartwell was at the centre of it, basking in the flattery of his friends and dispensing banalities as if scattering words of wisdom. Christopher was left to take stock of his surroundings. His eye took in every detail. The stage was high and framed by a proscenium arch, guaranteeing the play's visibility to everyone in the theatre. What Christopher was less certain about was audibility. Would the actors' voices reach all parts of the audience? More to the point, would those same spectators abandon tumult for a degree of silence so that the play could be heard?

The noise was deafening. As more patrons crowded into the boxes or elbowed their way into the pit, the cacophony steadily worsened. Laughter and ribaldry predominated, male guffaws counterpointed by the brittle shrieks of females, many of whom wore masks to hide their blushes or to conceal the pitiful condition of their complexions. Wives, mistresses and courtesans were dotted indiscriminately around a house that seemed to consist largely of braying aristocrats or indolent gallants. Prostitutes cruised for business among those in the pit while pert orange girls swung their hips and baskets with studied provocation.

Christopher noticed one orange-seller who was being used

as an emissary, taking a note from a pop-eyed man in a monstrous hat to a vizarded lady who sat in the front seat of a box. Other flirtations were taking place on all sides. The Theatre Royal was a giant mirror in which the assembled throng either preened themselves, got riotously drunk or made blatant assignations. A brawl erupted in the pit. An unseen woman screamed in distress. The wife of a visiting ambassador swung round to spit incautiously over her shoulder, unaware of the fact that someone had just taken the seat directly behind her and, providentially, unable to comprehend the language in which he began to abuse her. Swords were drawn in another box. An old man collapsed in a stupor.

It was at this point that the play began. Christopher had never seen *The Maid's Tragedy* before and he was not about to see it properly now for, though the pandemonium lost some of its rage when the actors appeared, it still bubbled mutinously, drowning out most of what was being said in the opening exchanges. Before the play was a minute old, the tall, stately figure of the King himself slipped into the royal box to take his place among his friends and to cause a ripple among the audience. His timing was impeccable. No sooner had he settled down than Harriet Gow, the object of his affections, came on to the stage in the role of Aspatia, the betrayed maiden.

A hush fell instantly on the whole auditorium. This is what they had come to see, a frail, delicate, impossibly beautiful creature who moved with natural grace and whose voice plucked at the heart-strings.

> '*My hard fortunes*
> *Deserve not scorn; for I was never proud*
> *When they were good.*'

It was all that she uttered on her first, fleeting appearance but it drew a gasp from every man present. Christopher Redmayne was among them, moved by her patent suffering, struck by her wan loveliness and captivated by that soft, lilting voice. In the space of a few seconds, he came to appreciate the magical qualities of Harriet Gow. Once she quit the stage, a heavy murmur returned to fill the air, punctuated by the occasional outbreak of hostilities in the pit or by some altercation in one of the boxes.

The Maid's Tragedy slowly unfolded. Beaumont and Fletcher's play was over half a century old but its theme had a curious topicality, a fact which led to the suppression of the piece when the manager, Thomas Killigrew, had tried to stage it earlier in the reign. The plot revolved around a lecherous King and his corrupt Court. Amintor breaks his engagement to Aspatia at the King's request and in her stead marries Evadne, sister to his friend, Melantius. On their wedding night, Evadne reveals to her husband that he will never enjoy her favours because they are exclusively the property of the King. Unwittingly, Amintor has been tricked into being a cuckold, betraying his true love, Aspatia, in the process. The seeds of tragedy are sown.

Those who could hear the play felt its deeper resonance. The King on stage bore a marked resemblance to the one who sat so calmly in the royal box. Charles II was not always discreet in his private life. It was well known that he had sometimes provided husbands for his mistresses in order to give them a cloak of respectability. More than one real-life Amintor had heard the dread confession from his wife on his wedding night. Henry Redmayne missed none of the innuendoes and sniggered time and again. Jasper Hartwell let out a high-pitched, asinine giggle, accompanied by a violent shaking of his body that made his wig tilt at a dangerous angle. A tragic situation offered much unintended comedy.

There were neither sniggers nor giggles when Aspatia swept in once more, accompanying the treacherous Evadne to the latter's bedchamber. Harriet Gow was a picture of despair, reflecting upon her woe with a sense of resignation rather than self-pity, then cutting through the taut silence with a song that touched even the most cynical listeners.

> *'Lay a garland on my hearse*
> *Of the dismal yew;*
> *Maidens, willow branches bear:*
> *Say I died true.*
> *My love was false, but I was firm*
> *From my hour of birth.*
> *Upon my buried body lie*
> *Lightly, gentle earth.'*

Christopher was entranced. Not only had he seen the small miracle of a rowdy audience being subdued to respectful silence, he had heard one of the most melodious and affecting voices ever to issue from a human mouth. Harriet Gow was truly a nightingale. The rest of the cast might display the full range of their abilities but the memory that would linger in every mind was that of Aspatia's sad song in the second act of the play. Christopher's mouth went dry and his eyes gently moistened. Aspatia's vulnerability left him tingling.

When she was offstage, the interruptions resurfaced and many of the lines were lost beneath the commotion but Christopher did not mind. He watched and waited for Aspatia to make another entrance, to impose order once more on the mild chaos and to trumpet the virtues of honesty and loyalty in a society that was bedevilled by vice. The play ended in a welter of deaths, Evadne's killing of the King being presented as a perverted sexual act that excited the senses of the dullest onlookers but it was Aspatia, yet again, who soared above them all, dying with such realism and poignancy that she set women weeping and strong men snuffling. Christopher was not ashamed of his own tears.

Thunderous applause was directed mainly at the hapless Aspatia, now gliding back to the centre of the stage like its undisputed jewel, luxuriating in the ovation and giving a gentle curtsey to the King who was leading it from the royal box. Christopher was a prey to swirling emotions. Pity for Aspatia welled up inside him along with deep affection for the actress who portrayed her. Envy soon took over, then a feeling of betrayal, then a sense of loss. Resignation finally claimed him. While she had been singing her plaintive song, Harriet Gow had been his and every other man's in the audience, reaching out to each one individually with the sheer power and musicality of her voice. Now she was indicating her preference very clearly. A royal nightingale for a royal bed.

'Well?' said Henry into his brother's ear. 'Was I right about her?'

'Oh, yes,' admitted Christopher. 'She is without compare.'

'I would give anything to make her mine,' said Hartwell effusively. 'Harriet Gow is the most beautiful woman in the world. Have you ever heard such a charming voice? It still echoes in my ears. She is absolute perfection.'

'Invite her to your new home, Jasper,' advised Henry.

'Do you think that she would come?'

'She might. If I delivered the invitation – by way of the King.'

Hartwell grabbed him. 'Would you do that for me, Henry?'

'That and much more, my friend. You will have one of the finest houses in London. It deserves to be celebrated with a banquet to which only the most distinguished guests will be invited. Do you agree?'

'Oh, yes!' said the other. 'Mightily!'

'Only one thing remains, then.'

'And what is that?'

'A practical matter,' said Henry with an arm around his shoulder. 'You must engage my brother, Christopher, to design the house for you. When she sees the result, Harriet Gow will snatch at your invitation. In Christopher's hands, architecture is an act of seduction in itself.'

'Then he is the man for me!' announced Hartwell.

'It is settled. Are you content, brother?'

'Yes,' said Christopher. 'Very content.'

But his smile of gratitude concealed deep misgivings.

Chapter Three

Jacob Vout was the ideal servant, always at hand if needed, wholly invisible if not. He moved around the house in Fetter Lane with quiet efficiency and kept the place spotless. Christopher Redmayne could find no fault in him. Jacob was a benign presence, fiercely loyal to his master, honest, trustworthy, kind, conscientious, attentive without being intrusive and obedient without being servile. Now in his sixties, he had learned everything and forgotten nothing about his chosen occupation. Christopher treated him like a friend who happened to work for him.

'Jacob!' he called.

'Yes, sir?' said the old man, materialising at his elbow like a spirit.

'Do we have any drink in the house?'

'A little, sir.'

'Give me a more precise inventory.'

'One bottle of brandy and six bottles of wine.'

'Is the wine of good quality?'

'*I* think so, sir,' said Jacob defensively, 'but your brother decided otherwise. I fear that Mr Redmayne's tastes are rather exotic. On his last visit here, he made disparaging comments about your cellar, but that did not stop him from consuming a whole bottle of the wine on his own.'

'Only one? Henry must have been on his best behaviour.'

'Mr Redmayne is given to excess.'

Christopher grinned. 'It comes from being the son of a senior churchman,' he said. 'Forget my brother. Fetch a bottle of wine from the cellar and set out three glasses. A celebration is in order.'

'Indeed, sir?'

'Yes, Jacob. My design has been approved by my client and

23

he is bringing the builder here this morning to meet me. This is an important moment in my career. I have finally reached the stage where a house of mine will see the light of day *and* be paid for in full.'

'That is cheering news, sir.'

'Look upon those bare shelves in the cellar for the last time. They will mock us no longer with their emptiness. We may at last be able to afford to fill them once again, if not with a vintage to Henry's taste, then at least with a tolerable wine.'

Jacob nodded then scuttled out of the parlour. Christopher looked down at the drawings laid out on the table in front of him. He had laboured long and hard to turn Jasper Hartwell's requirements into bricks and mortar, and he was pleased with the result. His fears about his client's unacceptable demands had been largely illusory. The exterior of Hartwell's new home would not, after all, reflect its owner's fantastical appearance in any way. He had been as willing to take instruction as to give it, resting gratefully on Christopher's superior knowledge of line and form, and eschewing any extravagance or vulgarity. The architect had been given the freedom to express himself without too much interference.

Christopher's visit to The Theatre Royal had borne rich fruit. Not only had he acquired a wealthy and indulgent client, he had been able to marvel at the art of Harriet Gow, an actress at the very height of her powers. It had been a memorable experience. The melancholy song from *The Maid's Tragedy* still haunted him and he hummed the tune aloud as he envisaged her singing the lament once again. Jacob showed less fondness for the sound. Returning from the cellar with a bottle of red wine in his grasp, he clicked his tongue at his master.

'You are doing it again, sir,' he commented.

'Doing what?'

'Humming that dirge.'

'It is no dirge, Jacob, but the most bewitching song I ever heard.'

24

'Then someone else must have been singing it.'

'Indeed, she was.'

'She?'

'A nightingale among women.'

'I've no time for birds who keep me awake after dark,' said the other, eyes twinkling beneath their bushy brows. 'Especially when they are so mournful. I prefer to hear happy songs in daylight.' He set the bottle on the table. 'Three glasses, sir?'

'Yes, please.'

'Your brother will not be joining us, then?'

'Henry will not even be up at this time of the morning, Jacob. His barber does not call until eleven. Besides, he has already played his part in this business. The rest is up to me.'

'Yes, sir.' Jacob took the wine into the kitchen, returning empty-handed to peer over Christopher's shoulder at the drawings. Scratching his bald pate, he let out a wheeze of admiration through his surviving teeth. 'Will there be anything else, sir?'

'Not for the moment. Though I should perhaps warn you.'

'About what, sir?'

'My client's appearance.'

'His appearance?'

'It is rather overwhelming.'

'I'm not easily overwhelmed, sir.'

'That is what I thought until I encountered Mr Jasper Hartwell. Suffice it to say that ostentation is his middle name. Prepare yourself, Jacob. When you open the front door, you will be met by a blaze of colour such as you have never witnessed before.'

'I'll bear that in mind, sir.'

He disappeared from the room and Christopher was left to examine his handiwork once more. Aspatia's song soon returned to his lips. He wondered if Harriet Gow really would attend a banquet at the house he had designed. It gave the commission additional lustre. His mind toyed with memories of the visit to the theatre and time drifted steadily by. The arrival of a coach brought him out of his reverie. Jacob opened the front door before the guests even had time to ring the bell. True to his boast, he was impervious to the vivid plumage before him. After conducting the two men into the parlour, the servant vanished into the kitchen to await the summons concerning the wine.

Jasper Hartwell was at his most flamboyant. Dressed in a suit of blue velvet adorned with gold thread, he doffed his hat, displayed the ginger wig to full effect, gave a token bow and offered a crooked smile.

'Forgive the delay, Mr Redmayne,' he said earnestly. 'Mr Corrigan arrived at my lodgings on time but we were held up in Holborn by the traffic. I've never seen so many carts and carriages fighting over so little space. It was quite unbearable. Something should be done about it. I may need to raise the matter in Parliament. Oh,' he added, extending a gloved hand towards his companion, 'let me introduce the man who will construct my wonderful new house – Mr Lodowick Corrigan, builder supreme.'

Christopher exchanged a greeting with the newcomer then waved both men to chairs. Several weeks had passed since their initial meeting and he had become habituated to his client's mode of address. Jasper Hartwell lived in a world of superlatives. Any architect he employed had, by definition, to be at the pinnacle of his profession; any builder was, by extension, unrivalled in his craft. While Hartwell burbled on excitedly about the project, Christopher sized up the man charged with the responsibility of turning a bold vision into reality.

Notwithstanding his client's fulsome praise, Lodowick Corrigan did not inspire confidence. He was a tall, wiry man in his forties, dressed like a gentleman but with more than a hint of incongruity. Rough hands suggested hard work and his weathered complexion was the legacy of long hours outdoors. Greying hair was divided by a centre parting and fell either side of a mean, narrow face. High cheekbones and a lantern jaw destroyed any sense of proportion and the obsequious grin was unsettling. Corrigan said nothing but his dark eyes were loquacious: they spoke of envy. Christopher sensed trouble ahead.

It was time to call for the wine.

It was no occasion for social niceties. Summoned to the inn by one of the watchmen, Jonathan Bale took in the situation at a glance. A big, beefy man with a red face had drunk too much too fast and become violent. Here was no ordinary tavern brawl. Patient entreaty only fed the man's aggression. Having knocked one customer unconscious, he beat the head of a second against a table then hurled a bench at a third. When the innkeeper tried to remonstrate with him, he was kicked in the stomach. The drunkard then went on the rampage, overturning tables, heaving a huge settle to the floor and generally terrorising everyone in the taproom. Watchmen were sent for but they arrived at the moment when the man chose to discharge a pistol into the ceiling, creating an impromptu snowstorm of plaster and extracting yells of rage from the couple engaged in strenuous fornication in the bedchamber above.

Jonathan marched in on a scene of chaos. Sword drawn, the man was stumbling around the room, swearing wildly, demanding a woman to take the edge off his lust and swishing his weapon in all directions. The sight of the constable only turned his tongue to even fouler language. Jonathan remained calm and waited for his chance. It soon came. The man staggered unsteadily towards him and tried to decapitate him with a vicious swipe of the sword. It was his last act of defiance. Ducking beneath the blade, Jonathan flung himself hard at his assailant, hitting him in the midriff and knocking every ounce of breath and resistance from him. The man was toppled like a tree. There was a resounding thud as the back of his head met the solid oaken floorboard then he plunged into oblivion.

A grateful silence followed. It was broken by a gulping sound as the drunkard began to vomit convulsively. Still nursing his stomach, the innkeeper walked across to Jonathan.

'Thank you, Mr Bale,' he said with feeling. 'He went berserk.'

'Do you know the fellow?'

'No, he's a stranger. And he won't cross the threshold of the Brazen Serpent again, that I can tell you.'

'If he does,' advised one of the watchmen, 'call me. Had it not been for the pistol, I'd have tackled the rogue myself.'

'Then he was lucky that he only had me to deal with, Abraham,' said Jonathan with an affectionate smile. 'You and Luke Peach here would have torn him to pieces between you and fed the scraps to the dogs. You are doughty watchmen.'

Abraham Datchett and Luke Peach did not hear the gentle irony in his voice. The two old men were dutiful officers but age and infirmity limited their effectiveness as agents of the law. They showed great bravery after the event but erred on the side of discretion whenever a crisis occurred. Fond of them both, Jonathan excused their obvious shortcomings and only ever assigned them tasks within their compass.

'Get him out of here,' he ordered. 'He has an urgent appointment with the magistrate. Lug him away so that this mess can be cleared up. I'll take statements from all witnesses then overhaul you.'

'Yes, Mr Bale,' said Abraham, pleased to be called into action. He bent over the supine figure. 'Grab his other arm, Luke. When I give the word, haul him upright.'

Jonathan helped them to lift the miscreant to his feet. Getting a firm hold on him, the two watchmen dragged him unceremoniously through the door, setting off a communal sigh of relief. The constable was brisk in his work. After taking statements from all who had been present during the outburst, he took possession of the discarded pistol and sword, refused the innkeeper's offer of a free tankard of ale and walked quickly after the others. The dazed offender was soon being charged by the local magistrate.

It was the third incident to which Jonathan had been called that morning and he knew that it would not be the last.

Baynard's Castle Ward, which he patrolled so sedulously, was an area rife with crime and disorder. The Great Fire had temporarily burned out some of its worst offenders but they were starting to trickle back now that rebuilding was under way in earnest and fresh pickings were available. If the streets were to be kept safe, Jonathan had to remain vigilant.

As he strode along Carter Lane with the sun on his back, he saw a figure emerge from a house ahead of him. The sight of the young woman aroused ambivalent feelings in him. Unsure whether she was a friend or a discarded acquaintance, he opted for a muted greeting, tipping his hat solemnly and rising to a noncommittal grunt.

'Good morning, Miss Hibbert.'

Mary Hibbert's pretty face lit up with unfeigned pleasure.

'Good morning, Mr Bale,' she said pleasantly. 'How nice to see you again! I hope that I find you well?'

'Very well, thank you.'

'How is Mrs Bale?'

'Extremely well.'

'I'm pleased to hear it.'

'You have just been visiting your uncle, I see,' observed Jonathan with a nod at the house. 'He has been ailing these past few weeks.'

'Alas, yes,' said the other sadly. 'My aunt sent me a note, imploring me to call. This is the first opportunity I've had to do so. My life has changed so much since I moved away from this ward. I am so busy these days – I have almost no free time. It means that some of my relatives have been rather neglected.' She gave a shrug. 'There is no help for it, I fear. I live in a different world now, Mr Bale.'

'So I understand.'

'I think that you criticise me for it.'

'It is not my place to pass judgement on you, Miss Hibbert.'

'Yet I can hear the disapproval in your voice.'

'It has no right to be there,' he apologised. 'Forgive me.'

Jonathan had always liked the Hibbert family. Daniel Hibbert was a skilful tailor, a small, anxious man who worked hard to support his wife and two children. The constable was sad to lose them when they moved from Carter Lane and distressed to hear that Daniel and his wife had been two of the first victims of the Great Plague. Mary, their elder child, had been in domestic service at the time. She was a kind, polite, obedient girl with attractive features. Jonathan recalled how hurt he had been to learn that she was now in the employ of Harriet Gow, an actress of such notorious reputation that even a God-fearing constable had heard of her. Looking at her now, he realised that he should not blame Mary herself. That would be quite unfair. She was one more victim of the Great Plague. Lacking the parents to guide her, she had gone astray.

Mary Hibbert seemed to read his thoughts. She shrugged again.

'It is only to be expected, I suppose,' she said.

'What is?'

'Your attitude, Mr Bale. My aunt is the same, except that she is more outspoken. She told me to my face that I had made a terrible mistake. But a girl has to take the chances that fall to her,' she added with spirit, 'and I do not regret having chosen the path that lay before me. It has opened my eyes to amazing new wonders.'

'I'm sure that it has,' said Jonathan evenly, 'though I suspect that your aunt and I might not describe them as wonders. That is not to condemn you. It is only natural that a young woman such as yourself is impressed by being able to wear fine clothes and travel in a carriage, but what price do you have to pay for such an experience?'

'What price?'

'Yes. What losses are involved? What dangers threaten?'

'Oh, there's no danger, Mr Bale, I do assure you. Our coachman takes great care of us. He is our protector. And nobody, in any case, would dare to hurt Miss Gow. When I am with her, I am completely safe. Have no fears for me, sir.'

'It is not physical danger that I speak of, Miss Hibbert.'

'Then what?'

'Moral danger.'

She gave a smile. 'You sound like my aunt.'

'Someone has to look out for you,' he said with concern. 'Since your parents died, that role falls to your relatives and to your friends.'

'But I can look out for myself.'

'That's a matter of opinion.'

'I respect yours, Mr Bale, but I'm afraid that I may have gone beyond the point when it has any relevance to me. My aunt told me bluntly that I have sold my soul to the devil when all I have done is to become maidservant to a talented actress.'

'Your aunt shares my distrust of the theatre.'

'Have you ever *seen* a play, Mr Bale?'

'Heaven forbid!'

'Have you been inside a playhouse?'

'I would not demean myself by doing so.'

'On what evidence, then, do you pour scorn on the theatre?'

'I have seen those who frequent such places, Miss Hibbert, and that is enough for me. During the Commonwealth, theatres were closed by law and the city was the better for it. There were standards of public behaviour. But now! All that is past. The drunken and the debauched flock to such places of resort. Women of the street parade their wares shamefully. Theatres are in a state of constant affray. They are sinks of iniquity and it pains me that you are associated with them.'

'It has done me no harm, I promise you.'

'It is bound to take its toll. However,' he said, making a conscious effort to sound more positive, 'the decision has been made and it is not for me to take you to task. I wish you well, Miss Hibbert. You deserve whatever success comes your way. To ride in a fine coach is a measure of success, I have to admit that. When you waved to us in Drury Lane some weeks ago, it crossed my mind that you had come a long way since your days of living here. Many would account you very fortunate.'

'I do so myself, Mr Bale.'

'Then let us hope that good fortune continues,' he said,

putting aside his reservations about her employer. 'Your aunt has a sharp tongue but she loves you dearly. Words spoken to wound you are well meant. Remember that. Mrs Hibbert has your best interests at heart.'

'What she conceives of to be my best interests.'

'Exactly.'

Jonathan managed a first smile. It was wrong to criticise Mary Hibbert for things over which she had no control. The corrupt theatrical world into which she had wandered seemed to have caused her little visible damage. To his eye, she still had the same friendly manner, the same unforced honesty and the same fresh-faced eagerness. Jonathan felt guilty at some of the doubts he harboured about her. Her parents would have been proud of Mary Hibbert.

'Goodbye,' he said, offering a friendly palm.

She shook his hand. 'Goodbye, Mr Bale.'

They parted company and he headed for home, ready for the meal which his wife, Sarah, would be preparing for him and having lots of gossip to pass on to her. Sarah would be interested to hear about the meeting with Mary Hibbert. As he plodded along the street, he rehearsed what he was going to say, noting with pleasure that his fondness for the girl had gradually subdued his apprehensions about her. Mary Hibbert's essential goodness would be proof against the temptation all around her. Jonathan was glad that the chance encounter had taken place.

It never occurred to him that he might not see her alive again.

Wine did nothing to improve Lodowick Corrigan. He sipped the contents of his glass slowly and deliberately, studying his companions through narrowed lids and nodding his agreement with all that they proposed or suggested. Jasper Hartwell drank freely, giggled incessantly and became ever more flamboyant in his gestures. Christopher, too, enjoyed the wine but he was very conscious that it was only making the builder more deferential. What worried him was that the deference was only on the surface. Corrigan's body might fawn obligingly and his tongue might release the odd word of ingratiation but his eyes were cold and watchful. When their employer was not present, Christopher suspected, then a very different Lodowick Corrigan might emerge.

Christopher tried to coax him out of hiding.

'What is your view of the site, Mr Corrigan?' he asked.

'It is well chosen, sir,' replied the builder.

'The best that money could buy,' added Hartwell, tapping his purse. 'Nothing less than perfection will satisfy me.'

'Why does the site recommend itself to you, Mr Corrigan?' said Christopher, pressing him for an answer. 'Give us a comment from the builder's point of view.'

'The builder merely obeys orders, Mr Redmayne. In this case, the orders are remarkably easy to obey because Mr Hartwell has chosen a prime site on which to set his house. It will be a privilege to work with him and, of course, with a rising young architect like yourself.'

Hartwell beamed. 'I knew that you would get on with each other,' he said, draining his glass. 'I sensed it in my bones.'

Christopher's bones were delivering a contradictory message. He was finding the builder both irritating and evasive. Behind his show of agreement, he caught worrying indications of the man's quiet conviction that, as the oldest and most experienced person involved in the project, he would have the power of decision. Far from obeying employer and architect, Lodowick Corrigan was lurking in readiness to frustrate and subvert them. He had firm ideas about how a house should be built.

Just before they departed, the builder finally showed his hand.

'There is only one thing that concerns me, Mr Redmayne,' he said casually. 'With respect to your position as the architect, I felt that I must raise the matter at this early stage.'

'And what matter is that?' wondered Christopher.

'The use of Caen stone.'

'It's what I recommend for the portico.'

'I know that, Mr Redmayne, but you were ignorant of the problems of supply when you made such a suggestion.'

'It's no suggestion, Mr Corrigan. It's a specification.'

'You might have to change your mind about that, sir.'

'Why?' said Hartwell. 'I liked the notion of Caen stone.'

'So do I,' insisted Christopher. 'I spent several weeks in Canterbury earlier in the year. Caen stone is used in abundance there, both in the ecclesiastical buildings and elsewhere. It is a clean, clear, well-defined stone. I noticed how easy it could be worked with chisel and hammer.'

'Other stone is even easier to work,' argued Corrigan. 'And it is more readily available here in London. I have shares in a stone quarry so I speak with authority here. If it were left to me . . .'

'But it is not.'

'Yet if it were . . .'

'If it were,' echoed Christopher, 'there would be no argument. You would have the stone of your choice and that would be an end to it. But that is not the case, Mr Corrigan, is it?' He paused meaningfully. 'As it happens, Mr Hartwell appreciates the virtues of Caen stone. On my advice, he wishes to have it incorporated into the façade of the house. I am confident that we will find a more than adequate supply of the material. Indeed, while I was there, I seized the opportunity to speak to one of the stonemasons in Canterbury to make sure that there were no difficulties with regard to delivery.'

Corrigan fumed in silence. He had lost the first of what would be many battles with the architect. With his employer present, he did not risk a second engagement but Christopher knew further hostilities would transpire in due course. The man wanted his revenge. Emptying his glass in one peremptory gulp, he glared at Christopher.

'How many houses have you designed? he asked pointedly.

'Several.'

'I'm not familiar with your work.'

'Nor I with yours, Mr Corrigan.'

'Walk down any of the major thoroughfares of London and you will see the work of Lodowick Corrigan. I am in great demand.'

'That is why I sought you out,' said Hartwell, adjusting his wig in a mirror. 'I wanted a builder without compare. Matched with an architect whose name will dance down the ages.'

Corrigan was sour. 'An architect is only as good as his builder.'

'Granted,' said Christopher. 'By the same token, a builder is only as good as his architect. If he is able to take direction, that is.'

'Oh, Mr Corrigan will take direction,' Hartwell assured him. 'They tell me he's the most obliging fellow in Creation. You'll have no cause for complaint, Mr Redmayne.'

'I'm pleased to hear it.'

'Lodowick Corrigan will hang on your every word.'

'Will he?'

It was a rhetorical question but the builder nevertheless answered it. The face which had for so long worn an obsequious smirk now became one large black scowl. The mouth hardened, the teeth clenched and the eyes smouldered like hot coals. Christopher Redmayne had been looking forward to the building of the house for Jasper Hartwell. It had seemed a wonderful assignment in every way. Until now. Much of the pleasure had suddenly drained out of the enterprise. In choosing Lodowick Corrigan as his builder, Hartwell had unwittingly confronted his architect with a major and perhaps insurmountable problem. The two men were natural enemies. As he looked into the angry face of his visitor, Christopher was left to wonder how much of the house he had designed would actually make its way from the drawing to the site on which it was to be built.

It was the worst possible time to interrupt him. Henry Redmayne was enduring the morning ritual with his barber when the servant burst into the room. Henry sat up in surprise, the razor slipped and blood spurted from a cut in his cheek. Henry's shriek was worthy of an amputated limb. It sent the barber into retreat.

'You're supposed to shave me,' he howled. 'Not execute me!'

'I'm sorry, sir,' mumbled the barber.

'It was your fault,' said Henry, turning upon the servant who had charged into the bedchamber. 'What on earth possessed you to come racing in here like that? Have you taken leave of your senses, man?'

'No, sir,' muttered the other.

'Then what other explanation is there?'

'An urgent message has come for you, sir.'

'Nothing is so urgent that it cannot wait until I have been shaved. Heavens!' he said, applying a fingertip to the wounded area to test the flow of blood. 'I might have had my throat cut. Look, man.' He displayed a reddened forefinger. 'I am bleeding to death here. Your master is close to extinction – and all that you can talk about is an urgent message. Damn and blast you! Take your hideous visage away from me.'

The servant held his ground. 'The messenger awaits a reply.'

'Let the villain wait.'

'But he is bidden to return to the Palace at once, sir.'

'The Palace?' Henry's self-pity gave way to alarm. 'The message has come from the Palace? Why did you not say that, you dolt?'

He snatched the missive from the servant's hands and broke the royal seal. It took him only a second to read the message. Jumping from his seat, he issued a stream of instructions before permitting the barber to stem the flow of blood from the cut on his face. Ten minutes later, he was mounting the horse which had been saddled for him and riding at a steady canter towards the Palace of Westminster. A royal summons demanded an immediate response. It swept everything else aside. Henry Redmayne was needed by his King. That was all that mattered.

Chapter Four

When they dined at the Dog and Partridge in Fleet Street, it seemed to Christopher that dogs and partridges were almost the only creatures that were not served as part of their meal. Fish, fowl and meat of every description were brought to their table in strict rotation so that Jasper Hartwell could inspect, admire, decry, sample, spit out, order or reject, according to his whim. He was a generous host, encouraging his guest to eat heartily and drink deeply. Hartwell set the tone, gourmandising shamelessly and barely pausing to allow one course to be digested before forcing another down his throat. Rich food made him more talkative, fine wine took him to the verge of hysteria. Hartwell's bizarre appearance already made him the unrivalled centre of attention. His wild laugh and excitable gestures ensured that everyone in the inn watched him with ghoulish curiosity.

Christopher Redmayne was at once pleased and dismayed. He was glad to be invited to dine by his client, especially as Lodowick Corrigan, the troublesome builder, had been deliberately excluded from the invitation. At the same time, however, he was worried by Hartwell's readiness to blur the line between employer and architect, to treat the latter as a friend with the same gluttonous appetite and the same vices. Christopher could simply not cope with such a huge meal on a regular basis. Nor could he show anything but polite interest in Hartwell's merry tales of his nightly visits to brothels and gaming houses. The suggestion that he might accompany his host on a nocturnal escapade was deftly deflected without giving any offence. It was an art he had perfected by dint of refusing similar blandishments from his brother, Henry, a man of rakish inclination with the money and the leisure time to indulge the wanton

37

urges that were his constant companions.

Eager to keep his relationship with Jasper Hartwell firmly on a professional basis, Christopher tried to guide him around to the subject of the house. It was not easy. Concentration had long since deserted Hartwell. He had reached the stage of giggling uncontrollably for no apparent reason. Stupor was only a few glasses of wine away.

'Why did you choose Mr Corrigan?' asked Christopher.

'Who?' replied Hartwell, pulling a face.

'Lodowick Corrigan.'

'Never heard of the fellow.'

'Mr Corrigan is your builder.'

Blank amazement. 'Is he?'

'You know he is, Mr Hartwell. You brought him to my home this morning so that I could meet him. We passed a pleasant hour or two together. Mr Corrigan seemed to be . . .' Christopher searched for a word to cloak his disapproval of the man. 'He seemed to be sound. Very sound.'

'The soundest man in the building trade.'

'You remember who he is, then?'

'Of course, of course,' said Hartwell, before guzzling some more wine. 'Lodowick Corrigan came with the highest recommendation. As did my architect. I pay for the best so I expect the best. If I had sufficient Latin, I'd translate that sentence and use it as my family motto. But I am no Classicist, alas. Latin baffles me almost as much as Greek. But the point holds, regardless of the language in which I express it. Only the finest of its kind is good enough for Jasper Hartwell. Well,' he said, chewing a mouthful of venison, 'you are living proof of the fact.'

'I'm flattered to hear you say so.'

'I recognise quality when I see it.'

'Thank you.'

'The Hartwell eye is unerring in its accuracy. Why, look at my apparel. Am I not the most elegant gentleman alive? I have the gift of selection. As with my clothing, so with my choice of employees. Pure instinct. No sooner did I catch sight of you at the theatre that afternoon than I thought, This young architect, Christopher Redmayne, is the man for me. That is why you are here.'

'I am deeply grateful, Mr Hartwell.'

'You are here but Corrigan, being of a lower order of creation, is not. A builder cannot enjoy the same privileges as an architect. He is a mere employee whereas you are also a friend. I will give the fellow a ride in my coach but I would not condescend to break bread with him. Apart from anything else, he has the most appalling hands. Did you notice all that dirt under his fingernails? No,' he continued, letting out a sudden laugh, 'Lodowick Corrigan is a prince among builders but he will never aspire to occupy a place among my intimates.'

'Who recommended him?'

'Several people. He has a fearsome reputation.'

'For what, Mr Hartwell?'

'Maintaining the dirtiest fingernails in Europe.' He shook with mirth and banged the table with both fists. 'Forgive me, Mr Redmayne. I am in humorous vein today. Let me be serious for a moment,' he said, making an effort to control himself. 'Lodowick Corrigan is renowned for building houses on time and to his clients' exact specification.'

'I'm glad to hear it.'

'You will have no problems whatsoever with him.'

'Good.'

Christopher was not as reassured as he sounded. The meeting with the builder had disturbed him profoundly. Instead of being able to work harmoniously with the crucial figure in the enterprise, he feared that he would have to fight every inch of the way to have his wishes fulfilled. Further discussion with Hartwell was pointless. The man now lapsed into maudlin reminiscence and all that Christopher could do was to compose his features into a semblance of concern and nod at regular intervals. Hartwell suddenly reached out to grab him by the wrist.

'I must confide in you, Mr Redmayne!' he gasped.

'About what, sir?'

'Affairs of the heart.'

'But you have been doing that for some time,' said Christopher.

'Those were mere trivialities. Passing acquaintances. The joyful conquests that all men need to remind them of their manhood. I speak now of true love, of devotion, of – dare I say it? – commitment. Nay, I would go even further and talk, for the first time in my life, of holy matrimony. That is how stricken I am. How ensnared. How desperate. I am even ready to contemplate the surrender of my bachelor life.'

'You have my warmest congratulations!'

'Sadly, they are premature.'

'Does not the lady in question requite your love?'

'She is not even aware of it as yet.'

'Have you not declared yourself?'

'Only with my eyes and with my palms. I have applauded her until my hands have been stinging with pain. She deserves it. She is sublime, Mr Redmayne. A saintly creature. Everything I could possibly want in a wife.' He gave an elaborate shudder. 'But there are certain drawbacks.'

'Drawbacks?'

'The lady is already married.'

'Ah, I see.'

'And she is beset by other suitors.'

'Does not her wedding ring keep them at bay?'

'No, it only seems to excite them all the more. A thousand wedding rings would not deter one particular lover. Indeed, were she not already in possession of a husband, the cunning fellow would certainly provide her with one forthwith then cuckold him mercilessly.' His whole body sagged. 'Do you catch my drift, Mr Redmayne?'

'I believe that I do.'

'A right royal obstacle blocks my path to happiness.'

'Then I can guess at the lady's name.'

'Is she not all that I have said?'

'She is, indeed!' said Christopher with enthusiasm. 'No

woman could be more worthy of your love.'

'Or of the house I am having built. It would be a fitting place for such beauty and grace. She could fill it with song. Bring it to life. Enlarge it with purpose. Tell no one of this,' he said, slurring the words. 'Jasper Hartwell does not wear his heart on his sleeve. I am too much a slave to fashion for that. But you know the truth, my friend. I worship her.'

'I can understand why.'

Hartwell spread his arms wide in a gesture of submission. 'I love Harriet Gow!' he confessed.

Then his arms dropped, his eyes closed, his head lolled and his whole body hunched forward. Jasper Hartwell's face rested gently on the plate in front of him. Christopher found himself sitting opposite a vast mountain of ginger hair. From somewhere deep in its interior came a series of resolute snores. The meal was comprehensively over.

The parish of St Martin's-in-the-Fields was one of the largest and most prosperous in London. Though not without its darker areas, it was, for the most part, distinguished by the luxurious residences of aristocrats, courtiers, gentry and their dependents, alongside the neat houses of respectable tradesmen and successful businessmen. Situated next to the Palace of Whitehall, the parish was the favoured address of ministers and civil servants alike. It had status and grandeur. In the church which gave it its name, it also had a magnificent edifice as its focal point.

Christopher Redmayne took a moment to appraise the church. Built over a century earlier, it had survived civil war, plague and fire intact, serving its parishioners faithfully and acting as a magnet to ambitious clerics once they realised what financial rewards could be reaped by the occupation of its pulpit. The spacious church had seating for a congregation of four hundred but, on the single occasion that Christopher had attended a service there, he estimated that at least twice that number were crammed inside St Martin's. It was a centre for urgent Christianity or for those who felt the need to be seen at prayer.

Critical of some Tudor architecture, Christopher had nothing but admiration for this example of it. The parish church of St Martin's-in-the-Fields was triumphantly what it set out to be – a solid, soaring paean of praise to the Almighty, rising above the community it inspired yet remaining essentially part of it, friendly, familiar, welcoming. Time had mildewed its stone and generations of birds had subtly altered its texture but it carried these signs of age lightly. Over eighty churches perished in the Great Fire. It was not only the parishioners of St Martin's-in-the-Fields who gave thanks that their church had been spared. Here was a symbol of hope. A beacon of renewal in the area of Westminster.

When he had gazed his fill, Christopher nudged his horse forward. He was still suffering from the effects of the monstrous dinner. Having helped to carry Jasper Hartwell out to the latter's coach, he had walked back to Fetter Lane, collected his mount, given Jacob some idea of his movements then set off to examine once again the site of the new house. It was only a few minutes' ride from the church. Occupying a corner, the site ran to the best part of an acre and offered a series of interesting challenges to both architect and builder. Christopher believed that he had met those challenges with some flair. Fortunately, his client agreed with him. Reaching the plot of land, he dismounted in order to walk over every part of the site while it was still virgin territory. Before long, he mused, a splendid new house and garden would rise up to take their place among the exclusive residences all around them.

Swelling with pride, Christopher was also assailed by doubts. It was one thing to create a series of remarkable drawings for a client but quite another to translate them into reality. Did he have the correct proportions, the ideal materials, the most suitable style? Had he made best use of the corner site? More to the point, could he control a difficult builder? Before he could even begin to answer the questions, he was diverted by the clatter of a horse's hooves and by a yell of brotherly rage.

'Christopher! Damnation, man! Where have you *been*?'

Henry Redmayne arrived at a canter, reined in his horse and leaped to the ground. Face perspiring beneath his wig, he lurched across to Christopher and pointed an accusing finger.

'It has taken me an age to find you.'

'I've not been hiding from you, Henry.'

'When I called at your house, that lame-brained servant of yours told me that you were dining with Jasper Hartwell, though he had no idea where. It was maddening!'

'Jacob is not lame-brained,' said Christopher loyally. 'He is the shrewdest servant I know. Do not blame him. When I left with my client, I had no idea where we were going.'

'No!' wailed Henry. 'That meant I had to work my way through Jasper's favourite haunts one by one. By the time I finally reached the Dog and Partridge, the pair of you had left so I returned once more to Fetter Lane. The ancient fool who looks after you at least gave me some idea of where you might be, although he could not supply the exact location of the site. The net result is that I have been charging around Westminster in search of you and getting more flustered by the minute.'

'Was it so important to find me?'

'Important and imperative.'

'Why?' asked the other. 'What has happened?'

'I received a royal summons.'

Christopher smiled. 'A promotion at last? A well-deserved reward for your years of service at the Navy Office? Ennoblement, even? Tell me, Henry – are congratulations in order?'

'No!' growled his brother.

'I am sorry to hear it.'

'Though I should perhaps be congratulated on tracking you down. It has taken me hours and, as you see, vexed me beyond measure.'

Henry's appearance bore out the description. He was panting with exasperation. His face was white with anger, his eyes bulging with resentment. The long, largely unproductive search had left him hot and dishevelled. His wig was awry and his hat clinging on at a perilous angle. The apparel over which he took such care was smudged and wrinkled. A self-appointed man of fashion was, for once, unkempt. It irked him.

'Look at the state of me,' he complained.

'It's hardly my fault.'

'Of course it's your fault, Christopher! But for you, there would have been no urgency, no madcap ride around London.'

'But you were the person who received the royal summons.'

'I *thought* I was,' said Henry darkly.

'What do you mean?'

'I was not even ushered into His Majesty's presence. After sustaining a vicious wound at the hands of my barber, I went to the Palace in great haste, only to be met by Will Chiffinch.'

'Chiffinch?'

'Page of the Bedchamber.'

'I thought I had heard the name before.'

'Anyone who wishes to get close to His Majesty is acquainted with Will Chiffinch. He is far more than a Closet-Keeper. He is the King's friend and trusted confidant, his pimp, pander and procurer-general. Chiffinch is also employed on the most secret and delicate business such as raising money for the royal purse or supplying information of a highly sensitive nature.'

'Then why did this Mr Chiffinch send for you?'

'In order that I could be dispatched to find my brother.'

Christopher was astonished. 'Me?'

'How many brothers do I possess?'

'But I have never even met this Will Chiffinch.'

'He controls the door to His Majesty. That is what makes this all so humiliating. I am hauled off to the Palace to be told that the royal summons is really intended for you and that my sole contribution is to hunt you down at once. In short,' said Henry, stamping a peevish foot, 'I am reduced to the status of a servant, a messenger, an intercessory. Why not approach you directly? Why involve me at all?'

'Did you not ask that?'

'I was not permitted to ask anything, Christopher. Besides, getting a straight answer out of Will Chiffinch is like trying to tattoo a bubble in pitch darkness with your hands tied behind your back. He is a master of evasion. Truth and he parted company such a long time ago that they no longer have anything in common.' He wiped the sweat from his face with a large handkerchief. 'The upshot of it all is this: now that I've located you, I must take you to the Palace of Westminster for a vital meeting.'

'With whom?'

'I was not told.'

'Why should I be summoned to the Palace?'

'I am beyond caring. All I know is that I must deliver you there with all due speed.' He hauled himself up into the saddle. 'Mount up, Christopher. This farce has gone on long enough. Come with me before I expire on the spot. It is so unkind, so cruel. They do me wrong to send me on such a mean embassy.'

'Is that what it is?' wondered the other. 'A mean embassy?'

Henry straightened his hat and adjusted his coat.

'There's only one way to find out,' he said balefully.

A servant conducted them through the labyrinthine interior of the Palace before handing them over to the Page of the Bedchamber. William Chiffinch was waiting for them. A tall, spare, dignified man in sober attire, he was quite elderly yet having a sprightliness that belied his years. There was something strangely nondescript about Chiffinch, an elusive quality which made it somehow impossible to remember the exact configuration of his features once you turned away from him. He was a walking paradox, an impressive figure who was yet almost invisible, a wielder of power who evinced no sense of his real influence. Introduced to the man by his brother, Christopher was struck by the dark, watchful, worldly eyes, taking everything in yet yielding nothing in return. He felt that he had been judged and found wanting.

'I am to take you into His Majesty's presence,' said Chiffinch.

'Not before time,' snapped Henry irritably.

'The invitation does not embrace you, Mr Redmayne. It is your brother who is in demand here. You were a convenient go-between.'

Henry was mortified. 'A go-between! A man in my position being used as a convenient go-between? This is intolerable.'

'On the contrary, sir, you have rendered a useful service.'

'Is that what you call it!'

'Lower your voice, Mr Redmayne.'

'Then do not give me cause to raise it, Mr Chiffinch. All that I ask for is a modicum of respect. Of simple human decency. Treat me as I have every right to be treated.'

'I may be forced to do just that,' said Chiffinch smoothly.

Henry blustered afresh. Christopher intervened swiftly.

'Calm down,' he said, patting his brother's arm. 'I am sure that a happy compromise can be reached here.' He turned to the other man. 'Mr Chiffinch, I am very sensible of the honour visited upon me, but it is only fair to draw attention to the crucial role played by Henry in getting me here in the first place. Where I go, my brother goes with me. If you acquaint His Majesty with that fact, I think that he may be ready to indulge us. Both of us are at his service.'

Chiffinch gave him a searching stare before letting himself out through a door. Christopher could not decide if he had surprised or annoyed the man. Henry had no doubts on the subject.

'You have just stepped on some significant toes, Christopher.'

'Have I?'

'It's not the way to endear yourself to Will Chiffinch.'

'I can live without his good opinion.'

'Not if you wish to befriend His Majesty.'

'I had to speak up for my brother,' said Christopher. 'You've been shabbily treated, Henry. I'll not stand by and let that happen.'

'Thank you.'

'We are in this together or not at all.'

'Bold words! You may live to regret them.'

'I think not.'

Chiffinch rejoined them to pass on a curt command.

'His Majesty will see you now – *both* of you.'

Christopher allowed himself a quiet grin and Henry basked in what he saw as a substantial triumph. Both of them followed Chiffinch into the Drawing Room. Having escorted them to the centre of the ornate carpet, the Page backed away so silently that it was impossible to tell if he had left the room or was lurking in one of its many recesses. Neither Christopher nor his brother dared to look round. Their gaze was fixed on the tall, immaculately dressed figure who sat opposite them. Framed in the high window, King Charles was staring dejectedly at a ruby ring on his left hand and ignoring the spaniels who were clambering all over him. One of them was perched on his shoulder, nibbling at the outer edge of his periwig and arousing the yapping jealousy of the other dogs.

The visitors waited until the royal head finally turned in their direction. Henry gave an extravagant bow but Christopher inclined his back with more restraint. Charles raised a morose eyebrow.

'You have come at last,' he observed.

'I had some difficulty finding my brother, Your Majesty,' said Henry apologetically. 'But I stuck to my task.'

'Good.'

'We are here at your command.'

'Henry.'

'Your Majesty?'

'Be quiet, please.'

'Oh, well, yes, naturally, if that's what—'

'Completely quiet,' insisted the King, quelling him with a stare before turning his attention to Christopher. 'We have

47

met before, Mr Redmayne. You rendered sterling service on that occasion.'

'As did my brother,' reminded Christopher.

'He is of no account here. You are, sir. That is why I sent for you, by means of a go-between.' Henry winced at the insult but wisely held his peace. 'Do you recall what I said at our last meeting?'

'I believe that I do, Your Majesty.'

'Well?'

'You were pleased with the way that I'd been able to render you some assistance and you were kind enough to say that you might call upon me again one day.'

'That day has arrived, Mr Redmayne.'

'Then it comes at an inappropriate time, Your Majesty.'

'Inappropriate?'

'I am heavily preoccupied with my work.'

'Royal business takes precedence over your career, however illustrious that may be. I should warn you that I am not accustomed to being thwarted. This is a matter of the utmost importance so I'll brook no obstruction.'

'Christopher was not being obstructive, Your Majesty,' said Henry.

'But you are, sir.'

'Without intention.'

'Hold your tongue or leave the room!'

'Of course, Your Majesty.'

'I only wish to hear from your brother.'

Henry recoiled from the rebuke and squirmed in silence.

'Is there nobody else who could take on this assignment?' asked Christopher. 'Work begins tomorrow on a house that I have designed. My presence on site is vital.'

'Not if the building is delayed.'

'There's no reason for that to happen, Your Majesty.'

'There's every reason. And before you ask again,' he said, lifting an imperious hand, 'there is nobody else who is so well fitted for the task before us. Great courage and discretion are required. You possess both qualities in abundance.

That is why I turn to you in this emergency.' He detached the spaniel from his shoulder and dropped it to the floor. 'No other names were even considered. I must have the two of you.'

Christopher was taken aback. 'Henry and I?'

'No, not Henry. That is a laughable suggestion. This is way beyond your brother's meagre capacities.' Henry bit back a protest and writhed afresh. 'The man I have in mind is that constable.'

'Jonathan Bale?'

'The very fellow. Surly but solid.'

'You have summed him up to perfection, Your Majesty.'

'The two of you worked well together.'

'Give or take a few disagreements.'

'Disagreements?'

'Nothing of consequence,' said Christopher dismissively, gliding over any mention of Jonathan Bale's republican sympathies. 'Constable Bale is a dedicated man. A brave one, too. He saved me from a beating.'

'You and he must pick up the trail at once.'

'The trail, Your Majesty?'

'Yes,' said the King, rising to his feet and scattering the dogs. 'The search must begin immediately. Thus it stands, Mr Redmayne. Someone very dear to me has been abducted. Circumstances compel me to pine for her in private. I need hardly tell you what those circumstances are. On one thing, however, I am decided. She must be found – alive and well – at the earliest possible opportunity.'

'May I know the lady's name?'

'All of London is familiar with it by now.'

'Indeed? Then she must be famous.'

'Deservedly so.'

'Who is the lady?'

'Mrs Harriet Gow.'

Christopher was stunned. The idea that Harriet Gow was in any kind of peril was a severe blow. He reeled. Unable to contain himself, Henry let out an exclamation of horror before clapping a hand over his truant mouth. The King began to pace the room.

'This is a bad business,' he moaned, 'and it must be resolved quickly. A precious life is at stake – a very precious life. Rescue must be effected.' He stopped in front of Christopher. 'All mention of me must, of necessity, be absent from this affair but I wish to be kept informed of any progress that you and Constable Bale make. Is that understood?'

'Yes, Your Majesty,' mumbled Christopher, still trying to absorb the shock of what he had heard. 'But can this be so? Mrs Gow kidnapped? Who could wish to lay rough hands on such a beautiful lady?'

'That is what you must find out, Mr Redmayne. Harsh punishment will await the malefactors, I can promise you that. I can also promise you and the constable a sizeable reward.'

'Saving the lady would be reward enough in itself.'

'Nobly said, sir!'

'I had the good fortune to see Mrs Gow in *The Maid's Tragedy*,' said Christopher, recalling the effect she had had on him at the theatre. 'A truly remarkable talent. That song of hers could charm a bird from a tree.'

'Then you will understand why I want her prised from the grip of her abductors,' said Charles, eyes flashing. 'The longer she is at their mercy, the more danger to her life. Act fast, Mr Redmayne.'

'Where will I start, Your Majesty?'

'That is up to you, sir.'

'But you've given me no firm information.'

'We do not have any, beyond the fact that Mrs Gow was travelling in her coach this morning when it was ambushed in a narrow lane. The coachman was overpowered, the lady seized and spirited away. A ransom note arrived soon after at the Palace.' He turned away to hide his consternation. 'What few details we have, you can learn from Will Chiffinch. Will?'

'Your Majesty?' said the other, emerging from a corner.

'Do what is needful.' He studied the ruby ring, distressed to think that the person to whom he gave its twin was in such peril. 'Mrs Gow occupies a special place in my heart. I'll not sleep a wink until she is safely returned to it. Please find her – *soon!*'

The King went back to the window and the audience was over. At a signal from Chiffinch, the Redmayne brothers tripped out of the Drawing Room. Christopher's mind was ablaze. All his reservations about taking on the assignment now faded away. Harriet Gow was missing. It was incredible and yet, when he thought about it, not entirely unexpected. Beauty as rare as hers, allied with talent as unique, was bound to attract envy and spite. Her enjoyment of royal favours would create another set of enemies. Which of them had kidnapped her? And how much were they demanding for her release?

Will Chiffinch took a deep breath then indicated some chairs.

'It might be better if you both sit down,' he said, marshalling his thoughts. 'What I am about to tell you is, of course, in the strictest confidence. Never forget that. You must be discreet. The ransom note, as you will see, warns of dire consequences if any attempt is made to rescue Mrs Gow. One wrong move could prove fatal to her.'

'You can trust me, Mr Chiffinch,' affirmed Henry with a hand on his breast. 'I am Discretion itself.'

'That is not His Majesty's estimation of you, Mr Redmayne.'

'Oh?'

'Hence the fact that you are relegated to the outer fringes of this inquiry. Remain there in silence, please. Otherwise, you delay us.'

'Tell us about the abduction,' urged Christopher. 'Where exactly did it take place? How violent were the kidnappers? Was Mrs Gow hurt?'

'We hope not.'

'Yet the King said the coachman was overpowered.'

'No question of that,' said Chiffinch with a sigh.

'What do you mean?'

'Let the fellow speak for himself.'

He crossed to a door in the corner and opened it to admit a big, brawny man of middle years in a torn coat that was spattered with blood. The coachman's craggy features were disfigured by bruises, and heavy bandaging encircled his forehead. A split lip throbbed visibly with pain.

'This is Roland Trigg,' introduced Chiffinch. 'He has been Mrs Gow's coachman for over a year now. His duties include more than simply conveying her from place to place. Mr Trigg is familiar with her movements and with those in her intimate circle. But let us return to the abduction itself. Hear it from one who was actually there. Mr Trigg?'

Roland Trigg ran a purple tongue over his swollen lip.

'She was took, sirs,' he said with a mixture of sadness and anger. 'Stolen from me in broad daylight. I fought hard to save her but I was outnumbered. Four of them in all. One with a pistol and three with cudgels. They left their trademark all over me, but no matter for that. Help me to find them, sirs, for I have a score to settle with that quartet.'

'A score?' echoed Christopher.

'Yes,' vowed the other, bunching his fists. 'I mean to kill each one of them with my bare hands. Slowly. Just for the pleasure of it.'

Chapter Five

It was an afternoon of mixed fortunes for Jonathan Bale. Though he cleverly apprehended the thief who broke into unoccupied premises in Knightrider Street, he failed to catch the man's accomplice, a nimble youth who got away with appreciable takings. The constable went on to stop a fight between two irate neighbours, adjudicate in a marital dispute over a dead cat and give evidence before the magistrate in three separate cases. When a breathless Abraham Datchett accosted him with the news that a corpse was bobbing about in the river, Jonathan rushed down to the wharf, only to discover that the watchman's failing eyesight had confused a piece of driftwood caught up in some tarpaulin with human remains. There were further examples of success and failure during his patrol of Baynard's Castle Ward. It was a typical day.

When his feet took him close to Addle Hill once more, he slipped home to see his wife and to take some refreshment. Sarah Bale was in the kitchen as he let himself into the house. Bare arms deep in water, she was washing some clothes for regular clients. Among the jobs she took on in order to supplement their finances was that of tubwoman, receiving filthy sheets and returning them with an almost pristine whiteness. It was hard work but Sarah revelled in it, singing to herself as she laboured and building up a steady rhythm in the tub.

Jonathan came up behind her to plant a kiss on her cheek.

'Are you still doing that, my love?' he said.

'It will keep me busy for a couple of hours yet.'

'You take on too much, Sarah.'

'I never refuse good, honest work.'

'You should.'

'We need the money, Jonathan.'

'We'll manage somehow.'

'You always say that.'

'Only because it's the truth.'

She broke off to dry her hands and to appraise her husband.

'You look tired,' she noted.

'It's been a tiring afternoon.'

'Have you called in here to moan about it?'

'I never do that, Sarah, and you know it,' he said solemnly. 'My work is left behind the moment I step through that door. This is my refuge. My place of sanctuary.'

'I wish I could say the same.'

She glanced at the washing with a wry smile. Sarah Bale was a plump woman with a round face that was full of kindness and character. His wife was almost twice the weight she had been when she married him but Jonathan was quite unaware of the transformation that had taken place. The happiness of their union imposed a benign form of blindness on him. Looking at her now, he marvelled yet again at her comely features and her youthful vitality.

Though he resented the amount of work she accepted, Jonathan saw the practical advantages. Apart from bringing a steady trickle of additional money into the home, taking in washing, sewing or doing other chores gave Sarah an insight into the lives of many families in the locality. Most of what she picked up was idle gossip but some of the information was extremely useful to her husband. Jonathan prided himself on the fact that he knew everyone in his parish by name but it was his wife who often provided significant detail about some of the people he nominally protected.

Jonathan poured himself a mug of beer to slake his thirst.

'Whose washing is that?' he asked, indicating the tub.

'Mrs Calcart of Thames Street.'

'When is her baby due?'

'You're behind the times, Jonathan,' she said, poking his ribs with an affectionate finger. 'She brought a lusty son into the world over a fortnight ago. There'll be even more work from Mrs Calcart from now on.'

'That sounds like bad news.'

'Not to me,' she said brightly. Sarah folded her arms and became serious. 'I've been thinking about what you said earlier.'

'Earlier?'

'That meeting you had with Mary Hibbert.'

'Yes,' he admitted, 'it's been preying on my mind as well.'

'Oh? Why?'

'Because I feel I was rather stern with her. Without cause. I tried to be friendly but my words were somehow tinged with disapproval. Why deceive myself?' he asked with a shrug. 'I *do* disapprove of what she's doing. There's no denying that. But it doesn't give me the right to condemn her.'

'That was my view as well.'

'I'm sorry I spoke out of turn to Mary.'

'She's still very young.'

'Young and vulnerable.'

'You should have been more considerate.'

'Should I?'

'More understanding.'

'About what?'

'Her situation. This position she managed to secure. Most people would think that Mary Hibbert has done very well for herself.'

'I'm not one of them, Sarah.'

'There you go again!' she teased. 'Running the girl down.'

'I'm worried about her, that's all. Deeply worried. Daniel Hibbert was a good friend of mine. Any child of his can call on me for help.'

'But that's not what Mary did.'

'More's the pity!'

'Aren't you forgetting something?' she said quietly. 'When the Plague ravaged the city, she lost two parents in a matter of weeks. Think on that, Jonathan. Yet she never complained or asked for sympathy. Mary and her younger brother kept struggling on. She did all she could to improve herself and her hard work finally paid off. Look what she's achieved. A place in the household of a famous actress.'

He was cynical. 'Famous or *in*famous?'

'Don't be so harsh.'

'I'm only being honest, Sarah. You think that Mary Hibbert has made something of herself but I shudder at what's happened. Her parents raised her to lead a life full of Christian endeavour, and where has it ended? In the playhouse! That veritable hell-hole. That public sewer called The King's Theatre.'

'Can it really be so bad?'

'Worse than I dare to describe.'

'But you said that Mary had not been corrupted.'

'Not as yet.'

'You told me how friendly and open she still was.'

'That's true,' he conceded. 'She had no airs and graces. Nor did I catch any hint of coarsening. It was a pleasure to talk to her.'

'It's a pity you didn't give her the same pleasure,' chided his wife, putting a gentle hand on his arm. 'You mean well, Jonathan, I know, but your strictures can be a little daunting at times.'

'Someone has to speak out.'

'There are voices enough to do that.'

'Mine will always be one of them.'

'Even when you're talking to an innocent girl? What harm has she done? What crime has she committed?' She watched him carefully. 'I'll warrant that Mary has *kept* her innocence, hasn't she? Did you find time to notice that about her?'

Jonathan pondered. 'Yes, Sarah,' he said at length. 'I did.'

'And?'

'Mary Hibbert has not been polluted.'

'Then why read her a sermon?'

'I've been feeling guilty about that ever since.'

'So you should.'

'Yet the girl needed to be warned.'

'Against what?'

'The dangers that surround her.'

Sarah gave him a hug. 'You spy dangers everywhere,' she said fondly. 'It comes from being a constable. You may claim that you never bring your work across that threshhold but it's not true. It follows you wherever you go. You're always on duty. You can't help being what you are, Jonathan, and I love you for it.'

'There's some consolation, then,' he said with a smile.

'You're a good man. Too good in some ways.'

'What do you mean?'

'You expect too much. You set standards that others can never meet. Stop trying to control people. They have their own lives to lead, Mary Hibbert among them. Leave her be,' she counselled. 'My guess is that she's under no threat. Not if she's the girl I remember. She has her wits about her.'

'You may be right.'

'I am right. Stop worrying about her.'

'I'll try, Sarah.'

'Have faith in the girl. Mary won't let herself down, I'm sure. Nor will she come to any grief. Just let her go about her own business in her own way,' she said softly. 'No harm will befall her.'

The flowers never ceased to delight her. Mary Hibbert walked among them like a child exploring a magic garden. Harriet Gow never lacked for floral tributes. Baskets of exquisite blooms arrived each day from close friends or anonymous admirers. The house near St James's Square was replete with Nature's beauty and charged with the fragrance of summer. A red rose caught Mary's eye, a flower so rich in hue and so perfect in composition that it took her breath away. She felt a vicarious thrill. No man had ever sent her flowers or even given her a posy. Yet she could take pleasure from the fact that her mistress attracted so much love and devotion. She could share indirectly in the joy of adoration.

It was early evening and Mary had been back in the house

for several hours now. She was glad that she had visited her sick uncle even though she collected a severe reproach from her aunt in the process, and, during her chance meeting with Constable Bale, some further disapproval. Mary could understand their attitude towards her and she was relieved that her brother, Peter, did not share it. Her aunt and her former neighbour could never appreciate the privileges of the world in which she now moved whereas Peter simply marvelled at them. Being surrounded by beautiful flowers was only one of those privileges. As she looked around the room with its costly furnishings, she offered up a silent prayer of thanks.

Hearing the sound of a coach, she crossed to the window to see if her mistress was returning but the vehicle rumbled on past the house. Mary was mystified. Mrs Gow should have been back some hours ago. Peter, too, should have arrived by now. Her brother was coming to get some money from her and he was rarely late for such an appointment. Mary had no idea where either of them might be. Mrs Gow's absences were routinely cloaked in euphemism. That was the rule of the house. In this particular case, her departure enabled Mary to pay the overdue visit to Carter Lane to call on an ailing relative. Enjoined to be back at the house by early afternoon, she wondered what had delayed her employer. Her apprehension grew.

She was relieved, therefore, when she heard the bell ring. Her mistress had come at last. Running to the front door, she flung it open with a welcoming smile but the greeting died on her lips. Instead of looking into the lovely face of Harriet Gow, she was staring at a complete stranger, a short, stocky individual in the garb of a coachman. The visitor tipped his hat respectfully.

'Miss Hibbert?' he asked.

'Yes.'

'We need your help, please. Mrs Gow has sprained her ankle and will not alight from the coach until you come. Follow me.'

'Wait!' said Mary guardedly. 'Where's Roland? He always

drives Mrs Gow's coach. Why isn't Roland here?'

'He, too, was injured in the accident, Miss Hibbert.'

'What accident?'

'Come with me and your mistress will explain.'

'But I see no coach.'

'It's just around the corner, a mere step away.'

'Why is it there?'

'Please,' he insisted politely. 'You're keeping Mrs Gow waiting.'

Against her better judgement, Mary went with him around the angle of the house to the vehicle that was parked in the next street. She came to a sudden halt. It was not her mistress's coach at all. Before she could protest, her companion grabbed her firmly by the shoulder. A second man, lurking in readiness in a doorway, came up behind her to drop a hood over her head and to push her forward. Mary was hustled swiftly into the coach. Strong arms imprisoned her while a rope was tied tightly around her wrists. She flew into a panic but the hood muffled her screams. Her flailing body was easily subdued by the people who trussed her up. It was terrifying. She heard a whip crack and felt the horses lunge into action. The coach soon picked up speed. As the vehicle rattled noisily along the street, Mary Hibbert continued to yell for help that she knew would never come.

'It is disgraceful! Wholly, utterly and inexcusably disgraceful!'

'Don't take it so personally.'

'How else am I to take it, Christopher? I've never suffered such embarrassment in my entire life. I, Henry Redmayne, a loyal servant to the Crown, a dedicated employee of the Navy Office. I've eaten with the King, drunk with him, gambled with him, walked with him, played tennis with him, watched plays with him, bowed and scraped before him at Court a hundred times and done just about everything else a man can do to curry his favour. Heavens!' he said, waving his arms like the sails of a windmill. 'We're practically on intimate terms. He calls me by name, knows me by reputation. And what does all this add up to in the end?'

'Try to rise above it, Henry.'

'Rejection! Total rejection!'

'That's not how I see it,' argued Christopher.

His brother was inconsolable. 'I know rejection when I feel it,' he howled. 'It's pure agony. You could hear it in His Majesty's voice, sense it in Will Chiffinch's manner. They give me no credit whatsoever. In their estimation, I am the lowest of the low, a messenger, a runner of errands, a base and unconsidered bearer of tidings.'

'You found me,' reminded Christopher. 'That was crucial.'

'Yes,' agreed Henry, 'but as soon as I did that, I was discarded. Cast aside. Abused. Insulted. Shamefully maltreated. Did I get any thanks? Did I earn any respect? No. It was akin to slow torture!'

Christopher let him rail on for another five minutes. Henry was still smarting so much from what he saw as his own humiliation that he could think of nobody else. After their interview at the Palace, they had returned to the house in Bedford Street to examine the situation and work out a plan of action. Henry was in such a state that he had to be given a cordial by one of his servants. Left alone with his brother in the drawing room, Christopher thought it best to let Henry's ire spend itself in a series of impotent protests. Fatigue eventually set in. Henry's voice became a mere croak and his body lost all its animation. He barely had the strength to remove his wig. Rational discussion could at last begin.

'Let us start with the key factor here,' suggested Christopher. 'Mrs Harriet Gow has been kidnapped. I think we should put aside personal concerns and address ourselves solely to that emergency.'

'But that is what I wished to do, Christopher. I revere that woman as much as anybody. I drool over her. It hurts me to think that she is in any kind of danger. Yet am I allowed to come to her aid?'

'Yes, Henry.'

'No. You listened to what Will Chiffinch said. I'm a disregarded bystander here. My opinion counts for nothing. When that hulking coachman told his tale, I was not even allowed to ask him a question. They've gagged me.'

'Remove the gag.'

'I was treated like dirt.'

'In that case, only one remedy will suffice,' said Christopher. 'You must prove them wrong, Henry. You must show that you're worthy of their respect and admiration. And the best way to do that is to help me in this daunting task of finding Harriet Gow.'

'You already have a partner in that enterprise.'

'Do I?'

'Yes. That plodding constable of yours, Mr Jonathan Bale. A stone-faced Puritan, if ever I saw one. He'd arrest a man for simply *thinking* about pleasure, let alone actually indulging in it.'

'You're being unfair to him. Mr Bale has fine qualities.'

'I've no use for them.'

'Well, I do, Henry. So does His Majesty. That's why he wants Mr Bale involved in this business. We two can achieve much together, but there are things that would be of enormous help to us. Things that only you could do.'

Henry jumped up from his chair. 'So that's all I am, is it?' he complained with renewed bitterness. 'Not even a royal messenger any more – but a constable's lackey!'

'Of course not.'

'My brother leads the search, Mr Bale blunders along in his footsteps, and there am I, ignobly bringing up the rear.'

'Nonsense!' said Christopher, adopting a firmer tone. 'This is a matter of life and death, Henry. Shake off your self-pity just for once and think about someone else. Keep the image of Harriet Gow before your eyes,' he urged, 'imprisoned by enemies. When I ask you to help us, I do so because I know how valuable your contribution will be, every bit as valuable as the one that I or Mr Bale could possibly make. We are equal partners here, all three of us.'

'Oh well, that's different,' said Henry, partially mollified. 'You are quite indispensable.'

'Am I?'

'Yes, Henry. Your assistance is critical. If we are successful, you will reap corresponding rewards. Think how impressed His Majesty will be with you. How much you'll astound Mr Chiffinch. And, most of all, what gratitude Harriet Gow will heap upon you.'

Henry was convinced. 'I'm yours,' he volunteered readily. 'Just tell me what to do.'

'First of all, give me your impression of what we've so far heard.'

'But I could make neither head nor tail of it, Christopher.'

'Go through it again now. Search for the logic.'

'Is there any?' wondered his brother, scratching his head. 'Harriet Gow is abducted. A ransom note is sent to the Palace. Five thousand pounds is demanded for the safe return of the lady.'

'That sounds logical enough.'

'Does it? Then you are not acquainted with the royal finances. They are in a parlous condition. His Majesty does not possess five hundred pounds, let alone five thousand. Every time he wants the most paltry sum, he's forced to go cap in hand to Parliament. There's simply no money to be had, Christopher. The Dutch War has bankrupted us.'

'But hostilities are now at an end.'

'Only because we were forced to sue for peace. Don't remind me of it,' Henry groaned, putting a palm to his brow. 'It was excruciating. But a few short months ago, the Dutch not only broke through our defences in the Medway, they sailed on to Chatham, sank three ships, towed away the *Royal Charles*, the pride of our Navy, raided Sheppey and destroyed the fort at Sheerness. It was my blackest day at the Navy Office. Crude as his metaphors always are, Sir William Batten was right. The Devil shits Dutchmen. We were well and truly buried in the ordure.'

'Come back to the ransom.'

'There is no way that His Majesty can pay it.'

'Not even when the life of a lady is at stake?'

'Especially then. It's one thing to beg money from Parliament for essential expenditure, but they would turn a deaf ear to any requests concerning one of his mistresses. Besides,' Henry observed, 'the terms of the ransom note were explicit. The transaction is to be kept secret. How can that happen if the House of Commons is involved?'

'I can see His Majesty's dilemma.'

'It is rather more complicated than that.'

'I know. There is the small matter of the Queen.'

'Her Majesty is the least of his worries. Other ladies bulk larger in his life than she does. Lady Castlemaine is the worst of them, as grasping and greedy a woman as ever clambered into the royal bed. A real viper when she is roused. Were it not for the fact that she would be more likely to kill than ransom Harriet Gow, I would not put it past her to be the author of this whole conspiracy.'

'Now we are getting somewhere!'

'Are we?'

'*Cui bono*: who stands to gain?'

'Lady Castlemaine would certainly gain from the removal of her chief rival, but she is not the only one. His Majesty spreads his favours far and wide. There are a number of ladies who would be heartily glad to have Harriet Gow removed from her pinnacle.'

'Make a list of them, Henry.'

'It may be quite a long one.'

'Every name is important. We'll work our way through them. But there's another area we must explore,' said Christopher, thinking it through as he circled the room. 'Her work at the theatre. Find out who her closest friends were. Ask when and where they last saw Mrs Gow. Sound them out about any potential enemies she may have. Oh, and above all else, speak to the manager.'

'Tom Killigrew?'

'He may give us valuable clues.'

'He'll be too busy tearing out his hair when he hears the news. Harriet Gow fills the theatre for him. Without her, his business will go slack. I don't relish passing on the bad tidings.'

'Then don't do so. Discretion is imperative here. Simply tell Mr Killigrew that Mrs Gow is indisposed. That's all he needs to hear.'

'When hundreds of playgoers are banging on his door, demanding to know why she does not appear on stage? What is the poor man to say? I must tell him *something*, Christopher.'

'Explain that she has been called away unexpectedly.'

'By the men who kidnapped her?'

'No!' exclaimed Christopher. 'Don't breathe a word on the subject. You read that ransom note. Break silence and you imperil Mrs Gow.'

'I'd hate to do that.'

'Then be ruled by me.'

'As you wish.'

'Start with Mr Killigrew. See what you can learn from him. Then talk to anyone at the theatre who was close to Mrs Gow. Do it carefully, Henry. Go armed and watch your back.'

'Why?'

'Brutal men are involved. You saw what they did to Roland the coachman. He was hired for his strength yet they got the better of him.' He recalled the sight of the battered servant. 'By the way, what did you make of the fellow?'

'I wouldn't care to bump into him on a dark night.'

'Nor I,' admitted Christopher. 'Trigg was a most unprepossessing character. Yet he seemed to be devoted to Mrs Gow and she must have found him satisfactory to put up with that ugly face of his. All that I'll venture is this: I'm grateful that Roland Trigg is on our side in this affair. I sense that he'd make a formidable enemy.'

'We may have enough of those, as it is.'

'Try to think who they might be, Henry. Rack your brains to tease out the names of anyone with a grudge against Harriet

Gow, or a reason to wound His Majesty by abducting her. You know the murky world of London far better than I do. Explore it to the full.'

'I'll do my best. Harriet Gow deserves nothing less.'

'My sentiments entirely.'

'What of you?'

'I'm off to look up an old acquaintance,' said Christopher, moving towards the door. 'Though I fear that he may not be overjoyed to see me again. Mr Jonathan Bale looks upon the Restoration as a form of moral plague. What is a dour Puritan like him going to make of the news that one of the King's mistresses has gone astray?'

'He'll probably raise three cheers.'

'It could be a difficult conversation.'

Christopher heaved a sigh then let himself out of the room.

Crime was no respecter of a constable's leisure time. No sooner had Jonathan started to read to his children from the family Bible that evening than he was summoned by one of the watchmen to deal with a new crisis. A warehouse had been set alight by a disgruntled apprentice. Although the blaze had been speedily controlled and the miscreant detained, a secondary crime was in the offing. Jonathan arrived on the scene in time to stop the owner of the warehouse from inflicting grievous bodily harm on the apprentice, who now cowered in a corner and pleaded for mercy. A combination of good-humoured firmness and diplomacy was needed to rescue the arsonist from the clutches of his former employer. Having hauled the young man in front of a magistrate, Jonathan took him off to be placed in custody. He was free to return home again.

Shadows were lengthening when he finally reached Addle Hill. Wanting to rest after a long day, he felt misgivings when he saw a horse tethered outside his front door. Sarah's greeting only intensified his concern. As he stepped into the house, her face was shining.

'We have a visitor, Jonathan,' she said with excitement.

'Do we?'

'Mr Redmayne.'

'What does he want?' grunted her husband.

'You'll have to ask him when he comes down.'

'Comes down?'

'Yes,' she said cheerily. 'Mr Redmayne very kindly offered to read to the boys. He has such a lovely voice. I could listen to it all day.'

'That's more than I can do!'

Jonathan was about to start up the stairs to interrupt the reading when he saw Christopher descending. The latter's polite wave gained only a brief acknowledgement. Jonathan was suspicious.

'What have you been doing up there, sir?' he asked.

'Reading to them from the Book of Judges,' said Christopher, 'the story of Samson. They seemed to like it at first.'

'At first?'

'It sent them both asleep.' He resorted to a whisper. 'I suggest that we keep our voices down and continue this conversation elsewhere.'

Jonathan gave a signal to his wife then led his guest into the parlour. Sarah went upstairs to check on her children. The constable was embarrassed and annoyed, uneasy at the thought of entertaining a gentleman in his humble dwelling and irritated at the liberties his visitor had taken while he was there.

'I'll thank you to leave any reading to me,' he said huffily. 'They're my sons and I give them a Bible story every night.'

'So I understand, Mr Bale, and I applaud you for it. But you were called away this evening and both Oliver and Richard were desperate for someone to read to them. I offered my services. Mrs Bale was only too happy to give me her permission. The boys seemed happy, too – until they dozed off towards the end.'

'I don't want it to happen again, Mr Redmayne.'

'Then I'll respect that wish.'

'Thank you, sir.'

Jonathan was standing awkwardly in the middle of the room. He waved Christopher to a chair then sat opposite him on a low stool. In spite of himself, he was not entirely displeased to see his guest again. He had developed a deep and lasting respect for him as well as a grudging affection. They could never be kindred spirits but an adventure had drawn them together in a way that was bound to forge a bond between them. It was one which put a friendly smile on Christopher's face. The constable's manner was more wary.

'What brings you to my house, Mr Redmayne?' he asked.

'I'll not pretend that it was the pleasure of reading about Samson, though that does have its charms. No, Mr Bale. I come on the most urgent business – at the express request of His Majesty.'

Jonathan quailed. 'His Majesty?'

'Do you recall what he once said to us?'

'How could I ever forget?'

'He said that he might need us again one day.'

'The words were like a hot brand.'

'Then steel yourself for more pain, Mr Bale. The call has come.'

'To you or to me?'

'To both of us. His Majesty was most specific about that.'

Great surprise. 'He remembered who I was?'

'By deed, if not by name.'

'But I'm only a humble constable.'

'I know, Mr Bale. I'm a struggling architect but that doesn't stop His Majesty from selecting the two of us for this assignment. It's a bizarre choice, I grant you, but not without its reason.'

'Reason?'

Christopher leaned forward. 'Before I say anything else, I must impress upon you the importance of secrecy. We are dealing with a very delicate matter here. Nothing must be heard outside these four walls.'

'You can rely on me,' came the brisk reply, 'and nobody will eavesdrop. When my wife comes downstairs, she'll go straight to the kitchen. You can trust Sarah. She understands.' His eyes narrowed. 'Now, sir, what exactly is this very delicate matter?'

'It concerns a lady, Mr Bale. A rather special lady.'

Christopher was succinct. He gave a clear account of the facts without embellishment. The effect on Jonathan was startling. He was, by turns, shocked, alarmed, scornful, interested, almost sympathetic then patently disgusted. One question burst out of him.

'Was the lady alone when she was abducted?' he asked.

'Apart from her coachman, Mr Trigg.'

'There was no one else in the vehicle with her, then?'

'Such as?'

'A maid, a companion.'

'No, Mr Bale. The coachman left us in no doubt about that. Mrs Gow was completely alone. That's what made her such an easy target.'

'I see.' Jonathan relaxed visibly before coming to a quick decision. 'Find someone else, Mr Redmayne. I'm not your man.'

'What are you saying?'

'That I've no wish to be involved. Why should I be? This crime has no relevance to me. It didn't take place in my ward and I can bring no particular skills to the solution of it. Someone else might. Seek him out and press him into service.'

Christopher was aghast. 'You are daring to *refuse*?'

'On a point of principle.'

'But this assignment comes with a royal command.'

'That's what appals me,' said Jonathan levelly. 'I'm sorry to hear that the lady in question has been kidnapped and I hope that she can be rescued before any harm comes to her, but I've no wish to be part of a scheme which has one obvious purpose.'

'And what's that?'

'Retrieving someone for His Majesty's bed.'

'You put it very bluntly, Mr Bale.'

'Bluntly but honestly.'

Christopher was stung. 'I make no comment whatsoever on the King's motives,' he said quickly, 'but this I can tell you. Harriet Gow's importance does not rest solely on her relationship with His Majesty. She is an actress of supreme talents, adored by all who have seen her perform or heard her sing.' He rose to his feet. 'I had the good fortune to witness her on stage myself and I've never been so moved by the sheer histrionic power. The lady is a genius. Let me nail my colours to the mast,' he said proudly. 'To save Harriet Gow, I'd go to the ends of the earth and endure any hazards. But I'll not succeed on my own. That's why I need your help.'

'It's not at your beck and call.'

'Nor even at His Majesty's?'

'There are other constables in London.'

'But none with your particular abilities, Mr Bale. How can you hold back, man? You're sworn to uphold the law. A dreadful crime has been committed and you're turning your back on the opportunity to bring the villains to justice.' Christopher was almost imploring him. 'Please consider your decision again. You simply must help me.'

'It's out of the question, sir.'

'But why?'

'I told you earlier. It's a point of principle. You may trumpet the lady's virtues but she inhabits a world of vice. Theatre is a symbol of all that's wrong with this city. I'll not subsidise corruption.' He got to his feet, his broad shoulders straightening as he did so. 'Nor will I provide a missing favourite for the King's bed. That's not what I call upholding the law, Mr Redmayne. It's condoning a vile sin in order to solve a crime.'

'The lady is in grave danger!' said Christopher angrily.

Jonathan was unmoved. He crossed the room to open the door.

'Then you'd better try to find her,' he said calmly.

Chapter Six

'Why are you asking me all these questions about Harriet Gow?'

'Idle curiosity.'

'I know you better than that, Henry.'

'The lady fascinates me.'

'She fascinates every man with red blood in his veins,' said Killigrew, twitching a lecherous eyebrow, 'but that doesn't make them interrogate me like this.'

Henry Redmayne dispensed his most charming smile. 'I ask purely in the spirit of friendship, Tom.'

'Friendship with me – or with Harriet?'

'Both, my dear fellow.'

'You're an accomplished liar, I'll give you that.'

'Then we have something in common.'

Thomas Killigrew laughed. He was too old and too experienced to be easily taken in. Now in his mid-fifties, he was a man of medium height, running to fat and showing candid signs of a lifetime of sustained dissipation. Viewing the puffy face with its watery eyes and drooping moustache, Henry found it difficult to believe that he was looking at the same man as the one who had been painted almost thirty years earlier by no less an artist than Van Dyck, the premier choice of Charles I, the most single-minded connoisseur of portraiture in Europe. Thomas Killigrew had moved in high circles. As a Page to the King and Groom of the Bedchamber, he was entitled to call upon the artistry of a true master. Anthony Van Dyck's brush had been precise.

Henry had seen the painting at Killigrew's house on a number of occasions. It showed a pale, slim, desolate young man in mourning over the death of his wife, Cecilia Crofts, one of the Queen's ladies-in-waiting. A bare eighteen months of marriage had ended in tragedy. Attached to the sleeve of the bereaved man was a gold and silver cross engraved with the intertwined initials of his dead wife. Around Killigrew's other wrist was a black band from which Cecilia's wedding ring dangled dolefully. The widower's expression was a study in dignified suffering. It was impossible to look at the portrait without being moved. Even someone as cynical and indifferent as Henry Redmayne had been profoundly touched when he first laid eyes upon it.

Van Dyck would paint a vastly different picture now. Tom Killigrew had lost his good looks in a steady flow of drink and debauchery. There had been hardship along the way. An unrepentant Royalist, he endured arrest, imprisonment and exile during the Civil War but he also contrived to find a second wife for himself, a rich lady whose wealth he enjoyed to the full and whose tolerance he stretched to the limit. The Restoration was the making of him, a chance to establish his primacy as a theatre manager, profiting, as he did, from his cordial relationship with the King and from his ability to judge the mood of his public in order to satisfy it time and again. Only one serious rival existed and Tom Killigrew had all but eclipsed him.

They were in the manager's room at The King's Theatre. One eye closed, Killigrew scrutinised his visitor through the other and stroked his moustache like a favourite cat. There was a mocking note in his voice.

'Do you wish to try again, Henry?' he said.

'Try what?'

'This foolish game of deception.'

Henry mimed indignation. 'Would I deceive *you*, Tom?'

'If you could get away with it.'

'I simply brought you what I felt was an important message.'

'Balderdash!'

'Mrs Harriet Gow is unable to appear on stage at the moment. I felt that you should know that at once. I must say that your reaction has been singularly uncharacteristic.'

'In what way?'

'Any other man in receipt of such intelligence would be frothing at the mouth. To lose any of your actresses would be a sorry blow. When the missing lady is Harriet Gow, there is a whiff of disaster in the air.'

'I've grown rather used to disaster,' said the other wearily.

'Aren't you at least disturbed?'

'Of course. Highly disturbed. Harriet was to have performed once more in *The Maid's Tragedy* tomorrow afternoon. I'll now be forced to rehearse someone else in her place.'

'How can you be so calm about it?' asked Henry.

'It's the calm after the storm, my friend. Had you been here an hour ago, you'd have caught me in mid-tempest.'

'Why?'

'That was when I first heard the news.'

'You *knew* already? But how?'

'By reading Harriet's letter.'

Henry gulped. 'She wrote to you?'

'That's what people usually do when they wish to send a letter. Hers was short but unequivocal. Sickness is forcing her to withdraw from London for a brief time.'

'Sickness?'

'No details were given.'

'And the letter arrived an hour ago?'

'Yes. Here at the theatre.'

'Who brought it?'

'I've no idea. It was left at the stage door for me.'

'Are you sure that it was written by Harriet Gow?' pressed Henry. 'Could it not have been a clever forgery? Did you recognise her hand?'

'Of course. It's unmistakable.'

'Was there nothing else in the letter? No hint?'

'Of what?'

'No entreaty?'

'None.'

'No second message between the lines?'

'Why should there be?'

'Oh, I just wondered, Tom.' Henry's tone was offhand but his mind was racing. A new piece of evidence had suddenly come to light. 'I don't suppose that you have the missive here, by any chance?'

'As it happens, I do.'

'Where?'

'It's in my pocket.'

'Ah.'

'And before you ask,' said Killigrew, anticipating his request, 'you may not view my private correspondence. Anything that passes between Harriet Gow and me is our business and nobody else's. Be assured of that. What you can do, Henry,' he continued, impaling his visitor with a piercing stare, 'is to tell me what brought you here in the first place. No lies, no evasions, no feeble excuses. What, in God's name, is going on? Why these questions? Why this subterfuge? Why come charging over to my theatre in order to apprise me of something I already knew?' He stood inches away from his visitor and barked at him. 'Well?'

Henry shifted his feet. His mouth felt painfully dry.

'Is that a flagon of wine I see on the table?' he murmured.

Christopher Redmayne was in a quandary. The lonely ride back to Fetter Lane gave him the opportunity to review its full extent. Plucked from a lucrative commission to supervise the building of the house he had designed, he was asked to track down and safely retrieve an actress who had been kidnapped in violent circumstances and who might already be a long distance away from London by now. What little information he had at his disposal had come from a coachman who had been beaten senseless and who was still stunned by the assault. Christopher's only assistant was his brother, Henry, erratic at the best of times, nothing short of chaotic at the worst. Jonathan Bale, the constable selected by the King to aid him in his search, had refused even to take a serious interest in the case because of its moral implications. It was lowering. To all intents and purposes, Christopher was on his own.

In an instant, the summons from the Palace had altered the whole perspective of his life. Instead of being engaged on site in the parish of St Martin's-in-the-Fields, he would have to begin the following day either by delaying work on the foundations or by yielding up control to Lodowick Corrigan. Neither course of action recommended itself. What excuses could he make? How would his absence be viewed? He blenched as he thought what sort of an impression his enforced disappearance would make on Jasper Hartwell. His client embodied a further complication. Here was a man, hopelessly in love with the very woman who had been abducted. What if Hartwell somehow caught wind of the kidnap? He would hardly thank Christopher for keeping such vital intelligence from him. It might sour their friendship beyond repair, perhaps even lose him the priceless commission to design the Hartwell residence.

Wherever he looked, Christopher saw potential hazards. His search for the royal nightingale could be the ruination of him. With so little in the way of clues, it was an intimidating task. He was groping in the dark. His one hope lay in a speedy solution of the crime but that seemed like a ridiculous fantasy. Without the resourceful Jonathan Bale at his elbow, he was fatally handicapped. It was an open question whether Henry would actually help, hinder or unwittingly subvert his enquiries.

He was still wrestling with his problems as he turned into Fetter Lane at the lower end and nudged his horse into a trot. Gloom was slowly descending on the city now, wrapping up its buildings and its thoroughfares in a first soft layer of darkness. When he got closer to his own house, however, there was still enough light for him to pick out the shape of the coach that was standing there. His ears soon caught the sound of a loud altercation in which Jacob seemed to be involved. Christopher dropped from the saddle and ran to investigate.

His arrival was timely. Jacob was trying to explain to his

visitor that his master was not at home but the man became aggressive and started to hurl threats at the old servant, waving a fist and accusing him, in the ripest of language, of wilful obstruction. Unabashed, Jacob gave tongue to such stinging obscenities that his companion was momentarily silenced. Christopher leaped into the gap between expletives.

'What on earth is going on here?' he demanded.

'There you are!' said Roland Trigg, swinging around to confront him. 'I need to speak to you, sir, but this idiot of a servant is trying to send me packing.'

'*I'll* send *you* packing if you can't speak more civilly, Mr Trigg. Anybody who abuses my servant must answer to me. Jacob is not an idiot. He's the most trustworthy man I know and he is waiting patiently for an apology from you.'

Trigg glowered at Jacob who responded with a gap-toothed smile. The coachman used Christopher as his court of appeal.

'But I've something important to tell you, sir.'

'It can wait until you've apologised to Jacob.'

'I came straight here when I found out about it.'

Christopher held his ground. Hands on his hips, he waited with tight-lipped disdain while Trigg argued, whinged, pleaded and blustered. In the end, the coachman realised that the servant had to be appeased before the master would listen to him. A reluctant apology tumbled out, stinging his swollen lip in the process.

'Thank you, Mr Trigg,' said Christopher evenly. 'Now that we've got that out of the way, perhaps you should step into my house. Stable my horse, please, Jacob. I'll not be going out again tonight.'

'Very good, sir,' said the other.

While his servant took charge of his horse, Christopher led his guest into the parlour. Trigg removed his hat to reveal the bandage. By the flickering light of the candles, he looked even more gruesome. Taking off his own hat, Christopher lowered himself into a chair and kept the coachman standing.

'What is it that you wish to say to me?' he asked brusquely.

'There's been more trouble, sir.'

'Trouble?'

'I didn't know who to turn to. Mr Chiffinch said I wasn't to bother him but I wasn't to talk to anyone else either. Apart from you, that is. He gave me this address so I come here.'

'And picked a fight with my servant.'

'I thought he was lying to me.'

'Jacob never lies, Mr Trigg. As you saw, I was not on the premises when you called. Well, come on,' he prompted, 'let's hear it. What's all this about trouble?'

'Someone else was took, sir.'

'Someone else?'

'Mary,' said the other. 'Mary Hibbert. Mrs Gow's maid-servant.'

'Kidnapped, you mean?'

'That's what it looks like, sir. Mary almost never stirs from the house except to go to the theatre with Mrs Gow. She should have been there. But when I got back, the door was open and the place was empty.'

'Had anything been taken?'

'Not so far as I could see.'

'Were there any signs of a struggle?'

'None, sir.'

'Then how do you know that Mary Hibbert was kidnapped?'

'It's the only explanation, sir,' gabbled Trigg. 'One of the neighbours told me he'd heard sounds of a scuffle and the noise of a coach being driven away fast. His wife thought she might have heard a woman's scream.'

'Might have?'

'Mary is in danger, Mr Redmayne. I *know* it.'

'The evidence is hardly conclusive.'

'She's such a dutiful girl, sir. Mary would never go out of the house when Mrs Gow was expected back. Nor would she leave the door wide open for anyone to walk in. Mrs Gow has many admirers,' he said with a touch of rancour. 'Too many for comfort. Some of them try to pester her at home. My job is to keep them at bay. If I'm not there to protect Mrs Gow, then Mary always is. Please, sir,' he begged. 'You must believe me.

I wouldn't have bothered you without real cause. Mary's been took.'

'Then it's a worrying new development,' conceded the other. 'You did right to bring the news to me, Mr Trigg. Thank you.'

Though he could not bring himself to like the man, Christopher took pity on him. In the service of Harriet Gow, he had taken a severe beating. He was plainly distressed that both of the women he was employed to safeguard had been snatched away from him. Shuttling between anger and remorse, Trigg was like a distraught father whose daughters had been abducted.

'When we met at the Palace,' recalled Christopher, 'you told me that you'd been coachman to Mrs Gow for over a year.'

'That is true, sir.'

'And before that?'

'I held a similar post with Sir Godfrey Armadale.'

'Why did you leave?'

'I was offered the chance to work for Mrs Gow.'

'How did that come about?'

'A friend put in a kind word for me.'

'You obviously take your duties seriously.'

'It's the best position I've ever had, sir,' said Trigg earnestly. 'Until today, that is. Mrs Gow treats me very well and I've grown fond of Mary Hibbert. They're almost like a family to me. I can't tell you how upset I feel because I've let them down.'

'Don't blame yourself, Mr Trigg.'

'I should've *saved* Mrs Gow,' he insisted, beating his thigh with a fist. 'I should have been there to protect Mary Hibbert. It's my fault, Mr Redmayne, and there's no getting away with it. That's why I want to do all I can to find them. Use me, sir – please. Call on me at any time. I must be part of the rescue.'

'You will be, Mr Trigg.'

Christopher appreciated the offer of help though he was not quite sure how best to employ it. The coachman's strength might certainly be an asset, especially as Christopher did not have the reassuring bulk of Jonathan Bale alongside him. Yet the sheer physical power of Roland Trigg could also be a handicap if used in the spirit of vengeance. During their earlier meeting, the coachman had made his feelings about the kidnappers quite plain. Murder had danced in his eyes. Christopher did not wish to be party to acts of random homicide.

'How are you now?' he asked, considerately.

'Hurt and upset, sir.'

'I was referring to your wounds. You were still somewhat dazed when we spoke at the Palace. You had difficulty collecting your thoughts.'

'Not any more.'

'Does that mean you've had time to think things over?'

'I've been doing nothing else, Mr Redmayne.'

'And?'

'I believe I know who might be behind all this.'

'You gave us a few possible names earlier.'

'I forgot the most obvious one.'

'And who's that?'

'Mr Bartholomew, sir.'

'Bartholomew?'

'Yes,' said the other with conviction. 'Bartholomew Gow. If you ask me, he's more than up to a trick like this. That's who you should be looking for, sir. Mrs Gow's husband.'

Sarah Bale had long ago learned to read her husband's moods. It enabled her to offer succour when it was needed, advice when it was welcome and understanding when it was appropriate. Jonathan wanted none of these things now. Having retreated into a reflective silence, he was temporarily beyond her reach. His wife respected his mood. When her work was finally done, she adjourned to the parlour to sit with her husband and to mend a pair of Richard's breeches by the light of the candle. Her needle was slow and unhurried. Though she was eager to hear what had passed between Christopher

Redmayne and him, she did not dare to raise the subject with Jonathan while he was preoccupied.

It was a long time before he even became aware of her presence.

'Have you finished your work?' he said, looking up.

'It's never entirely finished, I'm afraid.'

'But you're done in the kitchen.'

'For today, yes.'

'Good.'

'Did you want anything?'

'No thank you, Sarah.'

'Some cheese, perhaps? We've plenty in the larder.'

'Nothing, my love.'

There was a lengthy pause. Feeling that he owed her some kind of explanation, he struggled to find the right words. Sarah waited patiently. He cleared his throat before speaking.

'Mr Redmayne came on private business,' he said.

'I see.'

'He wanted me to help him with something but . . .' He gave a shrug. 'But I had to refuse. It was a question of conscience, Sarah. I simply couldn't bring myself to do what he was asking. It offended me. I know that Mr Redmayne thought it strange, even perverse. By his standards, it probably is. But I can only act as my conscience dictates.'

'That's what you've always done, Jonathan.'

'I had to speak my mind.'

'Is that why Mr Redmayne left so abruptly?' she probed, gently. He gave a nod. 'Do you want to tell me any more about it?' He shook his head. 'Another time, then. There's no hurry. I can see that it's shaken you somewhat.'

'It has, Sarah. I hated having to turn him away. Mr Redmayne is a good man at heart. It wasn't *him* I was rejecting.'

'I'm glad to hear that.'

'There was nothing else I could do.'

Sarah could sense the doubts that were troubling him, the second thoughts that were making him broach the subject in order to justify himself. She was fond of Christopher Redmayne. On the few occasions when they had met, he had been unfailingly polite to her, showing a genuine interest in her children and wanting to befriend them. It pained her that he had stalked out of her home in such disappointment. She hoped that she had not witnessed his last ever visit to their home.

Jonathan felt able to confide his anxiety for the first time.

'I hope I did the right thing.'

'Only time will tell.'

'He shouldn't have asked me.'

'No, Jonathan.'

'It was unfair. It's not my problem.'

But it clearly was now. Sarah did not ask for detail. Some of it was etched into her husband's brow. For reasons best known to himself, he refused to take on an assignment that involved Christopher Redmayne. It was not the end of the matter, Sarah knew that. Recrimination had set in. Jonathan would torment himself for hours. Whatever he had discussed with his visitor had affected him at a deep level.

In a vain attempt to cheer him up, Sarah starting talking about their neighbours, offering him snippets of gossip that she had picked up during the day. Jonathan was only half-listening. The most he offered by way of response was a tired smile. Even an account of the wilder antics of some of the denizens of Baynard's Castle Ward could not stop him from brooding. He was still miles away.

The banging noise brought him out of his brown study. Someone was pounding on the front door. Sarah reached for the candle and made to rise from her chair but he put out a hand to stop her.

'I'll go, my love.'

'Who can it be at this hour?'

'Someone who wishes to be heard,' he said as the banging was repeated. 'He'll wake the neigbours, if he goes on like that.'

'Is it Mr Redmayne again?' she wondered.

81

'It had better not be.'

Jonathan used the candle to guide his way to the front door. As soon as he started to pull back the bolts, the thumping stopped. He opened the door and found himself looking at a small, almost frail figure, silhouetted against the moonlight.

'Mr Bale?' asked a querulous voice.

'Yes,' said Jonathan, holding the flame closer to the face of the youth who was trembling at his threshhold. 'What do you want?'

'Don't you recognise me?'

'Why, yes, I do now. It's young Peter, isn't it? Peter Hibbert.'

'That's right, Mr Bale. Mary's brother.'

'You're shaking,' noted Jonathan. 'What's wrong?'

'Something terrible's happened.'

It took two large glasses of brandy to convert Henry's gibberish into intelligible English. Arriving wild-eyed and incoherent at the house in Fetter Lane, he had to be calmed and cosseted before his brother could get any sense out of him. Christopher had only just waved off Roland Trigg before his brother appeared on his doorstep. He and Henry now sat either side of the table with the bottle of brandy between them as their interlocutor. Henry succumbed to another upsurge of self-pity.

'Never, never do that to me again, Christopher!' he said.

'Do what?'

'Subject me to that kind of embarrassment.'

'What are you talking about?'

'That old fox, Tom Killigrew. It will take a far better huntsman than Henry Redmayne to run him to ground. He gave me the slip time and time again.'

'Did you learn anything useful?' asked Christopher.

'Several things.'

'Such as?'

'That I must have been demented to imagine I could coax any information out of Tom Killigrew without arousing his suspicions. I was hopelessly out of my depth.'

'Don't tell me that you gave the game away!'

'Almost.'

'That's the last thing you must do, Henry.'

'I know, but I couldn't help myself. What saved me was the fact that he was already aware of what I went there to tell him.'

Christopher blinked. 'Already aware?'

'Harriet Gow sent him a letter of apology.'

'When?'

'An hour before I arrived.'

'How could she do that when she's being held by kidnappers?'

'I think I've worked that out, Christopher,' said the other, pouring brandy into his empty glass. 'They must have forced her to write the note in order to throw Tom Killigrew off the scent. If he suspected for one moment what had happened to her, he'd raise a hue and cry.' He sipped the alcohol. 'Is this the best brandy you have in the house?'

'What did the letter say?'

'I need something stronger than this.'

'Tell me, Henry,' said his brother, shaking him by the arm. 'Did you actually see this letter from Harriet Gow?'

'No. It stayed in his pocket.'

Henry recounted his interview with Killigrew in detail, making much of the discomfort he suffered and the skill he'd had to employ in order to lead the manager astray. The letter of apology from Harriet Gow was what weighed with Killigrew. Christopher was reassured to hear that his brother had not, after all, betrayed his pledge to maintain strict secrecy. He was also pleased that the visit to the theatre had thrown up some interesting new names for consideration. Henry passed over a crumpled list.

'I recognise some of these,' said Christopher, perusing it with care. 'They are mostly members of the company. Who is Abigail Saunders?'

'An actress of sorts.'

'Of sorts?'

'A pretty enough creature who uses the stage to advertise

her charms rather than her talents, perhaps because she has an ample supply of the former and a dearth of the latter. Abigail Saunders is a young lady of high ambition.'

'Why have you drawn a circle around her name?'

'She will replace Harriet Gow in *The Maid's Tragedy*.'

'So she stands to benefit.'

'Greatly.'

'And is Abigail Saunders another nightingale?'

'More of a vulture,' opined Henry. 'An attractive one, I grant you, but she is all claw under those delightful feathers.'

Christopher was amazed to read the last name of the list.

'Sir William D'Avenant?'

'That was Tom Killigrew's suggestion.'

'I thought that you didn't discuss the abduction,' said Christopher in alarm. 'How did it happen then that the manager is identifying a suspect?'

'By doing so without even realising it. Now stop harassing me,' said Henry before downing the contents of the glass. 'Talk to Tom Killigrew and Sir William's name comes into the conversation time and again. It's inevitable. They are the only two men with patents to run theatres in London so they are deadly rivals. Tom Killigrew has the edge with The King's Theatre but Sir William D'Avenant has had many triumphs at The Duke's House. They'll stop at nothing to secure an advantage over the other. What's the worst thing that could befall Tom Killigrew?'

'The disappearance of Harriet Gow.'

'Which theatre manager would profit most?'

'Sir William D'Avenant.'

'Exactly. That's why I put his name on the list,' Henry said smugly.

'Is he capable of such desperate measures?'

'A man with no spectacles is capable of anything.'

'No spectacles?' Christopher could not follow this. 'Sir William?'

'Yes. The old lecher contracted syphilis so often in the past that it's eaten away his nose. He'll never balance a pair of spectacles on it, no matter how bad his eyesight.'

'Be serious, Henry. We're talking about kidnap here.'

'Then Sir William D'Avenant must be a suspect.'

'I wonder,' said Christopher doubtfully. 'Let's assume, just for a moment, that you may be right. Why should Sir William send a ransom note to the King when it ought more properly to go to the rival manager? He's the one who might be expected to buy her release.'

'Hardly!' said Henry with a harsh laugh.

'What do you mean?'

'Tom Killigrew's finances are in a worse state than the King's. Worse even than my own, and that's saying something. He had to beg, borrow and steal to raise the money to build his playhouse. Every penny that Tom had is sunk in The King's House.'

'Couldn't he find the ransom money somehow?'

'That would be a miracle beyond even him, Christopher.'

'I still cannot believe that Sir William D'Avenant is implicated.'

'Then you don't know him as well as some of us do.'

'Is he such a villain?'

'Try asking Miss Abigail Saunders.'

'Why?'

'She was his mistress.'

Henry took up his list and went through the names one by one, fleshing them out with detail and adding speculative comment. His knowledge of the theatrical world was impressive, his insight into the private lives of its leading members even more astonishing. When he had delivered his cargo of scandal and supposition, he sat back in his chair and used the back of his hand to suppress a yawn.

'I'm exhausted by all the effort I've put in today. Deception is such a tiring business. You always have to remember which lie you've told to whom and for what purpose. But enough of my travails,' he said as he reached for the brandy once more. 'What of you, Christopher? Have you spoken to the grim constable yet?'

'Yes,' sighed the other. 'For all the good it did me.'

'Did he not rush to the aid of a lady in distress?'

'Not exactly.'

Christopher gave him an edited version of the conversation that took place in Addle Hill, playing down Jonathan's rejection in order to rescue him from Henry's scorn. What he did talk about at length was the unexpected visit of Roland Trigg, the truculent coachman. Henry was troubled to hear of the second abduction.

'The maidservant taken as well?'

'So it seems.'

'This is a bad omen, Christopher.'

'I prefer to see it as a good one.'

'What goodness can there be in the kidnap of a young woman?'

'A little, I hope. I take it as a sign of consideration towards Harriet Gow. She must be in a state of absolute terror. Her kidnappers are at least providing her with some company to still her fears. She and Mary Hibbert are very close. Trigg kept telling me that.'

'He told you a great deal, apparently.'

'Some of it was very revealing.'

'If the fellow can be trusted.'

'Try to get behind that forbidding appearance of his,' suggested Christopher. 'The man might yet turn out to be a useful ally. Roland Trigg deserves the credit for one thing at least.'

'What's that?'

'Providing us with a name to go at the very top of our list.'

'Who might that be?'

'Bartholomew Gow.'

Henry was chastened. 'Her husband?' he said, eyes glistening. 'I never even considered him. He and his wife have lived apart for some time. I'm not even sure that Bartholomew Gow is still in London.'

'What manner of man is he?'

'An odd one. A fellow of moderate wealth and peculiar

disposition. Content to hug the shadows while Harriet courted the light – at first, that is, but he grew resentful. Never marry an actress, Christopher. They would tax the patience of a saint and Mr Gow is assuredly no saint.'

'Would he stoop to the kidnap of his own wife?'

'I don't know him well enough to form a judgement about it.'

'What does your instinct tell you?'

'Anything is possible.'

'Trigg was quite antagonistic towards him.'

'He'd be antagonistic towards anyone. I've never met such a bellicose individual. What did he have to say about Bartholomew Gow?'

'Nothing to the fellow's credit.'

'Did he tell you where the wandering husband was living?'

'No, Henry. But he has pointed us in the right direction.'

'Has he?'

'I think so,' said Christopher, indicating the list. 'Look at those names. They're giving us a false start. Instead of beginning with a list of those who might or might not have a motive to abduct Harriet Gow, we should work from the other end.'

'Other end?'

'The lady herself, Henry. Examine her character and way of life. That's where the clues will lie. Why, for instance, did she marry a man like Bartholomew Gow? How did she become involved with His Majesty? What hopes did she have for her future? In short,' said Christopher, getting up from the table, 'what sort of person is Harriet Gow?'

'You saw her for yourself at The King's House.'

'What I saw there was a brilliant actress, thrilling our blood and working on our emotions. She's in no position to do that now. Harriet Gow is no longer floating along on a cloud of applause, Henry. She's a very frightened woman, held against her will. How will she cope with that?'

'Bravely, I'm sure.'

Crossing to the window, Christopher peered out into the darkness.

'I hope so,' he said quietly. 'I sincerely hope so.'

Mary Hibbert was still in a state of abject terror. After the long, jolting ride in the coach, she had been taken to a house and locked in a small cellar. Tied firmly to a stout chair, she could scarcely move her limbs. The hood had been removed from behind by her captors so that she caught not even the merest glimpse of them as they slipped out of the room. The sounds of a key turning in the lock and of heavy bolts being pushed into position had been further hammer blows to her already bruised sensibilities. Too scared even to cry out, she sat in her fetid prison and sobbed quietly to herself. Another noise made her sit up in alarm. It was the snuffling of a rat in the darkest recess of the cellar.

Mary was beside herself with fear. Why was she being put through this ordeal, and by whom? What had she done to deserve such cruel treatment? Would she ever leave the building alive? It was at that point, when she was writhing in pain, being slowly overwhelmed by her misery and about to slide inexorably into total despair that a new sound penetrated the gloom of her dungeon. It was faint but haunting. She strained her ears to listen.

> *Lay a garland on my hearse*
> *Of the dismal yew:*
> *Maidens, willow branches bear*
> *Say I died true.'*

She revived at once. It was extraordinary. A song about death had effectively recalled her to life, had given her hope and sustenance. Only one woman could sing as beautifully and movingly as that. Mary Hibbert was not alone in her distress: Harriet Gow was sharing it with her. They were bonded by suffering. The voice rose, strengthened and sang on with mournful clarity. It was enchanting. Mary closed her eyes to listen to the strains of her beloved nightingale.

Chapter Seven

Henry Redmayne made such a determined assault on the bottle of brandy that it took the two of them to help him up into the saddle afterwards. He waved a perilous farewell then set off slowly in the direction of Bedford Street. Jacob watched the swaying figure merge with the darkness.

'Will he be safe, sir?' he said anxiously.

Christopher smiled. 'Have faith in the horse at least, if not in my brother,' he said tolerantly. 'The animal is well accustomed to carrying his master home when he has looked upon the wine at its reddest.'

'It was brandy this time.'

'Yes, and he had the gall to criticise its quality. I know, I heard him. That's typical of Henry, I'm afraid. He'll abuse your cellar then drink it dry. No matter, Jacob. He *is* my brother and his need was particularly urgent this evening.'

'So I saw.'

The servant led the way back into the house, clearing away the two glasses and the almost empty bottle into the kitchen. When he came into the parlour again, he saw that Christopher was unrolling some paper on the table. There was mild reproof in the servant's tone.

'You're not going to start work now, are you, sir?' he said.

'Bring me more light, Jacob.'

'You need your sleep.'

'Not when something is preying on my mind. I have to put my thoughts on paper. It's the only way that I can make sense of them.'

Jacob sighed but refrained from further comment. Lighting two more candles, he set them on the table with the others so that they threw a vivid rectangle of light on to the paper.

Christopher's charcoal was poised for action. He sensed that Jacob was hovering.

'I shan't require anything else now,' he said. 'You go to bed.'

'Not until you're ready to retire, sir.'

'There's no point in the two of us staying up.'

'There's every point,' returned the servant with a prim smile. He retreated towards the kitchen. 'Call me when you need me.'

'You may be in there a long time.'

'I've plenty to keep me occupied, sir.'

Jacob vanished from sight. Sounds of activity soon came from the kitchen as he began to clean some of the silverware. Christopher heard nothing. He was too absorbed in his project, drawing swiftly from memory and writing the occasional name on the paper. He was far too stimulated by the visits of Roland Trigg and of his brother even to consider going to his bed. In his own way, each man had sparked off Christopher's imagination. It was the coachman's evidence which guided his charcoal the most. Christopher was immersed for the best part of an hour before he sat up to stretch himself and massage the back of his neck. He was puzzled. As he stared down at what he had drawn, he felt that something was amiss but he could not decide exactly what it was.

The decision was taken out of his hands by the ringing of the doorbell. Jacob emerged at once from the kitchen as if his whole evening had been structured around this one particular duty. Christopher heard him open the door before engaging in a short dialogue with a man who had a deep, firm, resonant voice. The sound made Christopher rise with curiosity. He wondered why Jonathan Bale was calling on him. No visitor could be less likely in Fetter Lane. When the servant came back into the room, Christopher saw that he had, in fact, two guests with him. The burly constable was accompanied by a wiry, tousle-haired youth of no more than fifteen. Even in that light, Christopher could see the anguish in the boy's face.

Jacob sidled off to the kitchen again, leaving Jonathan to make an uneasy apology and to effect an introduction.

'I'm sorry to disturb you so late, Mr Redmayne,' he began, 'but this is something that wouldn't keep until morning. It may have some bearing on what we talked about earlier.' He turned to the boy. 'This is a young friend of mine, Peter Hibbert.'

'Hibbert?'

'His sister, Mary, is in service with Mrs Gow.'

'Then I'm pleased to meet you,' said Christopher with interest. He gave a kind smile. 'I'm Christopher Redmayne. You're welcome to my home, Peter. Do sit down for a moment.'

Peter Hibbert glanced at Jonathan as if requiring his permission. When the constable lowered himself on to the oak settle, his companion chose the stool in the corner. Perched on its edge, he looked smaller and more frail than ever.

'Peter has something to tell you, sir,' said Jonathan.

'Does he?'

'It's about his sister.'

'Then I'm eager to hear it.'

There was a long wait. Peter Hibbert was far too nervous to speak at first. Over-awed by Christopher and the fine house in which he lived, Peter's confidence dried up completely. He began to lose faith in the tale he had to tell. His eyes darted wildly. Jonathan tried to rescue him from his tongue-tied embarrassment.

'Go on, Peter,' he nudged. 'Say your piece.'

'You've come all this way to do it,' encouraged Christopher. 'I'll be interested to hear what you have to tell me about your sister.'

Hands knotted together, the boy stared at the floor and tried to summon up enough courage to speak. When the words finally came out, they did so in an irregular dribble.

'Mary – that's my sister, sir – is in service with Mrs Gow – Mrs Harriet Gow – she's a famous actress. They live in a big house near St James's Square. Mary is very kind to me, sir. She looks out for me.'

He came to a halt and shot a look of apprehension at Jonathan.

'Tell the truth, Peter,' said the other. 'Exactly as you told me.'

The boy nodded. 'I'm apprenticed to a tailor, sir,' he continued, aiming his words at Christopher via the carpet. 'It was my father's occupation though I'm afraid that I lack his skill. I'm poorly paid for my work so I get into debt quite often. Mary gives me money. I'll pay it back one day,' he said with a touch of spirit, 'but it may take time. Anyway, I arranged to call on Mary this afternoon, to collect some money from her. But when I got there, the door of the house was wide open and there was no sign of my sister.'

'A most unusual circumstance,' observed Jonathan. 'When her mistress is absent, Mary has responsibility for the security of the house. She would never leave it unguarded.'

Christopher had heard a version of the story from Roland Trigg, but he was grateful for corroboration. Peter Hibbert had come to the same conclusion as the coachman. Mary Hibbert was in some kind of terrible predicament. A creature of habit, if she made an arrangement to meet her brother, she never let him down. Mary knew how much he needed the regular gifts of money from her.

'What did you do, Peter?' said Christopher.

'I ran all the way to my uncle's house in Carter Lane, sir. I knew that Mary had called on him earlier in the day because he's been very ill. I wondered if she might still be there.' He shook his head. 'But she wasn't. Mary left hours before.'

'I can vouch for that,' added Jonathan. 'I was in Carter Lane myself this morning and I spoke to Peter's sister as she was leaving her uncle's house. We're old friends, sir. The Hibbert family used to live in my ward.'

'Let me hear it from Peter,' said Christopher gently.

'I was more worried than ever, Mr Redmayne, so I went back to the house. Mr Trigg was there. He's the coachman.

When I asked him where my sister was, he told me she'd gone away suddenly with Mrs Gow and that I wasn't to fret about her. But I do fret, sir,' said the boy, kneading his fingers. 'And I'm not sure that Mr Trigg was honest with me. He had these bruises all over his face and a bandage around his head.'

Christopher chuckled. 'That doesn't mean he was lying to you,' he said easily. 'As it happens, I've spoken to Mr Trigg myself and I accept his word. He's in the best position to know where your sister is, after all. Jacob!' he called. The servant was in the room instantly. 'This is Peter Hibbert. He looks very hungry to me. Take him into the kitchen while I talk to Mr Bale in private. Feed him well.'

Understanding the situation, Jacob whisked the boy off before the latter could protest. The kitchen door was shut firmly behind them. Christopher's relaxed manner evaporated at once. He lowered his voice to talk to Jonathan.

'The boy's fears are all too real,' he admitted, 'but he mustn't know that. We don't want him to spread the alarm or have his uncle and aunt getting anxious. Peter must think that his sister has gone out of London with Mrs Gow for a short while. Even though the plain truth is that she was most likely abducted from the house this afternoon.'

'Is that what the coachman said, sir?'

'He had no doubts about it.'

'Then the life of an innocent girl may be in danger.'

'Two lives are at risk here, Mr Bale,' corrected Christopher. 'I won't waste time arguing which of the ladies is the more innocent or guilty. Both need immediate help. The manner of their kidnap shows how bold and uncompromising the men who snatched them really are. They gave the coachman a sound thrashing.'

'I've changed my mind,' said Jonathan, getting up suddenly from his seat. 'I'm sorry that I had to refuse your invitation earlier on but matters are different now. I knew the Hibbert family well. I watched Mary and Peter grow up. Their father, Daniel, was a fine man and a good neighbour to us.' He thrust out his jaw. 'If his daughter is in the slightest danger, I'll help to rescue her.'

'That offer is music to my ears.'

'Just tell me what to do, Mr Redmayne.'

'The first thing is to calm young Peter down.'

'Leave that to me, sir.'

'It's a happy accident that you actually know one of the victims. You may be able to tell me things about her which supplement what I've already heard from Trigg.' He looked down at the table. 'Talking of whom, there's something you can do for me right now, Mr Bale.'

'What's that, sir?'

'Take a look at this map. It's rather crude, I fear, but I'm an architect and not a cartographer. Come over here – what do you see?'

Jonathan was impressed. 'A map of London, sir,' he said with a wheeze of admiration. 'As neat and tidy as you could wish. But that's London to the life, no question. You've moved one or two of the roads about by mistake and Fleet Street bends a trifle more than you've allowed. Otherwise, as far as I can judge, it's more or less accurate.'

'St James's Square would be up here in the corner somewhere,' said Christopher, marking the place with a cross. 'Now, if you had to drive a coach during the day from there to the Palace of Westminster, which route would you take?'

'The most direct one with the best roads.'

'And that would be?'

'Straight down to Charing Cross here,' said Jonathan, pointing with his finger, 'then south along King Street.'

'That was my feeling. Yet Harriet Gow was abducted when her coach was stopped in this narrow lane off the Strand – right here.' His own finger jabbed down. 'If Trigg was taking her to the Palace, why did he go by such a peculiar route?'

'Did he mean to call in at Drury Lane on the way?' suggested Jonathan. 'Perhaps she had business at The Theatre Royal.'

'The coachman assures me that she didn't. His mistress

had an assignation with someone though he refuses to tell me with whom. Given the circumstances, I naturally assumed that it was with His Majesty.'

'I've no comment to make on that, sir.'

'He and Mrs Gow have been very close of late.'

'Please keep me ignorant of such detail.'

'But it's critical, Mr Bale. You agree with me that there's only one sensible way to travel from St James's Square to Westminster. That leaves us with two alternatives.'

'Does it?'

'The coachman may have misled me.'

'Or?'

Christopher looked up from his rudimentary map of London. 'Mrs Gow had a rendezvous with someone else entirely.'

Night brought a few concessions for Mary Hibbert. She was given a candle and provided with food and water. The man who untied her was wearing a mask but she did not have the courage to look up at him. Grateful to have some source of light in the dark cellar, she picked at the bread and cheese. Her captor waited until she had finished then he pointed to the truckle bed in the corner. When he went out, the door was locked behind him with an air of finality. Mary shuddered. During the previous night, she had slept in a fourposter at the house near St James's Square. Now she was reduced to a filthy mattress in a dank prison. The scuffling of the rat made her resolve not to lie down anywhere.

Huddled into the chair, she sat in the tiny circle of light and prayed that her ordeal would soon be over. No relief came, not even the cheering sound of a song from her mistress. It would be a long, lonely, unforgiving night for Mary Hibbert. Her wrists were chafed by her bonds, her whole body aching from its confinement in the chair. Her prospects were bleak. Trapped in her cellar, unable to reach the woman whom she served, unaware of the identity or purpose of her captors, uncertain of her future, she was more despondent than ever.

* * *

Eager to make full use of daylight, Lodowick Corrigan arrived on site with his men shortly after dawn. Under the builder's supervision, posts were hammered into the ground to mark out the different areas of the property and materials were unloaded from carts before being stacked carefully in designated places. By the time that Christopher Redmayne rode up, workmen were already starting to dig the foundations. Overnight rain had left the earth soft and pliable. The picks sank deep and true. Pleased by the flurry of activity, Christopher was frustrated that he would be unable to stay in order to watch progress. Corrigan ambled over to him with an ingratiating smile.

'You're late, sir,' he commented drily.

'I had things to do, Mr Corrigan.'

'We like an early start.'

'So I see. You've certainly brought sufficient men.'

'The best I could muster.'

'They seem to know their jobs,' said Christopher with approval. 'That's not always the case, alas. With so much building going on in London, there's a desperate shortage of trained men. Fresh labour has had to be brought in from outside the city. Some of the newcomers are very raw and inexperienced.'

'I only employ men who know their trade,' boasted Corrigan. 'I'll not have anyone blundering around on one of my sites. If they work for me, they know the rules. I'm a hard taskmaster but I pay well.'

'It's a clear enough message.'

Corrigan unrolled a drawing and Christopher dismounted to take a closer look at his own draughtsmanship again. The builder had a dozen or more questions ready, all delivered in a tone of studied politeness but each one framed in terms that implied criticism. Corrigan was flexing his muscles, trying to secure minor changes to the overall plan in order to establish a pattern of amendment. Christopher resisted each suggestion with a mixture of reason and firmness, aware that even one concession to the builder would be viewed as a sign of weakness on his part. Unable to make any headway, Corrigan became more blunt.

'Some alterations will have to be made, sir,' he warned.

'Why?'

'Because that's what always happens.'

'Is it?'

'Problems arise, a client demands changes, the faults of an untried architect are exposed. I've seen it all before, Mr Redmayne.'

'Have you ever encountered a builder who was unable to take simple instructions? He would be the biggest handicap of all.'

Christopher's remark was all the more effective for being delivered in a pleasant voice. Corrigan tensed but said nothing. Rolling up the drawing, he went off to relieve his anger by berating some of his men with unnecessary relish. Christopher was grateful to have shaken him off but a new problem now presented itself. As a coach rolled up, the face of Jasper Hartwell beamed out at him. Attired with his usual flamboyance and almost buried beneath the ginger periwig, his client beckoned his architect across.

'Isn't this exciting?' he said with a childlike grin.

'Yes, Mr Hartwell. The first day is always rather special.'

'I'd not miss it for the world. And you, I daresay, will be here from dawn until dusk to watch your house take shape.'

'Alas, no,' confessed Christopher.

Hartwell was shocked. 'No? Why ever not?'

'Other business calls me away, sir.'

'But you're employed to supervise the construction of my new home. I can't have you deserting your post, Mr Redmayne.'

'That's not what I'm doing, I promise you. But further work is needed on my designs, small adjustments, subtle refinements. I can hardly do that here in the midst of all this frenetic activity. Besides,' he said, indicating the site, 'there is very little to see in the early stages. An architect is far better employed improving his design than by watching a group of muscular men dig a large hole in the ground.'

'There's some truth in that, I suppose.'

'Take my word for it, Mr Hartwell. I'll not be far away. From time to time, I'll ride over here to check that everything is in order. Your house will not be neglected. It occupies my full attention.'

'And so it must, Mr Redmayne.'

'Count on me, sir.'

'I do. I look upon you as a true friend.'

The voluminous wig prevented him from putting his head through the window of the coach so he crooked his finger to pull Christopher nearer to him. Making sure that they could not be overheard, he spoke in a conspiratorial whisper.

'I've decided to take your advice,' he said.

'My advice?'

'With regard to a certain lady. I touched on the matter when we dined at the Dog and Partridge yesterday.'

'Ah, yes,' said Christopher, amazed that the man could remember anything about the occasion in view of the amount he had eaten and drunk. 'I trust that you got home safely.'

'I awoke from dreams of pure delight, Mr Redmayne.'

'Dreams?'

'Of her. Of my angel. Of Harriet.'

'I see.'

'I don't think that you do,' said the other, reaching out to grasp him by the shoulder. 'Your counsel inspired me, my friend. I fell asleep a disappointed man and woke a happy one. You were so right. Why should I wallow in despair when I can reach for Elysium?'

'Elysium?'

'In essence, it stands right here before us.' Hartwell giggled as he pointed a forefinger. 'Until I confided in you, I was ready to give up all hope but you stiffened my resolve. I love her, I want her, I need her, I *deserve* her, Mr Redmayne. More than any man alive. If obstacles lie in my way, they can be removed. Mrs Gow may be married but she and her husband have been living apart for so long that it will not be difficult to put them asunder by legal means. If all else fails, Bartholomew Gow can be bought off and sent packing.'

Christopher was disturbed that Harriet Gow's name had come into the conversation and appalled that he was being identified as the person who had given Jasper Hartwell such ludicrous advice. The chances of her ever taking his proposal seriously were so remote as to be non-existent, yet that did not deter the single-minded lover.

'As for this dalliance with His Majesty,' said Hartwell dismissively, 'it is of no account. Harriet will soon tire of him and he'll be off after fresh conquests. None of that worries me. I'll not see her as the discarded mistress of a King but as the woman who has finally discovered a man worthy of her. Me!' Another giggle slipped out. 'Am I not the most fortunate of mortals? I've everything a beautiful woman could want, Mr Redmayne. Wealth, position, influence, taste and the handsomest face in the whole world. Harriet and I were fashioned expressly for each other. And the house you've designed will be our Elysium, our place of perfect bliss. Thank you for making it all possible.'

'I hadn't realised that that's what I'd done, Mr Hartwell.'

'You've given me a new mission in life.'

'Have I?'

'Marriage to my adorable Harriet. Then I'll bring her home in my arms. You've not just designed a magnificent new house, Mr Redmayne. You've created a gilded cage for my amorous nightingale.'

'Quite by accident, sir.'

'No matter for that. All things proceed to wondrous consummation. I'll court the lady in earnest and begin this very afternoon.'

'How?' asked Christopher.

'At the theatre, of course. Harriet is to perform once more in *The Maid's Tragedy*. I'll be there to woo her from my box then I'll lay siege to her dressing room until she agrees to see me.'

'That may be rather difficult,' cautioned the other.

'Difficult?'

'Mrs Gow will not be appearing today.'

Hartwell's face crumpled. 'Why ever not?'

'I fear that she's indisposed.'

'But I've banked all on seeing her this afternoon.'

'You'll have to be patient, Mr Hartwell. It so happens that my brother, Henry, was at the theatre yesterday, talking to the manager. Mr Killigrew gave him to understand that sickness was obliging Mrs Gow to withdraw from today's performance.'

'Sickness? The poor darling is ill?'

'According to the manager.'

Panic set in. 'I must go to her,' he declared. 'Nurse her. Tend her.'

'That's the last thing you must do, sir,' said Christopher, anxious to calm him down. 'What the lady most needs is rest from the hurly-burly of life in the theatre. The stage is an exciting place but it makes enormous demands on those who grace it with their talents. In any case,' he added, 'Mrs Gow is no longer in London. She had taken herself off to an unknown address to recuperate.'

'This is dreadful news!'

'I'm sorry to be the bearer of such tidings.'

'Not at all. I'm glad to hear them so early in the day. If my angel is sick, I want to be at her bedside. Tom Killigrew will know where she is. I'll to him to get the full details.'

'But the lady wishes to be left alone.'

'She'll want to see me,' said Hartwell, sitting back in his seat. 'I'll have privileged access to her. I'm not just one more lusty hound in the pack that bays at her heels. Harriet Gow is going to be my wife.'

He shouted a command to his coachman and the vehicle moved off. Christopher was covered in dismay. Not only was he being accused of having given advice that would never have issued from his lips, he was having to conduct a search for a woman who now had a crazed admirer on her trail. Jasper Hartwell's intervention could be ruinous. It would certainly hamper Christopher's own investigations. What concerned him more than that was the fact that it might also put the life of Harriet Gow in danger. Christopher was still trying to assimilate the new development when he became aware of Lodowick Corrigan at his shoulder.

'Was that Mr Hartwell?' asked the builder.

'Yes.'

'What did he say?'

'That he was pleased to see that work had started.'

'Why didn't you call me over?'

'He preferred to talk to his architect.'

'But I wanted to raise a few points with him.'

'Raise them with *me*, Mr Corrigan,' said Christopher, meaningfully. 'I'm the only point of contact between builder and client. Remember that and there'll be no friction between us. Forget it, however,' he stressed as he mounted his horse, 'and I fear that we may fall out. A sensible man like you would not wish that to happen, I'm sure.'

Before the builder could reply, Christopher rode off at a brisk trot.

Abigail Saunders was a revelation. When he rehearsed her that morning in the role of Aspatia, the most that Killigrew dared to hope for was a competent replacement for Harriet Gow. But the actress excelled herself. She knew the role well and exploited it to the full. Voice, movement and gesture could not be faulted. It was only the song which exposed her limitations. Abigail Saunders had a high, reedy voice that could offer only sweetness. It lacked the poignancy that Harriet Gow could achieve, the ability to fill the theatre with a sadness that was almost tangible. Killigrew did not complain. Though his patrons would be disgruntled at the loss of their favourite, they would be given a more than able actress in her stead. Pert, pretty and confident, Abigail Saunders was seizing her opportunity with the zeal of one who had waited for it for a long time.

When the rehearsal ended, it was not only Killigrew who

showered her with praise. The other actors on stage were quick to flatter her as well. Stepping into the breach, she was saving a play in which they now had a far greater chance to shine, liberated, as they were, from the dominance of Harriet Gow and the lasting impact of her song. None of them spared a thought for their missing colleague. All that concerned them now was the afternoon's performance. For making it possible, Abigail Saunders deserved their thanks and their approval.

One other person had watched the rehearsal with interest. When it was over, he put his gloved hands together in token applause. Killigrew broke away from his company to accost the intruder.

'Whatever are you doing here, Henry?' he demanded.

'Witnessing a miracle, Tom.'

'Abigail surpassed herself.'

'So I saw. It was almost as if she knew this chance was coming.'

'What are you implying?'

'Nothing.'

'Then why do you have that look in your eye again?'

'Sheer fatigue, I do assure you.'

Henry Redmayne had been forced to rise much earlier than was his custom in order to get to The Theatre Royal that morning. The visit had been worthwhile. It had certainly forced him to revalue Abigail Saunders as an actress. In the scene where Aspatia, disguised as her own brother, provoked the man who betrayed her into fighting a duel, Henry was so moved that he had been jerked fully awake at last. The whole experience left him with a new interest in the young woman who had replaced the absent Harriet Gow.

'No word from her, I suppose?' fished Henry.

'None,' said Killigrew. 'Harriet has gone to ground.'

'You make her sound like an animal.'

'She's an actress, Henry, and they are invariably one part human and three parts animal. If you worked with them as often as I do, you'd realise what vain and silly creatures even the best of them are. Actors are even worse,' he moaned.

'Rampant stallions. Did you know that I'm obliged to keep a woman at twenty shillings a week in order to satisfy eight of the young men in the house? Theatre management is a constant trial, sir. It's turned me pimp.'

'Harriet Gow is of a different order, surely?'

'Don't believe it.'

'She has such breeding and refinement.'

'A whore can pass for a nun on stage,' said Killigrew with a grim chuckle. 'That is the wonder of it. Harriet is neither whore nor nun but she is more akin to the former trade.'

'That's a scandalous thing to say!'

'I speak as I find, Henry. I love the lady to distraction but this is not the first time she's been wayward. Occasional disappearances have happened before.'

'Indeed?'

'She does it to vex me, I swear, or to remind me just how important she is to my company. Sick, indeed! I do not believe a word of that letter she sent. Harriet is the healthiest woman I know. She simply wanted a few days away from the theatre.'

'Why?'

'Why else? The pursuit of pleasure. A man of your proclivities must surely have guessed that. Sickness is the cloak behind which she hides but I know the truth of it. Harriet Gow is either lolling somewhere in a rich man's bed or sailing down the Thames in the royal barge.'

A deep sigh. 'I wish that you were right, Tom.'

'You've evidence to contradict me?'

'No, no,' said Henry, quick to extricate himself. 'I accept your word for it. Nobody knows the lady as well as you. I've only worshipped her from afar. Along with all the others.'

'Like that arrant fool, Jasper Hartwell.'

'Jasper? How is he involved here?'

'He was hammering on my door first thing this morning, begging me to tell him where Harriet was. When I was unable to do so, he first thrust money at me then threatened me with his sword. I tell you, Henry, it was all I could do to get rid of the dolt.' Killigrew threw both hands in the air. 'How did he *know* that Harriet was unable to play today? Has someone been issuing handbills to that effect?'

'I'm more worried about the passion that he showed.'

'Oh, that was real enough.'

'Jasper Hartwell? Aroused?'

'To full pitch. Harriet has certainly lit a fire in his breeches.'

'They're never doused, Tom,' said the other with a grimace. 'But they usually smoulder for some fair, fat wench in red taffeta. Jasper is a man who has to pay outrageously for his pleasures for no woman would oblige him out of love or curiosity.'

'Keep him away from me, that's all I ask.'

'I'll look into it.'

'And tell me why you're lurking in my theatre.'

'To pay my respects, of course.'

'To me, you lying dog?'

'No, Tom. To the new star in your little firmament. Miss Abigail Saunders. Excuse me while I have a word with the lady.'

Killigrew was about to protest but two of the actors suddenly pounced on him to demand their wages and an artist needed instruction about the scenery he was hired to paint. Henry dodged the manager and made his way to the dressing rooms at the rear of the building. He soon found the one occupied by Abigail Saunders. A tap on the door brought a short, dumpy, dark-haired woman into view.

'My name is Henry Redmayne,' he said in his grandest manner. 'A close friend of Tom Killigrew and a connoisseur of the theatre. I was privileged to watch the rehearsal just now and I just wished to add my congratulations to Miss Saunders.'

'Thank you, sir,' said the woman gruffly. 'I'll pass them on.'

'No, Barbara,' called a voice. 'Invite Mr Redmayne in.'

The maid stood reluctantly aside so that Henry could stride into the dressing room. Sweeping off his hat, he executed a low bow. Abigail Saunders watched him in her mirror.

'Your performance was a delight, Miss Saunders,' he said.

'Thank you, kind sir.'

'It will carry all before it.'

'That is what I intend.'

She rose from her chair and turned to appraise him. His voice had led her to expect a younger and more handsome man but her smile shielded her disappointment from him. Her life had been an endless series of Henry Redmaynes. She talked their language.

'Will you be at the performance this afternoon, sir?'

'Nothing would prevent me from missing it.'

'Pray, visit me in my dressing room afterwards.'

'I'll do so with a basket of flowers,' he said gallantly.

'Have you seen the play before?'

'Only once. It is a powerful drama and no mistake.'

'You watched Mrs Gow in the role, then.'

'Possibly, Miss Saunders. I've quite forgotten. You have made the part so completely your own, I can't imagine any other actress even daring to take it on.'

'You flatter me, sir.'

'I welcome a rising talent.'

He gave another bow and was rewarded with an outstretched hand. Taking it by the fingertips, he bestowed a light kiss before releasing it again. Abigail flirted mischievously with her eyes.

'All you've needed is your place in the sun,' he remarked.

'It's come at last, Mr Redmayne.'

'I hope that this is only the start.'

'Oh, it will be,' she said with quiet determination.

'You sound very certain of that.'

'I am, sir. Nobody likes to profit from the misfortune of others but that is the guiding principle of theatrical life. As one person falls by the wayside, another must take her place. I'm deeply upset, of course, that dear Harriet is indisposed but I know how much she would hate a play to be cancelled because of her.' She spread her arms and spun around on her toes. 'So here I am. Keeping the theatre open this afternoon when it might otherwise have been closed.'

'Tom Killigrew was overjoyed with you.'

'So he will be when he sees my full range.'

'Full range?'

'Yes, Mr Redmayne. Aspatia is only one of the roles in which I'll dazzle the patrons. There'll be many others.' She turned back to the mirror to examine her hair. 'After all, Harriet Gow may be indisposed for quite some time.'

Mary Hibbert slept fitfully until the sound of a key in the lock brought her rudely awake. The cellar was cold, damp and hostile. Since the candle had burned itself out, the room was plunged into darkness, robbing her of any idea of time. When the door opened, therefore, she was surprised how much natural light flooded in. It made her eyes blink. Mary was taken out to use the privy, an embarrassing business when a man in a mask is guarding the door but a necessary one all the same. Hauled back down to the cellar, she was given more food and water. Breakfast over, she was guided back up the steps, across the hall and up the wide staircase. Mary began to shiver uncontrollably. Was she going to be ravished by her mute companion?

When they paused outside a room, she tried to break free but he was far too strong, subduing her with ease and taking liberties with his hands that confirmed her worst fears. Mary felt as if she were being suffocated. She began to swoon. A door was opened and she was thrust roughly through it alone. Tumbling to the floor, she heard the door being locked behind her and quailed. Then she heard something else.

'Mary!'

Harriet Gow came running across the room to help her up.

'Have they brought you here as well?'

'Yes, Mrs Gow.'

Mary burst into tears, not knowing whether to be relieved at the sight of her mistress or frightened by the dire straits in which they found themselves. Rising from her feet, she flung herself into her employer's arms, each clinging tight and drawing comfort from the other. Harriet eventually took her maidservant by the shoulders.

'This is all my fault,' she admitted.

'No, no, Mrs Gow. Don't say that.'

'They've dragged you down with me, Mary.'

'I don't blame you, honestly. I'm just so glad to see you again.'

There was no gladness in her eyes. As she looked at Harriet Gow, she did not see the poised and graceful woman with whom she spent her days so happily. Her mistress was flushed and unkempt, her dress torn and her shoes discarded. Hair that was so lovingly brushed as a rule now hung in long, uneven strands. All of her jewellery had been removed. Her composure had also vanished. There was a hunted look about her.

'Where are we, Mrs Gow?' asked Mary, looking around.

'I've no idea.'

'Have they hurt you? Did they . . .'

'No, Mary. Nobody has touched me. Yet, that is.'

'They locked me in a cellar all night.'

'How dreadful!' She hugged the girl to her. 'My plight is little better but at least I have a comfortable bed and a garden I can look out on. Where exactly it is, I don't know. We were ambushed near the Strand. While they fought with Roland, someone put a hood over my head and pushed me into another coach. It seemed to travel for an age before we got here. All I know is that we're out in the country somewhere. It's no use calling for help. We're quite isolated.'

'I heard you sing, Mrs Gow.'

'What?'

'That's what kept me going. I heard your voice drifting down to the cellar and knew that you were here as well. It helped. I hate it that this has happened to you, but at least we're together now.'

'Yes, child.'

They exchanged a kiss and held each other tighter than ever.

'Mrs Gow,' said Mary at length.

'Yes?'

'Who are they?'

'I'm not sure.'

'What do they want?'

'They haven't told me.'

'Do you have no idea who they might be?'

'No, Mary.'

'Why are they *doing* this to us?'

By way of an answer, Harriet Gow eased her across to the little sofa and sat beside her on it. Letting the girl nestle into her, she stroked Mary's hair softly and tried to reassure them both in the only way that came to mind. She began to sing.

Chapter Eight

Jonathan Bale made up for lost time. Having committed himself to the search for the missing women, he began early next day by calling on the house in Carter Lane, ostensibly to reassure Mary Hibbert's relatives that she was safe but also to find out how much they knew about her life and movements. Having gleaned some interesting new details, he left the city by Ludgate and began the long walk towards St James's Palace. It gave him time to marshal his thoughts. Impelled by a desire to rescue Mary Hibbert, he was troubled by memories of the earlier meeting with her when, he now felt, his principles had got the better of his civility. Sarah Bale's comment had been apt: the girl was still young. Jonathan should have made more allowance for the fact.

He was also assailed by guilt about his attitude towards Harriet Gow. Personal interest had drawn him into the investigation but it was as important to find the actress he had never met as the maidservant he had known for years. Both lives were threatened. Both women deserved help. Jonathan chided himself for letting his conscience get in the way of his compassion. While he was worrying about his moral standards, a gifted actress was being held to ransom by brutal men. It had taken the kidnap of Mary Hibbert to bring him to his senses and he was keen to make amends. His stride lengthened purposefully.

St James's Square was still at a very early stage of its growth. Situated in fields to the north-east of St James's Palace, it was taking shape on land which had been leased by the King to one of his most trusted friends, Henry Jermyn, the enterprising Earl of St Albans, who, among other services to the nation, was credited with negotiating the marriage of Charles II. Plots of land around the square were let on building leases and snapped up by astute speculators. Large, well-appointed houses began to rise on all sides, their value increased by their proximity to St James's Palace. It was an area of high profit and aristocratic tone, the sort of suburban development that was anathema to a Puritan constable still shackled by notions of integrity and nostalgia for the Commonwealth.

When he finally reached his destination, therefore, he winced at the sight of the exclusive houses of the rich and titled, at the leafy parkland that surrounded it and at the extraordinary sense of space. Even since it was rebuilt, Baynard's Castle Ward was still a warren of cluttered streets and modest dwellings. St James's Square was a world apart, a frank display of wealth, a haven of Royalist sympathy, a dazzling manifestation of the true spirit of the Restoration. Jonathan fervently hoped that his business would not detain him too long in such an uncongenial part of the capital.

Harriet Gow's abode was at the end of a row of neat houses near the west end of the square. Smaller than most of the new residences that were being erected, they nevertheless rose to three storeys, had matching façades and boasted long walled gardens to the rear. Jonathan rang the front doorbell but got no response. Hearing a banging noise at the back of the property, he went under the archway that separated it from its neighbour and strolled down to the stable. Roland Trigg was inside, coat off and sleeves rolled up to reveal thick forearms. Using a hammer with the skill of a blacksmith, he was trying to beat a strip of iron back into shape on an anvil.

Jonathan sized him up quickly then stepped into his field of vision. The hammer immediately stopped swinging. Trigg straightened up and greeted the visitor with a defensive stare, wondering why a constable had come calling on him. The heavy implement dangled from his hand.

'Do you want someone?' he asked levelly.

'Are you Mr Roland Trigg, sir?'

'I could be.'

'Coachman to Mrs Gow?'

'Who are you?'

'My name is Jonathan Bale. I've been asked to help Mr Redmayne in a case of abduction. He's authorised me to talk to you.'

'Yes, yes, of course,' said Trigg, setting the hammer aside and relaxing slightly. 'I've said I'll help all I can, Mr Bale. Is there any news? Have you picked up the trail?'

'Not as yet, I'm afraid.'

'They want hanging for what they did!'

'Their days may well end on the gallows,' said Jonathan evenly. He looked down at the strip of metal. 'Doing some repairs?'

'The coach got damaged during the ambush when it was forced against the wall of a house. I want it as good as new by the time Mrs Gow comes back.' He hesitated. 'She is coming back, isn't she?'

'We've every reason to believe so. Now, Mr Trigg,' said Jonathan, taking a step closer. 'I'd like you to tell me exactly what happened.'

'But I've already been through it twice.'

'So Mr Redmayne said, but he also remarked on the differences between the two versions. When you spoke to him at the Palace, it seems you were still suffering from the effects of the beating.'

Trigg glowered. 'My pride was hurt the most.'

'Understandably.'

'Mrs Gow counted on me.'

'Did she?'

'I was her bodyguard.'

'Let's go back to the ambush,' said Jonathan.

'*Again*?'

'I appreciate how painful it must be for you to recount the facts once more. It can't be avoided, however. Mr Redmayne is a clever young man but he's not as used to gathering evidence from people as I am. I listen to witnesses all day long. I know what to ask, when to press for details, how to spot when someone is holding information back.'

'I held nothing back!' said the other belligerently.

'Nobody's accusing you of doing so.'

'They'd better not.'

'Mr Redmayne made a point of saying how helpful you've been.'

Trigg was appeased. 'I want them caught, Mr Bale,' he said. 'More to the point, I want to be there when it happens. I've got a stake in this, remember.' He pointed to his face. 'I didn't get these bruises by walking into some cobwebs.'

'How *did* you get them, Mr Trigg?'

'Now you're asking!'

'Tell me in your own words.'

The coachman perched on the anvil and spat into the sawdust. After looking his visitor up and down, he launched into a long account of the ambush, interspersing it with speculation about who his attackers might be and adding a description of his later return to the house.

'I knew it,' he emphasised. 'I knew they took Mary Hibbert as well.'

'That's not what you said to her brother.'

Trigg was checked. 'Who?'

'Peter Hibbert. He called here twice yesterday. Seeing the door wide open the first time, he became alarmed and ran to relatives in Carter Lane, hoping that he might find his sister there. But Mary was nowhere to be found. Peter hurried all the way back here and bumped into you. Or so he says.'

'It's true.'

'The boy had no reason to lie.'

'How did you find out about it?'

'The Hibbert family once lived in my ward, sir. I knew them well. That's why Peter turned to me when he felt his sister was in trouble.'

'He was very upset when he came back here.'

'Yet you did nothing to reassure him.'

'What could I do? Tell him that Mary had been took along with Mrs Gow? How would that have helped?' Trigg hunched his shoulders. 'I thought the best thing was to say as little as possible. So I pretended they'd both gone out of London for a few days.'

'Peter wasn't sure if he should believe you.'

'I wanted to get the lad off my back!'

'You might have done it more gently.'

'He was pestering me.'

'Returning to the ambush,' said Jonathan patiently, 'you've told me the exact point in the lane where you were set upon but you haven't explained what you were doing there in the first place.'

'Making my way to the Strand.'

'Down such a narrow thoroughfare? Surely there are easier ways to travel. And why go to the Strand? Mr Redmayne is firmly under the impression that you were heading for the Palace of Westminster.'

'Then he's quite wrong.'

'You had another destination?'

'We weren't going to the Palace that day.'

'Yet you ended up there.'

'Only because I was sent for, Mr Bale. The ransom note had arrived by then. They knew there'd been an ambush. I was hauled down there to explain what had happened.'

'So Mrs Gow was actually visiting someone in the Strand?'

'I didn't say that.'

'Do you dispute the fact?'

'I've no need.'

'What do you mean?'

'My job is to take Mrs Gow wherever she wishes me to take her. She has a lot of friends so I drive all over London. Well beyond it at times. I never know who she's going to see and I don't care. I simply do what I'm paid for, Mr Bale. That's all I'm saying.'

'Even though you could be hiding evidence?'

'Of what?'

'The motive behind the kidnap.'

'I've told you everything.'

'Except your destination yesterday. Don't you see how

important it is for us to know it, Mr Trigg? The person she was on her way to see might be able to help us. Perhaps someone had a grudge against him and used Mrs Gow as a means of revenge. One thing is certain, sir.'

'What's that?'

'You were expected. That ambush was laid in the ideal place.'

'So?'

'*You* mightn't have known exactly where you were going but someone else did. They knew the time of day you'd be driving down that lane and they knew just how many men it would take to overpower a strapping coachman and abduct a lady. Now,' he said, squaring up to Trigg, 'where were you taking Mrs Gow?'

'To see a friend.'

'Does he have a name?'

'She didn't say.'

'What about an address?'

'I've forgotten it.'

'So you were told?'

'I can't remember.'

Jonathan could not make out if he was dealing with sheer bloody-mindedness or with fierce loyalty to an employer. Either way, the result was the same. Willing to furnish any other information, the coachman was strangely reluctant to disclose the destination of his coach. It was time to try another tack with him.

'You mentioned the name of a suspect, I hear.'

'I mentioned several.'

'This one came as an afterthought. Mr Redmayne paid particular attention to it. He said I was to ask you about Mr Bartholomew Gow.'

Trigg nodded. 'He's tied up in this somewhere.'

'Why do you say that?'

'Because of the way things are between him and his wife.'

'But they don't even live together.'

'Exactly, Mr Bale,' said the other with a faint flicker of

lechery. 'How would you feel if a lady like that turned you out of her bed?'

'I'd never have got into it in the first place, I promise you!'

'Then you've never seen Mrs Gow. She's more than beautiful, I can tell you. It's a pleasure to be anywhere near a woman of her type. Mr Gow can't do that any more. He's been deprived. The last time he came to the house, she refused even to see him.'

'Oh?'

'He was very persistent. I had to move him on his way.'

'Is that one of the things you're paid to do, Mr Trigg?'

'Sometimes.'

'Moving her husband on his way?'

'Getting rid of undesirables,' said the coachman with a smirk. 'They buzz around her like flies. Swatting them is my job. But Mr Gow is the main problem. He's sworn to get even with her.'

'Was it a serious threat?'

'Mary Hibbert thought so.'

'What about his wife?'

'I think she'd gone past listening to him.'

'Why did Mr Gow bother her?'

'Ask him.'

'What was he after?'

'His wife.'

'But she turned him away and that made him angry.'

'Vicious, more like.'

'Wasn't she worried by his threats?'

'Not really, Mr Bale.'

'Why not?'

'I told you,' said the other complacently. 'She's got me.'

'Yes,' agreed Jonathan, annoyed by his manner. 'I'm sure that you protected her well – until you drove down that lane towards the Strand. Even your strong arm was not enough then, was it? They were waiting.' He leaned forward. 'Now who could possibly have known that you'd be taking that exact route?'

* * *

'I'm a very busy man, Mr Redmayne. I can only give you a little time.'

'Yes, Sir William.'

'I leave for the theatre within the hour.'

'Then I'll not beat about the bush,' said Christopher. 'I just wondered what you could tell me about Miss Abigail Saunders.'

'Abigail?'

'I understand that she was once a member of your company.'

'Briefly.'

'Why did she leave?'

'By common consent.'

'Miss Saunders is with The King's Men now.'

'That's of no concern to me,' said the other smoothly.

After studying the list provided by his brother, Christopher Redmayne elected to begin with the name at the bottom. Sir William D'Avenant was an eminent man with a lifetime of literary achievement behind him. Yet his career had been even more chequered than that of his rival, Thomas Killigrew. The godson of William Shakespeare, he was rumoured to be the playwright's illegitimate offspring and there were those who had hailed him as Shakespeare's natural heir. Civil war interrupted his promising work as a dramatist. A committed Royalist, he was captured twice but escaped both times. When the Queen sent him to Virginia, his ship was intercepted and D'Avenant was arrested once more. Held in the Tower, he was at least allowed to write and publish poetry. It enabled him to keep his talent in good repair.

Christopher called on him at Rutland House, his sumptuous home in Aldersgate, a place where he could not only enjoy the fruits of his success but where, on occasion, he had staged some of his theatrical events. D'Avenant was in his early sixties but looked at least a decade older. The vestigial nose, unfit to support spectacles, bore testimony to the goatish instincts of younger days and there were other indications in the gaunt face with its ugly blotches on leathery skin of an acquaintance with syphilis. Christopher found it hard to believe that such an elderly lecher could enjoy the favours of an attractive young woman.

'What is your estimate of Miss Saunders?' he asked.

'As an actress or as a person?'

'Both.'

'Abigail can decorate a stage nicely,' said the other, flicking a speck of dust from his sleeve, 'but she will never be more than a diverting piece of scenery.'

'Mr Killigrew disagrees with you, Sir William.'

'That goes without saying.'

'He's chosen Miss Saunders to take over a role vacated by Mrs Harriet Gow.' D'Avenant sat up with interest. 'She'll be seen this afternoon as Aspatia in *The Maid's Tragedy*.'

'Indeed?'

'Mr Killigrew has the highest hopes of her.'

'More fool him!'

'His judgement is usually sound.'

'Abigail has been promoted beyond her mean abilities.'

'That's not what my brother says,' said Christopher. 'He was at the theatre this morning and saw Miss Saunders in rehearsal. She left a profound impression on Henry. He could talk of nothing else when we met at a coffee-house a little while ago.'

'And you say that Harriet Gow vacated the role?'

'She is indisposed.'

'Do you know why, Mr Redmayne?'

'Sickness was mentioned.'

'Then it can be ruled out immediately,' said the other sagely. 'No actress would yield up as telling a role as Aspatia unless she were on the point of expiry. There's more behind this. Harriet Gow would never let an ambitious creature like Abigail supplant her, even for one afternoon, if it could possibly be avoided.'

'I take it that you admire the lady's work, Sir William?'

'Harriet? She is to Abigail as gold is to base metal. Let me be quite candid. Harriet Gow is the one member of Killigrew's

117

company I'd happily lure away to join The Duke's Men.'

'Not Michael Mohun or Charles Hart?'

'I have their equal in Betterton and Harris.'

'What about Miss Saunders?'

'Tom Killigrew is welcome to the lady. She causes more trouble than she's worth. In short, her aspirations greatly outrun her talents and that cruel fact never improves the temperament of an actress.'

'You sound bitter, Sir William.'

'Wise after the event, Mr Redmayne, that's all.'

The visit had established one thing to Christopher's satisfaction. Sir William D'Avenant was so patently surprised at the news about Harriet Gow that he could not in any way be involved in her abduction. Nor was he working with Abigail Saunders to further the career of a young woman who had, according to Henry Redmayne, been the old man's mistress. Whatever their true relationship had been in the past, it had left the theatre manager with harsh memories.

D'Avenant scratched at the remnants of his nose and regarded his visitor with growing suspicion. He flung a sudden question at him.

'What's your game, sir?' he demanded.

'My game?'

'Yes, Mr Redmayne. Why are you here?'

'I came to see you, Sir William.'

'To exchange tittle-tattle about actresses? No,' said the other with a cynical laugh. 'I think not. There's a darker purpose behind this visit, isn't there? Who sent you?'

'Nobody.'

'Tom Killigrew?'

'I came on my own account.'

'For what purpose?'

'The pleasure of meeting you, Sir William.'

'Pah!'

'It's the truth.'

'Don't talk to me of truth!' snarled the other, hauling himself to his feet. 'I'm old enough to remember a time when it hardly existed. When one thing was said but another meant. When we were all engaged in bare-faced lies of some sort in order to save our own skin.' He loomed over Christopher. 'I only agreed to see you because I know your brother, Henry, a disreputable character, to be sure, but he has a certain louche charm and he patronises my theatre without trying to tear it apart as some of those drunken gallants do. His name got you in through my door but I've yet to hear a reason why I shouldn't turn you straight out again.'

'Then perhaps I should declare my hand,' said Christopher, smiling apologetically as he groped in his mind for an excuse to cover his arrival. 'You're far too perceptive to be misled, Sir William. The fact is that my visit here is connected with my profession.'

'That of a spy, perhaps?'

'Not exactly, though a certain amount of listening, watching and gathering intelligence is required so I have something of the spy about me. I'm an architect, Sir William. I live by my talents.'

'Why trouble me with your company?'

'Because I heard a whisper that you plan to build a new theatre.'

'You've sharp ears, Mr Redmayne.'

'In my profession, I need them,' said Christopher. 'I've a particular fascination with theatre architecture and came to offer my services.'

'I'd look for more experience than you have to offer.'

'Enthusiasm can sometimes outweigh experience.'

'Sometimes,' conceded the other, looking at him with curiosity. 'An architect, you say? What have you designed, Mr Redmayne?'

'Domestic buildings, for the most part.'

'For whom?'

'The last was for Lord Staines. The project on which I'm currently employed is a house I've designed for Mr Jasper Hartwell.'

'Hartwell? That lunatic fop in the ginger wig?'

'He's a good client, sir.'

'And a rich fool into the bargain. That's the best kind of client you can have. Well, you must have earned your spurs if someone like Lord Staines sees fit to offer you a commission, and Jasper Hartwell would never live in a cheap house. You have definite credit, Mr Redmayne.'

'Enough to interest you, Sir William?'

'Tell me what you know about the design of a theatre.'

'I've visited Mr Killigrew's playhouse and your own, of course, in Portugal Street where you converted Lisle's Tennis Court into a theatre.'

'Successfully, do you think?'

'Yes, Sir William. You showed great invention. Your use of scenery was quite brilliant. That's what forced Mr Killigrew to build his new theatre near Drury Lane. His own converted tennis court in Vere Street could never match The Duke's Playhouse.'

Christopher expatiated on the architectural merits of all three buildings but he had criticism as well as praise. He took care to mention that he had seen several plays performed in France and learned much from their presentation. Convinced that his visitor's interest was real, D'Avenant was soon caught up in a heady discussion of his own plans, showing a deep knowledge of theatrical practicalities and a commendable grasp of architectural principles. In the course of their debate, he also introduced a fund of anecdotes about actors and actresses with whom he had worked in his long career. Christopher was entranced. Valuable new facts were emerging every minute.

'I am known as a master of adaptation,' said D'Avenant proudly. 'For one thing, I have the right to adapt the plays of my godfather, the revered William Shakespeare, a name that will always live on our stages. But, in a sense, Mr Redmayne, my whole life has been one interminable act of adaptation. Circumstances forced me to change time and again. I had to adapt or perish. Take the Commonwealth,' he went on, resuming his seat. 'Theatres were closed down, actors thrown out of work. But I found a way around the rules. Plays might be forbidden but there was no decree against opera. Adaptation came to my aid once again. I took a play called *The Siege of Rhodes* and, by the addition of music and song, turned it into an opera. Since I had no theatre, I adapted this very house for performance.'

'Your name is a by-word for ingenuity, Sir William.'

'So it should be. It's what sets me apart from that grubbing little charlatan, Tom Killigrew. That and the fact that I write plays of true wit whereas he can only manage comedies so scurrilous that even the most degenerate minds are offended by them. Enough of him!' he said derisively. 'The point is this, Mr Redmayne. After all those years of adaptation, I wish to create something wholly original, a theatre that is neither a converted tennis court nor a riding school, but an auditorium conceived solely and exclusively for dramatic entertainment, embodying all that I have learned about that elusive art.'

'Have you chosen a site?'

'It will be in Dorset Garden.'

'What about an architect?'

'You see him before you.'

'Someone will have to execute the designs on your behalf.'

'He's already engaged.'

'Does he require an assistant?' said Christopher hopefully, now fired with a desire to be somehow involved. 'I learn quickly.'

'Restrict yourself to grand houses, Mr Redmayne. That's where profit lies for an architect. My new theatre may take years to build and I have to confront one hideous truth.'

'What's that, Sir William?'

'I may not even live to see it open.'

He rose slowly to his feet and Christopher followed suit. Moving sluggishly, his host conducted him across the room. Christopher opened the door then turned to face him again.

'Thank you so much for suffering my company, Sir William.'

'You've a lively mind. That's always welcome.'

'I enjoyed hearing about your new theatre.'

'You had useful ideas of your own on the subject.'

'It was a privilege to share your vision.'

'Yet that's not why you came.'

Christopher was caught unawares. His expression betrayed him.

'I'll trespass on your time no longer,' he murmured.

'Give the lady my warmest regards.'

'Lady?'

'Harriet Gow. That's who you really came to talk about, isn't it? I could see it in your eyes.' His face crinkled into a tired smile. 'Stick to architecture, my friend. You're too honest to be a spy.'

Christopher was lost for words. A servant appeared in the hall.

'Please show Mr Redmayne out,' ordered D'Avenant crisply.

'Yes, Sir William,' said the man.

'Oh, and Gregory . . .'

The servant paused. 'Sir William?'

'Make sure that you don't let him into the house again.'

Jonathan Bale soon found the exact spot. The brickwork of the house had been deeply scored where the coach had scraped against it. The hasp that Trigg had been repairing was only one of the casualties on the vehicle. Jonathan ran a finger along the shallow grooves that had been gouged out of the brick. The impact must have been hard. He looked up and down the narrow lane, wondering yet again why such a route had been taken and seeing how perfect a place it had been for an ambush. Standing in the middle of the little thoroughfare, he tried to reconstruct in his mind exactly how it happened but his cogitations were interrupted by a sound from above. He glanced up quickly. The figure darted swiftly away from the upper window but not before the constable had caught sight of the man. Jonathan was being watched. He sensed that it was a hostile surveillance.

* * *

'There must be something we can do, Mrs Gow,' said Mary Hibbert.

'If only there were!' sighed her mistress.

'Have you tried to reason with them?'

'How can I when I'm not even allowed to speak?'

'What have they said to you?'

'Very little, Mary. When I asked a question, the man warned me to hold my tongue. I didn't argue with that raised fist of his. When the woman brings my food, she never says a single word.'

Mary was alerted. 'There's a woman here as well?'

'Yes, she's been keeping an eye on me.'

'All I've seen is one man. He wears a mask.'

'So does the woman. Her face is completely covered.'

'How many other people are here?'

'None, as far as I know.'

'Then we may have a chance.'

Mary crossed to the window. They were still alone together in the bedchamber. Reunited with Harriet Gow, Mary had recovered some of her willpower and all of her obligation to serve her mistress. She looked down at the garden below. It was empty. Open fields stretched beyond it to the horizon. The other woman joined her.

'It's too long a drop, Mary,' she said.

'There may be a way around that.'

'No, it's far too dangerous.'

'It's no more dangerous than staying here, Mrs Gow. They locked me in a dark cellar. It was horrifying. I'm not going to spend another night in there. I could hear a rat scampering about.'

'At least I've been spared that.'

'You're the person they need to look after,' argued Mary. 'That's why you have a proper bed and a woman to see to your needs. I'm glad of that. But I'm only a servant. They don't need to bother with me.' She stared through the window again. 'I've got nothing to lose.'

'What if they catch you?'

'I'll take that chance.'

'But what will you do, Mary?'

'Run as fast as I can to fetch help.'

'But we could be miles from anywhere.'

'Anything is better than staying here, Mrs Gow. I'm not asking you to come with me. You're safe enough here. They're treating you quite well because they know they have to. My case is different.'

'I'd much rather you stayed. You're such a comfort.'

'How long will they let us be together?'

Harriet Gow pondered. A woman of independent spirit, she found it galling to be deprived of her liberty. She was desperate to escape but she had grave doubts about the plan suggested by her maidservant. Getting down into the garden involved sufficient danger in itself. The chances of discovery seemed high. Even if Mary did get clear, she would be pursued as soon as her absence was noted. Harriet shuddered when she thought of the possible repercussions. She reached out to enfold her companion in protective arms, but Mary Hibbert was decisive.

'I'm going to try, Mrs Gow. It's our only hope.'

'But you could get hurt.'

'I'm not afraid.'

But Mary was trembling with fear and excitement. Feeling obscurely responsible for the predicament in which they found themselves, she wanted to do all that she could to get them out of it. She was young, fit and resolute. All she needed was a modicum of good fortune.

'It will work,' she promised.

'Will it?'

'It has to, Mrs Gow. Or we've no hope.'

'Somebody may come for us.'

'Who? Nobody even knows where we are.'

Harriet Gow nodded sadly. It was true. Her kidnappers had been swift, efficient and merciless. They would have covered their tracks.

Mary Hibbert held out her hands to her.

'Give me your blessing,' she said. 'Please, Mrs Gow.'

'I'll give you more than that,' replied the other, taking the brooch from her dress to hand it over. 'Have this as a keepsake, Mary. It may bring you luck.'

She kissed the girl impulsively. Mary pinned the brooch to her own dress. The two of them were soon knotting the bedsheets together.

Christopher Redmayne found time in a busy day to ride back to the site in order to assess progress. Neither Jasper Hartwell nor Lodowick Corrigan was there, though the bustling commitment with which the men were working suggested that the vigilant builder was not too far away. Satisfied that all was well, Christopher continued his round of calls before ending up in Fleet Street. It was early evening and he had arranged to meet up with Jonathan Bale outside the Lamb and Flag. A clock chimed, a distant bell boomed and the constable walked into view, arriving exactly on time.

Christopher dismounted from his horse to trade a greeting.

'What sort of a day have you had, Mr Bale?'

'Tiring.'

'Yet productive, I hope?'

'To some degree. What of you, sir?'

'Oh, I think I can claim to have made some headway. I've been looking more closely at some of the names on my brother's list. Sir William D'Avenant was the first.'

'Is he implicated in any way?'

'No, no, Mr Bale, I'm certain of that. But he taught me things about the theatrical way of life that shed much new light. It was well worth passing the time of day with him.'

He told the constable about his visit to D'Avenant's home, Rutland House, and his subsequent calls on some of the actors identified by his brother as possible sources of information. Jonathan was a good listener, absorbing salient detail and requesting clarification from time to time. He could see how assiduous Christopher had been and that pleased him.

When he finally paused, the architect pursed his lips in concentration.

'I still believe we must look to the theatre,' he said at length. 'That was Harriet Gow's world and that's where the clues that may save her will probably lie.'

'Then you must uncover them without me, sir,' warned the other. 'I'd be lost in that swamp. You and your brother must wade through it.'

'That's what Henry's doing at this precise moment. Watching a performance at The Theatre Royal.'

'The theatre!'

'Yes, Mr Bale.'

'I'm shocked to hear it.'

'Why?'

'Attending a play at a time like this!'

'It's not only for the purposes of recreation,' Christopher pointed out. 'Henry can do valuable work simply by keeping his ears open. Each to his own. My brother wallows in his swamp, I interview some of the possible suspects and you pursue your own lines of enquiry.'

'I try to, Mr Redmayne.'

'What did you find out?'

'That a certain coachman will never win prizes for civility.'

'Ah, you met the redoubtable Mr Trigg, I see.'

'He was a quarrelsome man, sir. I had to press him hard to get anything of value out of him. But it paid off eventually.'

'What did he tell you?'

Jonathan described the encounter and passed on the detailed account he had been given of the ambush. Christopher listened intently, noting slight variations from the earlier versions given by the coachman.

'Would you employ a brute like that?' he asked.

'No, sir.'

'Why not?'

'Because I wouldn't trust him.'

'Mrs Gow appears to do so.'

'He seemed to glory in that fact.'

'Where was he taking her when the coach was attacked?'

'That was the one thing even I couldn't prise out of him, sir. Not for want of trying. It was like talking to a brick wall. What Mr Trigg did insist on was that they'd not been heading for the Palace of Westminster.'

'I wonder.'

'What do you mean?'

'I had a second look at that map of mine, Mr Bale. It does seem odd that the coach would come into the Strand if it were going towards King Street, but there are other ways of reaching the Palace than by the obvious route.'

'I don't follow, sir.'

'The river. What better way to slip unnoticed into the royal apartments than by arriving in a boat? A woman could easily be smuggled inside to meet His Majesty.'

'It still doesn't answer our objection, Mr Bale. Had the coachman been driving towards one of the wharves, he'd most likely have come into the Strand from Charing Cross.'

'Not necessarily.'

'I took a close look at that lane, sir. I found the exact spot where the ambush occurred. There's barely room for a coach to get through. Mr Trigg must have had a very good reason to choose that route.'

'Do you have any idea what it might be?'

'I could hazard a guess.'

'Well?'

'We're searching for a destination that doesn't exist, sir, whether it be the Palace or somewhere in the Strand. Put yourself in the position of the coachman. Only one thing could take you down that lane.'

'What is it?'

'Think hard.'

Christopher snapped his fingers. 'The need to call at one of the houses there.'

'Exactly.'

'That's where Mrs Gow must have been going for her rendezvous. Instead of passing *through* the lane, they were planning to stop there. That raises the question of whom she was going to see.' Christopher thought hard.

'Impossible to be sure.'

'Quite so,' Christopher agreed.

'But I did my best to find out,' said Jonathan, reaching into his pocket to take out a grubby piece of paper. 'I didn't want to draw attention to myself by knocking on doors so I went into the tavern at the top end of the lane – the Red Lion. The innkeeper was a talkative man. He gave me the names of some of the local people who frequent his tavern.' He handed the list to Christopher. 'I think you'll find the one at the top the most interesting.'

'Why?'

'See for yourself, Mr Redmayne.'

Christopher looked at the shaky handwriting then gaped.

'Bartholomew Gow!'

Henry Redmayne stayed at the theatre long after the performance of *The Maid's Tragedy* ended. It had been only a qualified success. Incensed at the absence of Harriet Gow, some of the more obstreperous elements in the audience had stamped their feet in protest and barracked the actors. A few scuffles had broken out and Aspatia's first entrance went almost unnoticed. Abigail Saunders did not lose heart and her perseverance slowly won over the bulk of the spectators even though her tender pleas had to be delivered in a strident voice in order to be heard above the din. Much of the essence of the play survived and the company was given a rousing ovation at its conclusion.

After carousing with his friends, Henry had to remind himself that he was there on serious business; he made his way to the dressing room bearing the gift he had already bought from a flower girl. He was one of a number of admirers who jostled their way towards Abigail Saunders but persistence and combative elbows soon got him close to the actress. He presented the basket of flowers to her with a flourish and was rewarded with a proffered hand. Henry lingered over his kiss.

'You were divine, Miss Saunders!' he cooed.

'Thank you, Mr Redmayne.'

'The whole audience was enraptured.'

'I fought hard to earn their attention, sir.'

'You had mine from the moment you set foot on the stage. I could sing your praises all night, Miss Saunders. Sup with me and I will.'

'Unhappily, I already have an engagement.'

'Will you dine with me tomorrow, then?'

'I have another rehearsal to attend, Mr Redmayne.'

'Then I'll batter at your defences until they crumble,' he said with a broad grin. 'Crumble, they must. I'm resolved on it.'

A brittle laugh. 'I admire tenacity in a man.'

'And I admire quality in a woman,' he countered. 'It was on display out there on stage and it made me swoon with wonder. The pity of it is that your mentor was not there to appreciate it as well.'

'My mentor?'

'The man who inspired you.'

'And who might that be?' she asked.

'Why, Sir William D'Avenant.'

It was not the most tactful remark to make to the actress at such a moment. Her smile froze, her teeth clenched and his basket of flowers was tossed uncaringly aside. Abigail Saunders gave him a withering stare before turning her back on him.

'Goodbye, Mr Redmayne.'

Henry gabbled his apologies but the damage was irreparable. Ignoring him, she lapped up the flattery of all the other men who had crowded into her dressing room. Henry found himself slowly edged out of the room altogether. His attempt at befriending the actress had been hopelessly bungled. He would never get close enough to question her indirectly about Harriet Gow's disappearance now. Nor could he expect any kind of dalliance by way of compensation. Abigail Saunders had effectively rejected him on the spot.

There was worse to come. Rolling out of the theatre, Henry followed a group of playgoers who were tottering towards a nearby tavern. He needed some revelry to atone for his disappointment. A vision of his brother came before his eyes. Christopher would be angry that he had thrown away all chance of wheedling information out of the woman who stood to gain most from Harriet Gow's indisposition. Henry needed more alcohol before he could face his brother's censure. Licking his lips, he hastened after the others.

He did not get very far. As he walked past a sidestreet, two brawny men came out to grab him by the arms. Henry was given no time to call for help, still less to offer any resistance. Dragged into a doorway in the sidestreet, he was cudgelled viciously to the ground then kicked hard in the ribs by his two attackers. They were swift and proficient. When their work was done, they flitted nimbly away into the shadows, leaving Henry Redmayne in a groaning heap on the ground, lying helplessly in a pool of blood.

Chapter Nine

The summons was answered immediately. As soon as Christopher Redmayne heard the grim tidings, he mounted his horse and kicked it into a gallop, using the hectic journey to torment himself with guilt and arriving at the house in Bedford Street in a state of agitation. When he ran up to the bedchamber, he was shocked to see the condition that his brother was in. Henry seemed barely alive. His face was covered with bruises and lacerations, his head swathed in white linen. Traces of blood showed on the bedsheets. More bandaging had been wound tightly around the exposed chest. His bare arms were listless, his eyes scarcely flickering. He could manage no word of welcome.

The one consolation was that a physician was in attendance. The injuries were beyond the competence of a mere apothecary or surgeon and Christopher was glad to discover that a trained physician had been called in. Old and wizened, the man looked up with a half-smile.

'Are you his brother, sir?' he said.

'Christopher Redmayne,' replied the other.

'I've done all I can for him, Mr Redmayne.'

'How is he?'

'Very weak. He lost a lot of blood.'

'But he'll recover?'

'Oh yes, given time and careful nursing. Your brother is tougher than he looks, sir. He'll pull through, I've no doubts on that score.'

Christopher followed him to the door, asking for more detail of the injuries and seeking more reassurance. When the physician withdrew, the visitor rushed back to his brother's bedside and knelt anxiously beside it. He put a gentle hand on the patient's shoulder.

'Henry?' he said quietly. 'Can you hear me?'

'Yes,' came a faint whisper.

'Does it hurt you to talk?'

'A little.'

'What happened?'

Henry needed a few moments to gather his thoughts. Christopher felt a surge of remorse as he saw the extent of the wounds. Without his fine clothes and resplendent wig, his brother looked old, disfigured and positively decrepit. Words came out with painful slowness. Henry was patently suffering.

'I went to The King's House,' he said hoarsely, 'to see Abigail Saunders and to pick up what information I could. She acted well but she is no Harriet Gow.' A fit of coughing delayed him. 'When I came out into Drury Lane,' he continued, 'I was strolling along when I was set on by two bullies with cudgels.'

'Did you get a good look at them?'

'No, Christopher.'

'You'd never seen them before?'

'I don't think so.'

'Can you tell me *anything* about them?'

'Not really.'

'What did they say?'

'Nothing.'

'They just knocked you to the ground?'

'And kicked me in the ribs.' He rested a palm gingerly on his chest. 'I thought I was done for. I thought the rogues would kick me to death.'

'Were there no witnesses?'

'I've no idea. I was more or less unconscious.'

'Who found you?'

'Someone who was passing. He probably saved my life.'

'How did you get back here?'

'They carried me to the theatre. Tom Killigrew brought me home in his carriage.' A ghost of a laugh. 'I'm surprised he recognised me. I was covered in blood when they found me. Still, I suppose he's used to such a sight,' he croaked on reflection. 'There are often nasty brawls at his theatre. Broken heads and bleeding wounds are common enough.'

'I'm so sorry about this, Henry.'

'It couldn't be helped.'

'But it could. I should've been there with you. Or made sure that you had someone by your side. I did tell you to go armed.'

'What use are a sword and dagger when you've no time to draw them? They were too quick, too strong. They could have finished me.'

'No, Henry. This was only a warning.'

'Warning?'

'To me and to Mr Bale.'

'But they were probably just bullies, out for a fight.'

'Oh, no.'

'I got in their way by accident.'

'It was all planned.'

'Or I was the random victim of robbers.'

'There was nothing random about this.'

'They were looking for easy pickings.'

'Was your purse taken?'

'My purse?' He rummaged in his memory. 'I don't think so.'

'What about your rings?'

'They weren't touched either.'

'That proves it,' decided Christopher. 'They weren't after your valuables. You were singled out, Henry. Watched and jumped on at the right moment. It's all because of this investigation we've been dragged into. You should've had no part in it. I was wrong to involve you.'

'But I wanted to do my share.'

Another fit of coughing brought fresh pain to Henry. His brother waited until it passed then he adjusted the pillows for him. His heart welled up with sympathy. He and his brother were far too different in character and divergent in their interests to be really close, but adversity revealed his true feelings for Henry. Christopher wanted to reach out and cradle him. He also wanted to wreak vengeance on his behalf.

'We'll find them, Henry. I promise you that.'

'Be careful, brother.'

'Only cowards attack an undefended man.'

'I was off guard for once. Thinking about *her*.'

'Who?'

'Abigail Saunders.'

'Why?'

'She knows something, Christopher – I could feel it. She knows that Harriet Gow will not be back for some time and she's making the most of it. Abigail is too sure of herself.'

'What did she tell you?'

'Very little, unfortunately. I made the mistake of bringing Sir William D'Avenant's name into the conversation and after that, she wouldn't even speak to me. It cannot be pleasant for her to be associated with a gentleman who once suffered from such a visible disease.'

'She and Sir William are no longer close. That was something I gathered when I visited him at Rutland House. They parted on harsh terms. Sir William can be exonerated, Henry. He's not tied up in the conspiracy – that much I did establish.'

'And Abigail?'

'We'll need to take a closer look at her.'

'Go stealthily. She has barbarous friends.'

'You think that she instigated the assault?' said Christopher gently.

'Put it this way. One minute, I upset her. The next minute, I'm being cudgelled to the ground by those two men. And that was *after* I'd told her how much I'd admired her performance,' Henry joked miserably. 'If I'd dared to criticise it, she'd probably have had me cut into thin strips and fed to passing dogs in the street.'

'We don't know that Abigail Saunders is in any way caught up in this, Henry, so let's proceed with caution. Treat her as innocent until we have some evidence of guilt.' Christopher grew pensive. 'What is clear is that you were set on in order to send a message to us.'

'Why?'

'They know.'

'About what?'

'The fact that we're on their tail.'

'You may be, Christopher, but I have other priorities now.'

He managed a thin smile but the effort made him wince. His brother felt the pain with him. As he gazed down at the wounded man, he vowed that he would bring his attackers to justice. Pulled reluctantly into a search for a missing actress, he now had a personal score to settle. It made him burn with righteous anger. Every blow that his brother had taken had to be repaid in kind. The message needed a reply.

Henry dozed quietly off to sleep. It was ironic. No day passed without a hundred routine complaints from him. He would abuse his barber, terrorise his servants and protest loudly at everything his tailors did for him. Henry Redmayne was the sort of man who would have a tantrum if he got mud on a new shoe and plunge into hysteria if any garment of his became torn. Outrage was his natural element. Yet he had not raised the merest complaint against his savage beating. There was no whimpering, no reproach, no accusation. Christopher was touched by his stoicism. It was a new side to his brother.

Henry's eyes opened again. Sudden fear showed.

'Are you still there?' he asked.

'Yes, Henry.'

'I just had a frightening thought.'

'What's that?'

'For the first time in my life, I actually want Father to be here.' He drew in his breath sharply. 'I must be delirious.'

Harriet Gow was suffering a discomfort that bordered on agony. It was several hours since the departure of Mary Hibbert but she still had no idea if the girl had escaped or been recaptured. The descent from the window had been effected without setback. Harriet had hauled the sheets into the room again, quickly untied them and put them back on the bed. When she returned to the window, there was no sign of Mary. The brave young fugitive was either crouched in the bushes or making her way surreptitiously to a part of the garden where she could climb over the wall. Harriet wanted her back again, fearing for the girl's safety and blaming herself for agreeing to help in an escape bid that she was convinced would be doomed.

When the woman arrived with a tray of food, she was startled to see only one occupant in the room. The man was called at once and he conducted a more thorough search. Crossing to the window, he flung it open and glared out before racing from the room. The woman and the tray of food disappeared as well and the door was firmly locked. Part of her punishment had already been inflicted on Harriet. She was being deprived of her meal. They knew she must have condoned and assisted the flight of her maidservant. It would lead to privations.

The hours rolled by but no word came. Harriet shifted rapidly between hope and despair, believing that Mary had made good her escape then resigning herself to the thought that the girl had been tracked down. Racked by uncertainty, she paced the room, went obsessively to the window or hurled herself down on the bed. None of it brought relief. When evening shadows began to dapple the garden, her fears reached a new pitch of intensity. Where *was* Mary? Which direction had she taken? How far had she got? What possible chance did she have of outrunning the pursuit?

Night was falling when the door eventually opened. The woman entered and Harriet ran to her in the gloom, reaching out her hands.

'What's happened?' she begged. 'Is there any news?'

All she got by way of a reply was a hard slap across the face. Harriet staggered back in pain. The woman grabbed her and the man came in to help. Face still stinging, she offered no fight as they hauled her down the staircase then took her down the flight of steps that led off the hall. Harriet was pitched headfirst into the cellar. When the door slammed shut behind her, she was in total darkness. Mary Hibbert was not coming back; Harriet had replaced her in the evil-smelling cellar. Did that mean the maidservant had escaped or been taken somewhere else? Why would they not tell her? It was dispiriting. She groped her way to the chair, curled up in it and tried to pray. But the words would simply not come. She wondered if anyone was there to hear them.

It was late before Jonathan Bale was finally able to seek the refuge of his home and close the front door on another taxing day. Taking part in a search with Christopher Redmayne did not release him from routine duties in Baynard's Castle Ward and he had to cope with a number of incidents before he could retire from the streets. The last – a dispute between three different families over some stolen fish – was only resolved when the constable identified a stray dog as the real thief, leaving the aggrieved victims to patch up their differences with their neighbours and promise that they would not resort to false and over-hasty accusation again. By the time that he left them, all three families were engaged in vigorous reconciliation, united by a common desire to destroy the culprit.

'Where is the animal now?' asked Sarah Bale.

'Scavenging somewhere else.'

'There are too many stray dogs in the streets.'

'Stray cats, too,' said her husband. 'Not to mention gulls, pigeons and other birds with an eye for a tasty piece of fish. They were unwise to leave it in the kitchen like that with the door wide open.'

'As long as you solved the crime, Jonathan.'

'I wish they were all as easy as that, my love.'

A simple meal with his wife revived him. He listened to the rich crop of gossip she had harvested during her day and threw in amused comments along the way. Too late to read to his sons, he wanted to know how well they had behaved themselves.

'Oliver was quiet for once,' said Sarah.

'That's unusual.'

'I was afraid that he might be sickening for something but he seems healthy enough. He ate all his food.'

'So he should.'

'Richard was noisy enough for the two of them.'

'He's a growing boy, full of noise and mischief.'

'Is that how you were at his age?'

'I don't know, Sarah,' he said, diverted by the thought. 'It was such a long time ago. I suppose I must've been. There were four of us children, always squabbling. My father beat me a lot, I remember that.'

'You, a naughty child?' she teased. 'Never!'

'It's true.'

'Did you cause trouble, tell lies?'

'Probably.'

'What turned you into such a pillar of honesty?'

'Marriage to a certain Miss Sarah Teague.'

'You blame me, do you?'

'No,' he said with a grin. 'I *thank* you, my love.'

They talked on for half an hour or more before it was time to climb the stairs to bed. After the exigencies of the day, it was a relief to be able to chat about domestic concerns but Jonathan was never entirely freed from thoughts about the kidnap. His mind kept returning to it time and again but he did not confide in Sarah. He might entertain her with the tale of the purloined fish but the abduction of two women was another matter, especially as his wife knew one of the victims. Tired from her own exertions, Sarah was the first to get into bed. Her husband was not allowed to join her. The clatter of hooves took him to the window. What he saw there made him snatch up the candle and hurry out of the room.

Jonathan opened the front door before Christopher Redmayne could knock on it. The constable had never had a coach at his doorstep before. It loomed menacingly out of the darkness.

'A thousand apologies, Mr Bale,' said his visitor, 'but I'm afraid I have to disturb you. There have been developments.'

'Of what nature, sir?'

'It grieves me to report the first of them. My brother, Henry, was attacked and beaten outside The Theatre Royal today.'

Jonathan stiffened. 'Not seriously hurt, I hope?'

'He'll be in bed for a week or more.'

'Does he know who the attackers were, Mr Redmayne?'

'They cudgelled him to the ground before he so much as got a glimpse of them. But I fancy I've seen their handiwork before. So have you, Mr Bale.'

'On the face of a coachman, perhaps?'

'Yes.'

'But why assault your brother?'

'To send a warning to us.'

'They *know* we are after them?'

'Alas, yes.'

'How, sir?'

'I can't say.' He glanced over his shoulder at the coach. 'But the other development is this. When I got back to my house, a messenger was waiting. We're bidden to the Palace.'

'Now?' said Jonathan in disbelief.

'As a matter of urgency.'

'But I was just about to retire to bed.'

'I, too, hoped to be asleep by now.'

'You go, Mr Redmayne. On your own.'

'The letter insists that I take you.'

'Me?'

'You're mentioned by name.'

'I've no call to go off to the Palace of Westminster at this hour.'

'A royal summons can't be denied.'

'No, no,' said Jonathan evasively. 'It's a mistake. They don't really need me. You can answer for both of us, Mr Redmayne. Find out what this is all about then report to me in the morning.'

'I daren't go without you, Mr Bale.'

'You must.'

'The letter was unequivocal.'

'Explain that you represent the two of us.'

'No excuse will be accepted.'

'It's unfair to call on me like this, sir,' complained Jonathan. 'I can't just go off into the night. What will I tell my wife?'

'What you always tell her at such times. You're a constable. Duty calls. Mrs Bale will understand.'

'How do I explain this coach?'

'Convincingly. I'm sure you can do that.'

'No,' said Jonathan, making a last attempt to wriggle out of the commitment. 'You know my feelings about the Palace, Mr Redmayne, and those who live in it. I'd rather not set foot in the place, if you don't mind. I did so once before and it left me feeling corrupted.'

'Prepare to be corrupted afresh,' warned Christopher with a grin. 'You'll not only enter those portals, you'll arrive there in a coach sent at the King's command. That'll be an experience for you.'

'My blood curdles at the very thought.'

'Are you so easily offended?'

'To the marrow.'

'Then there's an easy solution here, I suspect. If you balk at the notion of travelling inside with me, I'll ask the coachman to let you sit beside him instead. And if that still troubles your conscience, carry a link and run alongside the vehicle.'

'You mock me, sir.'

'My brother was beaten senseless, Mr Bale,' said Christopher seriously. 'Looking at his bruises left me in no mood for mockery. We've been summoned to the Palace because something very important has occurred and the sooner we find out what it is, the better. So please,' he ordered, 'let's have no more delay. Make your excuses to your wife and come with me.'

Jonathan hesitated. He grasped at one last straw.

'The city gates are closed. The coach will not be allowed through.'

'Nobody will dare to obstruct *this* coach, Mr Bale.'

* * *

The ride to Westminster was an uncomfortable one for him but it did give Jonathan Bale the opportunity to voice some of his concerns. As the vehicle rocked and scrunched its way along, he confided his thoughts to Christopher Redmayne in the half-dark of its interior.

'I've been wondering about that house, sir,' he said.

'What house?'

'The one belonging to Mrs Gow. It must have been expensive.'

'Very expensive,' said Christopher. 'Be certain of that. I've friends who live in the area and I know how much they paid for the privilege. There are no cheap properties around St James's Square. Everything is at a premium.'

'Can Mrs Gow afford such a residence?'

'Presumably.'

'With a coach and coachman to go with it?'

'She's a lady who enjoys living in style.'

'But who supports that style?' said Jonathan thoughtfully. 'Mrs Gow could hardly do so on her income from the theatre. Actresses may be well paid but not to that degree, surely?'

'Go on.'

'That brings us to her husband. Since they appear to live quite separate lives, it's unlikely that he's footing the bill. So who is?'

'You obviously have a view on the subject, Mr Bale.'

'It's only a suggestion, sir, but I think we should at least consider it.'

There was a long silence. Jonathan was slightly embarrassed by what he was about to say and needed time to work up to it. He prefaced his remarks with a sincere apology.

'If I malign the lady, I'm deeply sorry because I don't intend to cast aspersions on her. But when I think of that fine house, one suspicion does cross my mind.'

'Some anonymous benefactor maintains her in it?'

'That, too, is possible,' he conceded. 'From what you tell me, there seem to be a number of "benefactors" in Mrs Gow's life. We're on our way to meet one of them now, and others

141

lurk on every side. Mrs Gow doesn't seem unduly concerned about her marital vows.'

'So what's your suspicion?'

'A fleeting thought, no more.'

'Well?'

'Could it be that Mrs Gow was not really abducted at all, sir?'

'Of course she was!'

'I wonder.'

'You heard the coachman.'

'Oh, Mr Trigg believes that she was kidnapped. He bears the bruises to prove it. But what if the lady devised the whole scheme herself? What if she sacrificed her coachman to achieve her end?'

'And that is?'

'To secure money, sir. Money to sustain her in the style that she prefers. We only know of the ransom note to His Majesty. Suppose that some of her other "benefactors" have received demands for lesser amounts? If only a few of them were frightened into paying, Mrs Gow would make a handsome profit on the scheme.' He sensed Christopher's disapproval. 'I know it's unjust to hold someone I've never met in such low esteem, but she wouldn't be the first woman to attempt such a cunning trick.'

'You're forgetting two things, Mr Bale.'

'Am I?'

'It's not just Harriet Gow's disappearance that we investigate. There's your erstwhile friend, Mary Hibbert, as well. Unless you think that she's in on this conspiracy?'

'No, sir. I'd absolve her of any duplicity.'

'Then why was she snatched from the house?'

'Can we be sure that she was, sir?'

'Roland Trigg had no doubts.'

'I have a few about him.'

'Then there was Peter Hibbert.'

'He was a frightened boy, thrown into a panic. I can see how it must have looked to Peter and to Mr Trigg, but the open door of a house is not conclusive evidence of a kidnap.'

'Granted. But it's part of a distinct pattern.'

'Is it?'

'You remarked a moment ago how grand the house was. Would anyone be careless enough to leave such a property unlocked and at the mercy of any passer-by?'

'No, Mr Redmayne.'

'The other factor you overlook concerns my brother.'

'I knew nothing of his plight when I first had these thoughts.'

'Well, you do now, so ask yourself a question. If this is all a game concocted by a grasping woman to squeeze money out of her lovers, why does she need to have a blameless individual like Henry battered to the ground?' Anger showed through. 'Another trick to convince us? That would be taking verisimilitude too far!'

'My suspicions are obviously unfounded.'

'I think they are, Mr Bale.'

'Pretend I never put them into words.'

'Very well. They annoy me greatly.'

'The truth is that I've never encountered a lady like Mrs Gow before, sir. You can guess at my views on the theatre. I revile it, hence I'm bound to have prejudices against anyone who works in such a place. Unjust ones, I daresay, but nonetheless real.'

'You were right to tell me.'

'I withdraw all that I said.'

'No need.'

'I was too quick to think the worst of her.'

'Harriet Gow is no saint,' Christopher admitted with a sigh. 'That's what makes this case so baffling. Most people are content to find one person to love them. Mrs Gow obviously enjoys having several admirers at her feet. In fact, the more we delve into her private life, the greater their number seems to be. Without knowing it, Mr Hartwell may have coined the perfect name for her.'

'Mr Hartwell, sir?'

'Jasper Hartwell,' explained Christopher. 'The man for whom I've designed a house. If only I had the time to watch it being built! He, too, has more than a passing interest in Harriet Gow and his description may turn out to be the most apt.'

'What was it?'

'He called her a nightingale.'

'A nightingale?'

'An amorous nightingale.'

Harriet Gow had never felt less amorous in her entire life. Locked in a dark cellar, deprived of the comforts she had enjoyed before, shorn of the company of the one person who had restored her spirits, she was now quite desolate. Uncertainty about Mary Hibbert continued to plague her. The later it got, the more fearsome her imaginings. Recriminations scalded their way through her mind. It was too long a time. If Mary had managed to get away to raise the alarm, help would surely have arrived by now. But none came. None might ever come. Wrapping her arms tightly around her body, she sat in the chair and wondered who could be inflicting such torture on her and to what end.

Did someone really hate her so much? Who could it be? As she addressed herself to the problem yet again, the same names flitted past. The men who bore them might have cause to resent her, but would they subject her to such pain and indignity? Harriet could not accept it. Accustomed to being loved and desired, she could not believe that anyone could detest her enough to abduct and imprison her. What was the next stage in her humiliation? How soon would it come?

In a vain attempt to cheer herself up, she tried to concentrate on happier times, on the charmed life she led, on her status as Harriet Gow, actress and singer, on her recurring triumphs in the theatre and her effortless conquests outside it, on her reputation. She was the mistress of a King, his unsurpassed favourite. She was at the height of her powers in the theatre. Such memories only served to throw her present situation into relief. Instead of lying in the luxury of the royal bed, she was sharing a cellar with the stink of damp and the scrabbling of a rat. Had she risen so high to be hurled down so low?

Snatching at her memories, she clung to the moment when she had been feted as Aspatia, the forlorn lover in *The Maid's Tragedy*. The thunderous applause still echoed in her ears. She had won the hearts of her audience. Her plaintive lament had ensnared a King and enchanted scores of other men. Yet her beautiful voice was meaningless now. This was something which brought the most anguish. Harriet Gow, the theatre's own nightingale, had a horrid fear that she would never be able to sing again.

William Chiffinch's lodging was close to the Privy Stairs, the usual mode of access for ladies on clandestine excursions to the Palace. Meeting them as they alighted from their boat, Chiffinch could conduct them discreetly into the building and along to His Majesty's apartments, next to which his own were conveniently set. Speed of entry and secrecy of movement were assured. When opportunity presented itself, Chiffinch was not above making use of the route for his own purposes. A man so dedicated to the King was bound to ape him in some ways.

He was not lurking near the Privy Stairs now. When the coach at last arrived, he intercepted it at the Palace Gate and took charge of its occupants. Accompanied by two servants with torches, the three men walked past the Banqueting Hall and briskly on towards the Chapel. Unhappy at being back on what he felt was polluted ground, Jonathan maintained a sullen silence. He left it to Christopher to tender their joint apologies.

'You're unconscionably late, sirs,' said Chiffinch sharply.

'We were delayed.'

'That much is obvious, Mr Redmayne.'

'The cause may not be,' said Christopher. 'My brother, Henry, was the victim of a violent assault today. When the message arrived at my house, I was away in Bedford Street.'

'That's no excuse, sir.' Chiffinch was unmoved by the mention of the attack on Henry Redmayne. 'You should have made more haste.'

'Mr Bale took some persuading to come.'

'Indeed?'

'But, as you see, he is here. As am I, Mr Chiffinch. We're sorry for any delay but it could not be helped. I do hope that His Majesty will forgive us.'

'His Majesty is in no position to do so.'

'Why not?'

'He is not here at present.'

'But the letter was signed by him.'

'At my request.'

'We haven't been brought here to see His Majesty, then?'

'You were summoned,' said the other. 'That was enough.'

Reaching the Chapel, they shed the two servants and stepped into an anteroom that was lit by candles and perfumed with frankincense. Jonathan was ill at ease. Chiffinch scrutinised him for a moment.

'So you are Constable Bale,' he said at length.

'Yes, sir.'

'And you have misgivings about coming here?'

'Several, sir.'

'Don't waste my time by telling me what they are, Mr Bale, for they would bore me to distraction. They are, in any case, irrelevant.' He inhaled deeply and tried to bring his guest to heel. 'You're here at my behest. I serve the interests of His Majesty. They are paramount here.'

'I disagree,' said Jonathan.

'It is not a permitted option.'

'I'd have thought the safety of two women came before all else, Mr Chiffinch. With respect, that's what brought me here tonight. Not the interests of His Majesty.'

'Those interests are bound up with the abduction.'

'That's a private matter, sir.'

'Is he always so quarrelsome?' asked Chiffinch, turning to

his other visitor. 'I wonder that you managed to get him into the coach.'

'It took some doing,' said Christopher with an affectionate glance at Jonathan. 'Mr Bale has a poor memory. He has to be reminded who sits on the throne of England.'

'I've no need to be told that!' retorted Jonathan mutinously.

'I spoke in jest.'

'It was out of place,' reprimanded Chiffinch. 'Indeed, bandying words like this is somewhat unseemly in the circumstances. I'm sure you've realised that only an event of some magnitude would oblige me to bring the two of you here like this. We have heard from the kidnappers.'

'So did my brother.'

'I'm sorry to learn of his beating, Mr Redmayne. Please convey my sympathy to him – though I cannot imagine why they should single out a man who is not engaged in this investigation beyond the status of a go-between.' An eyebrow rose enquiringly. 'Unless, of course, he'd been promoted against my instructions to a higher position?'

'He was attacked. That is all that concerns me.'

'Quite rightly. You're his brother. However,' he said, looking from one man to the other, 'we're not here to listen to a report on Henry Redmayne's condition, distressing as it may be. Something even more disturbing confronts us. A message has been sent.'

'May we read it?' said Christopher.

'It did not come in the form of words, I'm afraid. Their calligraphy was rather more vivid this time. Follow me, gentlemen.'

He crossed to a door, opened it gently then led them through into a small chamber. Even on a warm night, the place felt chill. There was a stone slab in the middle of the room. Lying on top of it, covered in a shroud, was a dead body. Candles had been set at the head and foot of the corpse. Herbs had been scattered to sweeten the atmosphere. A compassionate Jesus Christ gazed down sadly from His cross on the wall.

'The body was delivered at the Privy Stairs,' said Chiffinch.

'It came here by boat?' asked Christopher.

'So we assume.'

'Did nobody see it arrive?'

'We've yet to locate a witness.'

Jonathan stared at the slab. 'Is it Mrs Gow?'

'No, thank heaven!'

'Then who?'

'We don't rightly know, Mr Bale. That's why I sent for you and Mr Redmayne. I hoped that you might throw some light on her identity.'

Jonathan exchanged a worried look with Christopher.

'*Her!*' he repeated.

'It's the body of a young woman.'

Chiffinch was too squeamish a man to view the corpse himself. Taking the edge of the shroud fastidiously in his fingers, he drew it back to expose the head of the victim. Christopher was shocked to see such an attractive young woman on a slab in a morgue but he had no inkling who she might be. Jonathan recognised her immediately.

'Mary Hibbert!' he gasped.

'Are you sure?' said Chiffinch.

'No doubt about it, poor girl.' He bent anxiously over the body. 'What did they do to her?'

'Her neck was broken,' explained the other, not daring to look down. 'That's why the head is at such an unnatural angle and why . . . those other features present themselves.' He twitched the shroud back over the girl and wiped his hand on his thigh. 'It's a small consolation, I know, but the physician who examined her assured me that she would have died almost instantly. There'd have been little suffering.'

Jonathan was roused. 'Mary Hibbert ends up on a slab and you tell me there was little suffering?' he said with vehemence. 'Look at her, Mr Chiffinch. The girl was murdered. Did you see a smile on her face?'

'Perhaps we should discuss this outside,' suggested Christopher.

'I was about to say the same thing,' said Chiffinch gratefully, taking them back into the anteroom before shutting the door behind him. 'I didn't mean to offend you by my remark, Mr Bale. I merely passed on what the physician told me. I was as stunned as you when I first saw the unfortunate creature. It was an appalling sight.'

'She was such a lovely girl,' said Jonathan.

'Maidservant to Mrs Gow,' explained his companion to Chiffinch. 'We had some indication that she might have been abducted yesterday from her house but we never anticipated this.'

Jonathan shook his head. 'How could anyone do such a thing?'

'It's one more crime to add to their account.'

'A harmless child like that.'

'Did you know her well?' asked Chiffinch.

Christopher took over again. 'The Hibbert family used to live in Constable Bale's ward. They were neighbours of his. He'd seen Mary and her brother, Peter, grow up. They were friends. I met the boy myself. He was proud of his sister. She'd done extremely well for herself to secure a position with Mrs Gow.'

'Too well,' said Jonathan, bitterly. 'Look where it got her.'

'It's a tragedy,' agreed Christopher.

'Peter will have to be told.'

'That's out of the question,' said Chiffinch.

'You can't keep this from them, sir. Not from her relatives. They've a right to know what happened to Mary.'

'In time, perhaps.'

'No, at the earliest opportunity.'

'Discretion must be our watchword, Mr Bale. If we voice this abroad, we only endanger the whole investigation. The ransom note insisted on total secrecy. This regrettable event stresses that point.'

'Regrettable event!' said Jonathan, rounding on him. 'Mary Hibbert has been brutally murdered, sir. That fact may not trouble your mind overmuch but her brother will be shattered.

So will her uncle and aunt. They'll see it as more than a cause for regret, I can tell you.'

'Calm down, Mr Bale, I pray you.'

'Then show some more respect for the dead.'

'We must temper respect with expediency.'

'I agree with Mr Bale,' said Christopher. 'The girl's family deserve to know the worst. It's a cruelty to keep it from them.'

'A necessary one.'

'No, Mr Chiffinch. The body should be released.'

'It must be,' affirmed Jonathan. 'I see your objection, sir, but it can be answered. The true facts must not be leaked out. Nor need they be. Peter can be told that his sister met with an unlucky accident. I'll pass on the same tidings to Mary's uncle and aunt. It will spare them some of the anguish but it will also enable the girl to have a decent burial.'

'I support Mr Bale to the hilt,' said Christopher.

'We won't be denied.'

Chiffinch was nonplussed for once. He had not expected to meet such united opposition. Skilled in the issue of orders, he was used to obedience. He was less adept at coping with blank refusal. He eyed Jonathan with an amalgam of irritation and interest.

'Could you really persuade them that the girl died by accident?' he said. 'Can you soften the truth so effectively?'

'Yes, sir,' replied Jonathan. 'My work has often required me to break bad news to relatives. I'll find the right words.'

'Trust him, Mr Chiffinch,' urged Christopher.

'It looks as if I may have to,' said the other with slight asperity. He reached a decision. 'Very well, Mr Bale. Take charge of the arrangements. Tell me where the body is to be sent and it will be released.'

'Thank you, sir.'

Chiffinch saw an advantage. 'It will at least solve the problem of what we should do with it,' he said with relief. 'We could hardly keep it here indefinitely. Exercise prudence, that's all I ask, Mr Bale. Be politic in what you say.'

A brief nod. 'May I spend a little time with Mary, sir?'

'You want to go in there *again*?' asked a shocked Chiffinch.

'Please, sir. Alone.'

'That is more than I would care to do.'

'Mary Hibbert was a friend, Mr Chiffinch. I'd like to pay my respects. I'd also like to take a closer look at her injuries. You may be repelled by death but I've looked upon it many times in my walk of life. There may be signs I can pick up, little clues that could have eluded your physician.' He moved towards the door. 'May I have your permission?'

But he did not wait for it to be granted. Letting himself into the morgue, he closed the door silently behind him. Chiffinch gave a slight grimace and looked across at Christopher.

'Mr Bale is a strange man,' he remarked.

'You won't find a more honest or reliable fellow.'

'A touch of deference might improve his character.'

'Try telling him that,' suggested Christopher with a smile.

'He seems to think he's a law unto himself.'

'Oh, he is. Without question.'

'Be that as it may,' said Chiffinch sternly, 'I am glad of a moment alone with you. Unlike the constable, you appreciate His Majesty's deep personal interest in this matter. He's displeased, Mr Redmayne. Progress in such a short time was too much to expect, but he did want a report from you. Yet we heard not a word.'

'I was too preoccupied with the search.'

'A maidservant abducted, a brother attacked. These are not minor matters. We should have been informed of them. What else have you been keeping from us?'

'Nothing of note.'

'Where has your investigation led you?'

Christopher gave him a brief account of progress so far, omitting any reference to Jonathan's earlier refusal to help and instead praising the constable for his readiness. He listed the names that Henry had collected during his researches at the theatre and mentioned the curious fact Jonathan had unearthed in the Red Lion. William Chiffinch was intrigued.

'Bartholomew Gow?'

'Apparently he lives somewhere in the lane.'

'Why should his wife be going to see him?' asked the other. 'The two of them have parted. It's against nature. Ladies like Harriet Gow do not have assignations with discarded husbands.'

'We have no proof that she did on this occasion.'

'But it's a worrying coincidence.'

'That's why we mean to look into it.'

'Her coach is ambushed close to Mr Gow's house? That can surely be no accident, Mr Redmayne. Find the man.'

'We mean to, sir.'

'And send a report to me when you do.'

Christopher nodded. Jonathan Bale came out of the room, face ashen and head lowered. Whatever he had learned during his vigil, he was keeping to himself. Chiffinch did not press him. Escorting the two men out, he handed them over to the waiting servants whose torches lit their way back to the coach. It was only when the vehicle was well clear of the Palace that Jonathan broke his silence.

'I'm ashamed of myself, Mr Redmayne,' he admitted.

'Ashamed?'

'Of those suspicions I had. Mrs Gow is a true victim, I concede that now. An unscrupulous woman might try to trick money out of the men in her life but she would never go to these lengths.' A deep sigh escaped him. 'Mary Hibbert loved working for Mrs Gow. It shone out of her. And it was obvious that her mistress treated her well. She would never be party to what happened to the girl.'

'The same fate may befall Harriet Gow if we don't find her soon.'

'We'll find her,' vowed Jonathan, '*and* the men who killed Mary Hibbert. I've a word or two to say to them on her behalf.'

'So have I,' said Christopher, gritting his teeth. 'They're the same villains who attacked my brother, remember.'

'Callous rogues, sir. Far too fond of those cudgels.'

'What do you mean?'

'You didn't see Mary's body, sir,' said Jonathan quietly. 'I

152

did. I felt dreadful, having to look at her lying naked on that slab. But it had to be done. The physician was lying, Mr Redmayne.'

'What do you mean?'

'Mary suffered a great deal. Her whole body was covered in bruises where she'd been cudgelled unmercifully. I think she was beaten to death. My guess is that they only broke her neck afterwards. These men are animals,' he said with rancour. 'They didn't just murder the girl. They *enjoyed* it.'

Chapter Ten

After a long and largely sleepless night, Harriet Gow dozed off in the chair, still agonising over her decision to condone her maidservant's bold escape bid. Her slumbers were soon interrupted. The door was unlocked and unbolted then flung open to allow the man and the woman to come bustling in. They wasted no time on a greeting. Harriet was grabbed and lifted bodily from her chair before being dragged out. As they hustled her up the steps, she found her voice again.

'Where are you taking me?' she bleated.

'Be quiet!' grunted the man.

'Who are you?'

'Never you mind.'

'You're hurting my arm.'

'Be glad that I don't do worse.'

'What's going on?' she cried.

'You'll be told in time.'

'Where's Mary?'

'Forget about her.'

'Tell me!'

The man ignored her. Harriet tried hard to assert herself.

'You can't do this to me!' she protested with as much dignity as she could muster. 'Do you know who I am? What I am?'

'Oh, yes,' said the man with a throaty chuckle. 'We know.'

The dialogue took her up the staircase and along the landing. They were marching her back to her room. The change of accommodation was welcome but her relief was tinged with apprehension. Mary Hibbert's fate took precedence over her own immediate comfort. Harriet continued to ask about her until the door of the bedchamber was opened and she was pushed into it. Turning to continue her pleas, she found the door shut firmly in her face. At least she had been rescued from the cellar. What had prompted that? She could not believe that her captors had taken pity on her. Both of them – the man *and* the woman – had been consistently brusque with her. They spoke only to give her commands and they had no compunction about laying violent hands on her.

Evidently, they were acting on orders – but who was giving them? Was there someone else in the house, supervising her imprisonment and controlling any punishment she needed to suffer? Her two captors wore masks to avoid being recognised. Did that mean she had seen them before, or were they merely concealing their identity as a precaution against being picked out by her at a later date? And what of their master? Why did he not put in an appearance, if only to taunt her? What made him keep so carefully out of the way?

Harriet asked the same burning questions over and over again until she at last noticed something. Changes had been made to the room. Strips of wood had been nailed across the window, obscuring some of the light and making it impossible to open. Most of the furniture had been removed, leaving her with no option but to use the bed or the floor if she wished to sit down. Her comforts had been dramatically reduced. It was the sight of the bed that really harrowed her. Not only had it been stripped of all its linen to ensure that she could create no makeshift rope for another escape attempt, it had acquired a tiny object that glinted in the early morning light.

She was transfixed. The brooch that lay in the middle of the bed was the keepsake she had given to Mary Hibbert just before the girl had lowered herself into the garden. It was more than a reward for her bravery. It was a sign of her mistress's affection and gratitude. To have it brought back could mean only one thing: Mary had been caught. She would have no need of the brooch now. Rushing to the bed, Harriet snatched it up and held it to her bosom then she swung round to run across to the door. Beating on it with both fists, she yelled as loudly as she could and without any fear of the consequences.

'What have you done with Mary? Where *is* she?'

Christopher Redmayne was up at daybreak, refusing the breakfast that Jacob had prepared for him and ignoring his servant's admonitions as he headed for the stable. Cocks were still crowing with competitive zeal as he rode off down Fetter Lane. Henry's condition was his primary concern and he made for the house in Bedford Street at a canter, swerving his horse through the oncoming carts, waggons and pedestrians who were already streaming towards the city's markets. In the year since the Great Fire had devastated the capital, London had regained much of its old zest and character. There was a communal sense of resilience in the air.

When he reached his destination, Christopher found that his brother was now sleeping soundly after a disturbed night. He tiptoed into the bedchamber to look at Henry but forbore to wake him. Pleased to hear that the physician was due to call again that morning, he promised to return later himself then set off for the site in the parish of St Martin's-in-the-Fields. The short ride brought him to a scene of almost ear-splitting activity. Picks, shovels and other implements were being used with force, more building materials were arriving to be unloaded and stacked, horses were neighing, a dog was barking as it darted playfully between the piles of bricks and timber, workmen were cursing each other roundly and Lodowick Corrigan was in the middle of it all, bellowing above the tumult and pointing a peremptory finger.

Christopher took careful stock of what had so far been done. Even in a day, they had made perceptible progress, marking out the perimeter of the house and digging most of the foundations. He waited until the builder ambled across to him.

'I thought we'd seen the last of you, sir,' said Corrigan tartly.

'No, I'll be here from time to time.'

'You should stay all day, Mr Redmayne. If you did that, you might learn something.'

'About what?'

'How a house gets built.'

'But I already know,' said Christopher, icily pleasant. 'You find a talented architect to design it and an agreeable builder to put it up. All that they have to do is to trust each other.'

'That's what it comes down to in the end. Trust.'

'What do you trust in, Mr Corrigan?'

'My long experience.'

'Of disobeying the instructions of an architect?'

'When I started in this trade,' sneered the other, 'there weren't quite so many of your profession, sir. Master-builders were the order of the day – men like my father who did everything themselves. My father could design, construct and decorate a property entirely on his own.'

'Those days have gone.'

'They're sorely missed.'

Christopher did not rise to the bait of his implication. Instead, he tried to make use of the other's much vaunted experience. After discussing what would be done on site that day, he surprised his companion by resorting to some mild flattery.

'You know your trade, Mr Corrigan,' he said. 'I took the trouble to look at some of the houses you've put up in the city. Soundly built, every one of them. They're a credit to you.'

'Why, thank you, Mr Redmayne.'

'And a credit to the architect who designed them, of course.'

'They were all amenable men,' said Corrigan.

'Amenable?'

'To my suggestions.'

'Nobody is more amenable than I. Any suggestion of yours is always welcome. The problem is that I've not heard one yet that I thought worth taking seriously.'

'That's because your head's still in the clouds, sir.'

'Oh?'

'You're a true artist. All that concerns you is your reputation.'

'Naturally.'

'Other architects had a sharper eye for the possibilities.'

'Of what, Mr Corrigan?'

'Profit. Gain. Advancement,' said the builder slyly. 'Take your insistence on the use of Caen stone. It'll be expensive to buy and difficult to transport. The quarry in which I have a stake could provide stone that's similar in type and colour but costs half the price. Mr Hartwell doesn't know that, of course. Persuade him to change his mind about the portico and you could pocket the difference between the Caen stone and the kind I supply.'

'What's in it for you?'

'The pleasure of teaching a young man the ways of the world.'

'The ways of *your* world, Mr Corrigan. Mine is very different. It includes quaint concepts like honesty, fair dealing and mutual confidence. Proffer any more lessons in cheating a client,' he warned, 'and I'll be forced to report the conversation to Mr Hartwell.' The builder's smirk vanished at once. 'Now, give me some advice that I can use.'

'I don't follow,' said the other resentfully.

'Have you ever built a house in the vicinity of St James's Palace?'

'Two in Berry Street and one in Piccadilly.'

'What interests me are some properties in Rider Street.'

'Why?'

'I'd like to know who built them. I understand that there's only a small row of houses there at present, but they're well designed and neatly constructed. How could I find out who put them up?'

'By asking the man who owns them.'

'They're leased out, then?'

'If it's the houses I'm thinking of, yes.'

'Do you happen to know who the landlord is?'

'It used to be Crown land, Mr Redmayne,' said the other

with a knowing grin. 'So the King must be getting an income from them. If you want to live in one of those houses, you'll have to kiss His Majesty's arse.' A crude cackle. 'Watch out for those royal farts, sir, won't you?'

Jonathan Bale's day also began at dawn. After breakfast with his wife and children, he went off to acquaint Peter Hibbert with the sudden death of his sister. He was not looking forward to the assignment but someone had to undertake it and his link with the family made him the obvious choice. That was why he had volunteered so assertively in front of William Chiffinch. Horrified by Mary's death, Jonathan hoped that he might in some small way alleviate the distress that the tidings were bound to create. Peter was not the most robust character and his uncle was still very sick. Both would need to be helped to absorb the shock that lay in wait for them.

The boy was apprenticed to a tailor in Cornhill Ward and it was there that the constable first presented himself. Peter Hibbert was already at work, cutting some cloth from a bolt. After an explanatory word with his master, Jonathan took the boy aside and broke the news as gently as he could. Peter burst into tears. It was minutes before the boy was able to press for details.

'When was this, Mr Bale?' he whimpered.

'Some time yesterday.'

'Where did it happen?'

'Her body was found in Drury Lane. It seems that she was struck by a coach as it careered along out of control. Mary had no chance. It was all over in seconds.'

'What was my sister doing in Drury Lane?'

'I don't know.'

'I thought she and Mrs Gow had left London.'

'They must've returned without warning. My guess is that Mary was on her way to The Theatre Royal.'

'Where's the body now?'

'Lying in a morgue,' said Jonathan. 'I saw it late last night and identified it. This was the earliest I could make contact with you.' He saw the boy about to topple and gave him a hug. 'Bear up, Peter. This is a terrible blow, I know. Mary was a good sister to you.'

'She was everything, Mr Bale.'

'For her sake, try to be strong.'

'How can I?'

'Try, Peter. Mary is with the angels now, where she belongs.'

'That's true,' mumbled the boy.

Informed of the circumstances, the tailor gave permission for his apprentice to take the day off and Jonathan accompanied him to Carter Street, where he had to mix fact with deception again. The uncle was numbed into silence by the news but his wife let out a shriek, sobbing loudly and bemoaning the loss of her niece. She laid responsibility for the death squarely on Mary Hibbert's involvement in the tawdry world of the theatre. Jonathan was able to agree with her heartily on that score but he did not labour the point, preferring to soothe rather than allot blame, and anxious to leave Peter in the reassuring company of his relatives. Uncle and aunt soon rallied. Grateful to the constable for telling them the news, they willingly accepted his offer to speak to the parish priest in order to make arrangements for the funeral.

'Will you come back, Mr Bale?' asked Peter meekly.

'In time.'

'I'd like that.'

Jonathan gave him a sad smile. It was outside that very house that he had last seen Mary Hibbert and he was still prodded by uncomfortable memories of their conversation. He was determined to be more helpful and less censorious towards her brother. Peter had now lost a mother, a father and only sister in the space of two short years. He needed all the friendship and support he could get.

Jonathan's next visit was to the vicar, a white-haired old man who had lost count of the number of funeral services he had conducted. Mary Hibbert no longer lived in the parish but the fact that she was born there gave her the right to be buried in the already overcrowded churchyard. After discussing details with his visitor, the priest went scurrying off to Carter Lane to offer his own condolences to the bereaved. Jonathan felt guilty at having to give them only an attenuated version of the truth but he was relieved that he had not confronted them with the full horror of the situation. Peter Hibbert, in particular, would not have been able to cope. It was a kindness to spare him.

Having discharged his duties regarding Mary Hibbert, the constable could now begin the pursuit of those who murdered her. He left the city through Ludgate, walked along Fleet Street then quickened his pace when he reached the Strand, the broad thoroughfare that was fringed on his left by the palatial residences of the great, the good and the ostentatiously wealthy. Jonathan was too caught up in his thoughts to accord the houses his usual hostile glare. He came to a halt at the place where the ambush had taken place, wondering yet again why that route had been taken by the coachman. Walking to the top of the lane, he found the landlord of the Red Lion supervising the unloading of barrels from a cart.

'Good morning to you,' said Jonathan.

'Good morning, sir.'

'There's no room for anything to get past while this cart is here.'

'They'll have to wait,' said the other cheerily. 'We must have our beer or I'll lose custom. I daresay you don't have lanes as narrow as this in your ward. Not since the fire, that is.'

'Every street, lane and alley that was rebuilt had to be wider, sir, by order of Parliament. It's a sensible precaution. Fire spreads easily when properties are huddled so closely together.'

'Then keep it away from us.'

The innkeeper was a short, stout, red-faced man with a bald head that was encircled by a tonsure of matted grey hair. There was nothing monastic, however, in his coarse appearance and rough voice.

'So what brings you back to the Red Lion?' he said.

'Something you told me yesterday.'

'I think I told you quite a lot, sir.'

'You gave me a list of people who live in the lane.'

'That I did, Mr Bale.'

Jonathan was surprised. 'You remember my name, then?'

'A good memory is an asset in my trade, sir. People like to be recognised. It makes them feel welcome. I always remember names.'

'The one that interests me is Bartholomew Gow.'

'Ah, yes. He wasn't a regular patron of my inn but he did come in often enough for me to get to know him a little.'

'How would you describe him?'

'Pleasant enough, sir. Kept himself to himself. He always moved on if things became a bit rowdy. Mr Gow was too much of a gentleman to put up with that.'

'What age would you put him at?'

'Well below thirty still, I'd say,' replied the man, exploring a hirsute ear with his little finger. 'Handsome fellow. The tavern wenches were all keen to serve Mr Gow. He had a way with him, see. My wife remarked on it a few times.' He gave an understanding chuckle. 'She wouldn't admit it to me, of course, but I think she misses him.'

'Misses him?'

'He hasn't been in to see us for weeks.'

'Why not?'

'Who knows? Maybe he found somewhere more to his taste, sir. The Red Lion can get a bit lively when drink has flowed. Mr Gow was never at ease when that happened.'

'Where exactly does he live?' said Jonathan, glancing back down the lane. 'Do you know which house?'

'No, sir, but it's towards the bottom. That's where the best lodgings are to be found and I told you he was a gentleman.'

'Lodgings? He doesn't own the house, then?'

'Oh, no. He had a room, that's all.'

Jonathan squeezed every detail he could out of the man before thanking him for his help and moving off. When he got to the lower end of the lane, he began knocking on doors systematically in his search for Bartholomew Gow. The fourth house was owned by a big, fleshy woman in her thirties with a prominent bosom taking attention away from a podgy face that was pitted by smallpox. She opened the door with reluctance and was clearly displeased to see a constable standing there.

'Good morning,' said Jonathan politely.

She was wary. 'What can I do for you, sir?'

'I'm looking for a Mr Bartholomew Gow.'

'Then you've come too late. He moved out.'

'When?'

'Week or so ago.'

'But he did lodge here?'

'Yes.'

'What sort of man was he?'

'The kind that pays his rent. That's all I cared about.' She gave him a basilisk stare then tried to close the front door.

'Wait,' he said, putting out a hand to stop her. 'I need to ask you something. A couple of days ago, there was an incident right outside your door involving a coach. It scraped along the front of your house.' He pointed to the marks in the brickwork. 'Were you in the house at the time?'

'No, sir.'

'Was anyone else here? Anyone who might have heard the noise and rushed out to see what was going on?'

'Nobody, sir.'

'What of your neighbours? Did they see anything?'

'I don't think so or they'd have told me.'

'There must have been *some* witnesses.'

'I wouldn't know,' she said sourly.

Jonathan became aware that he was being watched from the upper room. It was the second time he had been under surveillance from that standpoint. When he stepped back to look up, he saw a figure move smartly away from the window.

'Did Mr Gow have the room at the front?' he wondered.

'Yes, sir.'

'Who lodges there now?'

'Another gentleman.'

And she closed the door this time before he could stop her.

'You've saved me a journey, Mr Redmayne. I was just about to come calling at your house in order to see you.'

'Why?'

'Because I wish to get to the bottom of this once and for all.'

'What do you mean, Mr Killigrew?'

'Something is afoot, sir,' said the manager waspishly. 'A worrying turn of events has occurred. First of all, I get a letter from Harriet Gow to say that she's temporarily indisposed. Then your brother, Henry, barges in here with the same news and does his best to pump me about the members of my company. Word somehow leaks out about her absence and I'm harried to death by her admirers, that moonstruck idiot, Jasper Hartwell, among them. Next minute, I find your brother peering over my shoulder while I'm taking a rehearsal then he springs the biggest surprise of all by turning up at my theatre, covered in blood.'

'It was good of you to convey him back to his home, Mr Killigrew,' said Christopher. 'That's one of the main reasons I called. To thank you for coming to Henry's aid and to give you a report on his condition.'

'How is he?'

'Weak but slowly recovering from his ordeal.'

'I thought we'd lost him when he was carried in here. Let me be brutally honest, sir. There've been times in my life when I could willingly have taken a cudgel to your brother myself. Henry can irritate so. But I repented my urge when I saw him lying there,' he said, recalling the gruesome image. 'No man deserves to be battered to a pulp like that.'

Thomas Killigrew was in a peppery mood when Christopher met him at the theatre. His visitor noted the disparity between this manager and the one with whom he had competed so strenuously for years. Killigrew had none of the easy charm of Sir William D'Avenant, the putative son of a humble Oxford innkeeper, who had risen to the status of a courtier and effortlessly acquired all the skills that went with it. The puffy Killigrew might have prior claim on the King's friendship but he lacked the studied grace of the older man.

'Let's not waste words, Mr Redmayne,' said the manager. 'I want to know exactly what's going on.'

'You have every right to do so, Mr Killigrew.'

'Then please explain.'

'First, let me offer an apology,' said Christopher. 'I feel that an unguarded remark of mine might have led Mr Hartwell to hound you here yesterday. He's developed a rare passion for Harriet Gow.'

'Show me a man who hasn't.'

'She's a remarkable woman. I count that performance of hers in *The Maid's Tragedy* as the most moving I've ever seen from an actress.'

'Abigail Saunders ran her close.'

'I'll come to Miss Saunders in moment.'

'Your brother was showing an interest in her.'

'Henry is not in a position to show an interest in any woman at the moment,' said Christopher sadly. 'It's all my fault for employing him to do a job that I was engaged to do myself.'

'And what job was that?'

Christopher saw no point in trying to deceive someone as worldly as the manager any longer. The disappearance of Harriet Gow had a direct effect on his takings at the theatre. It was in his interests to have her back on stage as soon as possible so that audiences would flock there again. That could be best achieved, Christopher judged, by taking the manager into his confidence. It would gain far more cooperation from Killigrew than Henry Redmayne had been able to secure by his more roundabout means. Swearing him to secrecy, Christopher gave a terse account of the situation. Killigrew was shaken to hear that his leading actress had been abducted and horrified to learn of the death of Mary Hibbert. When he fitted the attacks on Henry Redmayne and Roland Trigg into the picture, he saw how serious the predicament was.

One thing puzzled the manager. He frowned in wonderment.

'You're conducting this search on your *own*, Mr Redmayne?'

'No, I'm working in harness with Jonathan Bale, a constable.'

'An architect and a mere constable?'

'We were able to be of service to His Majesty in the past,' said Christopher modestly. 'That's why he sent for us. But the principal reason for using two men in this investigation instead of two hundred is that we will not arouse attention. At least, that's what I thought until Henry was assaulted. The ransom note insisted that no attempt be made to rescue Harriet Gow. Because we disobeyed, Mary Hibbert was killed by way of reprisal.'

'Doesn't that frighten you and this constable off?'

'Quite the opposite, Mr Killigrew. I feel guilty that anything I may have done somehow led to the girl's death and Mr Bale is not the kind of man who's ever scared away. He knew Mary Hibbert as a friend and neighbour. Nothing will stop him tracking down her killers.'

'How can I help?'

'In many ways.'

'Teach me what they are.'

'The main one is to tell us more about Mrs Gow's private life. You must have had some insight into it. Henry made a start for me. He managed to compile a list of people who were either close to her or who might be suspect in some way.'

'Do you have that list with you?'

'Of course,' said Christopher, producing it from his pocket to give it to him. 'Please disregard the last name.'

'If only I could!' said Killigrew, looking at it with disgust. 'I interviewed Sir William D'Avenant myself. He's not implicated.'

'He'd do all he could to seduce Harriet away from me.'

'Would he condone violence and murder?'

'He'd roast his grandmother on a spit in the middle of a stage if he thought it would increase his income at the theatre.

But no,' conceded the manager, 'not murder. I think the old crow would stop short of that.'

'What of the other names?'

'Henry has worked hard. He's got most of Harriet's close friends down here – and her enemies. In fact, there's only one person he hasn't put down and that's Martin Eldridge.'

'A friend or an enemy, sir?'

'Oh, a friend. No shadow of a doubt about that. Indeed, I have my suspicions that Martin Eldridge may have been elevated beyond the level of friendship by Harriet. She was deeply upset when I had to terminate his contract,' Killigrew said, lovingly caressing his moustache. 'She more or less pleaded with me to give Martin a second chance.'

'Second chance?'

'That's what Harriet called it. By my reckoning, it would have been more like a sixth or seventh chance.'

'Was he a member of the company here?'

'Yes. Martin was a clever actor – he might even have been a great one if he'd had the sense to apply himself, but he was too lazy. Too easily distracted. I'm a tolerant man, Mr Redmayne,' Killigrew announced with an intolerant scowl, 'but I'll not stand for wayward behaviour. I expect my actors to work at their craft. Martin Eldridge failed to do that.'

'What is he doing now?'

'What all unemployed actors do. Either look for work else-where, which means submitting themselves to that noseless monster who stalks The Duke's Theatre, or sponge off rich women.'

'How would I find him?'

'Talk to Abigail Saunders. She may be able to help you.'

'I was going to ask your permission to speak to the lady, in any case,' said Christopher. 'It crossed Henry's mind that she might somehow be involved in the abduction of Harriet Gow.'

'Abigail?' Killigrew shook his head. 'She'd never sink to that.'

'Miss Saunders is the main beneficiary of her absence.'

'But she isn't.'

'Then who is?'

'That rotting old lecher, Sir William D'Avenant. Can you believe that Abigail once granted him her favours? Well, yes,' he said with an oily grin, 'if you've the slightest knowledge of actresses, you can believe anything of them, I daresay. I certainly do. What a peculiar breed they are! Warrior queens with the faces of harmless cherubs.'

'Is Miss Saunders a warrior queen?'

'Decide for yourself, Mr Redmayne. Abigail should be here any minute for another rehearsal. She saved the day yesterday afternoon. And in view of what you've told me,' he sighed, 'she may have to come to our rescue for quite some time.'

The man rode hard along the deserted road. By the time he reached the house, his temper was up and his horse was lathered with sweat. The woman greeted him with a token curtsey at the door. She had removed her mask to reveal plain features lit by a pair of gimlet eyes. Storming past her, the visitor went straight into the drawing room where the other guard was waiting for him, his own mask now discarded. The newcomer was inches shorter and far slimmer in build but he was not intimidated by the burly figure of Arthur Oscott before him. Snapping his whip hard against his thigh, he glared accusingly at the man.

'Why did you let it happen?' he demanded.

'I was only following orders, sir.'

'Your orders were to keep both of them under lock and key.'

'The girl escaped,' Oscott said. 'We couldn't let her get away or she'd have raised the alarm. She had to be stopped.'

'Stopped and brought back here. Not beaten to death.'

'They got carried away, sir.'

'Carried away!' fumed his employer.

'When they caught up with the girl, she screamed and fought back. Smeek said they had to shut her up.'

'So they did – permanently.'

'I'd blame Froggatt, sir. Too eager with that cudgel. Ben Froggatt doesn't know his own strength. He's the one who done her in. When they came back, I gave him the sharp side of my tongue, I can tell you.'

'If I'd been here, he'd have had the point of my sword. Reckless fool! He could have ruined the whole plan.' He pointed the whip. 'And whose idea was it to deliver the body to the Palace?'

'Mine,' admitted Oscott. 'You told me I was to use my initiative.'

'That was when I thought you had a brain.'

'We had to frighten them, you said. Force them into paying the ransom. What better way to show them we weren't to be trifled with than by sending a message like that?' Oscott was unrepentant. 'I was trying to turn the situation to our advantage, sir. Thanks to Froggatt, we suddenly had a dead body on our hands. We could hardly keep it here. Smeek has his boat so I got him and Froggatt to row downriver to the Palace under cover of darkness.'

'Are you sure they weren't seen?'

'They swear it.'

'Where did they leave her?'

'By the steps.'

'And they got away safely?'

'Yes, sir. They're well versed in their trade.'

'I was told that you were as well,' snarled the other, 'but you let me down, Oscott. How on earth did that maidservant escape when two of you were guarding her all day long?'

'Knotted bed linen. She lowered herself into the garden.'

'Then the girl showed more initiative than you've managed.'

'It may all turn out for the best, sir,' argued the other.

'Mrs Gow was not to be harmed. I stressed that.'

'I know.'

'And I didn't just mean physical harm, you dolt! Think how she'll feel when she finds out what's happened to this Mary Hibbert. She'll be distraught. Keeping her locked up here is punishment enough in itself. There was no need to kill her maid.'

'It wasn't my fault,' said Oscott, thrown on the defensive.

'Of course it was! You hired Smeek and Froggatt – and that other bully boy who helped us in the ambush. Choose reliable men, that was my instruction. Not imbeciles.' He walked around the room to calm himself down, tapping the end of his whip into the palm of his hand. 'Well, let's hope we can retrieve the situation. Who knows? It might even serve our ends. It might just scare the money out of His Majesty's purse.' He came to a sudden halt. 'Where is Mrs Gow?'

'Sealed up in the bedchamber, sir.'

'Safely?'

'There's no way she can get out. The door is locked and the window has been boarded up. I saw to it myself.'

'Closing the stable door after the horse had bolted.'

'Mrs Gow is still here. She's the important one, isn't she?'

'Yes,' agreed the other. 'Mrs Gow is the only important one. As long as we have her, we can put pressure on them to hand over the money.' He looked upwards. 'What have you told her about Mary Hibbert?'

Oscott looked uneasy. 'Nothing, sir.'

'Are you sure?'

'We just let her know that the girl had been caught.'

'And how did you do that?'

'Mary Hibbert was wearing a brooch. We left it on Mrs Gow's bed.'

'Why didn't you leave the dead body while you were at it!' roared the other, charging back to him. 'You've as good as told her that the girl will have no need for the brooch again. Was this another example of your famous initiative?'

'It was my wife's idea.'

'Oh, was it now?'

'She thought we should punish Mrs Gow.'

'Whatever for?'

'Helping her maid to escape.'

'Your wife's every bit as stupid as her husband.'

'We've done what we're paid for,' reasoned Oscott. 'We set

up the ambush and brought Mrs Gow here. That's what you wanted.'

'Granted,' said the visitor. 'What I didn't want was the taint of murder on our hands. It was so unnecessary. Where are those two madmen now, Smeek and Froggatt?'

'Gone back to London.'

'Can they be trusted?'

'Yes, sir. They know how to keep their mouths shut.'

'I don't want any of this leading back to me.'

'Smeek and Froggatt don't even know your name, sir,' Oscott reminded him. 'No more do I. That was your stipulation. You're safe, sir. None of this can be connected with you.'

'It could if the trail led to this house.'

'Only the four of us know where it is.'

'That's two too many,' decided the other, rubbing his chin with the end of his whip. 'Smeek and Froggatt are liabilities. To be on the safe side, I think we'll move Mrs Gow.'

'Where to, sir?'

'Another hiding place.'

'But why?'

'They worry me, Oscott, those two friends of yours with the over-zealous cudgels. If they don't know where Mrs Gow is being kept, they won't be able to tell anyone where it is.'

'But they wouldn't do that, anyway,' insisted Oscott loyally. 'Smeek served in the Navy, sir. The man's as hard as teak and twice as reliable. Ben Froggatt's just such another. He knows how to earn his money. Have no fears about Smeek and Froggatt,' he said airily. 'They won't let you down.'

The Hope and Anchor was one of the many inns along the river that catered for sailors. With so many ships moored nearby, it was doing brisk business and its taproom was full. Smeek and Froggatt pushed their way through the crowd until they found a corner where they could raise their tankards in celebration. Short but powerful, Smeek had the weather-beaten complexion of a seafaring man. Froggatt was bigger, broader and even more rugged in appearance.

'We done well,' he said, drinking deep.

'Arthur Oscott didn't think so, Ben.'

'We shut the girl up for good. Pity we didn't have time to get some fun out of her before we did it, though. Pretty thing. I got a good feel of her body when we kidnapped her. I'd have enjoyed riding that little filly.'

'So would I,' said Smeek. 'One thing, anyway.'

'What's that?'

'She got us to the Palace. Never thought I'd set foot there.'

'Well, we did,' said Froggatt, jingling coins in his hand. 'And we got our reward from Arthur for doing it. He was pleased with us in the end. Leaving that body there would be another warning, he said.'

Smeek looked down at the money in his friend's huge palm.

'How long will it take us to drink through that, Ben?'

'Let's see.'

They shared a laugh, bought more ale then joined in the general revelry. The raucous atmosphere was home to them. Drinking heavily, they were quite unaware that someone was spying on them from the doorway. It was Froggatt who peeled off first to relieve himself. He made an obscene gesture to his companion then lurched out of the inn and around to the alleyway at the rear. Undoing his breeches, he broke wind violently then urinated against the wall.

The first blow was across the back of his neck. It made him double up in agony. Before he could turn, other blows from a heavy object rained down on his head. Froggatt flailed around madly, trying to grab his attacker, but his legs began to buckle. A final relay of blows from the cudgel sent him dropping to the ground in a pool of blood and urine.

Roland Trigg used a foot to turn the twitching carcass over.

'Hello, Ben,' he said with a grin. 'Remember me?'

Abigail Saunders was circumspect. Pleased to be introduced by Killigrew to a handsome young man, she balked slightly when she realised that he was Henry Redmayne's brother. The manager left the two of them alone in her dressing room so that Christopher could try to talk his way past her obvious reservations.

'I heard what happened to your brother,' she said with a degree of concern. 'It was dreadful. How is Henry?'

'On the mend, Miss Saunders.'

'Good.'

'I'm sure he doesn't regret it.'

'Regret what?'

'Coming here yesterday afternoon,' said Christopher. 'Even if it cost him a beating, he wouldn't have missed your performance as Aspatia.'

'Thank you,' she said, melting slightly.

'Everyone tells me that you were superb.'

'You'll have to judge for yourself, Mr Redmayne.'

'Will there be a chance for me to do so?'

'Possibly,' she said, turning her head to let him see her in profile. 'The play is very popular with audiences. Mr Killigrew is talking of staging it again next week.'

'What if Mrs Gow has returned by then?'

'There's no sign that she will. Harriet has vanished into thin air.'

'Have you any idea where she might be?'

'None at all.'

She turned back to look him full in the eye, almost challenging him to question her more closely on the subject. Christopher held back. Like Henry, he sensed that she knew more than she would ever divulge but, unlike his brother, he did not want to antagonise her with a thoughtless remark. He studied her face then gave a smile of approval.

'Henry was right,' he said gallantly. 'You're very beautiful, Miss Saunders.'

She blossomed. 'Thank you, Mr Redmayne,' she said happily. 'No disrespect to your brother but I find your praise more acceptable than his. Henry is too glib and well rehearsed. As an actress, I appreciate a capacity for rehearsal,' she continued, starting to relax. 'As a woman, however, I prefer a spontaneous compliment to a prepared one.'

'You must have plenty of both, Miss Saunders.'

'A woman can never have too many compliments.'

There was a teasing note in her voice. He did not respond to it.

'I believe that you're a friend of Martin Eldridge,' he said.

'Martin? Why, yes. We have a history.'

'History?'

'Not of *that* kind,' she reprimanded with a mock frown. 'Martin Eldridge and I could never be that close. But we did start out together in the theatre. We had our first parts in a play for The Duke's Men.'

'Is he a good actor?'

'I think so. And he was a staunch supporter of me.'

'Why did he leave the company?'

'Because he fell out with Mr Killigrew.' She looked towards the door. 'That's not too difficult to do, I'm afraid. He's a volatile character at the best of times. Martin upset him and his contract was not renewed.'

'Where might I find him?'

'Why should you want to do so?'

'A personal reason. His name was passed on to me.'

'I've no idea where he lodges presently but he's stayed with friends in Shoreditch before now. Somewhere in Old Street, I think.'

'I don't suppose you'd know the name of those friends?'

'No, Mr Redmayne. Martin has so many.'

'So I'm told. According to Mr Killigrew, he was close to Mrs Gow.'

'Too close, in my view!'

'Why?'

'Harriet did tend to gather young men around her, I'm afraid. We all like to do that to some extent, of course, but she took it to extremes. Martin was one of her attendants, always running errands for her. It was demeaning,' she said irritably. 'I told him so but he wouldn't listen.'

'What other young men did she have in her train?'

'I'm past caring.'

'So you did care at one point?'

'Mr Redmayne,' she retorted, 'I've a life of my own to lead and it gives me little time to pry into the affairs of others. Especially when one of them is Harriet Gow. I'd simply never be able to keep track of all her admirers. Harriet has changed,' she said ruefully. 'She's changed so much. I remember her when she first came into this cruel profession. Harriet was a nice, quiet, friendly girl with a husband she adored. Bartholomew went everywhere with her in those days – until she found him an inconvenience.'

'You sound as if you're sorry for him.'

'No husband should be treated like that. Somehow, he's managed to survive. Indeed, parting from Harriet may turn out to be a blessed release. When I saw him recently, he looked almost happy again.'

His ears pricked up. 'You saw Mr Gow?'

'Less than a week ago.'

'Do you remember where?'

'Of course. At Locket's ordinary in Charing Cross. I was dining there with a friend. Bartholomew Gow was sitting at the next table with his lawyer – a Mr Shann, as I recall. Bartholomew did introduce me. We only exchanged a brief word,' she said, 'but one of his comments made me burn with curiosity. Especially as his prediction turned out to be absolutely true.'

'Prediction?'

'Bartholomew told me that opportunity was at hand, and urged me to be ready for it. Harriet would soon be indisposed, he said, and I'd be asked to replace her if I'd studied her roles.'

'Were those his exact words?'

'More or less.'

'Did he say *why* his wife would be unavailable?'

'I didn't care,' she said coldly. 'Chances come along so rarely in this profession that you have to seize them with both hands. I'm very grateful to Bartholomew Gow.' She gave a dazzling smile, and added: 'He told me that his wife might be unable to appear on stage again *for quite some time*.'

Chapter Eleven

Jonathan Bale was a methodical man who liked to do things in correct sequence and at a steady pace. Punctual by nature, he was disconcerted to arrive at Ludgate precisely at noon and see no sign of Christopher Redmayne. Since he had abided by the exact time and place of their agreed meeting, he simply could not understand why the architect was not there as well. It was almost half an hour before the latter appeared on horseback to shower him with profuse apologies. Jonathan waved them away.

'I've no time to waste, standing around for you to come, sir. I could have been off elsewhere, doing something useful.'

'I know, I know, Mr Bale,' said Christopher, dismounting. 'But I got so engrossed in what Abigail Saunders was telling me – she's the actress who has replaced Mrs Gow – that I lost all purchase on time. I've so much to tell you about my visit to the theatre but I want to hear your news first. Where have you been?'

'My day began in Cornhill Ward, talking to Peter Hibbert.'

'Poor lad! How did he take it?'

'Not well, sir.'

Jonathan explained in detail how he had spent the morning. His attempt at tracing Bartholomew Gow had failed, but it had led him to an interesting discovery. It was one which the constable felt a little awkward about passing on. He lowered his voice.

'I knew that there was something odd about that house, sir,' he said darkly. 'The woman who answered the door to me was very evasive. She claimed that there was nobody in the house when that coach was ambushed right on her doorstep, but there's been somebody there the twice I've been to the lane. He's watched me from the upper room.'

'Bartholomew Gow, by any chance?'

'I don't think so. The landlady said that he didn't lodge there any longer but I'm wondering if he ever did live under her roof.'

'That innkeeper told you he did.'

'Only because Mr Gow called into the Red Lion from time to time. But that doesn't prove he was lodging in the lane.'

'I don't understand.'

'Neither did I until I watched the place, sir,' said Jonathan heavily. 'I kept out of sight in a doorway farther up the lane and just waited. A couple of hours, all told.'

'That *is* devotion to duty.'

'I wanted to be sure.'

'Of what?'

'My suspicions. It was the way that woman behaved. I could see that the last person she wanted outside her door was a constable. She hurried me quickly on my way.'

'But you lingered.'

'It was worth the wait, Mr Redmayne.'

'Why?'

'I saw a number of coaches stop there in all. A woman got out of the first and slipped into the house. A man soon followed her in the second vehicle. He left almost an hour later on his own. Soon after that, a third coach arrived with a man and a woman in it. They were let into the house as well.' He pursed his lips in disapproval. 'And so it went on.'

'What did?' said Christopher innocently. 'The landlady had a series of visitors, that's all. What's so unusual about that?'

'The way they took care not to be seen, sir. Those coaches stopped right outside the house so that the occupants could step straight in through the front door. I was only twenty yards away but I didn't get a proper look at any of them. They made sure of that.'

Christopher understood. 'I begin to see your reasoning, Mr Bale.'

'Mr Gow may never have lodged there.'

'Except for short intervals, that is.'

'Exactly, sir,' said Jonathan, ridding himself of a discovery that obviously disgusted him. 'The house is a place for covert assignations. Tucked away in that lane, it's very private, allowing people to come and go without being seen. It's an address of convenience. In my view, that's why Mr Gow used the premises occasionally. I think he had a rendezvous with a lady.'

'Not his own wife, surely?'

'That's not for me to say.'

'It would explain what her coach was doing in that lane.'

'Mr Trigg refused to comment on that.'

'He was only trying to save Mrs Gow's blushes, I fancy. On the other hand,' he remembered, 'he was very hostile towards her husband. Trigg more or less accused him of being behind this whole business. It seems unlikely that he'd deliver her into his arms like that.'

'Perhaps he didn't know who was waiting for her inside the house. Mrs Gow never told him. I shouldn't imagine a woman like that confides in her coachman, especially one such as Mr Trigg.'

'Well done, Mr Bale!' congratulated Christopher. 'I think you've stumbled on some valuable evidence. If that coach really was taking her to a tryst with her husband – bizarre as that seems – Mr Gow has to be implicated in the ambush.'

'All we have to do is to find him.'

'I managed to take a big step in that direction. That was why my talk with Abigail Saunders was so useful. She saw Bartholomew Gow less than a week ago.'

'Where?'

'At Locket's ordinary. Do you know the place?'

'Only from the outside, Mr Redmayne. I can't afford to eat there.'

'Mr Gow can. He was dining with his lawyer, apparently. That may be our best way to find him – through his lawyer.'

'Did you get the man's name, sir?'

'Shann. That's what Miss Saunders said and you may be sure she got the name right. Actresses have excellent memories – it's part of their stock-in-trade. The lawyer was called Mr Shann.'

'Let me chase him down,' volunteered Jonathan. 'I visit the courts all the time and I've many friends there. One of them is bound to have heard of a lawyer called Shann. It's not a common name.'

'I embrace your offer,' said Christopher gratefully. 'While you're doing that, I'll get on the trail of Martin Eldridge.'

'Who, sir?'

'A close friend of Mrs Gow's. And an intimate one, according to Mr Killigrew. Nobody in the company knew her as well as Martin Eldridge. He could prove a most helpful witness.'

'Do you have an address for him, sir?'

'Old Street.'

'Then I may be able to help there as well,' said Jonathan, pleased that his contacts were proving so useful. 'I know one of the constables in Shoreditch. Talk to him and he might save your legs a lot of walking. If there's a Mr Eldridge living in Old Street, the chances are that Jeremy Vye will come across him.'

'Thank you. I'll speak to Constable Vye this very afternoon, when I've paid another visit to my brother.'

'How is Mr Redmayne?'

'Still in some pain, I daresay. Several ribs were cracked.'

'Your brother was lucky. I saw what they did to Mary Hibbert.'

'Henry doesn't know about her yet,' said Christopher sombrely. 'I'm not sure that he should; it would only agitate him. He's already made his contribution to this enquiry. Henry deserves a rest.'

The physician held the vessel carefully to his lips and made sure that he drank all of the potion. Henry grimaced at the bitter taste. He mouthed a protest then sank back on the pillow. The old man turned to the servant who was hovering at the bedside.

'He's taking a turn for the worse,' he said softly.

'Yes, sir.'

'See that he has another draught of the medicine this evening.'

'Yes, sir.'

'What he most needs is rest.'

'We'll make sure that Mr Redmayne gets it.'

'Don't rouse him. Let him wake in his own time.'

'Yes, sir.'

'If he seems to dwindle, call me back at once.'

The servant nodded and showed the visitor out. Henry Redmayne heard nothing of their exchange. The potion had been unpleasant to swallow but its effect was immediate. His eyes closed, his body sagged, his mind emptied. He slid gently back into a deep and restorative sleep.

Sitting astride his horse, the man remained hidden under the trees, anxious to watch the departure but equally anxious that there was no chance of his being seen by Harriet Gow. The possibility was remote. When she was brought out of the house by Arthur Oscott and his wife, Harriet was blindfolded and her wrists were tied together. She had to be guided into the waiting coach. While his wife remained inside with the prisoner, Oscott climbed up into the driving seat. The man was satisfied. Everything had gone smoothly. When the coach drew away, he followed it at a safe distance. Harriet Gow was being transferred to some alternative accommodation. Tied up and unable to see, she would be increasingly anxious during the trip. The man escorting the coach had no sympathy for her. He wanted her to suffer. It was all part of his revenge.

Instead of pursuing his investigations in Shoreditch at once, Christopher Redmayne elected to return to Fetter Lane to snatch his first meal of the day, give instructions to Jacob then ride on to Bedford Street to check on his brother's condition. Going home was a serious mistake. Within minutes of his arrival, he had the first of three unexpected and unwanted visitors. Jasper Hartwell was in a frenzy of despair.

Clad in blue and gold, he leaped out of his coach with his ginger periwig swaying so wilfully that it all but parted company with the broad-brimmed hat that was balanced atop it. Christopher caught a glimpse of him through the window, gaining a few vital seconds to prepare his alibi. When Hartwell was conducted into the parlour by Jacob, therefore, the architect was bent studiously over the drawings he had just laid out on the table with such speed. He looked up nonchalantly.

'Why, Mr Hartwell,' he greeted. 'Good day to you, sir.'

'So this is where you are skulking,' complained the other.

'Not skulking, sir. Working on my designs, as you observe. Putting the last few finishing touches to your house.'

'I went to the site but you were nowhere to be seen. Mr Corrigan was deeply upset. There are a number of issues he needs to raise with you, Mr Redmayne.'

'He had an opportunity to do so earlier on,' said Christopher, 'when I rode over to the site to inspect progress not long after dawn. From what I saw, Mr Corrigan can manage very well without me.'

'Your place is in St Martin's.'

'That's exactly where I am, sir. In my mind's eye.'

Jacob suddenly came out of the kitchen with two glasses of wine. Without the slightest hint of gratitude, Hartwell took one of them, drank it down in a series of noisy gulps then handed the glass back to the servant. Jacob withdrew once more. The drink only seemed to intensify the visitor's apprehensions.

'Where is she?' he gasped.

'Who?' asked Christopher.

'Harriet, of course. My future wife.'

'According to report, the lady is unwell.'

'It's a lie, Mr Redmayne. I've spoken twice about her to Tom Killigrew and he didn't give me a satisfactory answer on either occasion. The truth is that he doesn't *know* where Harriet is. Neither does anyone else in the company. Think on that,' he said with a scandalised yelp. 'Harriet disappears and her own manager has no idea where she is or what drove her to be there. I fear skulduggery.'

'Never, Mr Hartwell.'

'I do. I felt it in my water.'

'An illusion.'

'Something untoward has happened to my beloved.'

'Surely not,' said Christopher, rising to his feet. 'Who could want to hurt such a beautiful woman as Mrs Gow? It's inconceivable.'

'Is it?' countered Hartwell. 'Who would want to hurt such an amiable fellow as your brother? Yet I gather from Killigrew that he was viciously assaulted yesterday outside the theatre. Beauty and affability are no protection against naked villainy. If a harmless man like Henry Redmayne can be picked on by bullies, then Harriet, too, may be marked out as a victim.'

'At whose behest, sir?'

'She has her share of enemies.'

'Do you know who they are?'

'They're too numerous to list, Mr Redmayne. Envy breeds many foes. My worry is that it may not be *her* enemies who are at work here but mine.' Hartwell plopped down into a chair. 'Sensing that I'm determined to make her my wife, someone has lashed out at me from sheer spite. It could be that husband of hers, of course, or it may just be a rival for her hand, consumed with chagrin because I've made her mine.'

'But you haven't, sir,' Christopher reminded him, delicately.

'How can I when she's vanished?'

'Mrs Gow has merely withdrawn. To recuperate.'

'From what?'

'That will become clear in time.'

'But she was a picture of health when I last saw her,' argued the other. 'At the start of the week, Harriet was singing her heart out for me on stage. Where is my nightingale now?'

'Resting, sir. Leave her be.'

'I must *find* her, Mr Redmayne.'

He went on at length, expressing his love for the missing actress and working himself up into a state of wild-eyed hysteria. Christopher was alive to the paradox. Having been engaged by the King to rescue Harriet Gow, he was now forced to pretend that she was not in any danger. Instead of continuing his search, he was being held back by the swirling infatuation of his client. Jasper Hartwell was luxuriating in his distress. Christopher wondered if the visit might yet have some practical value for him.

'Henry tells me that you're a connoisseur of the theatre,' he interrupted.

'It's my second home,' Jasper agreed.

'Then you'll know all the members of the company.'

'Both at The King's House and at The Duke's Playhouse,' he said proudly.

'I'm only interested in Mr Killigrew's company.'

'So am I since Harriet joined it,' said Hartwell wistfully. 'I can recall the very moment when she first stepped on to that stage. And as for that voice! Heaven has never fashioned such an instrument before.'

'What of the actors around her?'

'I never notice any of them when she is there.'

'Oh, come, sir. You cannot fail to notice men like Michael Mohun or Charles Hart. They're masters of their trade.'

'True. They lend quality and experience to the company.'

'What of Martin Eldridge?'

'A more slender talent,' said Hartwell dismissively. 'He relies too much on his good looks and not enough on his skill as an actor. Eldridge is able but no more than that.'

'Have you ever met him?'

'Of course. Most of them have supped with me at my expense. Actors are hungry people, Mr Redmayne, and they rarely earn enough to be able to turn down a free meal. Actresses, too, of course,' he added with a sigh, 'though Harriet has never accepted my invitation, alas. She is always spirited away from the theatre by someone else.'

'His Majesty?'

'When the mood takes him.'

'Who else?'

184

'Don't ask me to dwell on her other admirers, Mr Redmayne,' said Hartwell peevishly. 'I'm the only one who loves her properly and wants to take her away from that corrupt, dangerous, silly, shallow world.' He slapped the table. 'I do so hate it when I see them pounding on the door of her dressing room and demanding her favours.'

'Who?'

'The whole merry gang. Heartless rakes, one and all.'

'Lord Rochester, you mean? Sir Charles Sedley?'

'And the rest of them – Buckhurst, Armadale, Ogle. Yes, if ever a man was well named, it is Sir Thomas Ogle, for that's what he does. Well, he'll not ogle Harriet any longer. I'll rescue her forever from him and his drunken cronies. She's too good for any of them except me.'

Christopher encouraged him to talk about his endless visits to the theatre and pertinent information tumbled out time and again, much of it supplementing what his listener had already heard from his brother or from Killigrew, but some of it quite original. As Hartwell burbled on, one of the names he referred to kept coming back into his host's mind.

'You mentioned Armadale,' he noted.

'That's right. Sir Godfrey Armadale.'

Christopher was puzzled. He did not recognise the name and yet it sounded vaguely familiar. He had a strong feeling that he had heard it before and that it might be important to remember where.

Moving with his usual measured tread, Jonathan Bale nevertheless went far in a relatively short time. Enquiries among court officials soon gave him the address he needed. He presented himself at the building in Threadneedle Street and asked to speak to Obadiah Shann. Jonathan was allowed through into the lawyer's office. Niceties were brief. Shann barely looked up from the document he was perusing.

'What can I do for you, Constable Bale?'

'I wanted some advice about a client of yours,' said Jonathan.

'Then you seek it in vain. I never release confidential information about the people I represent.'

'I merely seek an address.'

'Of whom?'

'Mr Bartholomew Gow.'

'Why?'

'It's a private matter, sir.'

'Do you *know* Mr Gow?'

'No, Mr Shann, but I'm anxious to make his acquaintance.'

'How did you find out that I was his lawyer?'

'You were seen dining with him at Locket's ordinary.'

'Ah,' said the lawyer, taking offence. 'We're being spied on, are we?'

'Not at all, sir.'

Obadiah Shann eyed him with a blend of caution and dislike. Gaunt, grey-haired and wearing a pair of spectacles, he was a tall man whose back had been arched by many years of bending over a desk. Jonathan noticed the blue veins standing out on the backs of his hands and caught the distinctive whiff of tobacco in the room.

'I'm sorry that I can't help you, Constable,' said the lawyer.

'Then you may be compelled to, sir.'

Controlled anger. 'You dare threaten me with compulsion?'

'No, Mr Shann.'

'I think it best if you leave, sir.'

'Not until I know Mr Gow's whereabouts.'

'I have a right to protect my client's interests. Tell me what this is all about and I may be able to help you. Otherwise, depart in peace and let me get on with my work.'

'I need that address,' said Jonathan doggedly.

'For what purpose?'

'A most serious one.'

'You have a warrant for his arrest?'

'No,' admitted the other.

'You're here on legal business of some kind?'

'Please tell me where he is.'

'I'm not sure that I should, Mr Bale.'

'You're withholding crucial information, Mr Shann.'

'I don't answer to a mere constable,' said the lawyer, removing his spectacles to glare at his visitor. 'Who do you think you are, coming in here like this and issuing demands? Goodbye to you, sir! It seems to me that you've overstayed your welcome.'

Jonathan moved to the door. 'I have, sir,' he conceded freely. 'I may be a mere constable but I speak for a higher authority. Far higher than even an exalted lawyer like yourself. I can see that I'll have to get a warrant to force you to help me.' He gave a warning smile. 'Don't be surprised if it bears the name of the Attorney-General.'

'One moment,' said Shann, caught between alarm and disbelief. 'We're being too hasty here. I've no wish to be obstructive, I simply reserve the right to protect a client's confidentiality. Why are you so desperate to find Bartholomew Gow that you wave the Attorney-General at me? Surely you can give me some hint of what is in the wind.'

'A matter of some gravity.'

'Involving what?'

'Murder,' said Jonathan flatly.

'Murder?' echoed the other, jaw dropping.

'Among other things.'

'But Mr Gow is the most law-abiding man you could meet.'

'Then he has nothing to fear from me, sir, does he?'

Obadiah Shann hovered between surprise and suspicion. He wondered if Jonathan really did have the power of a senior law officer behind him. His visitor tried to nudge him along.

'Does he, for instance, live in Greer Lane?' he said.

'Where?'

'Greer Lane. It runs between Tavistock Street and the Strand.'

'No, Constable. Bartholomew Gow doesn't live anywhere near there and, to my certain knowledge, he never has.'

'Then where *does* he live?'

Jonathan eschewed politeness. The lawyer was needlessly delaying him. Searching for the killer of Mary Hibbert, the constable was in no mood for the prevarications of Obadiah Shann. His eyes glinted.

'Do I have to come back with a warrant, sir?' he said.

It took Christopher an hour to calm down Jasper Hartwell and convince him that Harriet Gow was not in jeopardy, a considerable feat in view of the reality of the situation. Wanting to call on his brother again before resuming his search, Christopher accepted the necessity of soothing his visitor. Hartwell was, after all, paying him a lot of money to design the new house and that bought him the architect's indulgence as well as his artistic skills. There was another salient point. Ridiculous as Hartwell's romantic ambitions were, they were easily understood. It was at a performance of *The Maid's Tragedy* that Christopher first met him and first came under the spell of Harriet Gow himself. Though he had never succumbed to any fantasies about marrying her, he had spent more than an idle hour savouring her beauty and singing her melancholy song.

No sooner had he dispatched one unwelcome visitor than a second came banging on his door. Jacob answered the summons and a heated exchange followed. Guessing who had called, Christopher interrupted the argument and detached his servant from the doorstep but he had no intention of inviting Roland Trigg across it. The coachman touched his cap in a courteous gesture and took the aggression out of his voice.

'Is there any news of Mrs Gow, sir?' he asked eagerly.

'None to raise any optimism,' confessed the other.

'But you're still searching for her?'

'Oh, yes. In the light of recent events, with more vigour than ever.'

'Recent events?'

'They know that we are after them, Mr Trigg. So they did their best to dissuade us from continuing our work. First of all, my brother Henry was attacked by two men in Drury Lane.'

'Never!' exclaimed Trigg. 'Why pick on him?'

'Because he was helping me in my search.'

'Was he badly hurt, Mr Redmayne?'

'Very badly,' said Christopher. 'I suspect that the men who gave you a beating also administered one to my brother. I don't need to tell you how proficient they are with their cudgels.'

'No, sir,' said the coachman ruefully. A grin formed. 'But I got my revenge on one of them. I chanced upon the rogue in a tavern and gave him a taste of his own medicine. He deserved it, too,' he added, pointing to his wounds. 'He was the man who really set about me. So I showed him that I can handle a cudgel as well.'

'Where is he now?'

'Nursing his broken bones, probably.'

'You let the villain go?'

'I had to, sir.'

'Why ever didn't you capture him?' said Christopher irritably. 'If he was involved in the kidnap, he should be arrested and held for trial. More to the point, he could have been interrogated about Mrs Gow's whereabouts. It was madness to release him.'

'They gave me no choice, sir.'

'Who?'

'The sailors who came out of the tavern. Half-a-dozen of them. When they saw what I'd done, they gave me no time to explain. They came at me to tear me to pieces so I took to my heels.' Angling for praise, he gave another grin. 'I paid him back, sir. He won't be assaulting me, your brother or anyone else for a very long time. Did I do well?'

'By your own standards,' said Christopher drily, 'I suppose that you did. But I'm annoyed that you let the man slip through your fingers like that. He should have been apprehended. Why didn't you go for help?'

'There wasn't time. He was leaving the tavern.'

'Which one?'

'The Hope and Anchor, sir.'

'Is that down by the river somewhere?'

'Thames Street.'

'What took you there, Mr Trigg?'

'It was only one of a number of places I went,' explained the other. 'That's where their sort go, sir – the men who ambushed us. Hired villains with a taste for violence. I had a feeling I might just stumble on one of them in a tavern along the waterfront or, if not there, in the stews of Southwark. I was working my way through them when I came to the Hope and Anchor and had some luck at last.' A growl of a laugh. 'My good luck was his misfortune.'

'Thank you for coming to tell me this, Mr Trigg,' said Christopher, keen to move him on his way. 'I'm relieved to hear that there is one less villain on the loose, though I would have preferred to see him behind bars where we could get some facts out of him. I hope that my own hunt is as successful as yours. When I've been to see my brother, I'll get back to it.'

'Let me come with you,' urged the other.

'I work more effectively on my own, Mr Trigg.'

'But you need protection, sir. Look what happened to me and to your brother. These men will stop short of nothing.'

'Not even murder.'

'What do you mean?'

'There's something I haven't told you,' said Christopher sadly, 'because we need to keep the details secret for the time being. But, given your position in Mrs Gow's household, I think that you have a right to know. Mary Hibbert has been killed.'

'Mary!' His face turned purple with rage. 'They killed that young girl? I can't believe it.'

'It's true, I'm afraid. I've seen the body myself.'

'How did they do it?'

'That's immaterial.'

'Not to me, Mr Redmayne, I want to know. I liked Mary Hibbert. She was always kind to me. *How*, sir? Was she stabbed, strangled or poisoned? Did they put a bullet in her head?'

'The girl was beaten to death.'

Trigg almost foamed at the mouth. 'I should've finished him off when I had the chance,' he said vehemently. 'I should've done for him.'

'That would only have led to your own arrest for murder.'

'Justified revenge. An eye for an eye.'

'I take a different reading from the Bible. "Thou shalt not kill".'

While the coachman struggled to master his anger, Christopher was left to question his wisdom in releasing the news about Mary Hibbert. He was glad when the man's fury seemed to abate. Roland Trigg held out his hands to plead.

'I beg you, Mr Redmayne. Take me with you.'

'That won't be possible.'

'But you can't do it all on your own, sir.'

'I have Constable Bale to help me.'

'It's not enough. You need a bodyguard. I'm your man.'

Trigg straightened his shoulders and thrust out his chest. His strength could not be doubted. The coachman had been assaulted by the same men who had put Henry Redmayne into his bed for a week, yet he had already recovered enough to mete out his own crude form of justice. Roland Trigg was resilient and, by his own boast, seasoned in violence. Christopher could see his value as a bodyguard to Harriet Gow but it was her predecessor who popped into his mind. He suddenly recalled where he had heard a certain name before.

'You served Sir Godfrey Armadale, didn't you?' he said.

'Yes, sir.'

'How long were you with him?'

'Some years, Mr Redmayne.'

'Sir Godfrey is something of a rake, I believe.'

'He enjoyed life,' conceded the other, 'but he was a good master. He gave me no cause for complaint. On the other hand, I was glad to be taken on by Mrs Gow – until the ambush, that is. In one way, it was just as well.'

'Why?'

'Because I like to be in London, sir. My roots are here, and all my friends. I couldn't take to anywhere else so I'd have had to leave Sir Godfrey Armadale in any case.'

'I don't follow.'

'He's moved away, Mr Redmayne.'

'Oh?'

'Quite recently, they tell me.'

'Where has he gone?'

'Back to where he was born, in the West Country. That's where Sir Godfrey hails from – down in Devon.' He swept the subject of his former master aside to make a final offer. 'I could warn you, Mr Redmayne. I know what those rogues look like. They're bound to try to strike again.'

'Then I'll be ready for them.'

Christopher did not have to waste any more time trying to get rid of his second visitor because Trigg was immediately supplanted by a third. A coach drew up outside the house and a stately figure in clerical garb alighted. Christopher's stomach lurched. Jasper Hartwell and Roland Trigg were unwanted callers, but each had nevertheless been able to impart useful information to him. The newcomer would not. In fact, his presence threatened to hamper the search altogether.

Christopher forced a smile and put false joy into his voice.

'Father!' he said, spreading his arms. 'How wonderful to see you!'

Clerkenwell's reputation had slowly changed over the years. Notorious for its brothels during the reign of Queen Elizabeth, it had been improved and developed by her successors, containing, for example, London's first piped water supply and attracting several aristocrats to build fine houses there. As the Court moved westwards under Charles II, many of the grand residences were abandoned to prosperous merchants or to skilled craftsmen who turned the area into a thriving centre for certain specialised trades. When he reached Clerkenwell after his long walk, Jonathan Bale was struck by the clear evidence of wealth. There were still abundant houses of resort in some of the darker corners, but the district was no longer as blatantly dedicated to sinfulness as in former times.

He eventually found the address with which Obadiah Shann had been reluctantly forced to part. It was a modest dwelling, smaller and far less impressive than the one in Greer Lane where, he had been led to believe, Bartholomew Gow actually lived. The place was neglected. As Jonathan looked at the perished brickwork and the cracks in the tiles, he understood why the man might arrange any assignations elsewhere. The grubby little house in the more insalubrious part of Clerkenwell was not a love-nest to tempt a discerning lady. A coach would be incongruous in the mean and filthy street.

Knocking on the door, he did not have long to wait for a reply. The servant who appeared before him was virtually a homunculus, a tiny man of uncertain years with a harassed look about him. The sight of the constable made him shrink back defensively.

'Yes, sir?' he whispered.

'My name is Jonathan Bale,' introduced the other, 'and I've come in search of a Mr Bartholomew Gow.'

'What makes you think that he lives here, sir?'

'I was given this address by Mr Shann.'

'The lawyer?'

'Yes. I've come straight from his office in Threadneedle Street.'

The diminutive figure retreated another step as he tried to weigh up his visitor. His scrutiny was intense, even slightly eerie, but Jonathan tolerated it with patience. The man eventually regained his voice.

'Wait here a moment, please,' he said.

'Is Mr Gow in the house?'

'I'll have to see, sir.'

Shutting the door gently in his face, the servant vanished from sight. Jonathan waited for several minutes. Tiring of the delay, he reached out to bang on the door with more authority but it swung obligingly open. Bartholomew Gow regarded him warily. He was a tallish man in his early thirties with apparel that was starting to fade and hair that was beginning to recede. Jonathan wondered why the innkeeper at the Red Lion had described as handsome a face that would have been pleasant at best even without the scowl on it.

Unhappy at being found in circumstances that caused him obvious embarrassment, Gow could rise to nothing more than brisk courtesy.

'Good day to you, Constable Bale. You wanted me?'

'Are you Mr Gow, sir?'

'At your service.'

'I hope that may be the case. May I suggest that we step inside, please?' said the visitor. 'I've come on business that should not be discussed in the street.'

Bartholomew Gow was unhappy to invite him in, mumbling an apology as he did so and ushering him into a small, low room with only a few pieces of furniture to hide its bare boards. Anxious not to detain Jonathan any longer than he had to, he did not offer him a seat.

'Well, Mr Bale?' he said with bruised dignity. 'What do you want?'

'I've come about your wife, sir.'

'Did Harriet send you?'

'Not exactly, Mr Gow. When did you last see her?'

'Some time ago. Why?'

'So you haven't been in touch recently?'

'No,' said the other. 'If you've spoken to my lawyer, you'll know that my wife and I live apart and have done so for a little while. That situation is unlikely to alter. I've no cause to seek her out and my wife certainly has no desire to get in touch with me.'

'I'm sorry to hear that, Mr Gow.'

'Are you?'

'I have a great respect for the institution of marriage.'

'Then your experience of it must have differed from mine.' He became almost testy. 'You've no business to come here to discuss my personal affairs. What's going on?'

'I wondered if you might tell me that, sir.'

'Me?'

'You're not easy to track down.' He glanced around the room. 'I hadn't realised that you lived in Clerkenwell.'

'This is only a temporary address until I can find something better.'

'Of course, sir,' said Jonathan, sensing the hurt pride that lay behind the lie. 'I was looking for you in Greer Lane.'

'Where?' Gow seemed baffled. 'Greer Lane?'

'It's just off the Strand.'

'Then it's well beyond the reach of my purse.'

'I was told that you lodged there, sir, but my guess is that you only use the premises on an occasional basis. A couple of days ago,' said Jonathan, deciding to confront him with the truth in order to gauge his reaction, 'an ambush took place in Greer Lane. Mrs Gow was abducted.'

'Harriet?' said her husband, mouth agape. 'Abducted?'

'I'm afraid so, sir. My job is to help in the search for her.'

'But who kidnapped her, man? And *why*?'

'I can only answer the second question, Mr Gow. Your wife is being held for ransom. To be honest, I was hoping that you might be able to throw more light on the circumstances of the abduction.'

'How can I?'

'It took place outside the house you visit in Greer Lane.'

'But I've never been near the place.'

'That's not what the landlady says,' argued Jonathan. 'Nor the innkeeper at the Red Lion. Do you deny you patronised the tavern?'

'In the strongest possible terms!' retorted Gow, going on the attack. 'Do you have the gall to tell me that you thought *I* was responsible for the kidnap? On what evidence? My wife and I may be estranged, Mr Bale, but I'd never wish her any harm.'

'Did you and she ever meet in Greer Lane?'

'No! How could we? I don't even know where it is.'

Jonathan felt suddenly ill at ease. Thinking that he would unravel the mystery when he cornered Bartholomew Gow, he realised that it had instead become more complex. The ousted husband was plainly telling the truth. He had nothing whatso-ever to do with the crime.

The dream made Henry Redmayne squirm and groan in his bed. He was sitting alone in a pew in Gloucester Cathedral, shorn of his finery and wearing sackcloth and ashes in its stead. Occupying the pulpit and gazing down at his elder son like a disgruntled prophet, was his father, the venerable Dean, pointing a finger of doom at him and accusing him of sinful behaviour and moral turpitude. What made Henry break out in a guilty sweat was the fact that his father was listing his peccadilloes with terrifying accuracy. It was as if every act of indiscretion, every visit to a gaming house, every night of inebriation and every lustful hour in the arms of a whore had been watched from a few feet away by the pious author of his being. It was mortifying. Henry came out of his nightmare with a cry of pain only to find that he had not escaped at all.

The Dean of Gloucester glared down from a bedside pulpit.

'What is the matter, Henry?' he asked solicitously.

'Is that you, Father?'

'Yes, my son. And it seems I came at just the right time to offer you solace. I was shocked when I saw you. Christopher and I have been praying beside your bed for almost half an hour.'

'That was very kind of you,' said Henry, closing his eyes in the hope of bringing the nightmare to an abrupt end before opening them again to find the Reverend Algernon Redmayne still bending over him. 'I know the value of prayer.'

'It has brought you back to us.'

Algernon Redmayne was a dignified man in his sixties with white hair curling to his shoulders and a large, curved, glistening forehead. Accounted a handsome man in his youth, he had features that were more akin to those of his younger son but their pleasing aspect had been subdued beneath years of sustained religiosity. Anything that was even marginally inappropriate in a devout churchman had been ruthlessly suppressed. The Dean of Gloucester was so completely defined by his rank and ministry that it was difficult to imagine his ever having been anything else. It was certainly impossible to believe that this tall, pale, solemn pillar of holy marble had actually fathered two children, thereby indulging in an act of procreation that indicated – against all the visible evidence – that he had, on two separate occasions at least, been a prey to fleshly desires that had no place in the cathedral precincts.

'How are you, Father?' asked Henry weakly.

'How are *you*, dear boy?' returned the other anxiously.

'I'm rallying, I think.'

'Brave man!'

'Have you come from Gloucester?'

'Yes, the Bishop and I have business here in London.'

'How is Bishop Nicholson?'

Henry did not have the slightest interest in the man but he wanted to keep his father talking while he assembled his own thoughts. The old man unnerved him at the best of times. Lying in pain in his bed, he felt as if he were locked in the pillory, utterly at his father's mercy. The Dean chose the moment to deliver a sonorous sermon.

'Bishop Nicholson is very much perplexed at the many impudent coventicles that have grown up in every part of our county. Not only do these Dissenters openly appear at their places of worship, they justify their meetings unashamedly to the Bishop's face. It is disgraceful,' said the Dean, letting his voice swell for effect. 'We have made complaints to the Justices in the Peace but they are dilatory in enforcing the law. When we have proceeded against the malefactors in the church courts, we have met with the most disrespectful behaviour.'

'I'm sorry to hear that, Father.'

'We are to take the matter up with Archbishop Sheldon. It is one of the reasons we are here.' He clasped his hands together. 'Let us put that aside for a moment, Henry.

Your condition disturbs me. Tell me, my son. What exactly happened to you?'

Entreating rescue, Henry looked across at his brother.

'I've told Father very little,' said Christopher, spelling out the potential for deception. 'Nobody has any idea how you came by your injuries because you've been unconscious until today. I daresay that you're still dazed by the experience,' he prompted. 'Aren't you, Henry?'

'Yes,' said his brother. 'I can only remember bits of it.'

'Tell us what they are,' encouraged the Dean.

'It was the last place I would have expected an attack, Father.'

'What was?'

'The church.'

Astonishment registered. 'You were in a *church*?'

'I visit it every day.'

'Which one?'

'That's the strange thing,' said Henry, manufacturing his story as he went along. 'I don't know. All that I can recall is that I was kneeling in prayer when I felt a tap on my shoulder. I thought it was probably the churchwarden, wanting a quiet word with me, so I followed him down the nave. Suddenly, I felt something strike me across the back of the head and I pitched forward. The blows came thick and fast after that.' There was a shrug in his voice. 'My purse was taken and so were my rings. That's what the villains were after. But to have it happen on consecrated ground!' he concluded, with a passable stab at indignation. 'It was sacrilege!'

The Dean of Gloucester's face was impassive. When he leaned in close to his elder son, however, his eyes gleamed knowingly.

'The injuries have patently affected your memory,' he said quietly. 'Wherever else you received them, it was not in a church. I have had time to look around your house and note the inordinate amount of wine and brandy in your cellars. I also took the liberty of inspecting your wardrobe. Nothing I saw even hinted at a man of religious conviction. Indeed, if you dared to wear any of that garish apparel in Gloucester Cathedral, Bishop Nicholson would call the verger and have you ejected for mockery.'

'Henry looks tired, Father,' interrupted Christopher, coming to his brother's aid. 'Perhaps we should leave him to rest.'

'Of course,' agreed the other. 'Let me just say one last thing to him. Listen very carefully, Henry.'

'I will, Father,' croaked the patient.

'Make use of this dreadful experience. Reflect on your life and wonder whether these injuries were not inflicted on you by way of just deserts. I am deeply sympathetic,' he emphasised. 'As your father, I am also upset to see you in such a condition. But your ordeal may yet have a curative effect. When you have recovered your strength and regained your memory, you may be ready to own that your tale about the church was a pretty fable devised to invite my approval. Next time I ask you what really happened,' he said firmly, 'I would like the truth.'

Henry Redmayne quivered and took refuge once more in sleep.

Chapter Twelve

As he made his way home on foot from Clerkenwell, Jonathan Bale reflected on the caprices of Fate. Bartholomew Gow had been a man of comfortable means, living in a fine house with a beautiful young wife and looking towards a future of uninterrupted happiness. Everything had changed dramatically. He was now embittered, short of money, living in a dingy abode with nothing more than a freakish servant for company and facing a bleak and lonely future. Jonathan could still not understand exactly how it had happened, but he did feel sorry for the man. The story had come out in fits and starts and it was only now that the constable was able to piece it together properly.

In his own estimation, Gow was a casualty of his wife's ruthless ambition. Since so much of it was activated by self-pity, Jonathan did not believe all that he had heard from the man. What interested him was Bartholomew Gow's ambivalent attitude towards his wife. Angry at her for the way she had treated him, he was genuinely concerned at the news of her abduction and fearful that she might be hurt in some way. Yet that concern was itself tempered by the feeling that justice may somehow have been done, that Harriet Gow was getting no more than she deserved for the way she had behaved. At one point, an almost complacent smile had touched Gow's lips.

Jonathan was baffled. His insight into a turbulent marriage upset him. He could not comprehend how two people who came together out of love and who took sacred vows at the altar could part with such enmity. Harriet Gow should certainly not take all of the blame herself. As he listened to the husband's meandering account of events, Jonathan saw the man's defects revealing themselves. Gow was spiteful, envious of his wife's talents, boastful about himself, mean-spirited, capable of bursts of temper and quite unable to accept that he had in any way been in the wrong. Though his visitor came to see how an outwardly personable man like Gow could have attracted an inexperienced girl to marry him, he also noted some of the shortcomings in the husband that must in time have irritated his spouse beyond measure.

When he turned into Addle Hill, he felt a surge of love for his own wife, a deep gratitude that he and Sarah had not bickered and battled with each other in the way that Bartholomew Gow and his wife clearly had. Jonathan and Sarah Bale had a different kind of partnership. It might lack the luxuries and the excitements that the other marriage had enjoyed at the start but it had endured. It was the core of Jonathan's life, the immoveable base from which he set out each day and to which he could return with the confident expectation of a warm smile and a loving welcome. A long conversation in Clerkenwell made him count his own blessings. He was not given to impulsive gestures as a rule, but when he let himself into the house and found Sarah in the kitchen, he wrapped her in his arms and gave her a resounding kiss.

'What have I done to deserve that?' she said, laughing.

'You're *here*, Sarah.'

'Well, of course I'm here. I've sheets to wash and clothes to mend and a dozen other chores to get through. I can't stir from the house until all that's done.'

'That wasn't what I meant, my love.'

'Then what did you mean?'

'Nothing,' he said.

The second kiss was brief but tender. Sarah busied herself with getting a meal for him. Eating times were irregular in the Bale household because she never knew when his duties would allow him to slip back to the house. She never carped about the fact. Though she might tease him at times, she rarely chided him about anything. What she had married was a good, honest, loving man who worked as a shipwright in their early years together. Her commitment was total. Sarah did not question his decision to become a constable even though it meant that less money would come into the house and that he would be exposing himself to constant physical danger. She was content to support him in whatever he chose to do.

'I hoped you might be back earlier,' she said, putting the food on the table. 'Where have you been?'

'Far afield.'

'Oh?'

'What about you, my love?'

'I've been far afield myself,' she joked. 'I went into the parlour, back into the kitchen, upstairs to clean the rooms, down again to start the washing in here then out to the garden to peg it on the line. You're not the only person who's travelled today, Jonathan Bale.'

He munched his slice of ham and smiled. She knew instinctively that he was engaged in a serious investigation but she did not press for details. Sarah would be told what was going on when her husband was ready to confide in her and not before. As she babbled on about the customers who had called at the house that morning, Jonathan felt sorry that he had to keep her in ignorance, but the case required absolute secrecy and there were some elements in it that he could never divulge. From the speed with which he gobbled his meal, Sarah could see how anxious he was to get back to his work. Collecting a kiss of thanks, she saw him to the door.

'When will you be back?' she asked.

'I've no idea, my love.'

'In time to read to the children?'

'I hope so.'

'They like to hear their father read,' she said. 'Though they did enjoy listening to Mr Redmayne, too. Oliver loved that story about Samson. Do tell that to Mr Redmayne, if you chance to see him again.'

'We may have other things to discuss,' Jonathan murmured.

He walked up Addle Hill towards Carter Lane, intending to

resume his task by following up some of the lines of enquiry suggested to him by Bartholomew Gow. Since the husband could now be excluded from the list of suspects, attention had to centre on someone else. Jonathan did not get far before he realised that he was being followed. The man must have been lurking not far from his home, waiting for the constable to emerge before trailing him. Jonathan did not look round for fear of frightening the stalker away. If someone had a reason to dog his steps, he wanted to know what it was, regardless of the hazards that might be involved.

The pursuit was relentless. Though he led the man on a twisting route, he could not shake him off. Jonathan eventually walked into Ave Maria Lane, part of the area around St Paul's Cathedral that had been stricken by the Great Fire and rebuilt in accordance with the new specifications. The lane had been widened to eighteen feet and some of its character had been lost in the process but the change had been necessary. Having helped to fight the fire himself in the previous year, Jonathan recalled how destructive and undiscriminating it had been. Not even the towering magnificence of St Paul's had been spared. He had taken a close interest in the reconstruction and had an intimate knowledge of every inch of the district. That knowledge was now put to practical use.

Swinging right into Paternoster Row, he headed for a narrow passage that led off to a tavern. It would be an ideal place for an attack. If his shadow were waiting for his opportunity, this is where he would take it. Jonathan was ready for him. Ambling along with apparent unconcern, he turned calmly into the passage then flattened himself immediately into the first doorway. Footsteps quickened and a stocky man came running around the corner with a cudgel in his hand, ready to strike. With no quarry in sight, he came to a halt and gazed around in astonishment, unaware that the constable was directly behind him. Relaxing his grip on the weapon, he let it dangle by his side.

Jonathan was on him at once. Leaping out of his hiding place, he threw one arm around the man's neck and used the other hand to grab the wrist that held the cudgel. The man struggled fiercely and it was all that Jonathan could do to hold him. He managed to twist the cudgel from the man's grasp and it fell to the ground but his adversary was wily as well as strong. Unable to dislodge the constable, he gave a sudden heave backwards and slammed him against the wall of a house. The impact made Jonathan release his grip and the man wrenched himself free. He retrieved his cudgel and raised it to hit out but Jonathan parried the blow before it gained any real force.

They grappled, punched and lurched violently to and fro. Jonathan had to take a couple more painful blows from the cudgel but he was not deterred. The man in his arms was most probably one of the assailants who had beaten a coachman, assaulted Henry Redmayne and, worst of all, helped to murder a defenceless girl. The thought of Mary Hibbert lying on a slab put extra strength and urgency into the constable. Bringing a knee up sharply into the man's groin, he made him double up with agony. Jonathan seized him by the neck and swung him headfirst against the nearest wall, splitting open his skull and depriving him of all interest in continuing the brawl.

It was Jonathan's turn to hold the cudgel now. He hauled the man upright, pinned him roughly against the wall and held the weapon at both ends so that he could press it against his adversary's throat. Dazed and bleeding, the man spluttered helplessly. His eyes began to bulge. Jonathan applied more pressure on his windpipe.

'Who sent you?' he demanded.

The arrival of his father clouded his mind and robbed him of valuable time. Christopher Redmayne had distractions enough without having to cope with the Dean of Gloucester. Much as he loved his father, he could not imagine a more untimely moment for the old man to descend on him. Paradoxically, the unexpected appearance of Algernon Redmayne might work to the advantage of his elder son. Swathed in

205

linen and covered with bruises, Henry was able to draw heavily on his father's compassion. Had the visitor caught him in his more usual guise as a sybarite, the wounded man would have attracted abuse rather than sympathy.

Christopher rode towards Shoreditch at a steady canter. Henry's condition had been a help to his brother as well. Anxious about the state of his elder son, the Dean had sent for the physician and insisted on remaining at the bedside until he came. Christopher was released to continue with work which, his father assumed, would take him to the site in the parish of St Martin's-in-the-Fields. Instead, the architect was heading in the opposite direction.

Jonathan Bale's advice was sound. It did not take Christopher long to find one of the local constables. Jeremy Vye was as unlike Jonathan as it was possible to be. A short, stumpy, jovial man in his forties with a red nose and bloodshot eyes, he was drinking ale in a tavern when the visitor tracked him down. Vye was keen to help.

'So, then,' he said cheerily, 'Jonathan Bale sent you?'

'Yes, Mr Vye.'

'Give him my compliments.'

'He sends his to you,' said Christopher. 'He also assured me that you would know almost everyone who lived in Old Street.'

'Know them and love them, Mr Redmayne. I was born and brought up in Shoreditch. Never been more than a few miles away from the place. Old Street? I can tell you the names of every man, woman and child,' he bragged. 'I can even tell you what they call their cats and dogs.'

'I'm not after a pet, Mr Vye.'

'Then who are you after?'

'Mr Martin Eldridge.'

The constable blinked. 'Eldridge? That name *is* new to me.'

'This man is an actor.'

'We have a few of them in Shoreditch, sir. Out of work, mostly.' He rubbed his nose thoughtfully. 'But this Mr Eldridge of yours must be a stranger to the area or I'd have met him.

My guess is that he lodges at the far end of the street, sir. Mrs Lingard took in a lodger recently – her dog is called Blackie, by the way – and there's a gentleman who's just taken a room with Mrs Passmore. Oldish fellow with a squint.'

'Then he's not the man I want. Martin Eldridge is still relatively young and handsome. He'd bear himself well.'

'Then he has to be Mrs Lingard's lodger. Be careful of that dog of hers when you call there, sir. Blackie can give you a nasty bite.'

He led Christopher out of the tavern and gave him directions. After riding to the address he had been given, Christopher dismounted and knocked on the door of a neat house of medium size, owned by someone who evidently took a pride in it. When he knocked, he heard a dog bark. The landlady soon answered the summons. Mrs Lingard was a pleasant woman of middle years and ample girth. Keeping her dog under control with an affectionate kick, she listened to her visitor's request before inviting him in.

'Mr Eldridge has a lot of visitors,' she explained, leading the way up the stairs. 'I can see why. He's a most charming gentleman.' She tapped lightly on a door and called, 'There's someone to see you, Mr Eldridge. A Mr Redmayne.'

After a short delay, the door opened and Martin Eldridge came into view. Christopher recognised him at once as the actor who had played Lysippus, brother to the King in *The Maid's Tragedy*, a comparatively small yet telling role and one which allowed him the final cautionary lines. Mrs Lingard was hovering. Eldridge dismissed her with a smile.

'Thank you, Mrs Lingard.' He stood back from the door. 'You'd better come in, Mr Redmayne.'

Christopher went into a room that was large and well appointed. The actor was a man who liked his comforts. Bottles of wine stood on a table beside the script of a play. Eldridge was excessively courteous. He motioned his visitor to a chair then spoke in a rich, cultured voice.

'You don't look like a man of the theatre,' he observed.

'Nor am I, Mr Eldridge.'

'I won't pretend that I'm not disappointed. You see before
you a man who is, I regret to say, temporarily separated from
his art. I await the call, Mr Redmayne. I hoped that you might
have brought it.'

'No, sir,' said Christopher. 'As it happens, it was Mr
Killigrew who drew my attention to you, but not because he
wished to engage you again.'

'Killigrew is a money-grubbing old lecher!'

'Yet not without a perceptive eye for talent. In a performance of *The Maid's Tragedy*, I saw an actor give a most
excellent account of the role of Lysippus. My congratulations,
sir.'

'Why, thank you,' said the other, warming to him. 'I flatter
myself that I acted to the limit of my ability in that play. Not
that anyone would have noticed with Harriet Gow alongside
me. She dwarfed us all.'

His tone was affectionate and quite free of envy. Given his
cue, Christopher took it at once. He sat forward earnestly in
his chair.

'It is about Mrs Gow that I've come,' he said.

'Why?'

'I was wondering if you knew where I could find her.'

'At her home, I daresay.'

'She does not seem to be there, Mr Eldridge.'

'Then you'd better ask Tom Killigrew where she is.'

'Mr Killigrew is as puzzled as I am, sir. The lady has
disappeared.'

'Harriet would never do that,' argued the other. 'Not
without due warning, in any case. She's wedded to her art. It's
always come first with her. If you've seen her act and heard
her sing, you'll know how gloriously she blossoms on a stage.'

'Oh, yes,' agreed Christopher. 'She was captivating.'

'Yet you say she's disappeared?'

'I'm afraid so.'

'Since when?'

Christopher gave him a shortened version of events, leaving
out any mention of the King, the ransom note and the murder

of Mary Hibbert. The more he heard, the more alarmed Martin Eldridge grew. Christopher watched him carefully to see if the alarm was sincere and not simply called up by the skill of a trained actor. There was something about Eldridge that was faintly troubling. The man was too plausible, too ready with his responses, too expressive with his emotions. Christopher had the strong feeling that he was hiding something from him.

'When did you last see Mrs Gow?' he asked.

'Not for some time, Mr Redmayne. As Tom Killigrew must have told you, I'm no longer a member of the company. He dismissed me.'

'Mr Killigrew said that you were a good friend of Mrs Gow's.'

'I was and still am,' replied Eldridge with feeling. 'When she first joined the company, she turned to me for advice and I was able to help her a little. At that time, of course, she was still married to Bartholomew.'

'Did you ever meet her husband?'

'Regularly. He came to the theatre to collect her.'

'How did you get on with him, Mr Eldridge?'

'Tolerably well,' said the other. 'We all did at first. Then things began to turn sour between them and we saw the results. Bartholomew was spiky and resentful. He came to the theatre less and less.'

'Was he a vengeful man?'

'I think that he could be.'

'On what evidence?'

'I can't rightly say, Mr Redmayne. But any man who lost a wife like Harriet Gow would be entitled to feel vengeful. Bartholomew always claimed that she slowly emptied his purse then cast him aside because he could no longer afford to keep her in such style.'

'Have you seen the house where she lives?'

'Once or twice.'

'I take it that Mrs Gow neither owns nor rents it.'

'No,' said the other smoothly, 'and it's none of my business who does. Acting is a precarious profession, Mr Redmayne.

We all of us have to make concessions or reach compromises to stay afloat. Harriet Gow has earned everything she has, believe me. I admire her for it.'

'Some of her colleagues at the theatre do not.'

'Mindless envy.'

'Would you describe Abigail Saunders as envious?'

'I'm a gentleman, Mr Redmayne,' said the other pointedly, 'which means that I lack a vocabulary coarse enough to describe Abigail to you. We first acted together at The Duke's Playhouse and I took her to be my friend then. I gave her a lot of support but she chose to forget that in time. The kindest thing I can say about Abigail Saunders is that she is a pretty little bloodsucker.'

'Would she be capable of sucking Mrs Gow's blood?'

'To the last drop!'

'You have a low opinion of the lady.'

'The woman,' corrected the other. 'Harriet Gow is a lady; Abigail is the inferior version that we call a woman. But why sit here talking to me when you should be out trying to find Harriet?' he said with sudden desperation. 'What have you learned? Who have you talked to? Do you have no clues at all, Mr Redmayne?'

'Several, sir.'

'Then act on them. Harriet must be found!'

'I appreciate your anxiety, Mr Eldridge, but I have the feeling that you may be able to help me rather more than you've so far been willing to do.' Christopher fixed him with a stare. 'I suspect that you and Mrs Gow were *extremely* close friends. She confided in you: that means you know things that are germane to this investigation, facts that might help to guide our footsteps.'

'What more can I tell you?'

'To begin with, you can be more precise about the date when you last saw Mrs Gow. A man as fond of a lady as you patently are would not be parted from her for too long. I think you know the day and the hour when the two of you last met.' An inquisitive smile. 'Don't you?'

Martin Eldridge seemed relaxed to the point of nonchalance but his mind was working busily. He appraised Christopher for some time, noting his visitor's strong build and air of determination. He also eyed the sword and dagger that Christopher wore. The architect would not easily be sent on his way. Other measures needed to be adopted.

'You're right, Mr Redmayne,' he admitted sadly. 'There are things that I've held back. From the best of motives, as you will see. Let me show you a letter from Harriet. It may explain a lot.' He moved to the door. 'Wait here a moment while I fetch it.'

'Very well.'

Eldridge went out of the room and left his guest to examine it with more care. It told him much about the character and habits of the actor. When he crossed to the table to pick up the printed text, he saw that the play was Shakespeare's *Othello*. Was Martin Eldridge planning a return to The Duke's Men? Only the company run by Sir William D'Avenant had the right to stage revivals of Shakespeare's plays. The sound of the front door opening alerted Christopher. Setting the play aside, he went swiftly over to the window and was just in time to see Martin Eldridge darting up Old Street before vanishing around a corner. Instead of going to fetch a letter, the actor had bolted.

Christopher was furious with himself for being so easily duped. He hurried to the door, flung it open and descended the stairs at speed but he was not permitted to leave Mrs Lingard's house. Blocking his way and barking fiercely at him was a large, black, angry dog with its eyes ablaze and its fangs bared.

'He doesn't like strangers,' explained the landlady helpfully.

The physician completed his examination and stood up from the bed.

'His condition is stable,' he announced.

'Can you not be more specific, sir?' asked Algernon Redmayne.

'Your son is neither better nor worse than when I was here

211

earlier. Rest is the only true physician. He took a fearful beating and has several cracked ribs. They will take time to heal. As for the bruises,' said the old man, 'they will vanish more quickly. Give him a week and you may recognise your son once again.'

'Unhappily, I'm not able to remain at his bedside for a week,' said the Dean of Gloucester, 'though I would willingly do so if it would be of any practical help to him. I'm just grateful that his dear mother never lived to see him in such dire straits. It would have broken her heart.' He addressed the physician with lofty condescension. 'When will Henry's mind clear enough for him to tell me the full details of the assault?'

'Your guess is as good as mine, sir.'

'A day? Two?'

'I've known cases where memory has been affected much longer,' explained the physician. 'We are not talking about a happy experience here but one that brought untold pain. The mind is a strange organ. It sometimes blocks out unpleasant recollections in order to spare a victim having to relive the agony. Be patient with him.'

'I *am* patient, man! I'm his father.'

'Don't expect too much too soon.'

'What are you telling me?' asked the other sharply.

'Mr Redmayne must not be harried. It will only add to his distress and may even delay recovery. The simple truth is,' he concluded, 'that your son may never fully regain his memories of the assault.'

Pretending to be asleep, Henry Redmayne heard every word and he could not stop himself responding to the physician's welcome words. His eyes remained firmly shut but his face gave him away. The Dean of Gloucester stared down at it with mild exasperation.

'Good heavens!' he declared. 'He's *grinning* at us!'

Smeek was sullen and uncooperative. Taken before a magistrate by Jonathan Bale, he was charged with felonious assault on a constable and held in custody, pending further charges that might well include kidnap and murder. Jonathan waited until they reached the gaol before he resumed his interrogation. Two hefty turnkeys went into the gloomy cell with the constable but Smeek was not intimidated. His years at sea had toughened him against all eventualities.

'Who hired you?' demanded Jonathan.

'I don't know.'

'Someone paid your wages.'

'Did they?' asked Smeek with a defiant smirk.

'What was his name?'

'I don't know.'

'Why did he set you on to me?'

'Nobody set me on to you.'

'Then why did you attack me?'

'Because I didn't like the look of you.'

The prisoner gave another smirk. Bleeding had been stemmed from the wound on his skull but his coat was still stained with blood. Smeek's temples were pounding. He vowed to be as obstructive as he could when questioned by the man who had given him the headache.

'Do you know what will happen to you?' said Jonathan.

'Who cares?'

'You should. Gaol can break most men.'

'I've never found one that broke me,' boasted the other.

'You'll only be held here until the trial. Kidnap is a more serious offence than assault. Doesn't that worry you?'

'No.'

'It should.'

'Nothing worries me, Mr Bale.'

'Not even the thought that you'll be tried for murder?'

'Murder?' There was a first note of alarm in his voice.

'A girl called Mary Hibbert was beaten to death,' said Jonathan. 'I viewed the body so I know exactly the kind of monsters they were. Mary Hibbert was a friend of mine and I have a personal interest in bringing these monsters to justice. The men who killed her will hang.'

'I wasn't involved.'

'Are you sure?'

'I swear it!'

'Yes,' said the other with heavy sarcasm, 'and you'll swear that you didn't attack a man called Roland Trigg. Nor one called Henry Redmayne, to say nothing of myself. It wasn't you, was it? Your cudgel has a life of its own. It did all that damage by itself.'

'I did not kill the girl!' protested Smeek.

'We'll prove that you did.'

'No! I'll answer for what I did, but not for someone else's crime.'

'You were involved. That's enough for me.'

'Not in the murder, Mr Bale. You must believe me. I went after the girl, I admit,' he said, wiping the back of his hand across his mouth, 'but only to track her down. That was our orders: to catch Mary Hibbert and take her back to the house. But she fought agin us. That upset Ben. He tried to quieten her down.'

'I saw how she was quietened down,' said Jonathan grimly.

'Not by me!' insisted the other. 'I hardly touched her.'

'Then who did?'

Smeek clammed up. He sensed that he had already said too much.

'Who did?' repeated Jonathan, stepping right up to him. 'You called him Ben, didn't you? Ben who? Tell me the name of the man who beat Mary Hibbert to death. Ben *who*?'

The prisoner regained some of his bravado. He folded his arms and leaned his back against the wall of the cell. He taunted Jonathan.

'Don't ask me, Mr Bale,' he said innocently. 'I swear that I don't know anyone by that name. Do you, sir?'

The house was smaller than the first one in which she had been confined. Harriet Gow wondered why they had transferred her. The new prison was also situated in open countryside. When she peered through the cracks in the shutters of the bedchamber, she could see nothing but a herd of sheep grazing in the fields. Her two guards were marginally kinder to her. The man and the woman still wore masks and still refused to answer her queries but they were less brusque with her. Harriet was handled with a little more respect. It was as if they had been reprimanded and told to treat her differently. She could see that they resented the order.

Mary Hibbert's fate still dominated her mind. Fearing the worst, she found it impossible to rest, still less to sleep. She kept thinking about her maidservant, remembering how willing and dependable she was, how proud to work for a renowned actress. Those days seemed to have gone for ever. Harriet knew in her heart that Mary Hibbert would never serve her again. Guilt stirred once more. It was only because of her that the girl had been thrown into jeopardy in the first place. Had she remained in her former employment, she would be alive and well.

When the door was unlocked, the woman brought in some food on a tray. Her husband remained in the doorway to make sure that the prisoner did not make a run for the exit. Harriet crossed over to the man.

'How long will I be kept here?' she asked.

'Until the ransom is paid,' he said coldly.

'And what if it isn't?'

He waited until his wife left the room before he answered. 'Then you won't leave here alive, Mrs Gow.'

Christopher Redmayne was forced to cool his heels at the house in Addle Street before Jonathan Bale returned. The constable was pleased to see him for once and grateful that it was far too early for him to have taken over the daily reading from the Bible to the two boys. When Sarah had taken them out of the parlour, Jonathan was left alone to exchange news with his guest. The constable came as near to expressing real excitement as he could manage.

'I caught him, Mr Redmayne,' he said with pride.

'Who?'

'One of the villains who wielded a cudgel. He tried to use it on me but I got the better of him near Paternoster Row. The fellow is in custody and will not trouble us again.'

'Tell me all,' urged Christopher.

He was thrilled to hear of the arrest, though his great delight was lessened by the fact that the prisoner had failed to confess or provide them with the names of his accomplices.

'One thing I know,' boomed Jonathan, recalling his visit to Clerkenwell. 'Those accomplices did not include Bartholomew Gow.'

'You found him?'

'Eventually.'

'And?'

'It was rather a sad tale, Mr Redmayne.'

Christopher listened to the comprehensive recital of facts, admiring Jonathan's methodical approach but wishing that he could be more succinct. At length, one suspect was eliminated from their enquiries.

'How odd!' he commented. 'The landlord of that inn was so certain that Mr Gow lived in Greer Lane.'

'So was the woman at that house,' said Jonathan. 'She assured me that he'd lodged there until quite recently. I still believe that he only used her premises on occasion but the fact remains that he denied even knowing where Greer Lane was.'

'Did you believe him, Mr Bale?'

'Implicitly.'

'Then I trust your judgement.'

'Thank you, sir,' said Jonathan, settling back into his chair. 'What of your own investigations in Shoreditch? Have you made progress?'

'Unhappily, no.'

'Why not?'

'I was badly hampered,' said Christopher. 'Before I could leave my house, I was cornered by Mr Hartwell, my client, a man with a legitimate claim on my time. And as he left, Mr Trigg arrived to ask how we were getting on and to pass on some rather startling news. And then, worst of all, when I was least ready for him, my father chose that moment to arrive from Gloucester to pay a call on me.'

'You mentioned startling news.'

'Yes, from the coachman.'

'What did he say?'

'You were not the only one to meet a man with a cudgel.'

Christopher's account was swift and concise. Jonathan's eyebrows lifted with interest when he heard that the other probable killer of Mary Hibbert had been brought out into the open.

'Why didn't Mr Trigg get help to arrest the villain?'

'He was more interested in revenge.'

'The man he assaulted must have been the accomplice to the rogue who attacked me. I'll wager he answers to the name of Ben. What was the tavern where this happened?'

'The Hope and Anchor.'

'Then we may be in luck, Mr Redmayne.'

'Why?'

'I know it well from my days as a shipwright. The place is not unused to brawls but it's not often that someone is beaten senseless on its doorstep. Someone will know who the victim was. I'll ask around.'

'Let me come with you,' volunteered Christopher.

'I'd rather go alone, sir. No disrespect,' he said, looking at his visitor's smart apparel, 'but you would not exactly blend in with the patrons of the Hope and Anchor. Seafaring men can be suspicious of outsiders and that's what you are. I'll go myself tonight, though not in the office of a constable. I'll find out what I can about the beating that Mr Trigg claims that he handed out.'

'I'm sure that he wasn't lying. He was so gleeful.'

'I don't see any occasion for glee.'

'Nor do I,' admitted Christopher. 'My visit to Shoreditch was not as productive as your sojourn in Clerkenwell.'

'Did you meet Jeremy Vye?'

'Yes, and your friend was most helpful. He picked out the right house for me and even warned me about Blackie.'

'Blackie?'

'Mrs Lingard's dog.'

Christopher launched into a second attenuated account. The details of his adventures in Old Street kept his host entranced. Christopher did not spare himself from blame.

'I was a fool,' he confessed. 'Martin Eldridge tricked me. While I was waiting for him to fetch that letter, he was legging it down the street. Blackie made sure that I couldn't pursue him immediately.'

'What do you conclude, Mr Redmayne?'

'That the slippery actor is embroiled somehow in this affair.'

'But he's a close friend of Mrs Gow's. You said yourself that he spoke very warmly of her. Why should he want to harm a lady he obviously cared for, Mr Redmayne?'

'Why should he take to his heels and run?'

'That still doesn't make him party to a kidnap.'

'No,' agreed Christopher, 'but it does put him on the list of people I'd like to question. Only next time, I'll have the sense to stand between him and the door.' A self-deprecating smile. 'And to take a bone with me for Blackie.'

'It's been a day of exchanges,' mused Jonathan.

'Exchanges?'

'Yes, sir. We lost one suspect – Mr Gow – and gained another in the person of Mr Eldridge. We lost one villain – this man called Ben – and traded him for an accomplice who made the mistake of attacking me.'

'But why, Mr Bale?'

'I've been wondering about that.'

'How did they know who you were and where you lived?' said Christopher, running a hand through his hair. 'My brother Henry was more visible. He was seen making enquiries at the theatre. But you've been far more discreet. How did they know you were working with me?'

'I'll ask this fellow, Ben, when I catch up with him.'

'It's almost as if someone is *watching* us.'

'Mr Eldridge, perhaps?'

'No, someone else. It unsettles me.'

'What next, sir?'

'You pay a visit to the Hope and Anchor while I try to find a missing actor. I won't let him slip away again, I promise you.' Christopher rose to his feet then paused. 'I've just had a curious thought.'

'What is it, Mr Redmayne?'

'Why was the ransom note sent to His Majesty?'

'The King is not unknown to Mrs Gow,' said Jonathan with evident distaste. 'And who else could command that amount of money?'

'Oh, there are gentlemen in her life with wealth enough to pay such a demand. Yet they, as far as we know, were not approached. The kidnap was arranged with the express purpose of embarrassing His Majesty.'

'So?'

'Three separate intentions may lie behind the abduction.'

'What are they?'

'First and foremost, to secure the ransom money.'

'They'll obviously kill to get that,' said Jonathan ruefully. 'Five thousand pounds is a vast figure. It could set someone up for life.'

'Let's move on to the second intention,' advised Christopher as he cogitated. 'Someone wishes to strike directly at His Majesty, to hurt his feelings and to wound his pride by seizing his favourite companion from right under his nose.'

'If only it was simply the royal nose she was under!'

'Now, now, Mr Bale.'

'Truth will out, sir.'

'Ours is not to pass moral judgements.'

'Perhaps not. What is the third intention, Mr Redmayne?'

'The most intriguing in some ways.'

'Why?'

'Because it doesn't concern money at all. Perhaps not even revenge. It turns on one avowed purpose. To bring a decisive end to the friendship between His Majesty and Harriet Gow.'

'An end?'

'The lady will hardly wish to continue a relationship which has brought her such suffering. And I suspect that His Majesty will wish to disentangle himself as well. What I believe,' said Christopher, 'is that we're looking for a man with a passion for Mrs Gow that's been over-shadowed by her involvement with the King. The obvious candidate was the embittered husband.'

'Bartholomew Gow can be acquitted. I'm certain of it.'

'That leaves us with another man who's enjoyed her favours but who, since His Majesty's interest was sparked off, has been pushed completely into oblivion.'

'What's his name?'

'I've already told you,' said Christopher. 'Martin Eldridge.'

Roland Trigg was in conciliatory mood for once. Confronted by an angry visitor at the house in Rider Street, he did his best to pacify the man. They were in the stable at the rear of the property. The coachman had been grooming the horses when he was interrupted.

'Calm down, Mr Eldridge,' he soothed. 'Calm down, sir.'

'How can I be calm at a time like this?'

'I know how you feel, sir.'

'Who's behind this kidnap?' demanded Martin Eldridge, shaking with fury. 'Tell me, Mr Trigg.'

'If only I could. I'd like his name so that I can get my own back for this,' he said, pointing to his injuries. 'I managed to take some revenge, though. One of the men who attacked me was given a sound beating of his own. He'll be more careful around Roland Trigg from now on.'

'One of the kidnappers?'

'Yes, I recognised him.'

'Has he been apprehended?'

The coachman told him the story that he had already related to Christopher Redmayne and the actor's expression changed from hope to disappointment. Eldridge was no nearer finding out who the real culprit was for the abduction of Harriet Gow. He became more agitated.

'Why did you bring me that message?' he asked.

'Because I was told to, sir.'

'By Harriet herself?'

'Who else? I take orders from nobody but Mrs Gow.'

'Why should she wish to cancel the arrangement?'

'She didn't say.'

'And why not send me a letter?'

'There was no time, Mr Eldridge. It was a decision taken at the last minute. That's why I arrived in Shoreditch so early in the day. Believe me, sir,' said Trigg fervently, 'I'm as eager as you are to have this mystery explained. Not only because of the beating I took. There's the business of Mary Hibbert.'

'Mary?'

'They killed her.'

'Surely not!' exclaimed Eldridge.

'No question about it. They wanted us to know how serious they were in their threats. We're left in no doubt now.'

'Why did Mr Redmayne make no mention of this?'

'I've no idea.'

'He only told me about the abduction and the beatings.'

'Strange!'

'I'm glad I know the truth,' said Eldridge, looking around uneasily. 'It shows how precarious Harriet's position is. Tell me all you know, Mr Trigg. I've the feeling that Mr Redmayne held a number of things back.'

'I can't add anything,' said the other cautiously. 'I'm only a victim of the kidnap. Mr Redmayne is the man to speak to, sir.'

'He was asking too many uncomfortable questions.'

'Someone has to.'

'But why him? What's his interest in Harriet Gow? He's only an architect. I know that his brother was cudgelled outside the theatre but is that really enough to make him abandon his work to take up this case?' Eldridge was baffled. 'Who *is* Christopher Redmayne?'

'He could be our salvation, sir.'

'In what way?'

'Mr Redmayne is a dedicated man. Whatever his reasons for getting involved, I admire him. He's our only hope,' Trigg stressed, clenching his teeth. 'Christopher Redmayne is the one person who may get to Mrs Gow in time to save her.'

His second meeting of the day with Jonathan Bale had been productive and reassuring. One man was in custody and a second might be found by means of enquiries at the Hope and Anchor. Christopher was still smarting at the way he had let Martin Eldridge escape his clutches and he was determined to make amends for his error. Finding the fugitive actor was his main priority but he first decided to return home in case any important messages had been left for him. He rode into Fetter Lane with some trepidation, fearing that he might be caught again by an irate client, a truculent coachman or an inconvenient parent but there were no coaches outside his house. He allowed himself to relax until he noticed Jacob emerging from the front door.

'I saw you through the window,' explained the servant. 'Thank goodness you've come back!'

'Why?'

'Your visitor has been waiting the best part of an hour.'

'It's not Mr Hartwell again?'

'No, Mr Redmayne. Nor that foul-mouthed Mr Trigg.'

'My father, then?' said Christopher, bracing himself against what might turn out to be the worst of the three. 'Who is it, Jacob?'

'The gentleman wouldn't give his name.'

'Yet you let him into my house?'

'He has an air of such authority about him, sir.'

'We'll see about that,' said Christopher, dropping from the saddle and handing the reins to Jacob. 'Tether him. I'll be leaving again soon.'

He went purposefully into the house to confront his anonymous guest but stopped dead when he saw who it was.

'Mr Chiffinch!'

William Chiffinch rose from his chair and gave a faint nod.

'I'm glad you've come back at last,' he said.

'It's only a brief visit. We have picked up the scent this time.'

'Then you should have had the grace to send us a report to that effect. His Majesty is in a state of continuous anguish. Tell me something that can at least allay his anxiety.'

'I'll try, Mr Chiffinch.'

Christopher told him in outline what had transpired since their last encounter. Chiffinch showed a flicker of approval when he heard of the arrest of Jonathan Bale's attacker, but the flight of Martin Eldridge only gained a look of scorn. He seemed faintly disappointed by the vindication of Bartholomew Gow.

'So the husband may be cleared of involvement?'

'According to Mr Bale.'

'It seems that the worthy constable has been appreciably more successful than you in his work,' said Chiffinch, letting his eyebrow issue a muted reprimand. 'What do you intend to do about it, Mr Redmayne?'

'Redeem myself by finding Mrs Gow.'

'That's not an option that will remain open for long, I fear.'

'Why not?'

'I come here with grim tidings. His Majesty was most insistent that you heard the news at once. That's why I took the unusual step of arriving on your doorstep in person.'

'I guessed that your mission must be important.'

'Very important, Mr Redmayne.' Taking a letter from inside his coat, he handed it over. 'That came to the Palace this afternoon.'

'From the kidnappers?'

'Read it for yourself.'

When Christopher did, he blenched. An already fraught situation had taken on a new and more menacing turn. He held up the letter.

'They may be trying to bluff us, Mr Chiffinch.'

'Was the murder of Mary Hibbert an act of bluff? No, sir. We have to take them at their word. You have less than twenty-four hours to unmask and capture the villains. They could not have put it more bluntly,' Chiffinch said, taking the missive back. 'If the ransom is not paid by sunset tomorrow, Harriet Gow will be executed.'

Chapter Thirteen

While their visitor was in the house, Sarah Bale made no comment on the rumpled condition in which her husband returned home. As soon as Christopher Redmayne left, however, she was able to take a closer look at Jonathan. She clicked her tongue in mock disapproval.

'Look at the state of you!' she chided.

'What do you mean, Sarah?'

'Your coat's dirty, your sleeve's torn, there's a bruise on your cheek and – yes,' she said, inspecting a stain on his shoulder, 'this looks like blood to me.'

'It's not mine, I assure you.'

'Where've you been, Jonathan?'

'Making an arrest.'

'Well, that sleeve will have to be mended before I can send you out again. And I'll want to brush some of that filth off. What will the neighbours say if you're seen abroad like that?' Anxiety took over. 'Do you have any other bruises?'

'One or two on my arms, that's all.'

'Do be careful, Jonathan.'

'I always am.'

'I want my husband coming back to me in one piece.'

'The man resisted arrest: I had to subdue him. He's in a far worse condition than me, Sarah.' He took off his coat. 'But I was going to change in any case. I have to go out again.'

'So soon?'

'I'm afraid so.'

'What about the children? I'm just going to put them to bed.'

'I'll read to them before I go.'

'Good,' she said, taking his coat and bustling off.

Jonathan went upstairs to his sons' bedchamber and took

out the old clothes that he wore when he worked as a shipwright. They still fitted. He smiled as pleasant memories of his earlier life flooded back. He had loved his trade. It brought him happy times and good friends. It also gave him the muscles and the stamina which made him such a formidable opponent in a brawl. He slipped a dagger into his belt and made sure that it could not be seen. When he went into the next room, Oliver and Richard were already tucked up together in bed, delighted that their father would be reading to them. Oliver stared at his bruise.

'What've you done to your face?' he asked.

'I bumped into something, Oliver.'

'Does it hurt?' said Richard, intrigued by the injury.

'Not any more.'

'What did you bump into, Father?'

'Never you mind, Richard.' Jonathan picked up the family Bible, the one book in the house. 'Now, what shall I read this evening?'

'Could we have some more about Samson?' said Richard.

'Yes,' agreed Oliver. 'He was a big, strong man. Mr Redmayne told us about him. He said that Samson was betrayed by a woman.'

'She cut off his hair.'

'Mother would never betray you, would she?' said the older boy. 'She'd never cut off your hair or you'd look funny.'

The two boys giggled. Jonathan quietened them down then read them a passage from the Book of Judges. They listened carefully. When he had finished, he said prayers with them, gave each a kiss on the forehead then stole out of the room. Sarah was already using a needle and thread expertly on the torn sleeve of his coat. She looked at his apparel and smiled.

'Just like the old days.'

'Not quite, Sarah.'

'Will you be late back?'

'I don't know.'

'Whenever it is, I'll wait up for you.'

'Thank you, my love.'

After giving her a valedictory kiss, he left the house and trudged off in the direction of Thames Street. It was early evening and still light. He walked parallel to the river, inhaling the familiar smells that drifted up from the waterfront and listening to the familiar sounds. The street was busy and he collected a number of waves or greetings while he was still in Baynard's Castle Ward. Once he moved into Queenhithe Ward, he was outside his own territory and took on a welcome anonymity. Passers-by hardly gave him a second look.

The Hope and Anchor was at the far end of Thames Street, well beyond London Bridge. It looked smaller than he remembered it and had acquired an almost ramshackle appearance. The one thing Jonathan had prised out of his attacker had been the man's name. Smeek would be at home in the Hope and Anchor, he decided. It was his natural habitat. The man bore all the marks of a sailor. Smeek was a tough, gritty, uncouth, fearless man who could look after himself in the roughest company and that was what the tavern offered him.

It was echoing with noise and bursting with bodies when Jonathan let himself in. A group of drunken sailors was singing a coarse song at one of the tables. Others were yelling threats at each other. Prostitutes mingled with potential customers, distributing the occasional kiss by way of blandishment. There was a stink of tobacco smoke and a thick fug had settled on the room. As he looked around, Jonathan could not suppress a smile at the thought of Christopher Redmayne visiting the tavern. He would be as completely and ridiculously out of place as the constable would be in a box at The Theatre Royal.

Jonathan bought a drink, shouldered his way to a corner and bided his time. It was important to blend into his surroundings. To accost the innkeeper at once and pepper him with questions would only arouse the man's suspicion. The constable had to be more casual in his enquiries. He fell in with a couple of sailors whose ship had just arrived from Holland. They were full of boasts about their exploits among

Dutch women. Jonathan forced himself to listen. When he saw that the innkeeper was on his own, he offered to buy his companions some ale and squeezed his way to the counter.

The innkeeper was a rotund man in his fifties with an ugly face made even more unsightly by a broken nose and a half-closed eye. As the man filled three tankards for Jonathan, the latter leaned in close.

'I was hoping to see some old friends in here,' he said.

'Oh?' replied the other. 'And who might they be?'

'One's called Smeek. We sailed together years ago. He told me that they came in here sometimes. Is that true?'

'It might be.'

'He and Ben were always together. Boon companions.'

'How well do you know them?' asked the innkeeper warily.

'Haven't seen either for a long time. That's why I thought I'd drop in at the Hope and Anchor – in case they'd been around lately. It's the kind of place they'd like, especially Ben. Nice and lively.' He paid for the drinks and bought one for the innkeeper himself. 'Have you seen any sign of either of them?'

'They were in here yesterday, as it happens.'

'Oh?'

'Throwing a bit of money around.'

'That sounds like them,' said Jonathan with a chuckle.

'Smeek might come back,' explained the other, deciding to take his customer on trust, 'but you won't see Ben Froggatt in here for a while, that's for sure.'

'Why not?'

'He came off worst in a fight. Right outside my back door.'

'Ben Froggatt? He could handle himself in a brawl. I'd like to see the man who could get the better of him.' Jonathan took a sip of his ale. 'Was Ben hurt very badly?'

'He must be. I'm told he's taken to his bed.'

'Poor old Ben,' said Jonathan, expressing a sympathy that was masking a deep hatred. 'I must call on him and try to cheer him up. Do you know where he lodges?'

'No,' said the innkeeper. 'But I think that Lucy might.'

'Lucy?'

228

The man nodded in the direction of a tall, angular woman with a heavily powdered face and a loud giggle. Sharing a drink with a grey-haired man, she fondled his arm with an easy familiarity.

The innkeeper gave a lop-sided grin of appreciation.

'Ben has taste,' he grunted. 'Lucy's his favourite.'

'I haven't the slightest clue where you could find Martin Eldridge.'

'Where would he go if he wanted to lie low?' asked Christopher.

'Who cares?'

'Please, Mr Killigrew. I need your help.'

'The only person I'm interested in finding is Harriet Gow,' said the manager, banging on the table. 'Harriet is the one you should be after, not a damnable actor who's too lazy to learn his craft properly.'

'Martin Eldridge might *lead* me to Mrs Gow.'

'What gave you that idea?'

'He's involved in some way,' said Christopher firmly. 'I know it. He was so evasive when I talked to him. He was hiding something.'

'Well, it wasn't his talent because he doesn't have any.'

Hoping for good news from his visitor, Thomas Killigrew was downcast when Christopher admitted that they still had no clear idea where the missing actress could be. The enquiry about Martin Eldridge only served to enrage the irascible manager.

'You shouldn't have let him trick you like that, Mr Redmayne.'

'I know.'

'He's a cunning devil, Martin. I wouldn't trust him for a second.'

'But some people do. His landlady told me how many friends he has. They are always calling at his lodging in Shoreditch. What I want from you is the name of those friends,' explained Christopher. 'My guess is that he'll stay with one of them in order to hide from me.'

'Then you'll never find him.'

'Why not?'

'Because it would take you weeks to get round all of Martin's friends. There are scores of them. Mostly women, of course, because a man with that silvery tongue and those good looks is bound to make the best of them. Martin Eldridge could charm the clothes off a countess. Yes,' he said enviously, 'and he could probably charm some money out of her into the bargain. That would be typical of him. He gives all his best performances in the bedchamber. If only he could act that well on stage!'

'I thought he was well cast as Lysippus.'

'He did rouse himself for *The Maid's Tragedy*,' confessed Killigrew, 'but only because Harriet Gow was in the play. For her sake, Martin always made an effort. When she was not in a cast, he'd simply walk through his part. Forget him, Mr Redmayne. He's not your man.'

'Then why did he take to his heels?'

'Perhaps you said something to upset him.'

'I'm serious, Mr Killigrew.'

'And so am I, sir,' retorted the manager. 'Harriet's been gone for days now. The company is getting nervous. My patrons are starting to turn nasty. They disrupted the performance this afternoon. That lean-witted booby Jasper Hartwell even had the audacity to storm in here and threaten to sue me unless I brought her back instantly. He said he wanted to hear his nightingale sing again.'

'Mr Hartwell has an obsession, I'm afraid.'

'So do I, Mr Redmayne. And my obsession is more immediate than his. Not to put too fine a point on it, Harriet Gow is my bread and butter. She sets food on my table. Without her, my takings will plummet.'

'Then help me to find her.'

'You'll not do that by means of Martin Eldridge. He adored Harriet. She's probably the only woman he ever really cared for. What would he stand to gain by her abduction?'

'I don't know.'

'Nothing!'

'I wonder.'

'Look elsewhere, sir.'

'Such as?'

'At her husband, for a start. Bartholomew Gow.'

'He's already been cleared of involvement.'

'Then I can do the same for Martin. Painful as it is to do him a favour, I can give you my assurance that he's not the villain here.'

'I reserve my judgement on that.'

Christopher would not be deflected from his purpose. He wanted to speak to the actor again. Unable to get assistance from one theatre manager, he decided to turn to another. He bade farewell and headed for the door. Killigrew had a rush of sympathy and called out to detain him.

'How is your brother?'

'Recovering very slowly.'

'I'll try to make time to call on him.'

'Thank you, Mr Killigrew,' said Christopher, fearing an encounter between his father and the disreputable manager. 'Not for a day or two, please. Henry can receive no visitors at present. His physician has forbidden it.'

'Tell him I asked after him.'

'I will.'

'What of the men who cudgelled him?'

'There's brighter news on that front. One is already in custody and the other may soon join him. In fact,' he recalled, 'a colleague of mine is attending to that matter right now.'

Ben Froggatt was in constant pain. His broken arm was in a splint, his eyes blackened, his head covered in lumps and crisscrossed with deep gashes. His hair was matted with dried blood. Every part of his body seemed to ache. Propped up on a mattress in the dingy, airless room, he swigged from a stone bottle and vowed to get his revenge. A mouse came out of its hole and ran across to search for crumbs on the platter beside him. Froggatt spat at the creature to send it on its way. There was a tap on the door. He tensed at once. Putting the bottle aside, he used his free hand to reach for the cudgel under the sheets.

'Who is it?' he growled.

'Lucy,' she answered.

'What kept you?'

'I've brought a friend of yours, Ben.'

She opened the door to lead in Jonathan Bale. His friendly manner vanished at once. He dashed across to the wounded man, caught his wrist as the cudgel was lifted and twisted the weapon out of his hand. Froggatt howled with rage at Lucy, who backed against the wall in alarm. Jonathan showed no compassion for the man's injuries. He was standing over someone who had sent Mary Hibbert to an agonising death. When his prisoner tried to punch him, Jonathan dodged the blow and took the dagger from his belt. The point was held at Ben Froggatt's throat.

'Smeek sent me,' he said.

'He'd never do that. He's a friend.'

'Not any more. Since we locked him up in gaol, he doesn't feel quite so loyal towards you any more. Smeek says that you murdered that girl all on your own.'

'That's a lie! He was there as well.'

'But you did the damage.'

When the dagger pricked his throat, Froggatt drew back. 'Who *are* you?' he hissed.

'I'm the man who arrested Smeek,' said Jonathan. 'I think it's high time that you joined him, don't you?'

The pangs of hunger were too strong to resist. Henry Redmayne was famished. Having feigned sleep in the hope that his father would leave, he realised that he could not dislodge the Dean of Gloucester so easily. There was something intimidating about the old man's presence. It was not merely the odour of sanctity which he gave off, nor even the sort of oppressive piety with which he filled the room.

Algernon Redmayne was sitting in judgement, poised to pass sentence on his wayward son. It was unnerving. Henry had no right of appeal.

Relations with his father had always been strained. Less than dutiful, Henry was also more than disloyal at times. His epicurean life was a brash denial of all the values that his father had inculcated in him. Though he had a comfortable income from his sinecure at the Navy Office, he also enjoyed an allowance from the Dean, a man of private wealth and generous disposition. Henry had abused that generosity so many times that he was in danger of seeing it withdrawn. It was a fate too hideous to contemplate. Living beyond his income, Henry needed the money from the parental purse to fund his reckless expenditure.

The pain in his stomach gradually overcoming his fear of the bedside judge, Henry opened his eyes, blinked and pretended to be confused.

'Where am I?' he asked.

'Back with us again, my son,' said his father. 'How do you feel?'

'Hungry.'

'That can only be a good sign.'

'I haven't eaten a thing since the assault.'

'You remember the incident?'

'Vaguely.'

'Good, good. I long to hear the details.'

'They seem very hazy at present, Father.' He looked around the bedchamber. 'Where's Christopher?'

'He's returned to his work on that new house. It's comforting to know that I have one son who has gainful employment.'

'So do I, sir. I have a position at the Navy Office.'

'Your brother is forging a career, you merely occupy space. At least, that is what I suspect. Christopher caused me many anxieties, I'll admit, but he does seem finally to have found his true path in life. All the money I invested in his education is paying off.' He bent over his elder son like a swan about to

233

peck an errant cygnet. 'But what of you, Henry? Oh dear, sir. What of you?'

'I need some food, Father.'

'I'm talking about spiritual nourishment,' said the other sternly. 'This house seems singularly devoid of it. There is the unmistakable whiff of sin in the air. You have strayed, Henry.'

'Once or twice perhaps.'

'Dissipation is writ large upon this building. It is the house of a voluptuary, sir. A hedonist. An unashamed sensualist.'

'Oh, I writhe with shame, Father. I assure you.'

'This is not a suitable environment for a son of the Dean of Gloucester. Too many temptations lie at hand for an idle man. Illicit pleasures beckon. I shudder at the thought that I might actually be paying for some of them.'

'No, no, that's not true at all.'

'Then where does that allowance go?' pressed the old man. 'On gaudy clothes and expensive periwigs? On wine and brandy? On some of those irreligious paintings I see hanging on your wall?'

Algernon Redmayne hit his stride. As his father's rebuke turned into a stinging homily, Henry could do nothing but lie there defenceless. In mind as well as body, he was suffering. He resorted to the only thing left to him. Against all hope, his prayer was answered. After knocking on the door, a servant entered with a potion for him.

'The physician said that you were to take this sleeping draught, Mr Redmayne.'

'Yes, yes!' agreed Henry willingly.

'But I wish to talk to you,' said his father testily. 'I want to hear the full story of your assault.'

'The physician was most insistent,' argued the servant.

'There's no hurry for the medicine.'

'There is, Father,' said Henry, making a mental note to reward his servant for his kind intervention. 'We must obey his wishes.'

He took the tiny vessel from the man and lifted it to his

mouth. Within seconds, his eyes began to close and his body to sag. The Dean of Gloucester finally gave up. Leaving instructions with the servant, he gave his son one last look of disappointment then left the room. Henry came awake at once. Spitting out the potion into a cup beside the bed, he panted with relief then issued a command.

'Bring me food at once!' he urged. 'And some wine!'

William D'Avenant stood in the middle of the pit at The Duke's Playhouse and surveyed the stage like a triumphant general looking proudly out across conquered land. He was a striking figure in dark attire, a wrinkled wizard of the theatre, a living link between the world of Shakespeare, his godfather, if not his actual parent, and the witty, vibrant, stylish and often shocking fare of the Restoration. Seeing the manager in his natural milieu, Christopher Redmayne could not fail to be impressed. D'Avenant was less impressed with his unannounced visitor. He spun round to confront the newcomer with a frown of disapproval.

'What are *you* doing here, Mr Redmayne?' he demanded.

'I came to see you, Sir William. Since you've barred me from your home, your playhouse was the only place I could try.'

'A pointless journey. Our debate on theatre architecture is at an end. I've nothing to add on that or on any other subject.'

'I wanted to talk about a play.'

'The performance was over hours ago.'

'There's only one actor I'm interested in,' said Christopher, 'and I'm sure he's known to you. Mr Martin Eldridge.'

'Eldridge?' repeated the other, covering his surprise well. 'What dealings do you hope to have with him?'

'That's a matter between the two of us. I understand that he was once a member of your company.'

'Not any more.'

'I suspect he has ambitions of rejoining the fold.'

'Does he?'

'Yes, Sir William. When I was at his lodging earlier, I

happened to notice a copy of Shakespeare's *Othello* on his table. That's the play I'm here to talk about. Why would an actor read it unless to work up some speeches from the drama? And why do that if not to win his way back into your favour?'

'You're a perceptive man, Mr Redmayne.'

'Mr Eldridge's hopes must centre on this playhouse because you have a monopoly on the work of Shakespeare.'

'I adapt it with distinction to suit the tastes of the day.'

'Will you take on a new actor for the performance of *Othello*?'

'Possibly. Possibly not.'

'You doubt his ability?'

'No,' said D'Avenant. 'Martin is an able actor. At least, he was when I was shaping his career. Who knows what damage that blundering fool, Tom Killigrew, has done to his talent? Martin's art may be beyond repair.' He studied Christopher shrewdly for a full minute before offering an unexpected concession. 'Linger a while and you may judge for yourself.'

'Why?'

'Because, as luck will have it, he is on his way here this evening. It's the only time when the playhouse is empty enough for me to hear him, and I no longer care to turn my home into a theatre. That's why you see all these candles lit, Mr Redmayne,' he said with an expansive gesture. 'They are here to shed light on the talent of Martin Eldridge.'

'You may be disappointed, Sir William.'

'More than likely.'

'No,' explained Christopher, 'not in the quality of his performance, because you're unlikely to see it. Mr Eldridge will not even turn up.'

'We made an appointment. It must be honoured.'

'He's on the run and has most likely gone to ground.'

'On the run? From whom?'

'Me, Sir William.'

'What's his offence?'

'I'm not sure until I can question him.'

D'Avenant was peremptory. 'Well, you'll not do that until

236

I've heard him give his account of Iago,' he insisted, tossing his white hair with a flick of his head. 'Interrupt that and I'll have you thrown out.'

'There's no need. He won't even come.'

'Mr Redmayne, let me tell you about actors. When there is the faintest chance of employment, they'll take it. Be they on the run from you, from the law, from their wives, their families or creditors, they will attend their auditions.' He turned back to the stage. 'He'll be here.'

Christopher was unsure what to do. Direction soon came.

'Mr Redmayne,' snapped the old man over his shoulder.

'Yes, Sir William?'

'Stay out of sight.'

Hovering between deference and resentment, Arthur Oscott led him into the drawing room. Oscott's wife stayed listening outside the door. The newcomer slapped his whip down on a table.

'Is she secure?' he asked.

'Completely, sir,' said Oscott.

'No more escape attempts?'

'None.'

'Good.'

'Mrs Gow doesn't have the heart for it, not since we caught her maidservant. She's very low.'

'I hope you've treated her well, Arthur. I'll not have her abused by anyone. Do you understand that?'

'Yes, sir.'

'Does your wife understand it? Harriet Gow is a very precious commodity to us. We have to guard her with care. It's not long now. We'll soon be able to divide the takings and celebrate.'

'Will we?' asked Oscott sceptically. 'There's no sign of the ransom money yet. I'm beginning to wonder if it'll ever come.'

'Of course it will, man!' returned the other vehemently. 'They'll have to pay now. My second ransom note left them with no option. We'll have the money by dusk tomorrow.'

'I'll believe it when I see it.'

'What do you mean?'

'Well, I don't wish to question your judgement, sir, but you said that the money would be paid immediately. All we had to do was to kidnap Mrs Gow and hold her for a short time.' He looked straight into his employer's eyes. 'What went wrong?'

'Nothing.'

'You boasted they'd never dare try to find her.'

'I know, but they've paid for their impudence. Henry Redmayne was soundly beaten and Mary Hibbert's body was sent to them. Not that I authorised her murder,' he said rancorously, 'but it was an effective way of getting a message through to the Palace.'

'It wasn't that effective,' said Oscott sourly. 'It hasn't stopped them from trying to hunt us down. They're still on our tail.'

'They won't be after today. Smeek will see to that.'

'Smeek is under lock and key in Newgate, sir.'

The other man was stunned. 'Who put him there?'

'Jonathan Bale – that constable you sent him to attack. He wasn't such an easy target as Henry Redmayne, sir. In other words,' he said meaningfully, 'Mr Bale is still trying to pick up our scent. I don't like it. Neither does my wife. She wonders if we should cut and run.'

'Cut and run!' roared his companion. 'We'll do nothing of the kind. All we have to do is to sit tight until the money is paid. If they want to see Mrs Gow alive again, they must and will pay the ransom.'

'Unless we're tracked down first.'

'How can we be?'

'Smeek may talk. And if they've got him, they'll soon take Ben Froggatt into custody as well. Tongues can be loosened in Newgate.'

'So what? Smeek and Froggatt know nothing.'

'They know that I hired them.'

'Forget them.'

'They know where we took Mrs Gow the first time.'

'But they have no idea where she is now, do they? You're getting soft, Arthur,' he warned, snatching up his whip. 'That's dangerous. I need people around me I can trust – not cowards who start to shiver at the first setback.'

'I'm no coward!' asserted Oscott, hurt by the charge.

'Then stop sweating, man. We hold all the cards.'

'Do we?'

'Yes, Godammit!' snarled the other, striking the table with his whip. 'And we'll play this game through to the bitter end so that we can collect our winnings. Hear that, Arthur? Our winnings. Nothing can stop us. They'll pay up, mark my words. They *have* to.'

Martin Eldridge failed before he even started. Desperate to give of his best, he did quite the opposite. His mind was distracted. Instead of concentrating on Iago's lines, he was thinking about a missing friend. His timing was off, his gestures uncertain, his grasp of the role poor. He stumbled over every speech that he attempted. Standing in the pit, Sir William D'Avenant kept inviting him to try again. Eldridge took it as a sign of kindness at first then realised that the manager was deliberately prolonging his ordeal, enjoying the humiliation of an actor he never seriously meant to employ in the first place. When he forgot the opening lines of Iago's most famous speech, Eldridge did not wait for a comment. He ran off the stage and stalked out of the theatre.

Coming out into Portugal Street, he walked quickly past Lincoln's Inn Fields in the direction of Holborn. He was soon overtaken by a horseman who reined in his mount to block his path. Before Eldridge could complain, he had Christopher Redmayne's rapier at his throat.

'Don't run away from me this time, Mr Eldridge.'

'I can explain that.'

'That's what I'm hoping. And by the way,' he said, nodding towards the theatre. 'I'm sorry if my presence hampered your performance just now. I did my best to stay out of sight.'

Eldridge was horrified. 'You *saw* that travesty of acting?'

'Lysippus was a far more suitable role for you.' Christopher dismounted and sheathed his sword. 'Where shall we talk?'

'In the nearest tavern. I need some wine.'

'Lead the way.'

Christopher had no fear that he would bolt again. The disastrous visit to The Duke's Playhouse had taken all the spirit out of him. Eldridge said nothing until they were sitting at a table in the White Rose. Two glasses of wine were bought at Christopher's expense. The actor sipped his gratefully.

'Thank you, Mr Redmayne,' he said.

'Supposing that you tell me the truth?' suggested Christopher.

'I might say the same about you.'

'Me?'

'When you called at my lodging, you made no mention of the fact that Mary Hibbert has been murdered. I was shocked when I heard.'

'And how did you do that?'

'By talking to Roland Trigg.'

'So that's where you went when you raced off.' Christopher tasted his own wine before he continued. 'Yes, I did conceal certain details from you because I thought it best to do so. But if you know about the girl, you'll realise the predicament that Mrs Gow is in. Unless we can find her very quickly, she may end up on a slab next to Mary Hibbert.'

'Don't say that!' exclaimed the actor.

'I simply want you to understand that time is not on our side. Don't waste any more of it, Mr Eldridge. I think I know what you have to say. Watching you on that stage this evening, it slowly dawned on me.'

'Go on.'

'You were the man in Greer Lane, weren't you?'

'Was I?'

'He went by the name of Bartholomew Gow but he was far too handsome to be Mrs Gow's real husband. When the lady went for an assignation in Greer Lane, she was coming to meet Martin Eldridge.' He put his face close. 'Am I right, sir?'

'You might be,' conceded the actor.

'In other words, on the day that she was abducted outside that house you used, Mrs Gow was on her way to meet you.'

'But she wasn't, Mr Redmayne.'

'Then what was her coach doing there?'

'I've no idea. She called off the rendezvous with me.'

'Called it off?'

'Her coachman brought word early that same morning. It wasn't the first time we'd had to change the arrangements,' he said, staring into his wine. 'Harriet was often in demand elsewhere. I accepted that. What I didn't know was that a kidnap was being set up in Greer Lane.'

'You mentioned arrangements, Mr Eldridge.'

The actor looked up at him before spilling out the truth in a continuous stream. Christopher had no qualms about his sincerity.

'Harriet and I have been close for some time,' he admitted. 'I loved her dearly, that's why she trusted me. I couldn't give her the things that her rich admirers could: Harriet knew that. What I could offer her was tenderness and understanding. She told me that it was in short supply elsewhere. Naturally,' he emphasised, 'we had to be extremely discreet. She could not be seen having assignations with a lowly actor. To cover my tracks, I used a false name.'

'Bartholomew Gow.'

'It seemed appropriate in the circumstances.'

'While you were playing the part of her husband, you mean?'

'I've told you, Mr Redmayne. I loved her. And I believe that she loved me. Why else would she take the risk on such a regular basis? We met twice a month in Greer Lane at specific times. It may not sound much to you but it meant everything to me. And to Harriet. She insisted on paying for the room in that house.'

'Who else knew about this arrangement?'

'Nobody apart from her coachman. And he was discreet.'

Christopher was less certain about that but he said nothing. 'Why did you run out on me at your lodging?' he asked.

'Because of the situation,' said the actor. 'I didn't want to admit that we had assignations – and I'm relying on you to say nothing of them to anyone else. Please, Mr Redmayne. I beg of you.' Christopher gave an affirmative nod. 'Thank you. I shouldn't have bolted like that but I was in a panic, afraid that I was somehow responsible for the kidnap because I wasn't in Greer Lane when I should have been.'

'You were told not to go there.'

'I begin to see why now.' He took a longer sip of his wine. 'I was different from the others, you see. That's what Harriet liked about me. I wasn't just another part of her collection.'

'Collection?'

'All those wealthy admirers. Harriet enjoyed collecting them like pieces of porcelain. She's a wonderful lady, Mr Redmayne,' he said fondly, 'but she has her weaknesses as well. Harriet was so proud when she added the most illustrious admirer of all to her collection. Even then, she would still meet me for an hour in Greer Lane.'

'Didn't you mind sharing her with someone else?'

'Why should I? A tiny piece of Harriet Gow is worth far more than the whole of another woman. I never aspired to own her like the others,' he explained. 'That was something she could never be. The exclusive property of one man.'

'Tell me more about this collection of hers.'

'It was rather extensive.'

'We've already found that out.'

'Besides, I'm not the person to ask, Mr Redmayne. There's someone who knows far more about it because he had to stand by and watch his wife putting her collection carefully together. That's the Bartholomew Gow you ought to speak to. The real one,' he said with a twinkle in his eye. 'Not the impostor.'

Jonathan Bale was simmering with quiet excitement when he left Newgate Gaol. He was so eager to pass on what he had discovered that he all but broke into a run. When he reached Fetter Lane, however, he found that Christopher Redmayne was not there. Jacob suggested an alternative address.

'He said that he would go back to his brother's house, Mr Bale.'

'That's in Bedford Street, isn't it?'

'Number seventeen,' confirmed the servant. 'That was the message he left for you. Mr Redmayne was worried about his brother's condition. You're to meet him there.'

'Oh, I see.'

Jonathan's step had lost its spring by the time he reached the larger and more imposing abode of Henry Redmayne. He hesitated before knocking, wishing that he could speak with Christopher at the latter's home but necessity compelled him to swallow his feelings of social awkwardness. Since he was still in his shipwright's attire, he was looked at askance by the servant who answered the door. Loath to admit him, the servant was amazed when Jonathan's name was sent upstairs and brought Christopher tripping down them. Delighted to see the constable, he escorted him into the house and up to his brother's bedchamber.

Henry Redmayne was sitting up in his capacious fourposter.

'Goodness!' he protested as the visitor was brought in. 'Am I some kind of peepshow that you bring people in off the street to stare at me?'

'Mr Bale is entitled to be here,' said his brother. 'He's the brave man who captured one of your attackers and, I hope to hear, has tracked the other to his lair. Is that correct?'

'More or less, Mr Redmayne.' Hat in hand, Jonathan managed a polite enquiry of the patient. 'How are you now, sir?'

'All the better for the news of your bravery,' said Henry. 'Who are the villains? And why did they have to pick on me when I was wearing one of my best coats? It was sodden with blood afterwards.'

'They're both in custody now, sir.'

'Excellent,' congratulated Christopher, patting him on the

arm. 'Tell us the full details. Did you go to the Hope and Anchor?'

'Yes, Mr Redmayne.'

Still slightly embarrassed by the situation, Jonathan gave a much shorter account of his movements than he might otherwise have done. Christopher was delighted and Henry, restored by a solid meal and two glasses of wine, was pleased to hear that the wheels of justice had rolled over the two men who had assaulted him.

'Where are the devils now?' he wondered.

'In Newgate, sir,' said Jonathan. 'I could get nothing out of Smeek when I questioned him, but Froggatt was more talkative. I hit on the idea of putting them in the same cell, knowing that they'd each accuse the other of committing the murder. It was a wise move,' he said modestly. 'They yelled at each other and gave away information without even realising they were doing it. When they came to blows, we had to pull them apart. Even with one arm in a splint, Ben Froggatt's a violent man.'

'Did they say who put them up to it?' asked Christopher.

'They don't know, Mr Redmayne, that's the pity of it. I got the name of the man who hired them – Arthur Oscott – but he didn't organise the abduction. That was someone else's doing.'

'How can we find this character Oscott?'

'By going to the house where Mrs Gow is held.'

'You know where it is?' said Christopher, tingling all over.

'Not exactly,' confessed Jonathan, 'but I managed to get some details out of them. They were responsible for taking her there. The house is in Richmond, just off the main road. Ben Froggatt said that it wasn't too far from the Palace.'

'We'll find it!'

'Richmond,' mused Henry. 'Who has a house in Richmond?'

'Anyone on that list of names you gave me?' said his brother.

'Nobody that I can think of, Christopher. And there must be several houses not far from the Palace. It could take you an age to get round them all. Wait a minute,' he said, hauling himself up gingerly. 'Yes, *he* used to have a property in Richmond, if memory serves.'

'Who?'

'That scurvy member of the merry gang.'

'Give us a name, Henry.'

'Sir Godfrey Armadale.'

'I never agreed to be party to murder, Sir Godfrey!' protested his irate visitor. 'You swore it would never come to that.'

'I never expected that it would.'

'Mary Hibbert was a harmless young girl.'

'She escaped from the house. She could have raised the alarm.'

'Does that mean she had to be beaten to death?'

'No, of course not. My orders were to bring her back.'

'What went wrong, Sir Godfrey?'

'Smeek and Froggatt lost their heads.'

'Ben Froggatt, in particular, I daresay. As I know to my cost.'

Days after the assault, Roland Trigg still bore vivid mementoes of his beating. He had travelled to the house in a state of towering anger, still stricken by the news about Mary Hibbert and worried about the consequences for himself. Sir Godfrey Armadale let him rant on until the sting of his fury had been drawn then he asserted his authority. He was a slim, elegant man in his late thirties, fashionably dressed and wearing a brown wig that matched the colour of his curling moustache. His face had surrendered its once handsome features to long nights of revelry and indulgence. Deep lines had been gouged, pouches had formed beneath the eyes and the skin had taken on a sallow hue.

'Have you quite finished, Trigg?' he said at length.

'They should have stuck to the plan, Sir Godfrey.'

'You were the idiot who didn't do that,' accused the other bitterly. 'Your orders were simple enough yet you couldn't obey them, could you? Why on earth did you have to attack Froggatt like that?'

'To get my own back.'

'And lose me one valuable man.'

'Ben Froggatt was a bad choice from the start.'

'Not according to Arthur Oscott.'

'I warned him against Ben but he wouldn't listen. They were supposed to ambush the coach and shake me up a little. That was the plan, Sir Godfrey. Instead of which,' he complained, 'Ben Froggatt sets about me with his cudgel as if he wants to kill me. I'm not standing for that from anybody.'

'So you throw the whole scheme into jeopardy.'

'No!'

'Yes, you did!'

'Ben had to be dealt with, Sir Godfrey.'

'Then why, in God's name, couldn't you wait until this business was over before you did so? You could have carved him up for dinner then, for all I cared. But no, you couldn't wait, could you? Thanks to you,' he said with withering scorn, 'Smeek was taken and Froggatt is rotting beside him in Newgate.'

Trigg was alarmed. 'They've been captured?'

'Yes,' said Armadale, regarding him with disgust. 'Because of your hot blood, I had to send Smeek to do a job that Froggatt would have done properly. Smeek blundered and was arrested by that constable.'

'Jonathan Bale?'

'We underestimated him.'

'You should have sent me to deal with Mr Bale.'

'After the way you've behaved so far, I wouldn't trust you to do anything. If you'd done as you were told, none of this would have happened. The whole thing would've been over and done with and nobody would have been any the wiser.'

'I did my share,' bleated the coachman. 'I kept an eye on Mr Redmayne and that constable. Yes, and who was it who told you about Mr Redmayne's brother making those enquiries?'

'You did,' conceded the other.

'I worked hard, Sir Godfrey.'

'You were very helpful at first. Until you lost your temper.'

'Ben Froggatt was the one who lost his temper. Battering to death an innocent girl like that. If I'd known about it when I gave him his own beating, he'd never have got up again, I swear it.'

'That's enough!' decreed Armadale, stamping a foot. 'Stop this ridiculous boasting. What's done is done and there's no use worrying about it. There's certainly no point in allotting blame all over the place. If we hold steady, the plan might still work.'

'Might?'

'It will work. Without doubt.'

'It hasn't worked so far.'

'No more impudence!' yelled Armadale, rounding on him with such rage that the coachman backed away and cowered. 'Don't you dare say another word, you miserable cur. It's not your place to criticise me. Remember who you are, Trigg, and what you were when I first took you on. You owe *everything* to me.'

'It's true, Sir Godfrey.'

'Then follow your orders and keep your mouth shut.' Trigg gave a penitent nod. 'That's all you have to do, is that clear?'

'Yes, Sir Godfrey.'

'Leave the decisions to me,' insisted Armadale. 'I spent months planning this kidnap and it's cost me a lot of money. Four men were hired, not to mention Oscott's wife. And there were many other items of expenditure. I'm not going to have all my careful work ruined by a hot-headed coachman who has to settle a grudge.'

There was a long pause. Trigg stood with his head down.

'Sir Godfrey?' he asked meekly.

'What now, man?'

'They will pay the ransom, won't they?'

'Of course!' said the other with confidence.

'But if they don't . . . what will you do to Mrs Gow?'

Sir Godfrey Armadale took up his stance in front of the fireplace.

'Get my revenge another way,' he said quietly.

Chapter Fourteen

It was not the ideal way to hold a conversation. Jonathan Bale was too preoccupied with staying in the saddle to hear everything that his companion was saying. An indifferent horseman, he clamped his knees too tightly against the animal and held the reins as if clinging to the edge of a precipice. He and Christopher Redmayne were riding towards Clerkenwell at a steady trot. In the interests of speed, Christopher had borrowed a horse for the constable from his brother. Henry Redmayne's bay mare was far too mettlesome for Jonathan. He feared that his mount would bolt at any moment. Amused at his discomfort, Christopher rode beside him with practised ease.

'Try to relax, Mr Bale. Let the horse do the work.'

'I prefer to travel on foot.'

'We must make best use of the last of the light,' said Christopher. 'And I think it's very important to speak to Mr Gow. That became clear after my conversation with Martin Eldridge.'

'The *other* Bartholomew Gow.'

There was a note of censure in his voice. As they left the house in Bedford Street, Christopher had told him about his reunion with the actor, confiding details that he did not wish to reveal in front of his brother. Jonathan had been shocked at Martin Eldridge's confession. It gave him no pleasure to learn that his assumption about the house in Greer Lane had been correct. The realisation that Harriet Gow, still a married woman, had a series of assignations with one man while involved at the same time in a dalliance with the King and, it was not impossible, with some of her other admirers as well, had offended his Puritan sensibilities deeply.

'It would not happen in my ward,' he asserted.

'What?'

'Using a house for immoral purposes like that. The magistrate would be informed. Action would be taken against the owner.'

'There's no law against inviting people into one's home, Mr Bale. Who are we to say what they get up to when they are left alone in a room? As for secret assignations,' Christopher pointed out, 'I'll wager they take place every bit as often in Baynard's Castle Ward as elsewhere.'

'Money changed hands in this case. That's the crucial point.'

'Can you prove it?'

'Why else would that woman provide the use of rooms?'

'You can ask her,' said Christopher, 'because you'll need to go back to Greer Lane before this business is over. My guess is that money changed hands for a more sinister purpose. That coach was ambushed right on her doorstep. The likelihood is that she was on the premises at the time and paid to look the other way. That's of far more interest to me than whether or not she assists the course of true love.'

'It's hardly true love!' protested Jonathan.

'It was in the case of Martin Eldridge. He worshipped Mrs Gow. I could see that. And she must have loved him to take such a risk.'

The bay mare gave a sudden lunge forward and caught Jonathan unawares. Rocking in the saddle, he tightened his grip on the reins.

'Go to Clerkenwell on your own, sir,' he advised.

'Why?'

'I'm not enjoying this ride.'

'But I need you to guide me, Mr Bale.'

'I could give you directions instead.'

'Why bother?' said Christopher. 'We need to go together. It's time we combined our forces instead of acting independently. Besides, you've already met Mr Gow. He trusts you.' He grinned as Jonathan's mare tossed its head mutinously. 'Rather more than you trust that horse.'

'I'm not sure what else we can learn from Mr Gow.'

'You think the visit is a waste of time?'

'No, Mr Redmayne,' said Jonathan. 'I just feel that we might be better employed searching for that house in Richmond.'

'In the dark? We'd never reach there by nightfall, especially if you insisted on travelling on foot. I'm as anxious as you to find that house, believe me, but we need more guidance.'

'Your brother mentioned Sir Godfrey Armadale.'

'Yes,' said Christopher, 'and it's a name I've heard in connection with Mrs Gow before.'

'Then the house may belong to him.'

'Let's not jump to over-hasty conclusions. I have it on good authority that Sir Godfrey Armadale is no longer living anywhere near London. He's moved back to the West Country.'

'Who told you that?'

'Roland Trigg.'

'And how would he know?'

'He used to be Sir Godfrey's coachman.'

As soon as he said it, Christopher realised that it was too great a coincidence to ignore. Jonathan reached the same verdict. Both jerked the reins to bring their horses to a sudden halt while their eyes had a silent conversation.

Carrying a sack, Roland Trigg let himself into the house with the key entrusted to him by Harriet, but he did not move about with the deferential tread of a servant this time. Pounding up the stairs, he went into her bedchamber and looked around for booty. Light was fading now but sufficient came in through the windows to save him from needing a candle. In any case, he had other plans for the silver candelabra. They were the first items to be placed in the sack. He crossed to the table on which an ornate mirror was set. It was here that Harriet Gow so often sat, but no beauty was reflected in the glass now. The big, bruised, sweating face of Roland Trigg could be seen as he scoured the table.

Most of the jewellery was in the largest of the boxes. He feasted his eyes on the contents, emitting a laugh of joy as he

251

guessed at the value. A second box followed the first into the sack then he found a third, a small, velvet-covered box, hidden away behind a pile of books. Opening it with curiosity, he let out a wheeze of surprise when he saw the ring that lay inside. Encrusted with diamonds, the large ruby sparkled with fire. Trigg held it on the palm of his hand to examine it. The ring was quite priceless. He suspected that it was a gift from the King himself. That gave it additional value in his eyes. The little box went into the sack, followed by the other items he scooped up.

Trigg worked quickly. He had somewhere to go.

'Why have you come to me?' said Bartholomew Gow irritably. 'I told Constable Bale all that I knew.'

'Yes,' said Christopher. 'He was struck by your honesty.'

'Why bother me again?'

'Because we thought you might actually be interested to know if your wife had been found and released yet.'

'Has she?' asked Gow with delayed eagerness.

'Unfortunately not.'

'Where *is* Harriet?'

'I'm hoping that you might be able to tell us, Mr Gow.'

'How would I know?'

The estranged husband was disconcerted when two visitors called at that time of the evening. Forced to invite them into the shabby little house, he was determined to send them on their way as soon as possible. Since there were only two seats in the room, Jonathan Bale remained standing. Christopher took the chair opposite his host. Sensing his reluctance to help, he tried to impress upon him the gravity of the situation.

'Mrs Gow is in serious danger, sir.'

'It's not my doing.'

'Don't you care?' he chided. 'Does your wife's safety merit no more than an afterthought? Mr Bale may have told you about the abduction but there are other crimes involved here.'

'There are,' agreed Jonathan, signalled into the conversation. 'Mr Redmayne's own brother was viciously assaulted and an even worse fate was visited on Mary Hibbert.'

'Mary?' said Gow. 'Harriet's maid?'

'She'll not be able to serve your wife any more, sir.'

'Why not?'

'She was beaten to death.'

Gow paled. 'She was *murdered*?'

'Now you see what we're up against, sir.'

'But why? Who could want to kill a girl like Mary Hibbert?'

'Their names are Smeek and Froggatt,' said Christopher, taking over again. 'Thanks to Mr Bale, both of them are in Newgate, awaiting trial. But they're only hired villains. We still don't know the name of the man who paid them to kidnap your wife.'

He gave Bartholomew Gow a few moments to absorb the new information. It made him thoughtful and uneasy. He looked at his two visitors with a degree of welcome.

'How can I help?' he offered.

'By giving us some names,' said Christopher.

'Names?'

'Yes, Mr Gow. We've been compiling lists of your wife's friends and enemies. To be honest, we weren't quite sure which category you fell into yourself. Perhaps neither.'

'I want Harriet to be saved,' affirmed Gow.

'Then we're working to the same end. The names we have were all suggested by people at the theatre. We wondered if you might add one or two more to the list. I know this must be embarrassing for you,' said Christopher delicately, 'and I apologise for that. What I can promise you is that Constable Bale and I will be very discreet.'

'It's too late in the day for discretion,' said the other wearily. 'Why try to hide it? Everyone knows that I'm the cuckolded husband of a famous actress. You want me to identify my wife's lovers, is that it?'

Jonathan shifted his feet, fearing what he was about to hear.

'I understand,' said Christopher, 'that some of her admirers gave her gifts and that she built up quite a collection.'

'That's right. I was part of it once.'

'I've told Mr Redmayne about your situation,' said Jonathan.

'I was squeezed dry and cast aside,' returned Gow. 'I couldn't afford to keep Harriet in the style she came to prefer so I was pushed out. Things went from bad to worse after that. I made some unwise investments, lost most of what little money I had, and am now reduced to living in this pig sty. It's demoralising.'

'What's your legal situation?' asked Christopher.

'I'm still trying to find out. My lawyer, Obadiah Shann, assures me that I can make a claim against Harriet but he's yet to explain how. I thought a wife was supposed to be part of a husband's chattels. Not mine. I was the chattel in that marriage. When she started to develop her collection, she tossed me out altogether.'

'Tell us about this collection,' encouraged Christopher.

'It began with small gifts. Baskets of flowers and so on. Then we were invited out together to dine but that didn't last,' he said ruefully. 'Harriet preferred to dine alone with her admirers. After that, the gifts became much more expensive. Sir Roger Mulberry gave her a necklace that must have cost all of two hundred pounds. Lord Clayborne gave her jewellery worth even more. And so her collection built until she had one of the most lavish gifts of all.'

'What was that, Mr Gow?'

'Somewhere in which to display it.'

'The house near St James's Square?'

'That came with royal compliments,' said Gow. 'How could a man of my means compete with all that? Harriet had already worked her way through most of my money. I couldn't buy her costly rings or fine clothes or a palatial house. And I certainly couldn't afford to buy her a coach.'

'A coach, sir?' said Jonathan, ears alerted.

'It was something she'd always wanted. Harriet pined for her own coach so that she could travel wherever she wanted. It was a gift that she cherished. He must have been besotted with her to spend that kind of money on her.'

'Who?' asked Christopher.

'Sir Godfrey Armadale.'

'*He* was one of your wife's admirers?'

'Among the most ardent,' explained the other. 'But Harriet only teased him. Sir Godfrey never got the rewards he was after from her. That's why his name probably won't appear on any of your lists. When she had what she wanted, Harriet discarded him.'

'Yet she kept the coach?'

'Oh, yes. And the coachman he'd provided.'

'Roland Trigg?'

'That's the fellow.'

Christopher did not need to exchange a glance with Jonathan.

'Surly beggar,' continued Gow. 'I had a few scuffles with him. When I tried to call at the house, Harriet told him to move me on. Trigg enjoyed doing that. He was her coachman and her bodyguard.'

'I suspect that he was something else besides,' said Christopher, standing to leave. 'Come, Mr Bale. I think we should pay a visit to Rider Street. Trigg has some explaining to do.' He paused at the door. 'One final thing, Mr Gow.'

'Yes?'

'Abigail Saunders met you in Locket's recently.'

'I remember, Mr Redmayne. I was dining with my lawyer. He was paying or I'd have been eating in a more modest establishment.'

'Miss Saunders was much taken with a remark you made.'

'What was that?'

'You told her that she might have an opportunity to replace your wife because Mrs Gow was going to be indisposed for a while. Do you recall saying that?'

'Yes. But I was only passing on what I'd just heard.'

'From whom?'

'Trigg,' said the other. 'I called at the house that morning but he sent me packing in no uncertain terms. And he warned me not to come back because Harriet would be going away for a while.'

'Going away?'

'That's all he said, Mr Redmayne.'

Christopher and Jonathan left at speed. The visit to Clerkenwell had delivered far more than they had dared to hope. As they headed off to their next destination, Jonathan was even starting to enjoy the ride.

Henry Redmayne was caught offguard for the second time. Wielded by his father, the cudgels were only verbal but they hurt just as much. The Dean of Gloucester strode without warning into the room to find his elder son, wide awake, sitting up in bed with a goblet of wine in his hand.

'Saints preserve us!' exclaimed the old man.

'Father!' said Henry, choking on his wine.

'I expected to find you fast asleep.'

'I expected that you'd be closeted with the Archbishop.'

'Indeed, I was,' explained the other, 'but I was worried about you and decided to make one last call before I retired. And what do I find, Henry? You are sitting up in bed with a smile on your face, consuming a goblet of wine.'

'A cordial, Father,' lied Henry, swallowing the dregs before his visitor could examine them more closely. 'A cordial prescribed by the physician to ease the pain.'

'What about the sleeping draught? That was supposed to have been prescribed by your physician as well.'

'Its effect somehow wore off.'

'You've been deceiving me, sir!' snapped his father.

'Why would I do that?'

'For some dark purpose that I intend to root out.'

'There *is* no dark purpose,' argued Henry. 'I've never had a dark purpose in my entire life. Ask Christopher. I'm the most opaque of men.'

'You pretended to be weaker than you really are in order to evade my enquiries about what actually happened to you. That is an act of gross deception. I feel betrayed, Henry.'

'You've no need, Father.'

'Thank goodness I had the impulse to call back here!'

'How was it that my servant didn't warn me of your arrival?'

'Because I ordered him not to,' explained the other. 'I wanted to steal upon you unannounced. In the event, it was a revelation.'

'That's not what I'd call it,' said Henry to himself, vowing to dismiss the servant who had allowed the parental assault on him. 'The truth is that I do feel slightly better, though my ribs still hurt whenever I breathe in. But my brain is still clouded.'

'With too much drink, probably.'

'Father!' he protested.

But he could not head off another sermon from the county of Gloucestershire. Delivered with blistering force, it left Henry stunned. He was not simply castigated for trying to deceive his father. All his other perceived or alleged faults were used to beat him into total submission. Henry was too cowed to defend himself. When the punishment had been delivered, Algernon Redmayne remembered his other son.

'Where is Christopher?' he said.

'Busy with his own affairs.'

'His place is here, beside you.'

'Oh, he's been very attentive,' said Henry, glad to shift the parental gaze away from himself. 'As it happens, Christopher was here earlier this evening with Constable Bale.'

'A constable? Why was he here? To arrest you?'

'No, Father. To bring me the glad tidings that the two men who attacked me were now in custody.'

'That is the first piece of good news I have heard since I entered this house. Was this constable instrumental in the arrests?'

'He overpowered both men.'

'Then I would like to speak to him. Having questioned the two villains, he will be able to give me more details of the assault than the victim is prepared to divulge.'

'My memory is still uncertain.'

'Then let me jog it for you, Henry.'

'It is not in the mood to be jogged,' said the patient, recoiling as his father bent over him with an interrogatory glare. 'I feel drowsy again. Wait until morning, please. I may then be more coherent.'

Algernon Redmayne's face was a mask of determination.

'I would appreciate some coherence *now*,' he said.

They arrived at Harriet Gow's house in Rider Street as night was starting to wrap a blanket of darkness around it. No candles burned within. Christopher Redmayne dismounted to knock at the door but there was no reply. Getting down from his own horse, Jonathan Bale led it down the side of the building to the stable. Both doors had been left wide open as if by a sudden departure. There was no sign of coach or horses.

'Trigg's got away!' said Jonathan in disgust.

'Only because he realised that the net was closing in on him. By the look of it, he cleared off while he still could.'

'He should be in Newgate with Smeek and Froggatt.'

'Oh, I agree,' said Christopher. 'He's the key figure. Our helpful coachman was helping someone else all the time. No wonder the villains knew who was on their tail. And no wonder Trigg could be so certain that Mary Hibbert was abducted. He was party to the kidnap. We were well and truly hoodwinked, Mr Bale. That beating he took made me think that Roland Trigg was a hapless victim.'

'That was the intention, sir,' said Jonathan. 'But I suspect that the kidnap didn't quite go to plan. Trigg was supposed to have been overpowered without being seriously hurt, but someone was too zealous with his cudgel.'

'Ben Froggatt, most likely.'

'That's why Trigg attacked him – to get his own back for a beating he shouldn't have taken. He didn't chance upon Froggatt in the Hope and Anchor at all. It was their regular meeting place: he knew they'd be there.' He gave a grim chuckle. 'Do you know what I'd like to do when I catch up with him?'

'What?'

'Throw him into a cell with Froggatt.'

'What a friendly conversation that might provoke!' Christopher reviewed the evidence. 'At least we now know why he wouldn't tell us where the coach was headed when it was ambushed. It was in Greer Lane by design – at a time when Mrs Gow would normally expect to visit Martin Eldridge.'

'Posing as her husband.'

'But he wasn't there. Mrs Gow didn't know that, of course. She didn't send Trigg to call off the arrangement with Mr Eldridge. She believed that she was on her way to meet him. Whereas, in fact,' he said with a grudging admiration, 'an ambush had been cunningly arranged. Trigg made sure that Mr Eldridge was out of the way then pretended to defend Mrs Gow when the coach was attacked. I blame myself for not suspecting Trigg earlier,' he confessed. 'I should've listened to Jacob.'

'Jacob?'

'My servant. In all the years I've known him, he's never uttered a crude word, yet Roland Trigg had him bawling obscenities like a drunken mariner. Jacob knew,' said Christopher. 'It's like a dog whose fur stands up instinctively when a plausible stranger walks into a house. I should have listened to Jacob's bark.'

'We were both taken in.'

'But we're on the right track now. That's obvious.'

'What do we do next, Mr Redmayne?'

'Nothing until first light, I'm afraid. My initial thought was that we should leave for Richmond at dawn.'

'I'll be ready, sir. Even though I dread the ride.'

'What I dread is following a false trail,' said Christopher. 'Trigg has laid quite a few for us in the past few days. I thought the name of Sir Godfrey Armadale might be significant until he assured me that the man had moved away to Devon. That was all a ruse.'

'I think we'll find Sir Godfrey in Richmond.'

'Along with Mrs Gow, if we're lucky.'

'If your brother will loan me the horse, I'll be ready at dawn.'

'Not so fast, Mr Bale,' warned Christopher. 'We don't want to go galloping around Richmond until we have more precise directions as to where Sir Godfrey lives.'

'How will you get those directions?'

Christopher pondered until a face popped into his mind.

'From a friend,' he said.

'Will he help us, sir?'

'Nobody has a better reason to do so.'

Lodowick Corrigan shifted easily from obsequiousness to resentment in a matter of minutes. He was standing near the site of the new house as he unloaded his complaints into the ear of his employer, buried, as it was, beneath the surging ginger wig. There was an aggressive subservience in the builder's manner.

'It's not right, Mr Hartwell,' he said with a scowl. 'I've never known an architect who was so lax before. I don't expect him to be here every second of the day, of course, but it's in these very early stages that I need to turn to him for advice. Mr Redmayne should be here.'

'I've taxed him on the subject, Mr Corrigan.'

'Perhaps it's time to do more than that.'

'More?'

'There are plenty of other architects in London, sir.'

'Replace him altogether?' said Hartwell, shocked. 'That would be going too far. His designs are exemplary and he's the pleasantest fellow you could wish to meet. You find him so, I'm sure.'

'Why, yes,' muttered the other. 'He's a personable young man, but is he fit for a project as large and testing as this? Mr Redmayne should be here, sir. I ask again – where is he?'

Still inside his coach, Jasper Hartwell looked over Corrigan's shoulder. A horseman was riding towards the site at a canter.

'Bless my soul!' cried Hartwell. 'I believe that he's coming.'

Corrigan turned round in disbelief and gritted his teeth when he saw Christopher Redmayne approaching. The newcomer gave both of them a cheery wave. Reining in his horse, he stayed in the saddle so that he could look down at the argumentative builder.

'Do you have any problems, Mr Corrigan?' he said.

'Not exactly, sir.'

'Can't you manage without me?'

'Of course,' retorted the other.

Christopher was curt. 'Then why don't you do so?' he said. 'I need to have a private word with Mr Hartwell. If you require any advice after that, I'll be happy to give it to you.'

'None will be needed.'

Lodowick Corrigan moved away to bellow at some of his workmen. Christopher turned to Hartwell and touched his hat in apology.

'I'm sorry I've not been here as much as I would have liked,' he said seriously, 'but that situation will change today.'

'It must change, Mr Redmayne. I've had complaints.'

'I could read them in Mr Corrigan's face.'

'He needs you on site.'

'He certainly does,' said Christopher, recalling an earlier exchange with the builder. 'He needs me to watch over him. Very closely. I have every confidence that I'll be able to do so when I get back.'

'From where? You're not deserting us *again*?'

'Not exactly, Mr Hartwell. I'll be acting on your behalf in a matter that's not unconnected with your new house.'

'My nightingale?' said the other, quivering with excitement.

'Yes, sir.'

'Where is she?'

'Not far away, Mr Hartwell.'

'Take me to her at once! I'll propose on the spot.'

'That would be far too precipitous,' said Christopher. 'Wait until the lady is back in London. As for her whereabouts, the truth is that I'm not entirely sure of them but I know someone who does. What I require from you is a little help to find the gentleman.'

'Gentleman?' Hartwell bridled. 'Not a rival for her hand?'

'I think not.'

'Who is the fellow?'

'Sir Godfrey Armadale.'

'Sir Godfrey?' said the other, scornfully. 'The filthy-fingered Mr Corrigan is more of a gentleman than Sir Godfrey Armadale. He's the most frightful character I've ever come across in my life and I wouldn't let him within a mile of my nightingale.'

'Do you know where he lives?' asked Christopher.

'Why should it matter?'

'Because I understand that he has information that could lead me to Mrs Gow. An architect should attend to every aspect of the house, Mr Hartwell,' he reasoned. 'That's why I'm so keen to assist you in your goal. I cannot imagine that anyone could better decorate the interior of your new abode than Mrs Gow.'

'Build the house *around* her.'

'I will, sir.'

'Find her, Mr Redmayne!'

'First, tell me how I can locate Sir Godfrey Armadale. Is it true that he has a house in Richmond?'

'He has properties all over the place. Including one in Devon.'

'I heard a rumour that he was going back to the West Country.'

'Not when he can carouse the nights away in London,' said Hartwell, trying to flick away a wasp. 'His main house is in Kew. A positively grotesque edifice, from what I hear. And not to be compared with my own wonderful new abode. That's where you'll find Sir Godfrey. At home in Armadale Manor.'

The wasp tried to take up residence in the wig, throwing Hartwell into a state of frenzied agitation. By the time he finally evicted the insect, he was too late to ask how Sir

Godfrey Armadale might assist the search for a missing actress. Christopher Redmayne had already galloped away.

Roland Trigg was given a poor welcome when he arrived at the house. Sir Godfrey Armadale came bursting out of the door to confront him. He was dressed to ride and an ostler was saddling his horse. Sir Godfrey hit the side of the coach with his whip.

'What the devil are you doing here, man?' he yelled.

'I had nowhere else to go, Sir Godfrey.'

'All you had to do was to remain where you were. That was the plan, you idiot. You were ordered to stay where you were until Harriet Gow was released. Then, because you felt you'd let her down badly by letting her get abducted, you would resign from her service. I devised it all so carefully,' he roared. 'By the time Mrs Gow worked out that you'd actually been an accomplice to the kidnappers, you'd have been well away, spending your share of the ransom. Instead of which, you make your escape and give the game away.'

'They were closing in on me, Sir Godfrey.'

'Who were?'

'Mr Redmayne and that constable.'

'They had no *proof*!'

'They had Ben Froggatt. He'd have pointed the finger at me out of spite. I'm lucky they didn't get me.'

'I'm beginning to wish they had,' said Armadale harshly.

'You don't really mean that.'

'Don't I?'

'Smeek and Froggatt may not know your name, Sir Godfrey,' warned Trigg. 'Neither does Arthur Oscott. But I do, don't I?'

'Are you threatening me?' howled Armadale, drawing his sword.

'No, no. I'm just pointing something out.'

'What is it?'

'We need each other, Sir Godfrey.'

Armadale made an effort to curb his anger. Putting his sword back into its sheath, he used the whip to beckon the coachman down from his seat. Trigg was unkempt and unshaven. Armadale could smell straw.

'When did you leave?'

'Just as it was getting dark.'

'Where did you spend the night?'

'At a tavern along the way,' explained Trigg. 'All the beds were taken so I slept in the stables. Don't worry, sir. Very few people saw me. I arrived and left in darkness.'

'The coach might have been noticed.'

Trigg grinned. 'I thought you'd like it back, Sir Godfrey.'

A reluctant smile flitted across Armadale's face.

'I do,' he conceded. 'I've waited too long to get it.'

'There's something inside for you as well,' said the coachman, opening the door. 'Go on, Sir Godfrey. Take that sack out.'

'Why?'

'Look inside it.'

Armadale prodded the sack with his whip then lifted it out of the coach to set it on the ground. When he opened it to peer inside, he was dumbstruck. Trigg enjoyed seeing the expression of amazement on his face. He smirked energetically.

'Well, Sir Godfrey?'

'Perhaps you're not as stupid as you look.'

'I felt that Mrs Gow owed it to us.'

The change of horses made all the difference. Christopher Redmayne rode the high-spirited bay mare from his brother's stable and gave his own horse to Jonathan Bale. The constable was far happier sitting astride a more obedient animal with a comfortable gait. Though the long ride tested his buttocks, he willingly endured the twinges of pain. Stopping at a tavern near Kew, they were given directions to Armadale Manor. It was less than a mile away. As soon as it came into view, Christopher saw what his client had meant about its grotesque aspect. Even from a distance, Armadale Manor was ugly.

Built out of sandstone almost a century earlier, it had none of the symmetry and beauty of a typical Elizabethan country mansion. A new wing had been added with hideous brickwork whose bright colour clashed with the gentle red hue of the façade. The upper part of the house had been restored by a slipshod builder who had made little effort to make his work blend in harmoniously. Other features of the house were even more unsightly. The architectural values that Christopher held most dear seemed to have been flouted.

'Who could live in such a repulsive house?' he asked.

'A repulsive man,' said Jonathan.

'At least we know that this is the right place.'

'How is that, Mr Redmayne?'

Christopher pointed. 'Look at the coach outside the stables. Isn't that the one belonging to Mrs Gow?' he asked. 'Trigg must be here.'

'Then I'll be happy to meet him again.'

Careful not to announce their arrival too soon, they tethered their horses among the trees and proceeded on foot. Jonathan worked his way round to the rear of the house. Christopher waited until his companion was in position before breaking his cover and strolling up the drive to the front door. The sound of the bell brought a servant into view.

'My name is Christopher Redmayne,' announced the visitor, 'and I've come to pay my compliments to Sir Godfrey Armadale.'

'The master is not here at the moment, sir.'

'Oh dear.'

'He rode off a while ago and may not be back for some time.'

'I see,' said Christopher, recognising the man's honesty. 'In that case, I'll not linger, though I may spend a few moments looking around this magnificent pile, if I may. I'm an architect by profession. Armadale Manor is quite unlike anything I've seen before.'

'Do as you wish, sir.'

The man closed the door behind him. Christopher went past the stables and turned down the side of the house. A yell of rage made him break into a trot. When he reached the back of the property, he saw Roland Trigg lying motionless at Jonathan Bale's feet. The constable glanced down at the prone figure.

'He tried to make a run for it. I got in his way.'

'What sort of a night did she have?' asked Sir Godfrey Armadale.

'Unsettled,' said Oscott. 'We could hear her, pacing up and down in the room. She never seemed to stop, Sir Godfrey.'

'She must be exhausted after all this time.'

'So are we.'

'You'll get your reward, Arthur.'

'When?'

'Today. I've told them where and how the ransom is to be paid. It's only a question of collecting it and all our troubles are over.'

'There weren't supposed to be any troubles.'

'I blame you for those.'

Oscott tensed. 'Me, Sir Godfrey?'

'Yes. You chose Smeek and Froggatt. They were the blundering fools who let us down. However,' he said, raising his whip to silence the protest he saw forming on the other's lips, 'we must put that behind us. I don't bear grudges. Smeek and Froggatt are out of this now. That means a larger share for you and your wife.'

'Oh,' said Oscott, relaxing slightly. 'Thank you, Sir Godfrey. My wife and I are very grateful. We've had to put in more work than we thought. It's been something of a trial.'

'That goes for all of us but we've come through it.'

'When will Mrs Gow be released?'

'When the ransom money is in my hands and not before.'

'She still has no idea who organised the kidnap?'

'No – and she never will,' said Armadale with a complacent grin. 'That's the beauty of it. I get my revenge and make a small fortune into the bargain. Yet nobody will ever know about it.'

The mood of self-congratulation was immediately dispelled. Flinging open the door, Oscott's wife ran into the room in a panic.

'There's a coach coming, Sir Godfrey!' she warned.

'There can't be.'

'See for yourself.'

The two men rushed to the window and looked out. Rolling up the drive and scrunching over the gravel was a coach. Armadale recognised it at once and glared up at the man who was holding the reins.

'It's Trigg!' he yelled. 'What the devil is he doing here?'

He and Oscott rushed out to welcome the coachman but there was a shock in store for them. When the newcomer raised his hat, they saw that it was not Roland Trigg at all but a complete stranger.

Christopher Redmayne beamed down from his high eminence. After a glance at them both, he turned his smile upon the shorter.

'Sir Godfrey Armadale, I presume?'

'Who are you?' growled the other.

'Christopher Redmayne.' Both men reacted with hostility to the name. 'I've come to collect Mrs Gow in her own coach.'

'Where's Trigg?'

'Tied up inside. He's coming back to London with us.'

'You're here on your own?' said Armadale with disbelief, one hand on the hilt of his sword. 'You're very bold, Mr Redmayne.'

'Trigg assured me that there were only the two of you here,' said Christopher easily, 'and that poses no problem to me.'

'What about three men?' Drawing his sword, Armadale turned to Oscott. 'Open the coach and untie Trigg.'

Oscott moved across to the coach and saw Roland Trigg inside, bound and gagged, threshing about wildly. When he opened the door, however, he discovered that the coachman was not the only passenger. Crouched out of sight on his hands and knees, Jonathan Bale now reared up and launched himself at Oscott, knocking the man to the ground before hitting him with a relay of punches. Before Armadale could go to the man's aid, Christopher tore off the coat he had borrowed from Trigg and hurled it into Armadale's face, drawing his own sword at the same time and leaping down to circle his adversary.

'I forgot to mention that Constable Bale was with me as well,' he said, feinting with his rapier. 'He's the man who arrested Smeek and Froggatt. Now it's Arthur Oscott's turn.'

Armadale came at him but Christopher parried his thrusts with skill, dancing back out of range before circling his opponent again. Jonathan pummelled away mercilessly until Oscott groaned in agony and lapsed into unconsciousness. His wife ran to tend him, swearing at the constable then turning her ire on Armadale.

'Shut up!' he snarled. 'I'll deal with you in a minute.'

'I claim pride of place, Sir Godfrey,' said Christopher.

'Come on, then.'

'Though I think that Mr Bale would like a word with you as well. He was a friend of Mary Hibbert. Your men killed her.'

Armadale turned his head towards Jonathan who was moving cautiously towards him with a dagger in his hand. A split second was all it took for Christopher to strike. His blade flashed, its point cut into Armadale's wrist, and the latter dropped his sword with a yelp of pain. Holding his wounded wrist, he darted into the house and tried to close the door after him but Jonathan was too fast, getting a shoulder to the door and forcing it open. When Armadale ran to the stairs, Christopher caught him before he could ascend them, holding the point of his sword between the man's eyes and making it clear that he was ready to use the weapon again. Blood was now dripping freely from his adversary's wrist. There was nowhere he could go. He was trapped.

'Where is Harriet Gow?' demanded Christopher.

'She's not here.'

'Don't lie to me, Sir Godfrey.'

'We moved her this morning.'

'Where *is* she?'

Christopher was about to jab his swordpoint in order to encourage an answer when it came from above in the most affecting way. The song was as clear and poignant as on the first occasion he had heard it.

> *'My love was false, but I was firm*
> *From my hour of birth.*
> *Upon my buried body lie*
> *Lightly, gentle earth.'*

Christopher looked upwards. The voice was inimitable. Though it was full of sadness, it was also celebrating its release. Harriet Gow was alive. Lowering his sword, Christopher gave a disarming smile.

'I believe that you have a nightingale in the house, Sir Godfrey.'

Devoid of his beloved spaniels for once, Charles II was in a sombre frame of mind, reclining in a chair and toying idly with the purses that lay in his lap. His dark attire suggested that he might be in mourning. After tapping on the door, William Chiffinch entered with the two visitors and brought them across to the King. All three waited until he was ready to look up at them with soulful eyes. Christopher Redmayne bowed from the waist and Jonathan Bale inclined a reluctant head. Coming out of his reverie, the King rose to share a warm smile between them.

'Thank you for coming, gentlemen,' he said, one hand playing with a rogue curl on his periwig. 'I wanted to express my gratitude in person. You have done me a profound service and rescued a dear, dear lady in the process. Such courage deserves a reward.'

'I've already had mine, Your Majesty,' said Jonathan bluntly. 'Apprehending the men who killed Mary Hibbert was my reward.'

'Yes,' said the King. 'A distressing result of this very

269

distressing business. I commend your bravery, Mr Bale.' He held out the purse. 'If you will not take the money for yourself, at least receive it on behalf of the girl's family. It might bring some small measure of relief to them.'

'Indeed it might,' admitted Jonathan, taking the purse from him. 'That's a kind thought, Your Majesty. Thank you for the suggestion.'

'How else could I get you to accept a reward from me?' He turned to Christopher. 'I hope that I meet no resistance from you, Mr Redmayne. Exceptional service deserves payment.'

'Then I gladly accept it, Your Majesty.' Christopher took the purse and gave a small bow of thanks.

'Allow me to add my own congratulations,' said Chiffinch smugly. 'You may have been dilatory in sending reports of your progress but I cannot fault your enterprise. You chose the right men, Your Majesty.'

'I always do, Will. It's my choice of ladies that sometimes lets me down. Not that I have any regrets in this case,' he said quickly, 'even though this incident has brought that phase of my life to a premature end. The lady in question has been saved. That is enough for me.'

'One was saved, Your Majesty,' Jonathan reminded him, 'but another was needlessly lost. Mary Hibbert might still be alive, had you simply paid the ransom in the first place.'

'Mr Bale!' reprimanded Chiffinch.

'His insolence has some foundation,' said the King, taking no offence. 'The girl was a friend – I appreciate his feelings. But there is a question of precedent here, Mr Bale,' he said, meeting the constable's stare. 'A man in my unique position must not give in to such demands. If I was seen to part with money in exchange for the release of a beautiful woman, we would be getting ransom notes by the day. Mrs Gow is, I have to admit, not the only remarkable lady who has attracted my interest. Besides,' he added sternly, 'I wanted the villains caught and punished. Sir Godfrey Armadale and his creatures will all swing from the gallows for daring to issue a demand to me. Their crimes are heinous.'

'Why were they committed, Your Majesty?' asked Christopher.

'Why?'

'I know that Sir Godfrey was embittered because he was rejected by Mrs Gow, but was that motive enough to put her through this ordeal?'

'No, Mr Redmayne, it was not. He had another victim in mind: one with royal blood in his veins. This whole affair has been an ordeal for me as well, as it was intended to be.'

'Did he act out of envy, then?'

'Revenge,' said the King casually. 'Sir Godfrey Armadale has been badgering me for favours ever since I returned to the throne. He's a persistent man, not easily shaken off. When he continued to pester me outrageously, I was forced to ban him from the Court. That upset him, didn't it, Will?'

'Yes, Your Majesty,' said Chiffinch. 'Mightily.'

'In abducting Harriet Gow, he was hitting two birds with one stone. A nightingale and an eagle. There was a time when I thought that we might have been two turtle doves,' he mused fondly, 'but that was a cruel illusion. Enough of this or the Palace will turn into an aviary!' He gave them another smile. 'Go with my heartfelt thanks, gentlemen. I will pay you the highest compliment that I can.'

'What's that, Your Majesty?' said Christopher.

'I shall willingly employ both of you again.'

Jonathan blenched. 'Is that necessary, Your Majesty?' he said.

'I hope not, Mr Bale, but it is a comfort to know that I possess, among my subjects, two men of such rare qualities.'

'We're happy to put them at your disposal, Your Majesty,' said Christopher. He looked at Jonathan. 'Aren't we, Mr Bale?'

The nod of agreement was only achieved with great effort.

With a languid smile, the King turned away to signal that the audience was over. Chiffinch waved the visitors towards the door but Christopher was not quite ready to leave. He took a step towards the King.

'I have a favour to ask of you, Your Majesty.'

Charles turned to regard him. 'Ask it, Mr Redmayne.'

'I do so on my brother's behalf,' said Christopher. 'Henry was an enormous help to me at the start of this investigation, but he suffered badly for his involvement. He still lies on a bed of pain.'

'I'm well aware of that,' observed the King solemnly, 'and I was very impressed with your brother's fortitude. I had no idea that Henry Redmayne possessed such a strong backbone beneath that bright attire of his. The favour will be granted. What does it concern?'

Christopher licked his lips nervously before declaring himself.

'The Dean of Gloucester,' he said.

The burial service took place at the parish church where Mary Hibbert had been baptised. Only a small congregation gathered to see her take leave of her earthly existence. Peter Hibbert sat between his uncle and aunt, each supporting the other. Jonathan and Sarah Bale were behind them with a few neighbours. Nothing could alleviate the grief of the family at that moment, but at least they had been spared the full details of the girl's death. Jonathan was glad of that and pleased that he had been able to hand over the purse of money to Peter Hibbert. It was small compensation but, in a sense, it was a ransom paid by the King even if it came too late to obtain the release of a prisoner.

When the coffin was lowered into the ground, tears flowed as mourners bade their last farewells. Jonathan had to put an arm around his wife's shoulders to comfort her. Turning to leave the churchyard, he was moved to see that Christopher Redmayne had also attended the service even though he had not known the victim. But it was another mourner whose presence touched him even more. Harriet Gow stood a little distance from the grave, sobbing quietly and trying to contain her feelings of guilt. Martin Eldridge took her arm and led her gently away.

* * *

Henry Redmayne had never known such continuous pain. Trapped in his bed and harangued by his father, he came to believe that he had died and gone to Hell. The Dean of Gloucester might not be dressed as a demon but his words stung like the prongs of a white-hot fork. All that Henry could do was to squirm in agony.

'I am much displeased with you, Henry,' said his father.

'That fact has been burned into me.'

'As my elder son, you should be setting an example. Consider your younger brother. What is Christopher to think when he sees your lewd behaviour? How could he pattern himself on you?'

'With difficulty.'

'Repentance is called for, Henry.'

'Oh, I repent,' said the other with feeling. 'Believe me, Father, I'm awash with repentance. I regret so many things in my past.'

'You misled me.'

'Not deliberately.'

'You did, Henry,' returned the Dean sharply. 'All that you told me about the assault was that it took place in Drury Lane.'

'That was the truth.'

'Yes, but it was not the *whole* truth, was it? What you carefully omitted to tell me was that Drury Lane is the site of a theatre and that you were leaving the building when you were attacked.'

'I'll not deny it, Father.'

'Why did you enter such a sinful place?'

'Of necessity.'

'Driven by uncontrollable desires?'

'Not exactly,' said Henry, trying to keep him at bay. 'But I wouldn't have gone there of my own volition. You're so right, Father. Corruption breeds inside a theatre. I thank God that I take no pleasure in the sight of young women disporting themselves on the stage or, what is worse, wearing masks so that they may mingle unrecognised among the wilder gentlemen in the audience to excite their passions.'

Algernon Redmayne clutched at the crucifix around his neck.

'Immorality on such a scale? Is that what happens?'

'I didn't stay long enough to find out, Father. My purpose in going was simply to speak to the manager and not to watch the play.'

'Then you didn't lurch drunkenly out into the street from an orgy?'

'If only there'd been one at hand!' said Henry to himself.

'Speak up!'

'Thank the Lord!'

Henry's exclamation was not in response to his father. It was provoked by the arrival of his brother, who tapped on the door and let himself into the bedchamber. Greetings were exchanged. When he had enquired after the patient's condition, Christopher offered something to his father. The Dean of Gloucester looked suspiciously at the missive.

'What is this?' he asked.

'A letter,' said Christopher, handing it to him.

'From whom?'

'Look at the seal.'

'By Heaven!' said his father, glancing down. 'It's from the King.'

'I had an audience with him only this morning.'

'You see, Henry?' said the old man, opening the letter. 'Your brother has been summoned to the Palace. Think of the honour that bestows on the family. Why can't you bring such lustre to the name of Redmayne?' He read the letter slowly then let out a cry of surprise. 'Oh, dear boy,' he apologised, reaching out to touch Henry's arm. 'I've wronged you. Now I see why you concealed so much from me. I have the details here,' he said, raising the letter. 'In the King's own hand.'

Henry caught Christopher's eye and received a reassuring wink.

'What does His Majesty say?' said Henry, tentatively.

'The truth,' replied his father. 'When you were assaulted, you were engaged in secret affairs of state. Your bravery is commended. This is a signal honour, Henry. I take back all that I said about you. Well, most of it, anyway. I misjudged you horribly.'

'His Majesty asked me to pass on his personal thanks, Henry,' said Christopher. 'Without you, we'd never have achieved the result that we did. You were superb. I'll strive to model myself on you.'

'Did you hear that, Father?' said Henry, basking in the praise.

'I heard and I saw,' answered the old man, clutching the letter as if it were the tablet containing the Ten Commandments. 'I must show this to the Archbishop. Royal favour displayed to both my sons! That will send me back to Gloucester a contented man.'

'As long as it sends you back there,' murmured Henry.

There was a flurry of farewells as the Dean took his leave.

'I'd have been here earlier,' explained Christopher, 'but I went to Mary Hibbert's funeral.'

'Had you come any later, it might have been Henry Redmayne's funeral. Father almost talked me to death. Thank you for rescuing me, Christopher. Now, what news?'

'You know the bulk of it. The villains are all in Newgate and a woman in Greer Lane is answering awkward questions about the fact that the man who lodged in her upstairs room was the fourth rogue involved in the ambush. Harriet Gow has her stolen property back, I can at last concentrate on my house and Mr Bale can pound the streets of Baynard's Castle Ward again. He was so kind to Peter Hibbert at the church,' he remembered. 'You'd have thought the lad was his own son. Oh, and one big surprise. Mrs Gow turned up there as well.'

'Quite rightly. Mary Hibbert was in service with her.'

'The real surprise came from her choice of companion.'

'It wasn't her husband, was it?'

'No, Henry,' said his brother, 'but it was a Bartholomew Gow. He goes by the name of Martin Eldridge. I think that this experience has taught our nightingale the hazards of consorting with exalted company. She may be better off with a humble actor.' He gave a sympathetic smile. 'It's going to be a huge disappointment for Jasper Hartwell.'

'Why?'

'He's so infatuated with her that he conceived the absurd notion of somehow dissolving her marriage in order to make her his wife.'

Henry was aghast. 'Jasper Hartwell married to Harriet Gow! That's obscene, Christopher. It's like the Dean of Gloucester marrying the Queen of Sheba. In fact, I'd say that Father probably has more chance of being accepted than the idiotic Jasper ever will.'

'I'm sure that Mrs Gow will let him down lightly.'

'What sane woman would marry a ginger periwig on legs?'

'Don't mock my client. I need him.'

'I know what I need,' said Henry lecherously, 'but how can I have it when I'm in this condition? It's so unfair. I've just survived three hours of Father in homiletic vein. I need someone to cheer me up.'

'The lady will be here in due course, Henry.'

'Lady?'

'Well, you don't think I forgot to mention you, did you?' said Christopher. 'Harriet Gow showered Mr Bale and me with thanks. I didn't want you to miss out on the praise so I told her how you took a dreadful beating on her behalf.'

'And?'

'She insisted on coming to see you this very evening.'

'Harriet Gow?' Henry was glowing. 'Alone in my bedchamber?'

'Just the two of you.'

'Wonder of wonders!'

'Ask her nicely and she might even sing you a lullaby.'

'That would thrill me more than anything else.'

'What would?'

'To listen to my own amorous nightingale.'

A mischievous thought put a broad grin on Christopher's face.

'We could invite Father here to share the experience,' he said.

Henry Redmayne laughed so much that his ribs ached for an hour.

If you enjoyed this book here is a selection of other bestselling titles from Headline

REYKJAVÍK

BY GIGI & FRIENDS

HANDPICKED

MAP

Don't get lost, look inside

———————→

REYKJAVÍK
DOWNTOWN

REYKJAVÍK

I am picky and I am dead serious when it comes to creating the best experiences possible.

We all want to get the most out of our visit to a new city or country, right? Go home with experiences and memories we can't get anywhere else. In my opinion the best thing is to have a local friend giving me advice and pointing out places I would never have found otherwise. But unfortunately that's not an option in most cases. Therefore I have collected experiences that I, and my friends, recommend to our visitors, giving them an exceptional blend of local, unique, green and fun options to enjoy. So hold on to the HandPicked guides because that's as close to a local friend you'll get.

Enjoy your trip!
Gigi, Founder and editor

P.S. Guðbjörg Gissurardóttir is my full name and when I lived in New York people would ask me to say it out loud for amusement purposes. Try it?

This book belongs to:

_____

Get the **HandPicked Iceland App** or go to our webpage **www.handpickediceland.is**

We are also on Facebook, Twitter and Pinterest. Oh, and don't forget to post pictures of your travels by using #handpickediceland.

Published by Í Boði Náttúrunnar Magazine – inspired by Icelandic nature, wellbeing and sustainable living.

Björk Guðmundsdóttir

or simply known around the world as Bjork, is the famous singer and songwriter who put Reykjavík on the world map! She is also famous for her creative outfits, i.e. the swan outfit she wore at the 2001 Academy Awards.

UNESCO

Reykjavík was the UNESCO City of Literature 2011. The Icelandic language has remained relatively unchanged for centuries and there is a near 100% literacy rate.

As one of the safest

cities in the world, you can often see babies sleeping in their carriage outside cafés or shops!

Bæjarins bestu pylsur

Icelanders love their hot dogs and they prefer them 'with everything'. The most famous hot dog stand in Reykjavík is Bæjarins bestu, where former US President Bill Clinton devoured one during his visit.

WHY REYKJAVÍK?

Well, where do we begin? The people... helpful, easy
on the eyes and everyone speaks English.

Local cuisine

Local delicacies such as rotten shark
meat, half a singed sheep's head,
fermented skate, smoked lamb and
stock fish and the famous skyr is worth
trying, really they are. However, don't
get your knickers in a twist; we do have
many, many, great restaurants you can
choose a 'normal' meal from.

Music and nightlife

Reykjavík never stands still, with
live performances and concerts all
year round in addition to its popular
festivals, Icelandic Airwaves. Björk,
Sigur Rós, Emilíana Torrini, and Of
Monsters of Men are only a few of
our great musicians that come from
Reykjavík and all have been active
in Reykjavík's nightlife scene at
some point, which by the way, has
a reputation for being one of the
hottest places to party!

Arts and Design

Bursting with creativity, the city
offers a wealth of culture with its many
art galleries, and not to mention the
number of craft shops and up-and-
coming designers.

Activities

Take a dip in one of the many geo-
thermal outdoor pools, enjoy a riding
trip on the friendly Icelandic ponies or
take a whale-watching cruise from the
harbour – you don't want to sit around
all day in your hotel room do you?

Nature

With low buildings and being
surrounded by sea and mountains,
nature is always present in Reykjavík.
Even the Northern Lights can sometimes
be seen in the city in winter and it's just
a short drive out of town to get in touch
with nature.

If this does not turn you on... just turn
the pages for more inspiration!

GOOD TO KNOW

Websites

handpickediceland.is On our website you'll find all our favourite places in Reykjavík and around Iceland plus their locations via Google Maps.

vegvisir.is Helps you to get from A to B, shows the distance, estimated time of travel, fuel expense, asphalt or gravel roads and routes.

aurora-service.eu Gives information about aurora activity and how the Northern Lights might behave while you are in Iceland.

visitreykjavik.is Practical information for travellers and you can buy a special pass that give you access to some museums, pools and the city's buses.

safetravel.is Information on how to drive safely in Iceland. Conditions can be quite unlike what you are accustomed to back home.

App

HandPicked Iceland is super helpful and easy to use, covers both Reykjavík and Iceland.

Veður is a useful app for weather forecast, free and available in English.

Emergency calls

Ambulance, Fire & Police 112

Currency

Icelandic Krona (ISK)

Embassies & Consulates

USA	(+354) 562 9100
UK	(+354) 550 5100
France	(+354) 575 9600
Germany	(+354) 530 1100
China	(+354) 527 6688
Japan	(+354) 510 8600

Transport

bus.is A map and timetable along with a price list where you can plan your trips, both within Reykjavík and outside. Single ride 400 ISK One-day card 1000 ISK.
Phone (+354) 540 2700

hreyfill.is A private taxi and person-alised guided tours for smaller groups. No tips!
Phone (+354) 588 5522

Tourist Information

The Official Tourist Information Centre
Phone (+354) 590 1550
Aðalstræti 2

Mobile Phones

Local SIM cards are widely available

Internet

Free wi-fi is available almost everywhere.

Tips for Travellers with Disabilities

Wheelchair-accessible hotels in Reykjavík: whenwetravel.com
Places accessible for wheelchairs in Reykjavík: wheelmap.org

Public Holidays

Be aware that many places and restaurants can be closed on these dates.

January	1st New Year's Day
March/April	Easter: Holy Thursday
	Good Friday
	Easter Monday
April	First day of summer
	(first Thursday after
	April 18th)
May	1st Labour Day
	Ascension Day
May/June	Whit Sunday & Monday
June	17th National Day
August	Holiday of Commerce
	(the first Monday in August)
December	24th Christmas Eve
	25th Christmas Day
	26th Boxing Day

Longest Day & Night

Summer solstice 20.–21. June
The longest day in Reykjavík with daylight for 21 hours and 10 min
Winter solstice 21.–22. December
The shortest day in Reykjavík with daylight for 4 hours and 10 min

Festivals and Events

Go to **www.visitreykjavik.is** for details:
Jan/Feb Dark Music Days
February Reykjavík Winter Lights Festival, Meditation week
Feb/Mar Food & Fun Festival
March DesignMarch, Reykjavík Fashion Festival, Sónar Music and New Media Art, EVE Fanfest, Reykjavík Blues Festival, Reykjavík Folk Music Festival, Icelandic Music Experiments
April/May Reykjavík Children's Culture Festival, Reykjavík Shorts&Docs Festival
May Raflost Festival of Electronic Arts
May/June Reykjavík Arts Festival, Secret Solstice Festival
July Ingólfshátíð Viking Festival
August Reykjavík Jazz Festival, Reykjavík Gay Pride, Reykjavík Culture Night, Reykjavík Bacon Festival, Reykjavík Dance Festival
September Reykjavík International Literary Festival
Sept/Oct Reykjavík International Film Festival (Riff)
November Iceland Airwaves International Music Festival, Reykjavik Young Art Festival, Craft and design tradeshow.

Did you know...

Reykjavík is the world's northernmost
capital city where there is only four
hours of sunlight in December, but
don't despair because there's 21 hours
of sunlight in June.

EAT

RESTAURANTS

Fish has been the livelihood of Icelanders through
the ages, or as the common saying goes, 'life is
salted fish'! (Meaning life has its ups and downs).
Fish is also Iceland's main export.

Restaurants in Reykjavík

Dining in cosmopolitan Reykjavík is becoming increasingly sophisticated and in only a few years, the collection of quality restaurants has exploded. Today, chefs place more emphasis on locality and quality of the available ingredients in a contemporary style. The most-used ingredients in Icelandic cuisine are fish or seafood, lamb and dairy along with seabirds and waterfowl, and then adding dried seaweed, herbs and berries for taste. You don't have to be a carnivore to enjoy Reykjavík's foodie scene though. Vegetarians or vegans can eat well – there is a healthy selection of vegetarian restaurants to choose from, and many include a veggie dish on their menu.

Did you know...

— **The tap water** is pure, free and drinkable.

— **Lunch is cheaper** than dinner in fancy places.
  Plan accordingly if you're on a budget.

— **We recommend** reserving a table when going out
  for dinner, especially at weekends.

....

A table for two
Borð fyrir tvo

....

....

Can I have the bill, please
Get ég fengið reikninginn, takk

....

ROADHOUSE

If you want a hearty meal made from scratch, you will just love this place. The menu reels off the best and juiciest burgers in town (including a veggie version), steaks and succulent baby back-ribs that are low and slow smoked on the spot, barbecued with their own Road-house sauce. It showcases the greatest of American dishes – with an Icelandic twist. Try the homemade fries from real potatoes topped with bacon and cheese for starters, and don't leave without downing the scrumptious milkshake, 'Peanut butter Lover', for dessert.

🕐 **Mon–Wed** 11.30am–21.30pm
Thu 11.30am–22pm
Fri–Sat 11.30am–23pm
Sun 12am–21.30pm

🏠 **Snorrabraut 56**
📞 **571 4200**
🌐 **roadhouse.is**

Cuisines American
Main Dish ISK 2.100–3.500

KAFFI LOKI

Go upstairs and enjoy the view over Hallgrímskirkja and the enormous wall painting from Norse mythology while letting your palate go absolutely native. Here the Icelandic culinary heritage, much cherished by islanders and visitors alike, is the focus. The freshly baked flatbread and rye bread, fish stew, and lamb soup are just a few must-eats and they taste exceptionally good in this unpretentious café – and so does their incredible rye bread ice cream for dessert!

🕐 **Mon–Sat**   9am–21pm
    Sun   11am–21pm
🏠 **Lokastígur 28**
📞 **466 2828**
🌐 **loki.is**

Cuisines   Icelandic
Main Dish   ISK 1500–3500

ARGENTÍNA STEAKHOUSE

A favourite steakhouse for many locals, serving dinner thanks to a mouth-watering menu, Argentinean style of course. Warm and cosy with a crackling open fire, Argentina offers quality Icelandic grass-fed beef, tender lamb and excellent seafood, all grilled on wooden charcoal. Only the best quality is good enough for their customers, and the same also goes for the service.

🕐 **Sun–Thu**   18pm–24pm
   Fri–Sat   17.30pm–1pm
🏠 **Barónsstígur 11**
📞 **551 9555**
🌐 **argentina.is**

Cuisines	Grill
	Steakhouse
Main Dish	ISK 3.900–7.200

HVERFISGATA 12

An eclectic mix of American rustic, old carnival and part museum, this pizza joint has multiple rooms, but still manages to give a sense of being private and personal. With a comfy bar and a restaurant that revolves around gourmet pizzas, starters, side courses, cocktails and draught beers. The pizza toppings are fresh, out of the ordinary and they summarize the dramatic interior by set designer Hálfdán Pedersen.

🕐 **Mon–Sun**   11.30pm–23pm
          Closes at 1am

🏠 **Hverfisgata 12**

📞 **437 0203**

🌐 **hverfisgata12.is**

Cuisines   Pizza
Main Dish ISK 2.100–2.850

DILL RESTAURANT

Small but stylish with its raw concrete interior, intimate vibes and sporting an open kitchen where you can enjoy watching pros at work. Gunnar Karl Gíslason is the executive chef at this restaurant inspired by the New Nordic Cuisine Manifesto.

Using what surrounds them and embracing the Old Icelandic traditions in their own way, the team here allows the ingredients to shine in their own simplicity and, most importantly, have fun while they are at it.

Wed–Sat 18pm–22pm

Hverfisgata 12

552 1522

dillrestaurant.is

Cuisines   European, Scandinavian

Main Dish   ISK 7.900–11.900

3, 5 or 7 course menu

GARÐURINN

The only pure vegetarian restaurant in town. Not a vego? You'll still be amazed at the tasty and satisfying fare served with freshly baked bread at this small, modest place. Open for lunch as well as afternoon refreshments, such as tea or organic fair-trade coffee with a delightful slice of cake. During summertime, check out the back garden.

🕐 **Mon–Fri**	11am–18.30pm
Wed	11am–17pm
Sat	12am–17pm

🏠 **Klapparstígur 37**

📞 **561 2345**

🌐 **heart-garden.is**

Cuisines	Healthy
	Vegetarian
Main Dish	ISK 900–2.800

SNAPS BISTRO

Whether you're in the mood for lunch, brunch or dinner, or just hanging out at the bar with some snacks, this is the place to visit. With French-inspired cuisine, your taste buds will be tickled by the first-rate menu and quality wine selection. Comfortable lighting, newspaper-covered walls and a relaxed and intimate atmosphere, it's popular among the local crowd.

🕐	**Mon–Sun**	7am–10am	📞	**511 6677**	
	Sun–Thu	11.30am–23pm	🌐	**snaps.is**	
	Fri–Sat	11.30am–24pm		**Cuisines**	French
🏠	**Þórsgata 1**			**Main Dish**	ISK 3.400–4.400

ÞRÍR FRAKKAR

Anything oceanic – fish, whales, even birds, has been the focus of this popular restaurant in Reykjavík since 1989. It is one of the few family-run restaurants in the city and will sustain you with ex-cellent, friendly service and fair prices (even better during lunch-time). The focus is on seafood, but they also offer soups and even a vegetarian dish. The fish stew is the best you will ever taste!

🕐 **Mon–Fri** 11.30am–14.30
        18pm–22pm
   Sat–Sun 18pm–23pm
🏠 **Baldursgata 14**

📞 **552 3939**
🌐 **3frakkar.com**
   Cuisines Seafood
   Main Dish ISK 3.600–5.800

OSTABÚÐIN RESTAURANT

A gourmand's paradise where cheese and other delicatessens laden the shelves, and where you can enjoy a healthy, tasty lunch in the nice restaurant downstairs. Slurp on the soup of the day or the fish which is always the freshest they can get their hands on, or enjoy an Italian bruschetta and a salad dish, depending on the chef's quirks. You won't be able to leave without being tempted by the deli on your way out.

🕐 **Mon–Sun** 10am–21pm

🏠 **Skólavörðustígur 8**

📞 **562 2772**

🌐 **ostabudin.is**

Cuisines	Fish
Main Dish	ISK 790–4.200

BERGSSON

A hip restaurant with a vision. Little in size but big at heart, it draws the smart crowd cherishing health and wellbeing above all. Salads, soups, homemade bread and delicious Mediterranean dishes made from the best raw ingre-dients they can get their hands on. Whether you want fast or slow food, cold or warm, it caters for your wish to stay healthy and full of energy through breakfast or brunch, and dinner during the weekdays.

🕐 **Mon–Fri**	7am–21pm	
Sat–Sun	7am–17pm	
🏠 **Templarasund 3**		
📞 **571 1822**		

🌐 **bergsson.is**	
Cuisines	Healthy
	Mediterranean
Main Dish	ISK 1.690–2.290

FISH COMPANY

Situated almost underground with stone walls, subtle lighting, wooden poles and a lounge by a raging open fire. The menu takes you on an imaginative journey around the island's fishing grounds and the world's herbal gardens. Whether it's for lunch or dinner, you'll leave content and maybe even amazed at the endless possibilities of preparing seafood or Icelandic lamb. Considered one of the best in seafood for years, enjoy an alfresco meal on their cobblestoned terrace in summer.

🕐 **Mon–Fri** 11.30am–14.30pm
            17.30pm–23.30pm
Sat–Sun 17.30pm–23.30pm

🏠 **Vesturgata 2a**

📞 **552 5300**

🌐 **fishcompany.is**

Cuisines	Seafood
	International
Main Dish	ISK 3.900–7.900

ICELANDIC FISH & CHIPS

When in Iceland, gourmands have no reason to stay away from delicacies such as fish and chips. Grab a bite at this open and perky place, next to the Volcano museum, where the chefs have developed this popular dish into a healthy meal. Using only Omega 3 oils, the freshest fish, spelt batter, oven-baked chips and the local skyr for different flavoured dips, you won't want to miss this organic bistro at Tryggvagata 11.

🕐 **All week**   12am–21pm

🏠 **Tryggvagata 11**

📞 **511 1118**

🌐 **fishandchips.is**

Cuisines	Seafood
Main Dish	ISK 1.290–4.790

KOPAR RESTAURANT

Cosy and romantic surrounded by stone-clad walls boasting a rustic chic interior and waterfront views smack on the old harbour. The fish is super fresh and this restaurant is possibly the only place in town with Icelandic rock crab on the menu. Emphasis is placed on local and sustainable fare, serving hearty, delicious meals for all – youngster or oldie, veggie or carni. If you want to get more sea bound, ask for their festive sailing tours.

Mon–Thu	11.30am–22.30pm
Fri	11.30am–23.30pm
Sat	12am–23.30pm
Sun	18pm–22.30pm

Geirsgata 3
567 2700
koparrestaurant.is

Cuisines	Contemporary
Main Dish	ISK 3.990–6.500

GLÓ

Health food that tastes rich and exotic – even mouth-watering! Nutritious, aromatic, colourful and pampering to your taste buds, this restaurant is truly one of a kind. Founded and run by the foremost raw-food cook in the world, Solla, your taste buds will thank you, whether your choice is the soup of the day, light meat dishes, vegetarian or raw. Try the juice Bar or sip a quality coffee or tea with a slice of cake or sample their exceptional raw-food dessert.

🕐 **Mon–Fri**	11am–21pm	🌐 **glo.is**	
Sat–Sun	11.30am–21pm	**Cuisines**	Healthy, Raw
🏠 **Laugavegur 20b**			Vegetarian
📞 **553 1111**		**Main Dish**	ISK 1.250–2.100

EXTRAS
EAT

Hornið
Italian
Hafnarstræti 15
551 3340
hornid.is

Coocoo's nest
Italian
Grandagarður 23
552 5454
Facebook

Grillmarkaðurinn
Steakhouse
Lækjargata 2a
571 7777
grillmarkadurinn.is

KBar
Korean
Laugavegur 74
571 6666
Facebook

Fridrik V
Scandinavian
Laugavegur 60
461 5775
fridrikv.is

Kol
Seafood
Skólavörðustígur 40
517 7474
kolrestaurant.is

Sjávargrillið
Seafood
Skólavörðustígur 14
571 1100
sjavargrillid.com

DRINK

CAFÉS AND BARS

Víking Gull 5,6% Lager the most popular beer in Iceland,
strong with lots of hops with both maize and sugar, which makes
it less filling but more refreshing such as European pilsner.
Gæðingur Pale Ale 4,6% Ale Unfiltered ale with a dregs
is fermented again after sealing it with a stopple,
which keeps the flavours developing further.
Kaldi 5% Lager The first micro brewed beer produced in
Iceland. Brewing based on a centuries-old Czech tradition.

A Drink or a Cup of Coffee?

In the middle of 18th century when coffee was first introduced to Icelanders, it was considered a luxury only for the wealthy. Then, a century later, standard equipment for coffee-making was found in every household with self-respect, and the public had caught the taste for coffee.

A common politeness in Iceland was, and still is, to offer a cup of coffee when people come to visit; it's a conversation opener and a welcoming gesture. When coffee houses started to pop up in Reykjavík in the middle of the 20th century we quickly caught up with the Italians. Now there are a few companies and some small coffee shops burning and grinding their own beans for maximum quality. Reykjavík also has plenty of pubs to suit a multitude of different moods and that cater to increasing demand for quality micro beer. Bars do not charge an entrance fee; however, expect to pay a small charge for entrance to live-music venues.

Either way, you're blessed for choice whether it's a beer or a brew.

Did you know...

— **Beer** was first allowed in Iceland in 1989

— **Icelanders** generally prefer coffee over tea

— **You can only buy alcohol** in special stores called Vínbúðin (locally called Ríkið) – government owned liquor stores

Cheers!
Skál!

Where are the toilets?
Hvar eru klósettin?

KEX HOSTEL

'Sæmundur í sparifötunum' is the gastro 'pub' at Kex Hostel, housed in an old biscuit factory and furnished with salvaged materials. Kex is extremely popular with the cool crowd, best known for its lively music scene where celebrated and upcoming musicians meet for concerts and jam-sessions. It is swanky with an exciting, ever-changing menu as the chef likes to use his creative flair while focusing on wholesome, local ingredients.

🕐 **All week** Until 23pm

🏠 **Skúlagata 28**

📞 **561 6060**

🌐 **kexhostel.is**

REYKJAVÍK ROASTERS

A cosy little café with grandfather chairs and old furniture where the aroma of freshly roasted coffee beans fills every corner. It's the freshest brew in town as the baristas do their own roasting and grinding on the premises. A real asset to Reykjavík's coffee culture with award-winning staff and yummy breads and cakes. Grab a bag of their freshly roasted coffee on your way out or you can sign up for a workshop on how to make better coffee at home.

🕐	**Mon–Fri**	8am–18pm
	Sat–Sun	9am–18pm
🏠	**Kárastígur 1**	
📞	**517 5535**	
🌐	**reykjavikroasters.is**	

SANDHOLT BAKERY

A family run bakery for almost a century! Great coffee and delicious pastries, cakes or cookies, or try out some of the light dishes at this surprisingly roomy coffee house with its comfy sofas and light décor. They make the best sourdough bread by using a unique 100 year old method, not to mention the assortment of lip-smacking chocolates handmade by Ásgeir Sandholt, pastry chef and chocolatier – the 5th in the World Chocolate Masters in 2011!

🕐 **Opens** 6.30am

🏠 **Laugavegur 36**

📞 **551 3524**

🌐 **Facebook**

MOKKA KAFFI

Espresso, art and cultural atmosphere since 1958. This old-fashioned café is run by the same owners and the unchanged interior is deep-rooted in Icelandic culture and has a special place in the heart of every bohemian, both as a café and an ambitious art gallery. The first in Iceland to serve real espresso, cappuccino, and café latte, and tempting you with their famous house waffles. Drink in the echoes of the '60s!

🕐 **Daily**   9am–18.30pm
   In Summer 9am–21pm
🏠 **Skólavörðustígur 3a**
📞 **552 1174**
🌐 **mokka.is**

LOFT HOSTEL

The café and bar on the fourth floor of this trendy new hostel is a hidden secret in central Reykjavík. It offers Chemex coffee, wine and beer from local breweries, as well as sweet and savoury treats. Awesome soup at lunch time frequently veggie style with sourdough bread. The hostel's 40-sq-ft balcony boasts a great view over the city and it's precisely the spot to enjoy bright summer nights or the Northern Lights during winter. Certified by Nordic Ecolabel, The Swan.

🕐 **All week**   10am–23pm
🏠 **Bankastræti 7**
📞 **553 8140**
🌐 **lofthostel.is**

EXTRAS
BAR

Kaldi Bar
Laugavegur 20b
581 2200/Facebook

Kaffibarinn
Bergstaðastræti 1
551 1588/Facebook

Microbar
Austurstræti 6
847 9084/Facebook

Slippbarinn
Mýrargata 2
560 8080/slippbarinn.is

Barberbar
Laugavegur 66-68
553 9366/Facebook

Ölstofa Kormáks og Skjaldar
Vegamótastíg 4
552 4687/Facebook

Ský Lounge & Bar
Ingólfsstræti 1
595 8545/skylounge.is

Skúli Craft Bar
Aðalstræti 9
519 6455/Facebook

EXTRAS
CAFÉ

Kaffifélagið
Skólavörðustíg 10
520 8420/kaffifelagid.is

Stofan
Vesturgata 3
546 1842/Facebook

Café Babalú
Skólavörðustígur 22
555 8845/Facebook

Iða/Zimsen húsið
Vesturgata 2a
511 5004/Facebook

Tíu Dropar
Laugavegur 27
551 9380/Facebook

Te og Kaffi
Austurstræti 18
660 7934/teogkaffi.is

Kaffi Tár
Bankastræti 8
511 4540/kaffitar.is

FUN

ACTIVITES

There are about 20 swimming pools in
the Greater Reykjavík area and even
more hot tubs. The hot water comes
from hot springs and when you are not
used to it, it can smell like rotten eggs!

Playtime

The Icelandic Sagas portray an intriguing picture of epoch-making events such as settlement and Christianity, but they also inform about what people did for entertainment back then – they fought, drank, sang and told stories, and challenged each other in various skills based on testing strength and agility. Competition in various sports and strength is still popular; along with singing, drinking and such, but having fun has also grown into so much more. You won't run out of things to do in Reykjavík – there's something for all ages.

Did you know...

— **Being an island** and a fishing nation, everyone in Iceland is required to learn to swim at school

— **Sea swimming** is getting more popular among locals, even in winter when the ocean temperature can plummet to minus 5 degrees Celsius (brrrrrrr...).

— **There are 23 different** species of whale around Iceland and you can watch these majestic mammals just outside Reykjavík harbour.

What's your name?
Hvað heitir þú?

This was fun!
Þetta var skemmtilegt!

SUNDHÖLLIN / SWIMMING

This geothermal swimming pool has served locals for decades. It has an indoor pool with two diving boards, two outdoor hot tubs and a sauna. Enjoy a walk to this fabulous destination for some serious fun and grab a classic Icelandic hot dog afterwards.

🕐 **Mon–Thu**   6.30am–22pm
   Fri   6.30–20pm
   Sat   8am–16pm
   Sun   10am–18pm
🏠 **Barónstíg**
📞 **411 5350**

Entering this barber shop is like step-ping back in time. Containing chairs that have served three generations, you just walk in off the street and have a haircut while listening to music and getting to know the barber, who is quite a character and also a musician and an assembler of amazing ship models that can be seen at the shop.

🕐 **Mon–Fri**   10am–18pm

🏠 **Laugavegur 62**

📞 **562 2240**

A break from the 'must see' hustle, this beautiful hidden spot is a perfect little detour from your stroll downtown. Here you can rest and view mystical and captivating sculptures in bronze casts by Iceland's first sculptor – Einar Jónsson. Open year-round and free of charge, entry is at the back of the Einar Jónsson Museum, just across the street from Hallgrímskirkja.

🕒 Eiríksgata

🏠 551 3797

📞 lej.is

SALSA ICELAND

This is for people who love to dance salsa or would like to learn. This dance studio offers free salsa nights every Thursday at RIO sports bar at Hverfisgata 46. Free drop-in lessons for beginners at 8pm, Taxi dancers (paid dance partners) from the student team, and open dancefloor for everyone from 9pm to midnight. Great fun!

🕐 **Thu**   8pm–12pm
🏠 **Hverfisgata 46**
📞 **511 2422**
🌐 **salsaiceland.is**

KOLAPORTIÐ / MARKET

Reykjavík's longstanding weekend
market, the merging point of rich and
poor, young and old. With a wonderful
seafood market and fresh farm produce Icelandic style, it also offers a
vast variety of stalls selling new and
second-hand goods. Quite the place
for excellent bargains, rare treats
and lots of fun.

🕐 **Sat–Sun**   11am–17pm

🏠 **Tryggvagata 19**

📞 **562 5030**

🌐 **kolaportid.is**

Why not explore Reykjavík from a different angle? At the same time you can go whale watching, observe cute puffins on the Puffin Express, enjoy adventures such as sea angling where the crew will barbecue your catch, or try the Northern Lights by boat tour if you're here in winter. Special Tours is a member of the Blue-Flag Eco-label and is a gold member in Vakinn, Iceland's quality system for tourism.

🕐 **Open daily** Check for booking

🏠 **Ægisgarður 13**

📞 **560 8800**

🌐 **specialtours.is**

43

REYKJAVÍK CITY HALL

Located at the north end of the capital's big pond, Tjörnin, you might stumble upon some cultural events here. Regardless, check out the huge topographical model of Iceland and you'll also find a tourist information desk and a restaurant. Enjoy the pond's birdlife through the vast windows while enjoying refreshments at the seafood restaurant Við Tjörnina.

🕐	**Mon–Fri**	8am–19pm
	Sat–Sun	12am–18pm
🏠	**Tjarnargata 11**	
📞	**411 1111**	
🌐	**reykjavik.is**	

NAUTHOLSVIK
GEOTHERMAL BEACH

Ylströndin is the only golden beach in Reykjavík and a very popular place for sea swimming and sunbathing in summer. Here you can find a manmade lagoon where the cold sea and hot water merge into one, plus an outdoor 38°C hot tub and steam bath. There's a service centre with a changing room and showers. Open year-round, check for opening hours. Afterwards try Nauthóll restaurant for a real treat.

🕐 Call for opening hours

🏠 Nauthólsvegur

📞 511 6630

🌐 nautholsvik.is

WHALES OF
ICELAND EXHIBITION

Take a journey through an 'ocean' of whales at the biggest whale exhibition in Europe. Here you can learn in an interactive way about these mammals in a magical space. Walk among more than 20 real-size models of the species found along the Icelandic coast, and take a closer look at these gentle giants of the sea.

🕐 **Open daily** 9am–18pm
   In summer 9am–19pm
🏠 **Fiskislóð 23–25**
📞 **571 0077**
🌐 **whalesoficeland.is**

EXTRAS
FUN

Kramhúsið
Dance studio
Skólavörðustígur 12
551 5103
kramhusid.is

Bíó Paradís
Indie Movie Theatre
Hverfisgata 54
412 7711
bioparadis.is

Reykjavík Bike Tours
Ægisgarður 7
694 8956
icelandbike.com

Viðey Island
By Ferry
Old Harbour and Skarfabakki Pier
533 3033
videy.com

EXTRAS
KIDS

The Family Park & Zoo
Laugardalur
411 5900
husdyragardur.is

Árbæjarsafn
Open-Air Museum
Kistuhylur
411 6300
reykjavikmuseum.is

The Icelandic Horse
Riding Tours
Sturlugata 3, Fjárborg
434 7979
islenskihesturinn.is

Laugardagslaugin
Outdoor Swimming Pool
Sundlaugarvegur,
Laugardalur
411 5100
laugardalslaug.is

CULTURE

ART & HISTORY

Leifur Eiríksson was the Icelandic explorer
who was the first to discover North Amerika
– 500 years before Christopher Columbus!

Something to Appreciate

Reykjavík is bursting with a vibrant arts scene that has been shaped through history by the roughness of nature, public closeness and innovative souls; it's dynamic, old-style and contemporary. Visual art in Iceland before the 20th century was mostly associated with literature. Today, however, it hosts an array of visual and contemporary art – Reykjavík is a treat for all art lovers.

Did you know...

— **Most museums** are free for those under 18 and are closed on Mondays.

— **The best view** over the city is from the tower of Hallgrímskirkja.

— **Ingólfur Arnarson,** a Norwegian refugee, and his wife Hallveig were the first permanent settlers of Iceland and gave Reykjavík its name in 874.

— **Reykjavík** means Smoky Bay. The city was named after steam rising from geothermal vents.

How do I get to...?
Hvernig kemst ég...?

Thank you
Takk fyrir

HALLGRÍMSKIRKJA

Andreas Warler

Not just a magnificent building that towers over central Reykjavík. It's a terrific vantage point (for a small fee) to view the city's colourful houses and scenery, but there's also a great music hall and a gallery. Check the church's program for events and services. It will be worth your while as Hallgrímskirkja has a vast 5275-pipe organ and one of the leading choirs in Iceland. Obviously music plays a big part in all services.

🕐 **Open daily** 9am–17pm

🏠 **Hallgrímstorg 1**

📞 **510 1000**

🌐 **hallgrimskirkja.is**

TÝSGALLERÍ

Walk through the orange door and
enter this tiny intimate space that
features ambitious individual art
exhibitions. Here you can also buy
a piece of art crafted by recognised
artists. It's the first to offer visual
descriptions to improve access
for the blind and visually impaired.

🕑 Thu–Sat   13pm–17pm

🏠 Týsgata 3

📞 699 5652

   842 5642

🌐 tysgalleri.is

MENGI/CULTURAL HOUSE

Björgvin Sigurðsson

A little bit of everything, hosting music, an art store and offering exhibitions that focus on experimental art. You'll find diverse musical events going on every Thursday, Friday and Saturday. On top of that they have their own record label.

🕐 **Wed–Sat**   12am–18pm
    Thu–Sat   20.30pm–23pm
🏠 **Óðinsgata 2**
📞 **588 3644**
🌐 **mengi.net**

KLING & BANG GALLERY

Take in the challenging impressions and contexts of creative thought by both young and older artists, national and international featuring cutting-edge exhibitions. The art space changes depending on the exhibition, so it's like entering a new frame every time you check out a show.

🕐 **Thu–Sun** 14pm–18pm

🏠 **Hverfisgata 42**

📞 **696 2209**

🌐 **this.is**

REYKJAVÍK MUSEUM OF PHOTOGRAPHY

A great way to get a sense of cultural diversity captured in contemporary photographs exhibited and accessible for all. In 2014 it was chosen as one of 10 best free museums in Europe according to The Guardian.

🕒 **Mon–Thu** 12am–19pm
Fri 12am–18pm
Weekends 13pm–17pm

🏠 **Tryggvagata 15 - 6th floor**

📞 **411 6300**

🌐 ljosmyndasafnreykjavikur.is

NATIONAL GALLERY OF ICELAND

Appreciate the principal collection of Icelandic visual art, mainly from the 19th and 20th centuries. Exhibitions are held regularly in three different spaces so you can be sure to find something interesting. Get a taste of Icelandic culture through local and international Icelander's perspectives. It's also great to visit the museum's beautiful building, shop and wonderful café.

🕐 **Tue–Sun** 11am–17pm
   In summer 10am–17pm
🏠 **Fríkirkjuvegur 7**
📞 **515 9600**
🌐 **listasafn.is**

THE NATIONAL MUSEUM OF ICELAND

Strap yourself in for a journey through history and see Icelandic treasures, a cultural heritage from the nation's earliest settlement to the modern day. Walk into the Viking Age or check out the new interactive exhibition that will delight all ages. Don't miss the museum shop or the café on the first floor.

🕐 **Tue–Sun** 11am–17pm

🏠 **In summer** 10am–17pm

📞 **Suðurgötu 41**

🌐 **530 2200**

thjodminjasafn.is

NÝLÓ
THE LIVING ART MUSEUM

Your artistic cravings will be satisfied here. Walk into this venue for a new kind of contemporary art. Nýló lures with events beyond art exhibitions such as live performances, music, poetry readings, theatre and so much more. It's a fun 30-minute ride on bus 12 from Hlemmur. Admission free.

🕐 **Tue–Sat** 12am–17pm
and by an appointment

🏠 **Völvufell 13–21**

📞 **551 4350**

🌐 nylo.is

EXTRAS
CULTURE

I8 Gallery
Tryggvagata 16
551 3666/i8.is

Hverfisgallerí
Hverfisgata 4
537 4007
hverfisgalleri.is

Kaffistofa Nemendagallerí
Student Gallery
Hverfisgata 42b
Facebook

Cultural House
Exhibitions
Hverfisgata 15
530 2210/Facebook

Saga Museum
Viking Wax Museum
Grandagarður 2
511 1517
sagamuseum.is

Árbæjarsafn
Open-Air Museum
Kistuhylur
411 6300
reykjavikmuseum.is

Literary and Culture Walks
Vesturgata 1
590 1520
bokmenntaborgin.is

The Settlement Exhibition
Aðalstræti 16
411 6370
minnjasafnreykjavikur.is

SHOP

DESIGN & CRAFT

The Icelandic 'lopapeysa' has kept the nation warm for more than a thousand years and you can be sure to find one at the oldest gift store in Iceland, Rammagerðin.

Innovation and Creativity

Local design has grown rapidly during the last decade and is now an important industry. History, local materials and a touch of nostalgia has influenced Icelandic designers during recent years in an attempt to define and celebrate their identity in a globalised world. Lack of material, resources and knowledge has given birth to a creative mayhem and a drive to be reckoned with.

Eco-consciousness has become an important factor among Icelandic designers who aim to create structures that last or can be re-used and strive to leave as few footprints as possible on the earth. March is a good time to visit Reykjavík and explore the craft and design scene. The Design March and Craft & Design exhibition, held in the City Hall, take place then.

Did you know...

— **The wool** of the Icelandic sheep is an even ratio of fine and coarse wool which makes it lighter, water repellent, and heat regulating, keeping the skin dry by letting out perspiration, and is easy to wash.

— **Design March** showcases the best of Icelandic diverse design scene and attracts foreigners as well as thousands of Icelanders

How much is it?
Hvað kostar þetta?

It's beautiful
Þetta er fallegt

GILBERT WATCHMAKER

Want to get into Gilbert's Hall of Fame? Tobey Maguire, Tom Cruise and Yoko Ono are among those who wear the exquisite JS watches, which are designed and assembled by hand in Iceland. Only the highest quality materials are used to produce the watches and every single detail has been given the time needed for perfection. Here you get a unique opportunity to meet the watchmakers and observe them assembling and testing their masterpieces.

🕐 **Mon–Fri**   10am–18pm

   Sat   10am–16pm

🏠 **Laugavegur 62**

📞 **551 4100**

🌐 **jswatch.com**

SPARK DESIGN SPACE

The only design gallery in the country, exhibiting outstanding Icelandic design projects. Every three months a new exhibition is produced. You can even purchase unique pieces from former exhibitions in the shop. If you are into design, this is the place to go to get an inside scoop from Sigga, the owner.

🕐 **Mon–Sat** 10am–18pm
Sat 12am–16pm
🏠 **Klapparstígur 33**
📞 **552 2656**
🌐 **sparkdesignspace.com**

Kogga is Iceland's most revered ceramic artist and innovator in her field. The gallery/studio has, in time, become a fixture of downtown's history, being at it for more than 30 years. Kogga's unique technique offers refined and beautiful designed ceramic objects that are timeless and are a vision for sore eyes. Ask for the popular pieces designed with motives from the work of her late husband, Magnús Kjartansson, one of Iceland's most loved painters. No two pieces are the same.

🕐	**Mon–Fri**	9am–18pm
	Sat	10am–14pm
🏠	**Vesturgata 5**	
📞	**552 6036**	
🌐	**kogga.is**	

RAVENS

Don't miss Ravens shop on your
leisurely stroll along Laugavegur. It is
a treasure trove of authentic Inuit art,
Arctic fur, exclusive bags, shoes, skin
rugs and custom-made knives. There
you can find nature collectables from
Greenland and Iceland along with a
variety of other exceptional curiosities,
including Greenlandic/Danish Isaksen
design. Fair triad is the goal with
everything exclusive and carefully
selected to radiate the warmth and
colour of the northern soul.

🕐 **Mon–Sat**   10am–18.30pm

🏠 **Laugavegur 15**

📞 **551 1080**

   ravens.is

🌐 **Facebook**   **Ravens**

AURUM

The award-winning jewellery designer
Guðbjörg K. Ingvarsdóttir is the name
behind the unique Icelandic brand,
Aurum. The jewellery collection is
classical, yet modern, exceptionally
feminine and rich in detail. It is
modelled on nature and her irregular
shapes. With fleeting snowdrops and
the movements of butterflies delicately
captured into the fine metal pieces,
this design challenges your sense
of balance and form.

🕐 **Mon–Fri**	10am–18pm
Sat	11am–17pm
Sun	12am–17pm

🏠 **Bankastræti 4**

📞 **551 2770**

🌐 **aurum.is**

KRAUM

Located in the oldest house in Reykjavík where contemporary designers and craftspeople display their traditional and modern Icelandic work. The joy of creativity is in the blood and you will be surprised at how many good artists, designers and craftspeople can be found here. Using wool, natural stones and wood, to livestock hides and bones, as well as fish skin; the innovative soul will always find a way to design a treasure.

🕐 **Mon–Fri**   9am–18pm
     Sat   10am–17pm
     Sun   12am–17pm

🏠 **Aðalstræti 10**

📞 **517 7797**

🌐 **kraum.is**

KIRSUBERJATRÉÐ

A historical general store with a new purpose offering a variety of Icelandic design and craft. A group of women with a different approach to creativity make the store a unique blend of styles in art, craft and design for those who long for originality, oddity and peculiarity. With its wooden floors, great windows, old cash register, spacious counters and shelves all the way up to the ceiling, you'll get the feel of the old trade while finding pleasure in contemporary design.

🕐 **Mon–Fri**   11am–18pm
    Sat   11am–17pm
🏠 **Vesturgata 4**
📞 **562 8990**
🌐 **Kirs.is**

KAOLIN CERAMIC GALLERY

A gallery run by nine ceramic artists each with their own unique style. Snug, bright and full of handmade treasures and sculptures where every piece has its own texture and unpredictable pattern depending on the artist – and some pieces just happen. Whether it's choosing a beautiful gift, or just cheering yourself up buying a unique cup for your morning coffee ritual, this is your place.

🕐 **Mon–Fri** 10am–18pm
   Sat 10am–16pm
🏠 **Skólavörðustígur 22**
📞 **555 2060**
🌐 **kaolingallery.com**

EXTRAS
DESIGN & CRAFT

Rammagerðin
Icelandic Gift Store
Bankastræti 9,
Skólavörðustígur 20
535 6690
rammagerdin.is

Orr
Modern Jewellery
Bankastræti 11
511 6262/orr.is

Gullkistan Jewellery
for the National Costume
Frakkastígur 10
551 3160
thjodbuningasilfur.is

Skúmaskot
Art and Craft
Laugavegur 23
663 1013
Facebook

Reykjavík Drapers Union
Handbags etc
Skólavörðustígur 17a
781 8801
Facebook

The Handknitting
Association of Iceland
Icelandic Wool
Skólavörðustígur 19
552 1890
handknit.is

FASHION

CLOTHES & ACCESSORIES

Icelandic design is both fresh
and fun to wear with a bold mixture
of colours and styles.

A Sense of Style

Fashion is a matter that is close to most Icelander's hearts and typically locals dress according to their sense of style, not the weather. When going out for a night on the town, they venture even further outside their comfort zone and the dress code is usually very stylish and upmarket. The contemporary Icelandic fashion is however, unconventional, rebellious and embraces a new way of thinking. It is a small, but fast-growing, industry where designers are not constrained by tradition. The annual Reykjavík Fashion Festival takes place in March and highlights the most recent works by Icelandic fashion designers.

Did you know...

— **The weather** changes several times in one day and you can practically experience all four seasons when taking a walk in town.

Do you have this in my size?
Áttu þetta í minni stærð?

How much is this?
Hversu mikið kostar þetta?

HERRAFATAVERZLUN
KORMÁKS & SKJALDAR

Men's shoes, shirts, suits, and hats, caps and canes. The trendsetter for gentlemen of all ages offers quality brands in ready-to-wear clothing and accessories as well as its own line of clothing. With a distinctive periodic theme and warm atmosphere built on the good values of quality products and customer service, this is the best kept secret in Iceland and keeps Reykjavík's men looking sharp.

🕐 **Mon–Sat**   11am–18pm

🏠 **Laugavegur 59 – Basement**

📞 **511 1817**

🌐 **herrafataverslun.is**

SPAKSMANNSSPJARIR

With an Icelandic designer of classical utilitarian clothes, this is one of the coolest shops in town. The unique designs are housed in sections, and you can wear them in a multitude of ways, separated into many pieces and pieced back together for a completely different look. Using only high-quality textiles and abstaining from fashion trends, the pieces will last a lifetime.

🕐 **Mon–Fri** 10am–18pm
Sat 10am–17pm
In June, July and August also on Sun 12am–17pm

🏠 **Bankastræti 11**

📞 **551 2090**

🌐 **spaks.is**

GLORIA

Gloria stands for modern simplicity – casual daily wear with a dash of unusual influences that suits women of all ages. It is the shop behind the popular JET KORINE label, locally designed and produced. Jerome Dreyfuss leather luxury bags, Forte Forte Italian chic street wear, Humanoid, and more. The accessories and clothing are exquisite, street-cool and original, including natural fabrics and leather in herbal-dyed and earthly colours. If you really want to stand out, you should check out the label's most famous piece, the Life Coat.

🕐 **Mon–Sat**   10am–18pm
   Sun   13pm–17pm
🏠 **Laugavegur 37**
📞 **571 7790**
🌐 **jetkorine.com**

SPÚÚTNIK / VINTAGE

When you are looking for something extraordinary, something to spruce up your wardrobe or personal style, Spúútnik is a second-hand heaven. For more than 25 years this immensely popular shop has specialised in an endless variety of vintage clothing for both men and women. Just like numerous others before you, you will be sure to find a treasure at a good price.

🕐 **Mon–Sat**   10am–18pm
   Sun   13pm–18pm
🏠 **Laugavegur 28b**
📞 **533 2023**
🌐 **Facebook**

Farmers Market is a cool brand that
merges old and new, romantic and
punk, farmstead and city life. An instant
success since it began in 2005 it works
in the best textiles from Iceland and as
far as Australia and India. You'll discover
clothing and accessories fit for all occasions. A visit to this beautiful lifestyle
store, set in a contrasting industrial
neighbourhood, is worth the trip.

🕐 **Mon–Fri**   10am–18pm
    Sat   11am–16pm
🏠 **Hólmaslóð 2**
📞 **552 1960**
🌐 **farmersmarket.is**

ORG

On and off the yoga mat this is the place to treat yourself and do some good at the same time, offering clothing and accessories – mainly for women. Indulge yourself with clear-cut fashion and be comfy and chic, dressing up in Kowtow and alike. Stock up with Manduka yoga products or enhance your beauty with cosmetics from Zuii – focusing on organic and fair-trade certified.

🕐 **Mon–Fri**   12am–18pm
   Sat   12am–16pm
🏠 **Laugavegur 58**
📞 **551 5800**
🌐 **Facebook**

EXTRAS
FASHION

Aftur
Women's Wear
Laugavegur 23
775 1000
Facebook

Steinunn
Men & Women's Wear
Grandagarður 17
588 6649
steinunn.com

Geysir
Family & Home
Skólavörðustígur 16
519 6000
geysir.com

Íglo & Indi
Children's Wear
Skólavörðustígur 4
571 9006
igloandindi.com

KronKron
Women's Wear
Laugavegur 63b
562 8388
kronkron.com

JÖR
Unisex Wear
Laugavegur 89
546 1303
jorstore.com

Krínólín
Men & Women's Wear
Grandagarður 37
551 0991
krinolin.is

Kíosk
Women's Wear
Laugavegur 65
445 3269

66°NORÐUR
Outdoor
Bankastræti 5
535 6680
66north.is

Eggert Feldskeri
Furcoats
Skólavörðustígur 38
551 1121
furrier.is

OTHER FAVORITES

NOT TO MISS

Ironically we love our ice cream in
any season or weather, and with
a chocolate dip... mmm delicious!

Picks and Preferences

Any specific interests – music, photography, delicacies, organic food, spiritualism, fragrance? Maybe it's a combination of all. Check out our favourite stores that didn't fit into any of the categories in this book You might be pleasantly surprised.

Did you know...

— **Icelanders** have a love for music that began in the 14th century with rhyme-chanting, the oral tradition of telling stories to pass the time, equally by men and women whatever their social status

What's the price for...?
Hvað er verðið á...?

It's a gift
Þetta er gjöf

LUCKY RECORDS

Looking for something rare in music? On vinyl or CD? New or second-hand? This is Iceland's biggest record store – by far. Selected the best three years in a row with more than 40,000 items covering a huge variety of musical genres, from jazz and soul to electronic and classical, and of course an impressive Icelandic section. It is the collector's paradise, basking in a friendly, chilled atmosphere. Browse the shop while listening to music and drinking free organic coffee. Located next to Hlemmur bus station.

🕐 **Mon–Fri**   9am–19pm

   Sat–Sun   11am–17pm

🏠 **Rauðarárstígur 10**

📞 **551 1195**

🌐 **Facebook**

GJAFIR JARÐAR
SPIRITUAL SHOP

Are you spiritually minded? Want to try healing or know about your future? Or are you just curious about the curative powers of crystals? You'll encounter serenity upon entering this spiritual store where you can also make an appointment with a healer or clair-voyant. It offers various stones and crystals and an assortment of jewellery, incense, relaxation music, meditative CDs, spiritual books, tarot cards, flower essences and more.

Mon–Fri   11am–18pm
Sat   12am–16pm
Laugavegur 50
517 2774
gjafirjardar.is

The owner of this tiny studio is not only an excellent photographer with a quirky eye for his subjects, as his book about Reykjavík proves, but also a collector of cameras and photographic artefacts displayed in his shop. His popular Reykjavík moments are sold in the shop and he also offers a collection of work from other superb contemporary Icelandic photographers, so you can take a piece of the city home with you.

🕐 **All week**   12am–18pm

   And on request

🏠 **Skólavörðustígur 22**

📞 **821 5600**

🌐 **Facebook**

SANGITAMIYA
THE NECTAR MUSIC

Almost like Aladdin's cave, this extraordinary musical-instrument store is full of musical treasures from all over the world, founded in the spirit of the artist and visionary Sri Chinmoy. You'll completely forget time once inside and it's hard to resist trying out the various (some strange looking) instruments peeking out from every corner. All of the staff is musically trained and

will be happy to assist. Music lover or not, this is just the place to visit and get some inspiration for your journey.

🕐	Mon–Fri	11am–18pm
	Sat	11am–18pm

🏠 Grettisgata 7

📞 551 8080

🌐 sangitamiya.is

MADISON ILMHÚS
PERFUMERY

In this fashionable house of fragrances they see perfume as a work of art. Madison is sure to provide you with the perfect fragrance or exquisite cosmetics. It's evident that the products are made with passion, everything carefully selected with a touch of class, the real beauty secrets of Europe. Be sure to take your time here, have a manicure or make-up for any event – you will walk out looking your best.

🕐 Mon–Wed	10am–18pm
Thur	10am–20pm
Fri	10am–18pm
Sat	11am–17pm

🏠 Aðalstræti 9

📞 571 7800

🌐 madison.is

OLD HARBOUR SOUVENIRS

Looking for something typically Icelandic? At Reykjavík's Old Harbour this inviting little shop has not only the typical souvenirs but a good selection of Icelandic design and craft. You'll find 100% authentic hand-knitted woollen sweaters, jewellery design, textile and ceramic design. It doesn't end there. Cosmetics and seasoning from Icelandic herbs and yummy chocolate are on offer and it's also a charming area to go for a stroll.

🕐 **All days** 11am–18pm

🏠 **Geirsgata 5c**

📞 **552-7777**

🌐 **reykjavikoldharbour.is**

BÚRIÐ / THE PANTRY

Just follow your nose – Búrið prides itself with the best 'stink' in town. Located in an up-and-coming area close to the harbour, you can get cheeses from around the globe, together with their own selection of divine jams, chutneys and nibbles, as well as cured meats and olives – heaven for food lovers. Búrið also runs popular workshops in English where you can learn all about the Icelandic skyr and delve into the country's cheese history.

🕐 **Mon–Fri**   11am–18pm
   Sat   12am–17pm
🏠 **Grandagarður 35**
📞 **551 8400**
🌐 **burid.is**

EXTRAS
OTHER FAVORITES

My Concept Store
Lifestyle Store
Laugavegur 45
519 6699
myconceptstore.is

Heilsuhúsið
Health Store
Laugavegur 20b
552 2966
heilsuhusid.is

Blue Lagoon Shop
Skin Care
Laugavegur 15
420 8849
bluelagoon.com

12 Tónar
Music Store
Skólavörðustíg 15
511 5656
12tonar.is

Paradís
Ice Cream
Njálsgata 23
555 4700
Facebook

Valdís
Ice Cream Parlor
Grandagarður 21
586 8088
Facebook

OUTDOORS

The Music Pavillion

The Music Pavilion was built in 1923 and the
first house in Iceland built specifically for
musical activities and is located in the public
park by the same name.

Fríkirkjuvegur 11

(Thor's palace) – constructed in 1908, this was
the first house with built-in plumbing in Reykjavík
– and the story goes that Thor had it made big
enough so he could upset and poke fun at the rich
people who lived on the other side of the pond.

Reykjavik Botanic Garden

A delightful outdoor collection of living plants, a beautiful and peaceful garden with trees, ponds and birdlife. Café Flora is a small café perched invitingly inside the display greenhouse. Check out the Family Park and Zoo close by.

The Music Pavilion Garden

The first organised public park in Reykjavík at the south end of Tjörnin, its formal name is the Pond Garden, a wonderful area for outdoor activities and games with a playground and benches.

Klambratun Park

One of the largest public parks in the city, a popular outdoor recreation area with a playground for kids, Frisbee golf course, basketball court and a beach volleyball court. Kjarvallsstaðir art museum is located at the north end of the park and has a welcoming café.

Austurvöllur Public Square

This downtown public square, lined by cafés, is a popular gathering place for locals, especially when the sun is shining.

The Old Cemetery

This is the biggest and the most beautiful cemetery in Reykjavík and falls under conservation status and is almost two centuries old – perfect for a nice walk.

The Hill

This manmade hill, by the artist Ólöf Nordal, is located at the waterfront by Reykjavík's old harbour. Take the stone path all the way to the top. This grass covered hill is 26 metres wide and 8 metres high, and at the top is a small shed to dry fish, but because it's an art piece, you won't see any dried (or wet for that matter)

WALKS

LANDMARKS

Harpa

is a new concert hall and
conference centre in Reykjavík
opened in May 2011, named after
a musical instrument – the harp.

Höfði

The house where Gorbatsjov and
Regan met in 1986 and their meeting
marked the end of the Cold War.

Imagine Peace Tower

This tower is a memorial to John Lennon from his widow, Yoko Ono. It's located on Viðey Island, close to Reykjavík and is lit annually from October 9 to December 8, December 21 to 31, February 18 and March 20 to 27. You can take a ferry to Viðey from Reykjavík for a guided tour.
www.videy.com
imaginepeacetower.com

Sun Voyager

The Sun Voyager is a sculpture that is an ode to the sun. It contains within itself the promise of undiscovered territory, a dream of hope, progress and freedom. Take a walk by the waterfront and snap a photo of yourself beside this massive steel contraption.
www.visitreykjavik.is/
solfar-sun-voyager

Hofdi House

Built in 1909 this is one of the most historically significant buildings in Reykjavík, currently used for official receptions and meetings. The house is believed to be haunted by a ghost named the White Lady. It's not open to the public but you can explore it from the outside.
www.visitreykjavik.is/hofdi-house

Harpa Concert Hall

A concert and conference centre, the hall's design is based on a geometric principle, realised in two and three dimensions. Reminiscent of the crystallised basalt columns commonly found in Iceland, the southern facades create kaleidoscopic reflections of the city and the striking surrounding landscape. Inside you'll find shops devoted to design, music and gifts, a restaurant, café, and information centre. You can also take a 45-minute guided tour.
www.harpa.is

The Pearl

A landmark building and restaurant, built on top of six hot-water storage tanks, overlooking the city. The restaurant is on the top floor and rotates, giving diners a 360 degree view. Scamper around outside and grab a cup of coffee or ice cream. The surrounding greenery is called Öskjuhlíð and is perfect for peaceful walks providing the planes are not departing or arriving from the nearby airport.
www.perlan.is

DAY TRIPS

OUT OF REYKJAVÍK

The Icelandic horse may be small in size but it's strong, friendly and sure-footed. It is five gated (the norm is four) and the tolt is its speciality, a natural four-beat gait making the ride particularly smooth but powerful. The Icelandic horse is one of the oldest and purest breeds in the world, and is famous for its stamina and endurance – they came with the Viking settlers around the year 900 AD.

Mount Esja Hiking Self-drive

This 914-metre-high mountain range is situated just outside the capital and is a popular hiking destination for locals. Several routes to choose from marked by difficulty, both up and around the mountain, with a spectacular panoramic view from the top.
www.esjustofa.is

Blue Lagoon Geothermal Spa Self-drive/Bus Tours

A unique lagoon in a lava field of geo-thermal sea-water where silica, algae and minerals reflected by the sun turn the milky water blue. At 38°C (100°F) and with its skin-healing properties, it's perfect for taking a relaxing soak in all year-round.
www.bluelagoon.com

Thingvellir National Park
Self-drive/Bus Tours

Here the parliament 'Althingi' was established in 930 AD. A UNESCO World Heritage Site since 2004, it oozes historical, cultural and geological importance. Almannagjá is a dramatic rift in the landscape formed by tectonic plates where the North American and European boundaries meet.
www.thingvellir.is

Krýsuvík Geothermal Area Self-drive

A remarkable 30-minute ride from the city to one of the most surreal land-scapes in Iceland with its colourful geo-thermal area, stunning cliffs and roaring Atlantic surf. A true hiking experience.
www.visithafnarfjordur.is

The Golden Circle
Self-drive/Bus Tours

The most popular route to discover Ice-land's most iconic natural and historical attractions in South Iceland, Thingvellir National Park, Gullfoss Waterfall, and Geysir hot spring area.
www.visitreykjavik.is/

Icelandic Horse Rental
Self-drive/Pick Up

A family firm offering riding tours within the city limits of Reykjavík all year-round. Customised riding tours in a colourful volcanic landscape, for beginners and experienced riders.
www.islenskihesturinn.is

On the HandPicked Iceland.is website you can find and map out your own day tour and tailor it to your taste from our recommendations. At visitreykjavik. is/activities you'll find many more day trips provided by tourist operators.

CHRISTMAS

DECEMBER IN REYKJAVÍK

There is not one but 13 Icelandic Yule Lads that come to town one by one 13 days before Christmas, depositing gifts in children's shoes that the kids place at their windows at night. If the children don't behave, they get a potato in their shoe instead of a treat – imagine the disappointment?
The Yule Lads are descendants from trolls and were supposed to frighten little children in the old days. Their parents are the most terrible ogres, Grýla and Leppalúði, and were a trick used by parents to frighten their children into behaving.

Ellidavatn Christmas Market

Just 15 minutes from the city centre in Heiðmörk, Elliðavatn lake boasts a traditional craft market during weekends in December, unique for its location and offers just the right amount of Christmas spirit. Here, you'll find Christmas choirs, harmonica players, a small cafe, writers reading from their new books and Santa keeping the kids entertained.
www.heidmork.is

Reykjvík Christmas Market

At Ingólfstorg square, downtown Reykjavík looks like a small village offering samples of local delicacies and hand-crafted goods from craftspeople and designers, as well as musical entertainment and visits from the Icelandic Yule Lads. It's open during the two weekends before Christmas.
www.visitreykjavik.is

Reykjavík Skating Hall

Why not take in some family fun and go skating when in town? In the Skating Hall at Laugardalur, located near the swimming pool and the Family Park and Zoo, you can roll along to music surrounded by disco lights.
www.skautaholl.is

Blue Mountains Ski Resort

It's just a 30-minute drive to Reykjavík's main ski resort. It's popular place and it's open when weather permits. There is ski rental and you can also refine your skiing skills with an instructor on weekends.
www.skidasvaedi.is

....

The Yule Lads

Played pranks on people in the old days, hence their names

Sheep-Cote Clod Sucked the yews in the sheep sheds

Gully Gawk Slurped the foam of cows' milk in the buckets

Stubby Snatched food from the frying pan

Spoon Licker Licked the spoon used to scrape the pots

Pot Scraper Licked food remains from the pots

Bowl Licker Licked the bowls clean

Door Slammer Slammed the doors

Skyr Gobbler Gobbled the skyr out of the skyr tub

Sausage Swiper Stole sausages when he had the chance

Window Peeper Peeped through windows (and sometimes stole toys)

Door Sniffer Sniffed the baking goods with his oversized nose

Meat Hook Snagged smoked lamb

Candle Beggar Longed for candles and begged children for them

TO DO

Places to visit and things to do

I'm staying in Iceland for _____ days

_____

_____

and in Reykjavík for _____ days

_____

_____

I'm travelling together with _____

_____

_____

I'm here to _____

_____

_____

My main objective is to _____

_____

_____

_____

_____

I LIKE

Places and things to remember

My Favourite experience _____

_____

_____

My Favourite restaurant _____

_____

_____

My favourite food _____

_____

_____

My favourite person _____

_____

_____

My favourite store _____

_____

_____

My favourite place _____

_____

_____

NOTES
SKETCHES
MEMOS

NOTES
SKETCHES
MEMOS

NOTES
SKETCHES
MEMOS

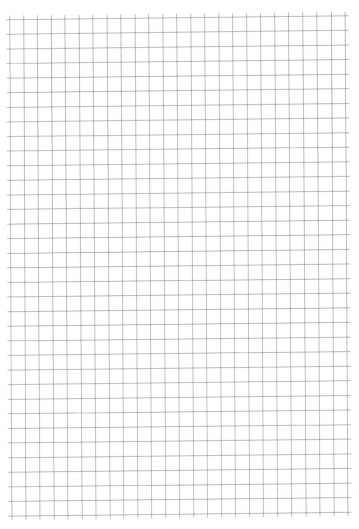

NOTES
SKETCHES
MEMOS

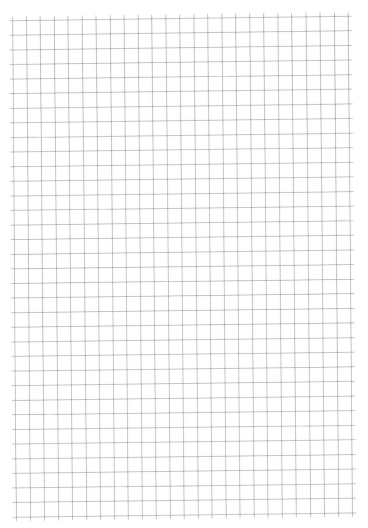

NOTES
SKETCHES
MEMOS

NOTES
SKETCHES
MEMOS

NOTES
SKETCHES
MEMOS

NOTES
SKETCHES
MEMOS

Concept and Art Director	Gigi - Guðbjörg Gissurardóttir
Text and Project Management	Rakel Sigurðardóttir
Design	Ármann Agnarsson
	Elsa Jónsdóttir
Illustrations	Elísabet Brynhildardóttir
Editor	Jason Flynn
Photography	Various sources
Photography Editor	Gigi - Guðbjörg Gissurardóttir

Í boði náttúrunnar

HandPicked Reykjavík 2015
Published and Distributed by
Í boði náttúrunnar – Magazine
(By Nature), Elliðavatn,
110 Reykjavík, Iceland

www.ibn.is
gg@ibn.is

Content is compiled based
on facts available in April
2015. Please check for
updates from respective
locations before your visit.

Printed in Iceland
Oddi ehf. Eco-labelled
printing company

If you liked our favourites in
Reykjavík then you'll be excited to
learn we have also made selective
choices around Iceland! Check
out our HandPicked Iceland app,
website or our cute little maps,
Eat&Sleep, Shop&Play and
Kids&Culture.